DAVIE BRYCE

Butterflies

12 1/2 weeks of recovery

Trigger warning!! Butterflies contains all of the following: multiple uses of profanity, one chapter contains sexual violence, one also tackles issues around racism, there is a character who masks his closeted sexual identity with horrible misogyny and this then develops into self-focused homophobia, there are chapters which depict fairly graphic sex scenes, and there are multiple references to drug use. No animals are harmed but there is one reference to puppy play as well as a collective group reaction to this.

First edition

ISBN (paperback): 9798301935336
ISBN (hardcover): 9798301968051

This book was professionally typeset on Reedsy.
Find out more at reedsy.com

Contents

1

No Man's Land

The bass from the clubs shook the street as Katrina dodged Jimmy's latest attempt to twirl her under his arm. His sunburn glowed neon in the UV lights, making her laugh despite herself. She'd joined this trip on a whim, desperate to escape Wexford and the whispers at work. She didn't care where she was or who she was with and for the first time in months, she felt free.

The hotel job had been a right of passage, straight out of University and it had been going well. She didn't even want to have a threesome, it hadn't even been that great, it just happened after a lock in one night. After a night drinking, post shift, with two of her more friendly colleagues.

Worse was afterwards, when the night shift manager was propositioning her at all times of the day or night, every shift, whilst the barman sent text messages declaring his undying love for her. If this had worked out vice versa then it might have gone to plan. It hadn't and as soon as the whispers started she knew it was time to go. She didn't even work her notice.

It was about the third night when she first spoke with Jimmy, or Victor as he'd introduced himself originally - along with his friend 'Jack' who were both from a wee place called Craiglang. This back story quickly unraveled as an attempt at preventing any unwanted follow up from their own visit to Ayia Napa. She hadn't been interested at first but he seemed harmless enough, as he danced around her.

Fiona, another one of the lads from Wexford, was smitten with Victor – Jimmy's pal Peter. Which progressed to daytime walks along the beach and lunches as opposed to just a dance and a grope in the dark each night.

It was here, playing wing man to her new found friend, that Katrina forgot the rules she'd set herself. She was charmed by Jimmy's quick humour and constant fun, as well as the attentive way he kept check on her. Soon enough, they were taking lunches without Fiona and Peter and eventually they were fucking like she'd never fucked in her life. Every night in Jimmy's apartment. 11 days holiday, 4 on her own and 7 days living with Jimmy. She disowned the lads right up until she met them back at departures and Jimmy sobbed like a baby as she got her flight home.

They exchanged long phone calls, emails, letters and romantic gifts for a few weeks, which felt like forever, until Jimmy booked her flights to come over.

Soon enough she packed her bag for four days and her heart for a lifetime as her Mammy dropped her at Dublin airport. She hugged her, hoping and knowing that she probably wouldn't be back. She knew she loved Jimmy and Jimmy had already made his intentions clear.

He met her at arrivals complete with a sign bearing her name and a huge bunch of flowers. They kissed and she was transported right back to Cyprus. Jimmy held her hand all the way back his flat in central Scotland, only dropping it to change gear.

There wasn't much to Falkirk and if she was honest with herself she was a bit disappointed that Jimmy's flat hadn't quiet been in the charming idyllic little lochside glen she'd pictured. More of a council flat similar to those she'd seen in Ferndale. Still Jimmy doted on her and his family made a fuss of her as they were introduced.

Jimmy paraded her like a new lioness to his pride.

Their second day flashed by in the blink of an eye. Jimmy had planned for them to meet up with his friends in a local nightclub called the Maniqui.

Oasis boomed throughout the flat as they got ready. Katrina attending to her makeup whilst Jimmy sang along to She is Love.

'Sure Liam Gallagher himself isn't in there with you'

Jimmy returned bare chested, towel draped around his waist like a kilt. He lay on the bed.

'You're gorgeous Katrina O'Shaughnessy. Absolutely fucking Gorgeous'

'Oh. Get over yerself. Passable at best' Katrina blushed.

'And what's the craic for tonight? Time will we be heading onto town?'

Jimmy seemed deep in thought.

'We don't have to go out, we could just stay in and watch a film. My mate Craig's lent me a copy of that Reservoir Dogs, it's to be minted'.

'After I've done all this makeup trying to make meeself passable. Are you ashamed or summit?'

'Not at all. Dinnae be daft, just wanting you all to myself'

'Well there will be plenty time later, for what you're after Mr Horny!'

Jimmy rose from the bed and stroked her shoulders as they talked in the mirror. Katrina reflecting bigger smiles back at Jimmy's.

'Can I get you a drink? A wee vino?'

'Sure that'd be grand but none of yer buckfast. I've been well warned by my Mammy'

Jimmy laughed as he poured her a glass of rose and opened a can.

Jimmy regaled in small talk with the taxi driver, as they headed into town, none of which Katrina understood fully. She was amazed at how quickly they spoke and how it sounded like a different language. She smiled when he looked her way and held his hand as she watched out the window, reminding herself that she was in Scotland now ...despite how much it still looked like Ferndale.

The nightclub queue was massive. Every girl in the place seemed to weigh more and wear less than Katrina. She hadn't felt as nervous meeting his Mam and Dad.

All he'd talked about was his pals from Camelon. How they'd be like brothers for him, more than his actual brother who was a bit of a junkie by all accounts.

The nightclub was suffocating. Katrina's heels stuck to the floor as she walked, the air heavy with sweat and cheap perfume. The music pounded in her chest, and every time she glanced at Jimmy, he was laughing too loudly, gesturing too wildly. She sipped her drink, trying to focus, but the whole night felt off.

'Alright Jimmy what's happening man? You daen alright pal? Is this the good lady you've been telling everybody about'

Jimmy's pal stood at least a foot taller than him. Completely bald so he could have been anywhere between 20 and 40 she thought to herself as he slid along the booth next to them.

Katrina was shaking hands and kissing cheeks as Jimmy's friends each chatted to her and then Jimmy.

Eventually one of the girlfriends of Jimmy's friends waved here over and she left Jimmy alone to chat with his pals.

They hadn't been as nice as she'd wanted and sprayed her with a volley of questions wrapped in barbs.

'Where in Ireland are you fae?'

'Wexford'

'Never heard of it. Is it full of IRA?'

'Jimmy's in the flute band, did he tell you?'

'Yeah he did that. It's not a big deal for me. We weren't a religious family'

'Met in Cyprus? I had a holiday romance too, but we never kept in touch'.

'We going to the toilet?'

The friend's girlfriends left to bitch about her in the toilet, she was sure. She sat and watched Jimmy holding court back at the booth before another guy approached her.

He was a tall lad with blonde hair in a middle parting, who seemed friendly enough.

'So your Jimmy's new Irish burd then? How's it going? Take it you showed him yer craic then?'

'You're too funny Mr. Yer mans got a good craic on himself too' She laughed back at him taking a swig of her drink.

'What your name?'

'Katrina. Everyone calls me Kat thou?'

'Hiya Kat. I'm Simon, although I've been called worse'

She laughed.

'Nice to meet you Simon. Why aren't you sat with the rest of the lads?'

'I was just getting myself a drink when I seen you sitting there on your Sweeney Todd. Didn't think it was nice him leaving you on your own.'

'There he is, we were just talking about you Jimmy' Katrina blushed as he stormed over. Jimmy clenched his fist tight in Simon's shirt and ran him against the wall.

'Get yerself tae fuck ya wee fenian cunt. Or I'll tear you apart'' Jimmy snarled, his voice low and sharp.

'Jimmy, stop it!' Kat yelled, tugging at his arm, but he didn't move.

Simon's hands flew up, palms open, but Jimmy didn't let go. The bouncers finally stepped in, pulling Jimmy back. Katrina's heart pounded in her ears. She didn't wait for him to explain. Grabbing her bag, she stormed out, hoping he'd follow....but not sure if she wanted him to.

A smirking bouncer held the door for her as she stormed out of the club, her heels clicking harder than usual on the pavement. She lit a cigarette, or tried to, her lighter refusing to cooperate. She glanced over her shoulder. He'd better follow her. If he thought he could talk to her like that, he had another thing coming.

'Fuck sake' she blasted.

A guy passing by offered her a light, which she gratefully accepted apologising for her outburst.

'Nae bother doll. Here you go'

He held out the lighter for her as took a few deep drags till her cigarette glowed bright orange.

She thanked him again just before he bounced off the concrete. It happened too quickly for her to comprehend. Suddenly there was her Jimmy, looking down on the guy who'd just lit her cigarette.

'Jimmy?'

'Are you okay?' he asked.

'Yes. The guy gave me a light, I was just saying thanks.'

Katrina dropped to check on him.

'Jesus Jimmy. He was only giving me a light, for god's sake'

'I though he was hassling you. I'm sorry'

'You need to calm that temper Mr. He's still not moved Jimmy?'

Jimmy and Kat both looked down on the guy. He was still motionless.

'He's not looking his best like.' Admitted Jimmy, panic starting to creep into his voice.

'Run' Katrina shouted as they both took off along the High St.

Soon enough they were back in a taxi and Katrina cuddled into Jimmy as they silently returned home.

Back at the flat, Katrina flashed into survival mode.

'Here get yer stuff off and have a shower'

'Kat I'm no exactly in the mood on account of me thinking I've maybe killed a boy aye?'

Katrina started pulling his shirt over his head.

'And in that case you wont be sitting in exhibit A when the guards come after you will ye?'

Jimmy finished stripping off and was quickly in the shower.

Katrina sat on the smart black leather sofa and folded his clothes silently.

Her mind whirred as she listened to Jimmy showering, thinking back to their week in Cyprus, how she'd made here heart up on Jimmy there and then. How this night had gone so wrong, so quickly.

Katrina froze when the door thudded. Her mind raced. *It hadn't taken them long*, she thought, glancing at the pile of Jimmy's clothes she'd folded. The shower dripped into the silence, each droplet landing like the ticking of a clock.

The knock came again, sharper this time, and she clutched the edge of the sofa, her knuckles white. Her breath caught in her throat. She turned her head slowly toward Jimmy, who stood in the bathroom doorway, pale and motionless, water still clinging to his skin.

'Central Scotland Police,' called through the letterbox.

Her lungs burned, but she didn't dare breathe. The extractor fan ticked faintly behind her. The shower dripped again, louder now, it seemed. Jimmy stepped closer, placing a hand on her shoulder, but neither of them spoke. They were frozen together, listening, waiting.

Finally, the letterbox snapped shut. A car door slammed. Then another.

The low growl of an engine rumbled into the night and faded into abandon-ment.

Neither of them moved for what felt like an eternity. The extractor fan stopped with a shudder, leaving the flat eerily still.

Jimmy held her all night, his arms wrapped tightly around her. They didn't speak, but neither needed to. They both knew exactly what the other was thinking.

2

Jack's Conscientious Rejection

'Are you on your way to do it now?'

'Aye man just driving through.'

'Could you no just phone her?'

'Nah man. She's better than that, plus I need to get my stuff.'

'Fuck's sake that's heavy. Can you no just tell her to post it thou?'

'Nah, I want to do it the right way man.'

'Will she know what's happening?'

'Ah think so. Conversation was kinda drifting that way.'

Jack's car hummed to a stop outside the block of flats, the buzz of Buchanan Street life fading into a muted backdrop. The air carried a chill, whispering through the narrow gap in his car window, mingling the scents of rain on concrete and distant city life.

'Aww fuck sake man. There's a polis car and an ambulance outside her flat. I better go.'

The speakerphone in Jack's car clicked off as he parked behind the police car. He walked by slowly. Looking in to see if it was empty, he looked up and down the street before he took a deep breath and pressed the buzzer, fearing the worst.

Denise answered.

'Hello' crackled through the speaker.

'Are you alright?'

Denise giggled.

'Is that you Jack?'

'Aye, are you alright?'

'Eh. I think so. I'll buzz you up.'

Jack pushed the door as the buzzer sounded and immediately took to the stairs two and three steps at a time. He knocked on the door and watched pensively before it opened slowly.

'What's up?' Denise smiled as she pulled open the door.

'Are you okay? I saw the polis car and ambulance outside and...'

'What. You thought I was giving you the dramatic send-off. Did you?'

'Well. Eh, aye... Kinda'

'Well, don't flatter yourself honey. I'm fine'

Denise turned and walked into the flat. She asked over her shoulder if Jack wanted a coffee, Jack watched her arse wiggling like two ferrets in a sack before reminding himself why he was there.

He followed her not knowing how to make himself look suddenly uncomfortable, in a place he'd been more than comfortable over the past few months. Denise immediately started making him a cappuccino, bouncing through small talk nonchalantly, as Jack's discomfort became real. She laid his drink on the coffee table, which had vinyl records melted into it. Jack tried his best to maintain uncommitted small talk. Nervous about what he was about to say.

'Do you like my dress?'

Denise asked, standing back to reveal her full slender frame as she brushed her hair back off her shoulders, presenting and demonstrating the full-length front zip on her black and white geometric patterned dress.

Jack looked her up and down and stood up as she began unzipping the dress, slowly from the bottom.

Denise waited till his hands almost touched her before she zipped its full-length closed shut and spun on her heels.

'I don't think so! Took your gift back to John Lewis and bought this in its place. Do you like it?'

As Jack's laughter faded into the warmth of his coffee, a storm of thoughts raged within him. Beneath the surface of his amusement, a whirlpool of love, regret, and resolve churned relentlessly.

'Look it's just not going to work.'

Denise was quiet, leaving Jack feeling like he had to work at explaining further.

'I need to tell you the truth. I've not been honest with you, there's someone else and it's complicated. Last time I was driving home from here I was guilt riddled, wondering if I should just crash the car and end it all, thinking everyone would be better off without me.'

Denise slipped out of character for a second.

'Don't be daft.'

Inhaling deeply, Jack felt the tide of Denise's restrained emotion wash over him; surprising, unsettling, yet oddly fitting. Drinking it all in and savouring it like embers on a cold night. He knew that she felt the same way about him, that there had been a magic between them, in the beginning. He knew too that she knew this was all wrong, it was...but he couldn't do this to her, not now.

'You've got to carve out your own path, Jack, even if it means putting yourself first. Good on you for that. Not many others have done that for you'

In Denise's voice, Jack heard a mix of admiration and melancholy. In her words, Jack heard not just an endorsement of his choice but a poignant reminder of his history of neglect that he'd managed miserably, she was yet another secondary victim.

Jack finished his coffee and stood up. He noticed that Denise had already packed his stuff in the hallway, it had been waiting for him to collect since before he'd arrived. He began to crumble.

The words 'I love you, Denise' spilled from Jack's lips, a confession, a plea, and a farewell all at once. Each syllable trembled with the gravity of what he was leaving behind, a testament to a love that could not be, yet would never fully leave his heart.

'I really do. I love you'.

'Go. Get your things and go.'

Denise pecked him on the cheek and rubbed his back.

Jack picked up his bags and turned to face her as she held the door open.

'I do love you.'

'And I love you too.'

Denise shut the door.

Jack burst into tears, stood there transfixed on the door mat. Staring at the closed door in front of him, eventually he realised the door wasn't going to open, no matter how hard he willed it. As he walked down the stairs the weight of his decision pressed down on him like a heavy coat.

Back in the solitude of his car, the reality of his choice began to concoct a heady mix of relief, sorrow, as well as a sliver of hope for a different future. Holding the steering wheel, he watched two paramedics struggle with an old fella into the back of the ambulance. He snorted at himself, and Denise, and set off onto his next disaster.

Every song on the radio, played like it was Steve Wright dedication. He turned off the volume and rang Dave back. Dave answered within one ring.

'What happened man?'

'Aww man. It was sad as fuck.'

'Had she hurt herself?'

'Naw man, naw. The polis n that wurnae for her. She was dead classy about it, like put me in my place and told me to go and be myself. '

'What are you going to do now?'

'I fucking miss her already Dave.'

'Drive back then ya daft cunt'.

'Naw I cannae. It's done, I've done it. Canny believe it but I did it.'

'I dunno what to say Jack. You know better than me, but she seems sound. Stevie's Mrs is all over the fucking place. Plus I can't see him reacting well to it all. What are you going to do?'

'Head to Tesco, wash my face, look like ah've no been crying and buy a big bunch of fucking flowers.'

That night Jack had drove over to meet with his on/off new flame. Who happened to be another colleague and was also, adding another level of precarious risk to this situationship, his boss's wife. Jack had told Dave all the sordid details from day one. How he'd been asking her to tell him who the boss was in her marital bed, each afternoon as he fucked her. How when he'd called in sick after a night out she'd taken the call and come over to nurse him back to full sexual health. How he'd talked her into leaving Stevie and how he was going to take her away to Scarborough and they were going to take things from there. Never looking back.

Dave had already watched Jack's peaks and troughs through each emotional roller coaster and as much as he tried to talk him around. Jack never listened, not at this point anyway. He was too far gone already.

3

Checked Out

Ryan stood there holding a basket, which should have been a trolley, waiting. The queue didn't move and he was staring daggers at the elderly couple who hadn't danced through pack and scan quick enough for his aching arms. He wondered if there should be a slow lane for them.

'Hey you' said a voice, surprising him out of his quiet distaste.

'Hello' he said back, ever polite, but not yet registering who'd stood in front of him.

'How are you doing?' She followed up, beaming him a smile which is way too familiar.

Play for time

'I'm doing great thanks. Struggling on. Yourself? You're looking well'

'Aww thanks. I knew you would be, you were always destined for great things'

Ryan's now beyond the point of clarifying who she is, so he smiled and said 'see you around' as she joined the queue behind him.

Desperate for a name to suddenly roll off the tip of his brain. A heavy-set young guy in long denim shorts and a black t shirt broke his concentration.

'Your turn' he announced gruffly, pointing towards a vacant till.

Ryan apologised whilst stealing an opportunity to look back at her again. She catches him looking and smiles.

Who is she?

Thinking over the useless information his brain holds right now and how he could benefit from a hard reset removing all the useful information stored somewhere more accessible. Instead he has the number for his house phone from 1991 still floating around uselessly.

She's now at the till behind him and he can practically feel her presence. Whilst he's still scanning his shopping, painfully aware of the series of beige meals for one belying the 'great things' he ought to be doing.

Who is she? How can you no remember THAT smile you daft prick.

He's looked up over the screen and caught her eye for a third time, she's clearly watching for his attention. He smiles back.

How do you know HER? Ya radge cunt, look at her. If you were smiling like that, at her, you'd be arrested.

He grudgingly gives up thinking as she slides out of his peripheral view and then, only then, it finally hits him. Like sod himself has just booted him square in the balls.

*It's only bloody **HER**. How could you forget **HER**? You are fucking clueless.*

Ryan exerts impatience by sighing and tapping his foot silently whilst waiting for approval of his alcohol-free beer.

Alison doesn't appear as happy to help as her name badge would suggest. She saunters over to Ryan, after checking out all her nails, and types in a code without even a glance to confirm that he's well over 25. Ryan takes note to challenge their challenge twenty-five policy for alcohol free drinks. But not today.

He packs the rest of what should've been a trolley into two bags and rushes into the car park. His racing heart sinks when met with a sea of cars, as if Sod's came back from his boot in the balls and now made the car park bigger... just to make things more interesting.

And yet there she is again, waving, as she drives past in a navy blue Vauxhall Astra. He waves before repeating the registration over and over as he makes his way back to his car. Trying not to drop the numbers out of his head whilst he grips keys in his mouth and opens the boot with the full weight of half a trolley in one hand.

Ryan throws the bags in the boot and then slams it shut, jumps in the car and begins writing what's left of the registration before his pen runs out and he ends up carving letters and numbers into his receipt.

He races out of the car park, thuddering across the speed bumps like they're not there and then drives in the general direction of where he thinks she once lived.

Eventually his blood pressure drops and he realises that this was, at best, a futile effort.

What were you going to do, follow her home? Weirdo.

More sensible, but defeated, Ryan drove home. Cursing his fully defragmented mind which can, now, not only place Susan in full gorifying digital technicolour but also appears to have found a re-run of her starring in his very own nightmare on any street.

He knew she'd come along, that's why he'd asked her in the first place.

He knew it was too early. He knew she was out of his league. But he'd got caught up in the moment. The feelings that he wanted to be sure she felt the same way. The feeling that he needed security, the feeling that she maybe wanted the same. The feelings that convinced him she did.

The way she turned when he dropped to one knee, the way their happy go lucky walk along the shore turned at that very moment. The way her whole demeanour shifted awkwardly, the way the gulls laughed at him as she pulled him up to his feet. Watching her apologise before she kissed his head and walked away. Before he turned and threw the ring into the sea, without a second's thought. Never even regretted it, not even today, despite the cost – it hurt still to much to think about it never mind look at it.

Ryan hadn't seen her since that day. And there she was still smiling that smile. Still thinking he could do great things. That made one of them, his hopes were pretty much dashed in that respect.

He opened a bottle of non-alcoholic Peroni and pushed up the laptop lid, before he searched for the registration number and confirmed the car type. Found out when her car was last sold, when it's MOT is due and when it had been in a category C accident before she even owned it. Each piece of information being unveiled as if he were making some sort of progress.

Before he realised that this was a load of pointless shite.

He made his beige meal for one and cursed that he'd never built on the promise he knew he had back then. He had the weekend there for the taking and then fucked it up on a Friday.

The air fryer beeped and he'd burnt his chips.

4

Stirling Mess

'Did you get milk?'

'Fuck Sake! I asked you when I was there if we needed anything.'

'I thought it was obvious that we needed milk.'

'Well it wasnae fuckin me that drunk all the milk, was it?'

'Naw it would have been your daughter. But you wouldn't have noticed her either, all you think about is drinking with your pals and ramming that shite up yer nose.'

'Well it's anything I can do to get away from your constant pish.'

'Well there's nothing stopping you from heading back to your wee whore.'

'Fuck sake Sarah it was two years ago, yet you still bring it up every fucking time. Is there something your hiding, that cunt from your work you're always texting?'

'What are you going through my phone now?'

'Aye to see what you were up to with that prick. '

'That prick just happens to be my boss. Not everyone has the same attitude to relationships like you do. I've never cheated, not once. You are such a dick Stirling'.

'And neither did I. I left.'

'Does that make it easier to tell yourself that? That you left and came back, whilst I sat at home and hid my crying from Kayleigh. You left us and never gave it a thought, so you could fuck a skank bitch.'

'It wasn't like that and well you know it'

'Oh was it not now? Enlighten me Stirling how was it any fucking different?'

Their daughter came into the kitchen. Sarah immediately ushered her back out the kitchen door.

'It's fine sweety. Mummy and Daddy are just having a discussion, he's going to get milk for your drinks from the shop. Aren't you?' Sarah commanded with her question.

'That's right wee doll. Can I get you anything else whilst I'm there?'

Stirling swung his car keys in his finger before he knelt and stroked her hair.

'I'll get you some of ice cream too?'

Kayleigh nodded enthusiastically and hugged her dad.

* * *

'Stirling'

'Stirling!'

'Stirling!!!'

Stirling woke up still bleary eyed, he could see Sarah in his face but was completely incoherent and unable to answer her with words.

'What the fuck is this?'

He stared at her blankly, still paralysed.

'This is the last straw. It's enough being a danger to yourself but our daughter. Fuck me, you've really done it this time Stirling.'

Stirling went back to sleep, still not sure what had happened but relieved the interruption was over.

When he finally woke up, only a flashback of this encounter with Sarah remained. He looked down, there on the coffee table were two neatly chopped lines of cocaine.

'Awww fuck sake. Fuck, fuck fucking fuck'

He lay back on the sofa and picked up his phone. No texts or missed calls. He rang Sarah, voicemail.

He started to text, quickly deleting everything whilst he tried to kickstart his brain.

He'd left to get milk. Bumped into Al in Tesco, they went for one pint. One fucking pint.

He checked his phone. He'd had a taxi ring him back at 6am. This is when he remembered.

He'd decided he'd stay awake, that he'd make Kayleigh's breakfast and then go to bed.

Cue the scene. Sarah waking up, already angry at his departure from earlier. Waking up to find him sparked out on the sofa with two lines of Colombians finest laid out for their daughter to find in front of her comatose father. In a long line of moments, this wasn't his finest. He pulled out the bag from his jacket pocket and carefully scraped both lines back into it.

He then walked through the empty house. Every movement seemed to jar against the hollow fabric of the building. He sat on the sofa and looked out of the window whilst tossing a cushion up and down.

He'd had some low moments but only just got to realising that there was only one common denominator throughout every single one of them. Having stood by a steady defence that; by the law of averages he couldn't possibly be in the wrong all of the time, he now realised that this was, in fact, actually the case. And not only that, he was well and truly fucked this time. This time she was serious, he'd just burnt his last life.

It was at times like this Stirling would've appreciated a Mam or Dad, a safety net to look out for him. But here he was again, in the doghouse and headed to weekend Dad central.

He swallowed the lump in his throat and phoned Al. Alan had a flat in Carronshore he had been planning to let out.

'Just a few months till I get things straightened out' he assured him.

5

Romantics Anonymous

Careless freedom, unexplained hand holding, unprotected hugs, your unquenchable thirst for THE one, a reckless sex drive coupled up with blissful abandonment. Unexpected consequences only hitting home years later, finally sobered up from being head over heels. Two kids and a mortgage later you think what happened? Your highs were encouraged relentlessly; Valentines cards, engagement parties, lavish weddings – and anniversaries all celebrating you finding your fix.

A cocktail of chaos bubbled away in your heart. When you fell in love, your brain released cupid's dose of chemicals; dopamine, oxytocin, and serotonin. Triggering the exact same neurotransmitters as some of the best class A drugs available today. The biochemical perspective supports why, much like substance dependence, you became addicted to the way love made you feel, leading to your obsessive and sometimes odd behaviour and then, almost inevitably.... your comedown.

Heartbreak is the cold turkey which darkly mirrors the high. Jealous rages, violent outbursts, you can't eat, you can't talk; dangerously stalking your ex's social media armed with a bottle of wine and a spiteful attitude. Don't think about work, they can wait till your heart is mended. But no one wants to know, she'll get over it; there's plenty more fish in the sea. The best way to get over someone is to get under someone else. Really?

Turns out Bryan Ferry and Robert Palmer were both right; Love is a drug and you might as well face it, you're addicted to it.

Romantics Anonymous. Mondays 8pm, Trinity Community Centre.

Dave had designed a website and put together a few social pages.

He'd asked Morag to get involved but she wasn't having any of it. Another one of Dave's follies. He'd been a salesman, a DJ, a festival organiser, a drive through barber not to mention an unsuccessful drug dealer and a fully confirmed high functioning alcoholic (now recovered). Inspired by his own spell in recovery and his pal's Jack's highs and lows in love he'd started his own counselling group.

He'd planned a simple structure for each week, closely following the structure of his AA meetings.

1/ Introductions and check-in.

2/ Some guidance and education around our relationship with romance.

3/Sharing.

4/Close.

And here they were week one. Jack, Stirling, Katrina and a guy called Ryan all booked to come along. He laid out a spare chair just in case anyone turned up unannounced, they didn't.

Dave made Jack sit outside as he paced the community centre room 'preparing' himself.

As soon as the clock struck 8pm he opened the door and Romantics Anonymous had began.

'Welcome, everyone, and thanks for coming tonight. Starting something new isn't easy, so give yourselves credit for showing up - half the battle is taking that first step.'

Dave pointed through a numbered list of prompts on a white board as the group sat in a semi circle of chairs.

'First we start with a quick introduction and a check-in regards where we are at with our relationship with romance then we move onto some guidance and education around some of our aspects which is accompanied by some sharing around the room before we close for that session.'

Dave looked around his newly formed group as they sat in silence. He waited just long enough for this to border on awkward before he pushed them along.

'As it's our first week I'll introduce myself. I have to reassure you all that this is a safe place and please treat the circle we're sat in as a circle of trust'

'I'm Dave. I started this group because I've been there. Love, breakups, addiction: it can mess you up in ways you don't see coming. But here, we'll unpack it all together, one week at a time. No judgment, just honesty and maybe a wee bit of support for each other'

Dave winced at how cringey the words fell out of his mouth. Undeterred he carried on.

'Jack are you okay to carry out your check-in next?'

'My name is Jack, obviously. I've had problems with romance all my life. The way you've described these issues Dave sounds like support that I need. I throw my everything into new love and this feels like it's matched in terms of energy until almost as suddenly it drops off, and regardless of how much pain it causes I find myself falling rapidly in love all over again or looking back and doubting decisions I've made were for the best.'

As Jack spoke, Katrina glanced at her lap, twisting the hem of her sleeve. Stirling leaned back, arms crossed, while Ryan's lips moved slightly, like he was rehearsing what to say next. Dave went to thank Jack but stopped as he continued...

'Just this week I finished things with my ex-girlfriend Denise. We hadn't been together long before I met another woman. We started off a thing, she was married, which escalated quickly and before I knew it we had plans to elope. She was leaving her husband for me and well I seem to have got caught up in a whirlwind and I'm not sure where it's going to land to be honest, not sure if I've made the right call'.

Dave looked around the room as Jack's honest introduction landed. Katrina was still fiddling with the hem of her sleeve while Ryan's brow furrowed as if he were doing mental soduko.

'I'm Katrina,' she began, her soft accent catching Dave's ear, it was definitely Irish, probably the South he thought.

'I'm here because...well, everyone around me seems to have moved on with their lives. But me? I'm stuck. My last relationship ended suddenly, a few years ago now, and I haven't trusted myself to fall in love again. I'm not even sure I can.'

She paused, brushing a stray hair behind her ear, and looked down at her hands. Dave nodded but stayed quiet, sensing she wasn't ready to say more.

Next to check in was Stirling. He'd seen Stirling clamber out of a hatchback in the car park and had him pigeonholed at first site. Stirling didn't disappoint or sway far from Dave's initial assessment.

'I'm Stirling and I'm here as I've fucked up many times before but find myself having moved from relationship to relationship fleetingly only to get stuck on my last relationship after my wee girl was born. I'd mistakenly thought I could keep living my life as I'd done previously but ultimately failed at both; failed at single life and couldn't hack family life. I'm now in a flat by myself whilst daughter and my ex are living with her parents. I seem to be focused on winning her back, but then scared that I actually do.'

Dave thanked Stirling for his check in and turned his attention to Ryan, who seemed to miss the pattern developing as Dave prompted him, gently, and asked if he could introduce himself.

Ryan took a noticeably, almost theatrical deep intake of air before he started.

'My name's Ryan,' he began, his voice too loud, as if rehearsed.

'I nearly got engaged a few years back. Since then...' He hesitated, adjusting his glasses.

'My confidence hasn't been the same. Susan, my ex, she...well, I thought she was the one. Turns out I was wrong. I guess heartbreak leaves a mark.'

He stopped, taking another theatrical deep breath.

'Anyway, they say there's plenty more ships in the night.'

Dave blinked. 'Isn't it fish in the sea?'

Ryan flushed. 'Yeah, that too.'

Dave wondered if Ryan was still a virgin, despite being probably 40. Jack's face said that he thought the same already.

'Thanks Ryan and thanks everyone for taking the time to introduce yourself. For our first week we'll look at the chemical reactions that happen in our bodies both when we find love and when relationships end. Feel free to sit and listen but if you feel that anything resonates with yourself and you feel like sharing, please do. '

Dave pushed back his chair and began his first session.

'When we fall in love, it's like a chemical cocktail hits our brains. Dopamine makes everything exciting and rewarding, oxytocin helps us bond and trust, and serotonin lifts our mood. It's no wonder we feel amazing, it's literally the same high you'd get from some class A drugs. But when it ends, the withdrawal hits just as hard. Our brains crash, stress levels rise, and that emptiness takes over.'

Dave looked around hopefully at their blank faces.

'It's why you can't stop thinking about your ex, replaying every memory, every mistake. Our minds are wired to hold onto that connection, even when it's gone. Sound familiar to anyone?'

Ryan raised his hand.

'Ryan, you don't need to raise your hand'

'But I wanted to ask a question?'

'That's fine go ahead'

'So this happens to everyone?' Ryan asked, leaning forward in his seat.

'That's right,' Dave replied. 'Anyone who's fallen in love and lost it; whether it's a breakup, distance, or death. The brain doesn't care about the reason; it just knows something's missing.'

Ryan nodded, but his frown lingered. Dave could see he wasn't entirely convinced, but at least it was a start.

Katrina was next to ask a question.

'And is this the same if you were away from a partner or if they died?'

'Yes, Katrina, that low after a breakup it's really real and it's deep, kind of like grief. Our brains don't really know the difference between different kinds of loss. Whether it's someone passing away, moving on, or just being away for a long time, all of these situation's mess with the connection we had with that person, and that can hurt.'

Katrina was nodding but said nothing. Stirling was next to volunteer a point.

'You mentioned earlier how you'd noticed similarities with drug use. Are people with other addictions more likely to suffer these same problems?'

'Great question, Stirling. Love and breakups hit us in a lot of the same ways addiction does. When we're in love, it's like getting a hit of something that makes everything brighter, sharper. Our brains get used to that high, that sense of reward. But when it ends, it's like going cold turkey. The joy, the comfort, that feeling of connection are all gone in one swoop, and our brains don't know what to do with that sudden emptiness. For someone who's been through addiction, the highs and lows of love can feel even more intense. Our brains are used to chasing big feelings, so when we fall in love, it might feel euphoric. And when it's over, it's like we're crashing. We might obsess, struggle to move on, all because those same pathways that kept us hooked before have been triggered all over again.'

The room sat in stunned thoughtful silence. Dave was quite pleased with his work and how things had gone, for a first week anyway. He sat down and opened his hands out.

'That's us for week one, folks. Thanks for coming along. Hopefully, you've found this session interesting and maybe even helpful. Over the next week, think about how your brain reacts to romance; the highs, the lows, and everything in between. Understanding what's going on up here,' Dave tapped his temple, 'can make navigating love just a little less messy. Same time next week?'

As the group filed out, Stirling paused by the door.

'See you next week?' Dave asked with a hopeful smile.

Stirling hesitated.

'Maybe' was all he offered, ducking under the frame off the door as he left.

6

Taking Stock Exchange

Patricia stood in the grand reception of the Stock Exchange Hotel in Manchester; she had doubted her instincts through the first class carriage window and through every stop from their home in Edinburgh. Surprising her husband was one way of putting it, she thought as she walked from reception across the foyer.

She forced a deep breath as she waited for the lift to arrive. Tapping repeatedly on the call button, knowing that the continued momentum would keep her moving on. Inside she went through the same motions again, tapping the button for the second floor impatiently until the doors closed and she forced another deep intake of air. Remembering her yoga instructors soothing voice, in and out, and out and in and hold and out as the lift zipped through the floors.

The doors opened on the other side of the lift which disorientated her for a second before she stepped into the corridor. The corridor was decorated like one of the rooms, pointless telephone tables with images of Manchester in black and white on each with green flowering plants which looked to be real, she thought.

Patricia checked the brass ornate sign with the room numbers and double checked the reservation details she'd emailed herself from Derek's laptop. She stood outside the door and forced another deep intake of air deep into her lungs.

In and out, in and out she replayed to herself again.

She knocked the door.

Silence boomed for what seemed like an eternity where she doubted even if she was there at all.

She then wrapped the door, hoping it wouldn't answer.

' A minute please'

Patricia recognised her husband's voice from behind the door. The door open slightly, before closing again.

'Move' she heard Derek muffle, following by further muffled responses which were unintelligible to her, in every aspect beside gender. She knew already what was happening behind the door. Her intuition noting every moment like x ray vision.

The door flung open elaborately and Derek flashed a smile over his belly, which flopped disappointingly over his shorts. She could smell the sex on him already, not her sex... the smell of disingenuous, forbidden, nasty sex. It was foul in every respect.

'Patrica. What a welcome surprise'

He lied.

He leaned in and hugged her unresponsive body, arms and all, as she scanned the room. Picking out every abnormality, every clue, the weight of evidence was enough for her to walk away right now but she didn't want to leave anything unproven this time.

An empty champagne bottle with two empty glasses.

The bed unmade on both sides, with every pillow used.

A pink trolley case.

Derek paced the room animatedly trying to shield her vision with his bulging frame. She held her silence whilst he muttered and blustered for defence. None of it landed for Patricia, her next move was already planned, it was just a matter of time before he finished shifting his pawns.

'You should have said you were coming down. I'd have made us reservations'

She watched his eyes following hers as she retraced all the evidence. He then fixed his eyes on hers, she saw his realisation drop as she moved to the bathroom door and attempted to open it.

It was locked.

It was only then she broke her silence.

'Open the door. I know whats been going on'

Derek dropped his realisation for a second and tried desperately to hang onto her last remaining shred of doubt.

'The bathroom is out of order Darling. Some awful carryon with the plumbing, I've been waiting for reception to call and fix it. I'd thought that was them arriving when you called'

Patricia wanted to believe him and almost let it slide, again, for a second before she raised her fist and banged on the door. She'd felt herself almost begin to shout, halted by a click from inside the bathroom as the door fell open. It opened slowly as a young face, half her age and size peered from behind the door. The face looked down and ashamed. Patricia thought she was quiet pretty if it hadn't been so ugly. Patricia smiled and said thank you, as she turned her venom towards Derek.

Disjointed from years previous, every single doubt she'd had, every misstep he'd made – all became clear in that moment, all looked ridiculously obvious in this fresh twenty twenty hindsight. How he'd refreshed and reflected every view back onto and into her. She didn't want to hear him speak.

The door closed as she made her way back along the corridor, resisting the temptation to volley each useless telephone table and their carefully position fake flowering plants as she passed. The lift hadn't even moved, the doors swished open as she lit up the button. She stepped into the lift and caught the lump in her throat as she made her way out of the hotel.

Spinning through the doors at the front of the hotel, she heard Derek careering after her.

' Patrica wait, let me explain'

She carried on through the doors and tried to flag down a taxi. Ignoring him when he caught up with her.

'It's nothing Patrica, nothing. I love you'

He continued to flail around her, trying to bother her. Like a wasp.

Patricia spun the rings on her fingers before she swatted his attempts.

'No Derek. We are nothing. We're done'

A black cab pulled over and Derek turned his attention to the driver , attempting to block her exit.

Patrica secured the driver's attention quickly enough.

'£50. To lock the doors and take me to the train station'

She never looked back at the doors locked with a thud and sped off towards the station.

7

Heart of Glass

There was Dave banging on what was still his old front door.

'Jack, Jack, Jack!!!'

The increasing desperation accelerating through each shout and bang on the door.

He hadn't answered a text in about three days and had a history of succumbing to whirl of depression. His elope to Scarborough had ended acrimoniously after Shelia fell for the owner of the hotel they'd stayed in, a lesbian who was feart of the cock by Jack's measure. He'd managed to recover the situation by returning to Mitchell's and spinning Stevie a yarn which he knew Sheila wouldn't contradict.

Eventually Dave pulled out his spare key. He hated the trepidation of what he was eventually going to find. Imagining how he'd done it. Mental images flickering as he prepared himself for Jack's lifeless body slumped over the couch, his blue face propped up on the table surrounded by discarded pills, or dangling from his belt hoisted up around the door frame...

He slid the key into the lock, heart pounding, and pushed the door open. The unmistakable smell of hash drifted out, sweet and earthy, a bizarre relief against the grim, rotting images his mind had conjured. Dave exhaled sharply, the tension in his chest releasing in a wave of irritation rather than affection.

He stepped over Jack's battered boots, their laces sprawled like they'd been discarded in mid-collapse, and swung open the vestibule door.

'What the fuck are you daen?' he barked, his voice cracking with a mix of anger and relief.

There, sprawled on the couch was Jack, very much alive, with an earphone dangling loosely from one ear and his eyes glued to the screen in front of him.

'What?' Jack muttered, glancing up briefly before returning to his game.

Dave leaned on the door frame, a sharp edge to his voice.

'I've been texting, phoning, banging on the door for ten minutes! Thought you'd done something stupid, ya daft cunt.'

Jack barely blinked, lifting the controller slightly.

'New FIFA came out. Champions League with Celtic. Some game, man.'

The weight in Dave's chest eased, but the residual frustration made his next words sharper than he intended.

'You're a fuckin' idiot, you know that?'

Jack smirked, eyes still locked on the screen.

'Good to see you too, mate.'

Dave sat down and refused a pass of a joint whilst Jack resumed focus on guiding Celtic through the Champions League group stages. The relief waving over him as his anger dissipated. Dave could never stay angry with Jack for too long, no one could.

Jack turned briefly as the game finished for half time.

'Thanks for worrying about me thou man'

'Can I get you a drink?' Jack asked as if he'd suddenly remembered his role as host.

Dave passed on account of the state of the place before he picked up a controller and challenged Jack to a game. Motivated by their competitive streak that swung like a sibling rivalry. Jack beat him with all the humility of a jealous wee brother.

'Take that ya ginger, Orange, Queen loving cunt'

Dave bowed out disgracefully, rage quitting mid replay at 2 nil.

He discarded the controller and walked around the flat that used to be his, memories of his and Morag's early romance filled the space, contrasting sharply with the empty takeaway cartons and the stale air of neglect. Renting it to Jack seemed like a great plan for them both.

Dave opened the blinds, to let some light in. He could see that Jack hadn't shaved in days and his bright eyes were dulled by an unspoken heaviness, despite his win.

'How you been doing man?'

Jack had a long list of things he was just about to start doing. His break up with Sheila had hit him harder than he was letting on, that much was clear. The fact that Denise had tried to make amends and he'd spurned her, in favour of Sheila, had only served to double his turmoil.

Backing away from his most vulnerable, Jack tried to return a volley of concern in defence.

'You still aff the drink?'

Dave had developed a medical condition which mean that after he started drinking he couldn't stop, it was called being a fucking absolute legend but despite this he was, indeed, still off it....

'Still counting the days. 772 exactly. I was thinking you might want to start coming back along to the groups? We've a few new members since your last visit and it might do you good to start talking about what's happened.'

Jack was nodding but still playing FIFA.

'Will do chief. Still Monday nights aye?' He shouted, earphones back fully encased. Dave leaned in for a half hug before he announced he'd let himself out, Jack waved as he popped the joint back in his mouth.

Dave shook his head as he stepped outside, the door clicking shut behind him. The crisp evening air hit his face, a sharp contrast to the stifling haze inside. He stood for a moment on the worn stone steps, his shoulders sagging with the weight of both relief and frustration.

Jack had always been like this, charming and infuriating in equal measure. Brushing off concern with a disarming grin and a flippant comment. Dave couldn't help but worry, though. He'd seen the cracks beneath Jack's surface, the moments when his bravado faltered and the weight of his choices seeped through. The whirlwind with Sheila, the lingering regret over Denise - it all painted a picture Jack wasn't ready to face.

As he walked down the path to his car, Dave replayed the conversation in his mind. He'd tried to keep it light, but he'd meant what he said about the group. Jack needed something to tether him, a way to process the chaos that seemed to follow him like a shadow. Dave wasn't sure if Jack would actually show up on Monday, but the offer was there. That was all he could do for now.

Sliding into the driver's seat, Dave started the engine and pulled away. The flat disappeared in the rear view mirror, but the image of Jack slumped on the couch, controller in hand, lingered. He sighed, gripping the wheel a wee bit tighter.

'772 days' he sighed to himself, unsure if he wanted to make it 773 yet.

8

Millie's First Week

For the first time since she arrived, Dave noticed the new girl, Millie, leaning forward with interest, slightly hunched as if to protect herself still but clearly interested. From the moment she'd made it through the door, he'd watched her shuffling nervously on her seat, trying to limit eye contact to an acceptable minimum with everyone in the room equally. He always found it painful watching members during their first few weeks, not sure where to sit, not sure what to say, not sure whether to stay or leave. Wondering if it was easier to put up with the heartache, they were trying to resolve in the first place. Millie was a textbook newbie: overdressed, over nervous and overthinking her every move.

But something changed when big Stirling had swaggered into the room. She looked up at all six foot something of him, dressed like one of they lottery winners that builds a quad bike course in their back garden, a lanky chav in yellow flip flops, grey joggers, and a blue stone island jumper. She was clearly enthralled by his glorious ensemble, maybe the mismatch of it all, but there was a grimace in it too. He carried himself with the full creep of a too-eager Tinder menace.

'Unfortunately, this week has been a problem for me,'

Stirling said with a certain casualness, stretching out his arms as if about to crawl into bed. Dave ducked out the way of one of his gangly arms as it swung towards him, catching an unmistakable gust of Lynx Africa as he did.

'You see, I'd been out on Saturday night and me and the ex had been texting. Long story short I woke up with her next to me on Sunday afternoon. I had to drop her back at her Mums and we sat in the car and talked for ages before she went back in, we kissed again, before she left, and we agreed we'd talk more during the week. She texted me later that day and I thought I would reply later. I didn't want to be too keen and push too heavily you see. That's been one of my problems.'

Dave grinned. 'Well, that's brilliant. Thanks for sharing, Stirling. That sounds like you've managed that really well. Just make sure you're managing your expectations.'

Stirling raised his hand.

'I'm no finished Dave.'

Dave's grin fell immediately. He should have known better than to think progress would be that straightforward. Stirling had split up with his Sarah, the mother of his child, prior to joining the group after she'd got sick of the way he'd been carrying on. He was a good lad, that was obvious, but it was clear that even though he diligently attended the meetings each week, Stirling had an obvious leaning for the social side of life, and that leaning rarely led to knowing when to quit while he was ahead.

'So 'I thought I'd play it cool. I'll respect myself, I'll give her time... all the shite we've talked about in here.'

Dave bristled at the notion of defending the group, but Stirling carried on.

'I'd put the phone in ma back pocket. I sat down on the sofa and pulled out my phone. I had another message from her. What is this? Some kind of fucking joke? And there above it was a picture, which I'd sent, of a lassy with her legs open, full Brazilian, two blue ticks and definitely no hers.'

'A private area?' Dave asked, screwing up his face as if to lessen the impact of his question.

Stirling unfortunately nodded.

'Aye, another burds fanny. I felt like I was in a nightmare. Like a state of shock. Even worse, I could see her writing. Boom the message hit me like a bullet: "What is this.... some kind of sick joke?" I just put the phone away.'

Dave was desperate to ask whose fanny it was, but he tried to remain professional. He looked around the room and it was clear everyone else was doing the same. They held their mouths closed that tightly they seemed to swallow their own lips. It was his duty to provide the group with some structure. He glanced over towards Millie, hoping she hadn't already decided the group wasn't for her. Millie was sat forward in her seat, captivated by Stirling's elaborate faux pas. Dave continued confidently.

'Well, Stirling. That certainly was an unfortunate accidental text and how are you feeling about it all now?'

'Like a fucking idiot. I keep pressing numbers on my phone to try and work out how it could happen. I'm at a loss. Problem is I actually love her, and we were talking about getting back together and all that. Aww fuck, I canny even talk about it any mare. I'm such a daft cunt. I've fucked it, Dave. Really fucked it this time. I eventually phoned her. She wasn't happy. I'd told her it was a mistake and that some of the lads in my WhatsApp group had sent the picture and I must have leaned on my phone and sent it to her by mistake.'

Even Dave, at his most optimistic, thought that was a bit weak.

'How did she react to that?'

Stirling looked defeated, all the animation from earlier drained from him now.

'She said the only mistake was her ever meeting me and hung up. And that was that. Now I'm here.'

This was standard fare for Romantics Anonymous, since Dave had first made a semi-circle of chairs in the middle of the Trinity Hall, the group had met each Monday evening, attended by a mix of steady regulars, desperate newbies and floating returnees who dipped in and out of service when their romancing got too much for them. The group focused on a mixture of cognitive behavioural therapy, education, spiritual support as well as the, obvious, benefits of group therapy. It was a lot of work, but Dave ran it all voluntarily. He wrote up the coursework, kept registers, and made sure they always had access to the hall.

That week, before the meeting, Dave sat down in his office (and by office he meant the desk crammed into his son's room) and logged into the

RA mail account. He smiled fleetingly as he remembered his password: MistyBrownEyes83. Fourteen emails, mostly spam were waiting for him, but his eyes were immediately drawn to a potential new enquiry:

Hi Romantics Anonymous,

I have had a chaotic and sometimes abusive relationship with Romance for a few years now and have finally decided to seek some support. I was hoping to come along to your next meeting if that wasn't too much trouble? If you could kindly, let me know if you have capacity within the group and if I need to send any details prior to attendance.

Kind regards

Millie

By the look on her face, it was clear she was regretting ever hitting send on that email.

'Millie. As a new member to the group, you don't need to share if you don't feel comfortable, but if you could introduce yourself, please?'

The room fell silent. All eyes trained on the new girl.

Unsure if she should stand or stay in her chair, Millie seemed to hover just above the plastic, her hands gripping the edge of the seat.

'Hi, I'm Millie. I am here to think more about my romantic relations and how they appear to, lately, conspire against me. I'm also looking for some techniques to help manage my reactions to romantic situations better. It's good to meet you all and thanks for being so friendly. Thanks so much.'

Dave was already impressed by Millie. She was an extremely attractive young girl and incredibly well spoken. He could see she was painfully nervous, but he tried to make eye contact with her, just long enough to make some kind of connection with her before he spoke.

'Nice to meet you too Millie and thanks for coming along. Hopefully, you find some help from within the group, some of our longer-term members act as sponsors and can help you through the most difficult situations, when they present themselves. You're never on your own.'

Dave watched as Millie gave a sigh of relief and relaxed a bit, sinking back into her chair.

'Unless you text your ex a picture of someone else's fanny.'

'Stirling, please,' snapped Dave.

Stirling pleaded his innocence with his eyes as he continued.

'It's true Dave. I called Tony and reached out for help on Sunday afternoon, immediately after it had happened.'

Thanks Tony, Dave mouthed silently as Tony tucked a heavy gold chain under the neck of his round neck white t-shirt before nodding back affirmatively. Re-pointing the creases down the middle of his jeans before he clasped his hands round the back of his head, leaned back, and shrugged off Stirling's lack of appreciation.

'Dinnae thank him. He suggested he take down his trousers and send me pictures of his bare arse and that I should do the same, then I'd send these over to her as evidence that we were having a laugh and that it was all just some changing-room banter.'

The room sat stunned.

Tony was only half embarrassed.

'I was trying to help! What else could I do?'

Dave was trying to think like Tony before giving up. He couldn't think of any circumstances that would have helped. Even anatomically that would have served no purpose. He immediately understood Stirling's frustration. But he had to keep things moving. To bring everyone back down to earth a little, Dave called upon ever reliable Katrina.

Kat was lovely and would do anything for you, for anyone. But Dave knew there was something, or at least he thought he did. Kat never seemed to have a problem but always had an answer for everyone and everything else.

She transmitted a smile across the group, as if she was a social worker being introduced to a problem family. Her ginger curly hair bounced around the room with her.

'Certainly, Dave. Hello everyone, old and new. My names Katrina, I have previously had issues with my love life and I consider myself an addict.'

And so she prattled on, the same rubbish each week: things were going well, work was busy, some rubbish about her cats. This week she'd concluded with a typical bland story about a train journey. It was ever reliable, ever boring.

The same could be said of Ryan. Ryan hadn't ever really found requited love. He'd had two girlfriends in his life and fell madly in love with them both, just before they dumped him. Once Dave had thanked Katrina for her story, Ryan was invited to speak.

Katrina and Ryan made a perfect double act. Put Ryan on after Stirling's accidental fanny story, and it'd feel like The Rolling Stones supporting Peter Andre. Dave knew it was best to deploy these two when the group was getting out of control, never in the headline spot, to bring any excitement down a little before the headline acts. Ryan dutifully obliged.

Conversely, Tony had been coming along for a few months now, joining the group after the first few weeks which had just been Jack, Ryan. Katrina and Stirling. He was different, to put it mildly.

'Can I just say firstly I was under pressure on Sunday afternoon,' Tony started, after Dave called on him to speak next.

'How many of you have had that call? Eh? Sorry Stirling, I didn't know what to suggest, you wouldn't even send me a picture of the fanny that you'd sent her. I didn't know what I was working with.'

'That's fine, Tony. Ma fuckup,' said Stirling reflectively.

Dave was looking at his watch, before he reminded Tony where he was.

'Hello all, I'm Tony. I'd like to extend a warm welcome to our new member Millie and our old friend Jack. Good to see some fresh meat arriving. I've been here with the RA for a few months now. I started coming after a recommendation I received after my bitch ex-wife kicked me out of my own home. I arrived here frustrated, desperate to see where I'd apparently gone wrong and looking for answers. I still am to be honest.'

'I spoke with my daughters, who now live with their Mum, over the weekend and, as we discussed earlier, tried to help a fellow member on Sunday afternoon. Can't do right for some folk.'

Dave piped in before they started again.

'And how are your daughters, Tony?'

'I've not seen them for a few months now, Dave. I give them a call but there busy with life and don't want their old Dad bothering them, but I phone each week to remind them I'm still alive and see how they are doing. Probably out getting shagged every weekend like their maw.'

Dave grimaced at Tony's lewd summary, even his own daughters weren't safe from his overtly sexually skewed view of the world. Normally, Dave brushed over Tony's remarks, as he'd either pretty much got used to him or grown to expect the worst. Before Tony could keep going, Dave thanked him for his contributions and moved around the circle.

'Thanks for coming along Derek, how have you been this week? Would you check in with the group too?'

Derek was a public schooled, successful business owner and utterly perplexed by his wife's inability to see beyond his adultery and the trappings of their life together.

'Like most of what everyone else has said David. Not too much happening, I've put a stop to my nights away working. But Patricia still hasn't relented. We're living separate lives but sharing a bank account and occasionally an awkward moment at the aga. It's been hellish to be honest.'

'And what is it you're finding most difficult Derek?'

'I suppose the hardest aspect is the frustration. I've tried explaining, I've tried apologising and I've made changes to my behaviour but she just doesn't get it'.

Dave watched as Katrina rolled her eyes. Not one to miss an opportunity, Dave seized the moment.

'Derek. Maybe the rest of the group can help provide a differing perspective for you?'

Teed up for her.... Katrina was ready to strike.

'Have you even spoke to her. Properly. Told her you can understand the hurt you caused cavorting around five-star hotels, spending BOTH of your money whilst she sat at home watching Tiger on her own. Have you ever seen it from her perspective?'

Dave watched as Derek sat carefully self-editing his response.

'Thanks Katrina. I hear what you are saying but I wasn't happy, that's why it happened. She must take some responsibility for that too?'

'I don't think so Derek. She wasn't the one who cheated on her partner. You should have spoken to her about how you felt, the fact that you still haven't is ridiculous. She's there in the house waiting for you to make amends, and here you are eight months later still crying about poor you. You need to get a grip.'

Dave shuffled in his seat, nervously on the fence before stepping in. Watching Derek recoil in his seat. Flicking the cuff links on his shirt as if he hadn't heard.

'As I've said before Katrina. It wasn't all one sided. It reached a point where I did what I did, but the problems were there well before then.'

'But you need to talk through those. And grovel, and apologise and apologise some more. Before crawling through broken glass just to hear her fart back at you over a walkie talkie. Cos that's all you deserve.'

Dave muted Katrina with a 'Thanks Katrina,' in his best teacher voice.

She reluctantly obliged.

Derek sat with the wheels spinning, he looked ruffled.

'Are you okay Derek?'

'Yes David. Absolutely fine. As you said it's good to hear other opinions and viewpoints, maybe not always the most eloquent but always good to hear'.

Dave felt like this was Katrina deployed at her best. He looked over at Jack, Jack was grinning menacingly knowing exactly how uncomfortable Dave was waiting for him sharing his headline moment. But first here was Lucy.

Lucy was an attractive girl, Dave thought. She definitely had the hips for the children she'd bore. She also had a habit of trying to accelerate every relationship through the gears and onto the next stage. In response, becoming devastated that her eventual rejection was a rejection of everything she held dear. Dave just wanted her to be happy, if anyone in the group deserved that, it was Lucy. She reminded him of a younger version of his wife.

'Hi everyone, I'm Lucy. I have had a problem with romance for the best part of a decade and after several attempts at love I decided I couldn't face another cold turkey coming off romance. That was a few months ago, and I feel like a much stronger person now and that's important to me and more so for my kids. Leaving me hurts enough but how someone could give up on them too still baffles me. I've had a quiet week. Not done much, just chilled really, nothing much to report. That is me just boring old me.'

'Thanks for sharing, Lucy. It is much appreciated and you're doing so well. Keep it up.'

Dave looked at his watch, again, and then to the next chair where Jack was sitting. He was not ready for Jack's share but, as was his calling, he kept pushing on.

'And next we have a returning member Jack, welcome back Jack. How are you? I know it's your first week back, but would you mind sharing?'

Jack was the archetypal floating member, his last flurry of attendances brought to a sudden halt several weeks ago. And each time, he'd re-emerge with a story full of soap opera twists and turns, flexing his shameless ability to make comebacks even Dirty Den himself would be proud of. His most recent disappearance had become less mysterious over the past couple of weeks, when Dave had first spoken with Jack and heard a story that had taken his breath away. The group was not ready for what they were about to hear. He knew that much.

'Hi Millie. Welcome to the group. Nice to see some old faces I recognise. I'm back but I didn't think I would be. Not this time, but here I am again. I had a thing you could have called a whirlwind romance, I helped pack up her stuff into her car and we drove off to Scarbourgh. A few days we had walks along the pier, games in the arcades, chippy teas and nights drinking in the wee bar till the small hours. Then suddenly, the next morning she decided to stop talking to me. Not. A. Single. Word.'

Dave was surprised, mainly by the gaping omissions in Jack's story. The fact that she was his bosses wife, the part where they'd been flirting with the landlady and had a threesome, as well as the fact that, to his best guess Jack had woke up in the middle of the night and urinated over two full suitcases of their clothes whilst brushing off her attempts to stem the hurried flow of his drunken pish. These, he felt, were critical aspects of the story that could have filled some gaps for the remaining members of the group.

He tried pressing Jack.

'Any reason why she might have stopped talking that you can think off?'

'Not one Dave. She was another heart breaker in a long line of heart breakers. I'm back on the wagon. I travelled back up the road and went tae work the next day.'

'And did your boss have anything to say about your unplanned vacancy?'

'It was a bad mental health week ….and that's the truth.'

Dave shook his head with a half-smile. Jack's ability to gloss over chaos never failed to amaze him. With a click of his laptop, Dave pulled up the evening's lesson.

Today was to be their first lesson in their eight personal rights. Dave had put together a quick PowerPoint, and had beamed it onto the wall, midway between two windows, whilst he talked over the contents.

They began with rule number 1: the right to say no.

'We all have that right to say no, and why is that important?'

Lucy put up her hand.

'Yes, Lucy?'

'So that we aren't putting ourselves in a position of danger or doing something we don't think is correct.'

'That is absolutely right. Thanks Lucy. We all have the right to say no to a situation we feel uncomfortable with, no matter how that might upset someone else or not align with their own interests. It's important that we all remember we have the right to say no.'

Tony piped up.

'I agree with that 100%. I was in the pub on Saturday night and some of the young team were trying to buy me a flaming shot called purple rain, but I was already too drunk for that.'

'Thanks Tony' said Dave, but Tony carried on.

'Still, they bought one for me, so I left the pub. They were phoning me and when I answered I told them I wouldn't be back in until they were gone.'

Dave was a bit disappointed that Tony hadn't really grasped the topic in a romantic sense. Before he could steer the group back on topic, Katrina joined in.

'They are disgusting. I had one up in Rialtos and straight away I felt like my cheeks had gone that way, you know, when you've blown up a balloon?'

Most of the group nodded.

'I should have said no too.'

'Thanks for sharing.' Dave smiled.

At the end of the meeting, once they'd stacked their chairs at the side of the room and everyone started filtering out, Dave made sure to check on Millie.

'Here, thanks for coming today. Some characters. Are you okay? Maybe see you next week?'

'I think so, David,'

Despite her initial nerves, she seemed to have a taste for the vulgarity, sitting further and further forward with each gory detail of their failed love lives.

'That's great, you can call me Dave, by the way.'

'Nice to meet you. I'm still Millie,' before she pulled a theatrical awkward face.

'And... thank you, Dave. I think this might be what I needed.'

9

Home Safe

Millie sat in the driver's seat of her car and immediately popped on the radio. It was tuned to Radio 1 despite her being nearly 30 now, and as the music blared, she wondered if there was a social cut off for Radio 1 listeners. If, perhaps, when you turned 25 that particular frequency should just be replaced by static. She turned it off.

But the silence didn't feel comfortable either. After driving along to the hum of the car alone, she eventually phoned her mum.

'How did you get on honey?'

'It was hilarious,' said Millie, 'but they were all mostly lovely.

'So, do you think you will go back?'

'I said I would. It's not as if I'm busy.'

'Okay honey. Well, I've left your tea on low in the kitchen, see you when you get in.'

Millie settled into her drive home and accepted the silence. She wondered to herself how she might react to being sent a picture of another girl's foo foo from her ex. She wasn't a prude, but she hadn't been happy with the word fanny being used to describe a woman's genitalia. Not as bad as cunt, she thought. The word cunt was horrible to her and, while she didn't hold it in the same 'c-bomb' regard as Americans did, and, honestly, still used it to describe everything from a guy with no name to any inanimate object she happened to hurt herself on, she didn't think it was appropriate for describing another lady's vagina. But honestly, her ex had sent her enough abusive texts that she'd have probably welcomed a foo foo pic.

Getting back to her Mum and Dad's she parked on the street, leaving enough room for her dad to get out in the morning. She felt safe being back at her Mum's. For the first week or two, even getting from her car to the front door came with a certain amount of looking over her shoulder, but now she didn't even look back as the car locked with a flash of its indicators. The only time Stevie had come near was Christmas day when he'd left a pair of Louboutins on her Mum's doorstep. She was still enamoured by the gesture, but he'd crossed the line that night and they were never getting back together.

She'd been back there for three weeks now, ever since Stevie had wrecked her flat in a jealous rage. After she'd left her place filled with fear and a shame she couldn't explain, she'd decided it was time to lie low. She wanted his remorse and general interest to burn out. She never had the energy to deal with anymore of his shit. He was a cunt she thought to herself.

She shouted hello to her Mum and Dad as she breezed through into the kitchen. The warmth hit her as soon as she opened the door; the radiators were always up full and her tea was still sat at the bottom of the oven. 'Your chips are in the air fryer,' her Mum called through as her dad popped open the fridge.

'You wanting a drink?' he asked.

'Irn Bru,' she replied as he pulled out a can of beer for himself and sat down at the table next to her.

'I'll sit with you; she's watching that soap rubbish. I canny be daen with it.'

Millie laughed a wee bit as she sat her plate down in front of her. Cordon Bleu it wasn't, lasagne and chips it was though and her dad made a mean lasagne. She was not convinced that half a ham stock cube in a jar of Dolmio qualified as a secret family recipe, but he was sticking to it.

'How did you get on, hen?'

'No bad,' replied Millie whilst blowing a fork full of chips and lasagne.

'Have you heard anything else from that cunt Stevie?'

46

'Dad!' she replied with faux embarrassment.

'Well, he is. If he gives you any more grief he's getting burst.'

She was pleased her Mum and Dad were here to look after her, whether that meant hot dinners or threatening to go round and batter him, but after Stevie had gotten over the shock of her leaving, he'd shown nothing but remorse, and was only interested in trying to win her back. That night though; she'd never forgive him for that.

They'd been having a drink at home, as was becoming their preference, that way she wouldn't have to deal with anyone casually glancing her way, and him feeling some need to step in and assert himself. She'd met Stevie at school and felt that she knew him better than anybody: he was misunderstood. He was dyslexic and angry with the world but fiercely honest and the most passionate man she'd ever met. She was smitten from when he first picked her for social dancing at school. Sure he was a bad boy to everyone else and a bit of a rogue, but he worshipped her. Through their younger years he'd been her hero. Since she was young, she'd suffered near constant racist abuse. It'd always been 'paki', never once did they enquire about her actual ancestry which was in fact half Indian. But this all stopped when Stevie and her started dating. No-one dared upset 'Stevie's bird.'

Even when she'd been accepted into Glasgow University, studying art and design, he appeared truly pleased for her. He was the one that suggested they both move to Glasgow and share a flat rather than her traveling through. She knew it was, in part, because Stevie hated the prospect of her sharing digs with other guys, but the security of his job delivering juice for Barrs and a flat in town wasn't any hardship for her. He supported her all the way through uni, taking on most of the rent and the bills, covering what he could on nights out, stretching his wage as far as it would go. But he needed a wee bit extra to keep on top of it all.

Stevie had started selling drugs even back when they were at school, bits of weed mainly that she'd even smoke a bit of herself, but when he moved to Glasgow he started taking Charlie. Every time they'd go to socialise with her new pals, they uni types, he'd nip off to the toilets and come back with his confidence boosted. She never noticed him dealing at first, just the flat got busier and he had more errands to run. And if she was honest, she didn't even notice him using for the most part. When she did, if she even thought of mentioning it, he got aggressive, so she did her best to not see it until it got really bad. That night it got really bad.

That night started out as a quiet Friday, they were having drinks in their flat and Stevie's friend Scott had popped around. It was obvious he'd only come to buy gear, but they all sat and had a few drinks whilst Scott and Stevie had a few social lines. Millie's heart started racing as soon as Scott had asked how uni was going, and she tried to play things down before Stevie interjected, 'She's a right wee brain box is Millie, designing clothes for Adler and Stevenson.'

She'd been offered a job with Adler and Stevenson after Stevenson himself had noticed her work at one of the year-end shows. Georgi Stevenson's clothing brand had been a hit all over the UK, She'd been selected for a full-time graduate role which began in July, before then Georgi was more than happy to have her in the office on a part time basis. Stevie hated Georgi. Georgi had the success and recognition which Stevie craved, but, more than that, Georgi's design work commanded Millie's admiration and, worse than that, for Stevie at least, Georgi could see the talent in Millie that would take her places. He had taken her under his wing and helped her develop out her first designs. Millie had been the first graduate to have her designs developed into apparel samples. Anytime he was mentioned, anytime he got in touch, anytime she worked, a slew of comments would be spat her way. It was becoming an obsession.

Scott had been impressed, he'd bought his girlfriend a dress from their Glasgow shop at Christmas and she'd been made up. He'd heard that Georgi was sound and drove a yellow Lambo. Again, Millie advised she didn't have too much to do with him but she had heard about the car. She said he was a fantastic designer despite his choice in car.

That was it, that's all she'd said! But as soon as Scott left, Stevie started on a line of questioning that he refused to let go, looking to escalate with each new dig. 'A fantastic designer, is he? Does he like Indian girls? Auld pervert!'

She'd soon had enough and phoned a taxi.

'Whaur are you going?'

Growled Stevie as he tried to block her exit. She forced by him, told him to stop being a dick and that she was going to her Mums.

'No, you're no!' scowled Stevie.

He followed her into the bedroom, knocking her open case off the bed. Millie looked up at him despondently, as she calmly righted the case where it fell before continuing.

'Really?' she ventured, still being careful not to mock him.

He was pacing up and down, wrestling with his anger before he suddenly left the room. 'Fuck it,' he bellowed as he slammed the living room door shut.

Shortly after, the stereo was booming. Beyonce's Drunk in Love was being drafted out for dramatic effect; the number of times it had been used this way had stripped away any emotional attachment for Millie. This was supposed to be their song but had now become just another item in Stevie's toolbox of coercion. Millie clicked the case shut, took one deep breath, and made her exit, knowing it wouldn't be too long before another of Stevie's trademark moves surfaced.

She clicked the door shut behind her and jumped into the waiting taxi. A wave of quiet relief passed over her as the driver pulled away. The driver didn't even have the radio on, and in the silence, Millie could hear the thumping in her chest fade, the rhythm of it beginning to slow. Then her phone started ringing. It was Stevie. Of course it was. She turned it off and popped it back in her bag resolving to give him the night to cool off. He needed to hit the gear on the head and stop being so jealous, but she still loved him. She couldn't help that.

By the time the driver pulled into her mum's street, Millie could already feel the tears drying. She gave one last sniff and rubbed her face in the crook of her elbow.

'You okay?' the driver asked as he cranked the hand break back into place.

'I'm fine, thanks.'

'You're Stevie's bird, are you no?'

'Yes,' she replied.

'He's a good friend of mine. Listen, you don't worry about the fair and have yourself a good night. If you're needing a lift back, just give me a phone. Take care doll.'

Millie arrived at her Mum's house. It was always referred to as her Mum's house, despite the fact that her dad had paid for it all and everything inside it. He doted on her Mum and this house had been their forever home. When the housing development started, Kim knew what she wanted and as soon as she saw the show home, she was smitten and, by proxy, as was Millie's Dad. It was always home for Millie. She opened the door and called through to them both, immediately setting aside any thought for her argument with Stevie. She could already tell they were a little bit drunk by the volume and eagerness of their voices.

'Oh hello dear, what brings you here?'

Her mum's voice slurred through from the living room.

'Is everything okay?'

'Yes, yes,' replied Millie, as she sat on the bottom stair and took her time taking off her shoes.

'Stevie's got all his pals' round to watch the boxing or something they were doing my head in, I though best to leave them to it and come out here. Are you no pleased to see me?'

'Aw of course we are.'

Before Millie could look up from her trainers, her mum was in the lobby with a hand on her shoulder that nearly drew a gasp out of her.

'In you come honey.'

Her Mum took her coat and popped it into her room, and by the time Millie went through to the living room, her dad was already pouring her a glass and talking at the same time.

'How's the new job going – you jet setting around the world yet?'

Millie looked around the living room, wondering if anything wasn't from Next. Next had been a byword for modern design in her Mum's mind and a sure-fire way of retaining her home's showroom status. It did just that. She laughed to herself as she imagined her poor Dad being dragged round the shops every weekend, then, when he finally got home, being continually badgered to tidy up after himself. She stroked a cushion on the sofa and thought to herself that it was actually quite nice before she tucked herself onto her seat and answered her dad.

'Not quite, but it's such a great place to work. Everyone is so nice, and the designers are given such free reign by Georgi to bring their own individualism to the collection, it's been great, exactly what I wanted to be doing.'

'And how's this Georgi been with you?' Her Dad asked, being her dad.

'Absolutely fine, his boyfriend Nic works with HR, and the two of them are lovely together you just wouldn't imagine them as millionaires.'

'That's good' replied her dad – satisfied with both the fact that he was nice, but also relieved that his daughter was safe from any millionaire admiring boss.

They had a few glasses of wine before Millie announced she was headed off to bed. Her Mum and Dad were well and truly drunk and sang away to Neil Diamond as she took herself upstairs. She brushed her teeth and then cuddled up in bed next to her bunny, still amazed that her Mum and Dad had kept him intact. She looked around the room thinking how she really must let them know that her old posters can go now, even knowing that her dad had already delicately removed them to repaint and then put them back up again, in exactly the same position. Even Bunny, the stuffed rabbit she'd had for as long as she could remember, was still balanced on her pillow. She unzipped her case, pulled out her mobile phone charger and plugged her phone in next to her bed, slightly embarrassed as she remembered how she'd insisted on having a plug charger next to her bedside table. Her Dad moved the plug socket to suit. He was a great Dad; she had amazing parents. All she really wanted was a home life like theirs.

She turned on her phone and it started beeping and beeping. Voicemail after message after voicemail after message.

Where are you? I love you I'm sorry. XX
Sorry can you call me? xx

Can you fone me? x
Fone me now.
Why have you left me?
Fucken fone me rite now.
Imigrant bitch. Fone
Fucken boot. Fine me
You at that cunt Georgi's?
Call me no x
I'll set his shop on fire.
Fone me ya boot. Or I'm torching his shop.
I'll do it.
That's your laptop fucked.
His shops next..
Fone me,. Paki bitc
That's his shop torched.

Millie sat and looked at the texts coming through with tears running down her face as each threat and each name hurt more than the last. How could he call her a Paki, Stevie of all people. She turned the phone back off and stared into the corner of the room. She turned off her light, lay down and kept staring at the same corner. Cuddling bunny tight against her, she already knew it was over.

She never slept that night. She got up early and sat with her Dad whilst they had breakfast. Her Mum liked to sleep in. He asked how things were going, she didn't have the heart to tell him the truth; the pain that she was feeling the horror around the corner for her, but she wanted to prepare him for the fact that she'd be back.

'Stevie's struggling, she said, he is like a fish out of water, and I feel like it's holding me back. He never wants to do anything, and I just think there's more to do with my life, would it be okay to come back here for a while, just whilst I sort out my life.'

'Of course, it is hen, I did think you were quiet last night and it's no normal for a young lassie to be hame with her Mum and Dad on a Friday night.

52

'Dad I'm nearly 30!'

They both laughed as he reminded her she was always his wee lassie. He asked if she wanted a run through to help with – she declined.

She jumped off the train and headed off down passed George Square, onto Buchanan Street. Thankfully, Adler and Stevenson flagship store was still standing, she instantly felt a bit better as she made her way down to their flat. But as she entered the street, she could instantly feel that something wasn't right. Her heart was racing as she punched the code into the flat entry system and made her way up the stairs. She passed one of the neighbours on the stair; he just kept his head down. She turned onto their level and noticed the door was slightly ajar, and the close was tinged with a smell like burnt plastic. She pushed the door and it swung open, slower than usual, clearing broken glass from the hall floor. One shard had got stuck underneath, and scraped a thin white curve into the laminate. She tiptoed through her broken flat. Remnants of pictures and her pieces from art school were torn up and scattered through the hallway, leading to the open bathroom door. Her work laptop was floating in the bath.

She couldn't believe he would do this. She made her way into the living room and found Stevie there, passed out on the sofa. She watched him sleeping, just for a second, watching him breathing calmly ...almost serenely, as if her Stevie was still in there somewhere. Stevie stretched and stirred prompting her to snap out of it, snapping herself out of the notion to care anymore. She began surveying the room; Every piece of furniture around him was slashed or burned, there were holes in every wall and blood sprayed everywhere. She placed a throw over him and made her way through to the bedroom, not even flinching at the disarray in front of her. Millie opened her case and started packing. She had to leave this time, leave behind the drama, the pain, the heartbreak of seeing Stevie lurch from one drama to another every time she moved on with her life. She didn't want to face any of it. She packed her case and walked out into the close.

'Millie? What's happened?' Scott was making his way back up the close.

'Tell him I'm leaving if you can wake him... I can't put up with his shit anymore. It's done.'

'Dinnae say that Millie, he'll be fine. You know what we are like. I'll have a word with him. I'll get him to phone you.'

'Don't' snapped Millie 'but tell him that I did love him and hope he gets help.'

She phoned her dad as she trudged off down the stair, the case whacking off the steps as she made her way to the close door.

'Dad? Could you pick me up please?'

He was already in the car.

10

Saturday Shift

Lucy was sitting half-dressed on the sofa, listening to the kids playing as it descended into a fight. She was pensively trying to gauge the meeting point between the axis of sofa sitting and intervening. She called an early warning shot up the stairs 'Archie,' then 'Ellie.' That was enough to turn their feud down to simmer as she resumed scrolling through TikTok. That was how she spent most of her time: spending way too long looking at the background of people's houses wondering why people would go to all the effort of putting a video out without putting the kids toys out of shot or even crop their video.

She looked round the living room and thought about how much cropping her videos would need, decided that was way too much editing and began to tidy away the pile of clean clothes she'd left on the sofa. She'd started leaving them there as a visible prompt to shame her into ironing and putting away said clothing. It had worked initially, but the sofa had now become the halfway house for any ironing which needed done.

She made her way into the kitchen and started rinsing off some plates. The smell of stale pepperoni pizza hung heavy in the kitchen. She had decided that the rest would have been a snack later, and then good for the birds, but it was now in the bin. 3 chances the pizza had had, and it was gone. Just then, her phone buzzed on the worktop.

It was Keith.

Keith and Lucy had had a thing, a brief romance which had ended suddenly when Keith had called her in a panic one day, apparently from the bathroom of his marital home asking if she could reply to his text suggesting she was a mate and they'd been having a laugh. She duly did and never heard from him again, until that morning. And now, she was texting back.

Hey stranger. How's you? How's the Kids? X

Her and Keith began texting back and forth. Telling her they were all good, that he hadn't been seeing them as much. How was she? Still as horny as ever?

Lucy put the tap off and left the dishes on the side. She returned to the sofa. As she walked, she caught sight of herself in the mirror. This was a fair departure from the vision Keith had in his head, she thought, but she decided to play along with his assumed mental image rather than the one reflecting back at her.

Always horny for you big boy. X

The texts became filthier, but Lucy still paused two or three times to shout up and placate Archie and Ellie. She eventually sent him a picture of her cleavage, heavily cropped and filtered to show her in the best possible light, as if an image from his imagination had suddenly materialised on his phone. His reply was almost instantaneous. He was impressed. He asked if she wanted to meet for a coffee on Saturday morning. Lucy was already skipping through what she might wear when she text her Mum to see if she would have the kids a few hours earlier. Lucy was starting a new volunteer position with the Samaritans on Saturday at 12. Her Mum was having the kids anyway, and it was just a coffee and a quick catch up. What harm could it do?

They were meeting for coffee.

Lucy's Friday flashed by in a whir. Come Saturday morning, she sprung out of bed before her alarm and started packing the kids' things before making them breakfast. She put on her makeup, just making herself presentable she told the kids. Archie told her that she was always lovely as she kissed him on the head. She pulled the door closed and walked the short distance to her Mums, hand in hand with Ellie and Archie. It was a nice sunny morning for September she thought to herself, already worrying she might be too close to sweating.

You're looking smart,' her Mum said, but she wasn't for hanging about. She left Archie and Ellie at her Mum's, ran back home and quickly pulled her top over her head before giving herself a healthy barrier of Mitchum. She checked her makeup one last time, smacking her lips in the mirror as she found her car keys and drove off to meet Keith.

She parked up at the palace car park, and immediately noticed Keith in his large navy-blue saloon car. He'd been waiting for her. They walked along to the coffee shop, him paying her compliments which she duly lapped up. He was still a fine-looking man.

He ordered them coffees as she found them a seat. She chose one in the window, looking out over the busy high street as she waited on him arriving with both cups. He slide the tray on the table and took the seat opposite her, his back to the passing shoppers. She took a sip, before asking 'So how's things with you?'

Keith went on about his change of jobs, about how busy he was, about not seeing the kids as often as he liked. He was so chatty. There was never an awkward silence. Her and Keith just seemed to bounce off each other. They ordered more coffee and Keith had some cake. And after what seemed like 10 minutes, Lucy's phone started ringing. She picked it up to answer but quickly checked the time. Her heart sank. That 10 minutes had been more like 2 hours. 'I'm late' she panicked. They packed up and finished their drinks whilst Keith settled the bill. They both walked as quickly as they could, testing Lucy's liberal Mitchum application further. Lucy got to her car and quickly apologised to Keith after deciding she'd better call them, Keith agreed and stood outside the car as she returned her missed call.

'Lucy, thanks for calling back. It is Mrs. Wright from the Samaritans. do you know what time it is?'

Lucy was already a bit perturbed by her patronising tone.

'I'm so sorry Mrs. Wright. I was having a coffee with a friend and I lost track of time.'

But Mrs. Wright was not happy. Edna hadn't had her lunch and they were already a staff member down; lunchtime was their busy period on a Saturday.

Lucy was very apologetic.

'I'm on my way just now, I'll be as quick as I can.'

Mrs. Wright told her not to bother. Their busy period had passed and well it was hardly a good first impression.

Lucy hung up the phone and started to cry, even though Keith was still stood beside her car. He gave her a sympathetic look and offered her a hug. She opened the door and stood up, he opened his arms to embrace her and she cried on his shoulder as she hugged him tight, his hands stroking her as she did. She could smell his aftershave, Fahrenheit, she thought. He asked if she was going to be okay and she confirmed she'd survive. She broke off from their hug and apologised whilst she blew her nose and stuffed the handkerchief back into her pocket.

'I must look such a mess,' she offered.

'Not at all,' replied Keith. Before he offered her another hug.

This time she noticed the pace of his hands stroking her slow down and slip gradually down her body, cupping her bum for a second before rising to stroke her back again. She looked up to see his reaction and he kissed her. She paused for a second before kissing him back. Eventually she allowed him to slip his tongue in her mouth, and before long he was licking the inside of his lips slowly. His hands groped her greedily but , eventually, they broke off and she began fixing her suit.

'Are you going to be, okay?' asked Keith again..

'That bitch was so rude. It was an honest mistake.' Lucy told Keith and herself.

Keith agreed. 'What's your plans now?'

Lucy immediately thought of her mum and kids' disappointment if she returned and told them how it went.

'I can't go and get the kids just now, they'll be devastated.'

'We could always go to yours?'

Lucy felt a fleeting pang of unease. Was this what she wanted, or just a distraction from everything she'd been trying to ignore? She silenced the thought as quickly as it came, giving in to the moment.

She got back in the car and began driving home, noticing Keith's eyes following her in her rear-view mirror. She realised that she didn't want to park her car outside her house, worried about Mum taking Archie and Ellie out for a walk and seeing her car. She indicated left and pulled over a few streets back, satisfied as she then watched Keith pull in behind her. She pointed to the passenger seat as she made her way around the front of his car. She opened the passenger door.

'Where are you going?' He asked.

'I was thinking we'd be best going in your car. Avoid any chance that my Mum might see my car parked outside and bring the kids around early!'

Keith agreed and beckoned her to 'jump in'.

Lucy pulled the door shout and looked around his car. It was nice she thought, although leg room was a bit cramped. She asked Keith how to put the seat back, he replied saying that it was only a short journey. As soon as they arrived and he pulled on the handbrake. She unclipped the seat belt before scanning the street and making a dash for it; encouraging him to be quick as she scurried up the path. She watched impatiently from behind a crack in the door, before he slipped inside, she then closed it firmly behind him. Double checking that it was locked, before she turned to smile at Keith.

The pair of them made out frantically on the stair. Keith undressed her as she made her way tentatively up each step, pulling the kids bedroom door closed as she backed into her own room. Lucy reached for his crotch whilst they kissed and noticed his cock was bristling with want in his jeans. She unclipped her bra and stepped out of her knickers as she lay back on the bed.

Keith greedily lapped away at her pussy and she moaned with delight, arching her back and grinding herself against his grinning face. She pulled him up, wanting him inside her. His face glistened with her want as they began kissing once more. She gasped as she felt him push up inside her and begin to fuck her. Soon, he grabbed her tight, grunted into her ear, buckled and came inside her. He stayed in position as Lucy hurriedly ground out her want against his expiring hardness. She eventually yelped and pushed against him as she felt the satisfaction of her climax wave through her body.

She was still lying there as Keith began piecing together his clothing.

'Is there somewhere I can?' he asked, pointing to his spent cock covered in their sex.

'Second door there on the left.' She sat back on the bed as he made his way to the bathroom. She lay back and contentedly listened to him washing up.

She was still naked in bed when he returned. He started getting dressed as she tried to make small talk, but he told her he'd lost track of time himself and was having to get back for the kids.

She was disappointed but what could she do. She began getting herself ready, and she could feel his cum dribbling from her as she pulled back the duvet and retraced her steps. She picked her clothes up off the steps and quickly wiped her pussy with her pants before tossing them into her laundry basket. Keith was already at the top of the stairs, nervously playing with his car keys and checking himself in the mirror.

'Well that was some consolation. Thanks Mr.,' she purred. Keith didn't make eye contact, but kissed her cheek and announced he had to go.

Lucy locked the door behind him and walked back up the stairs to her bedroom. She re-opened the kids' doors, remade her bed and opened the windows to air the place out a little. She got dressed, again, and walked back downstairs.

Keith had text already.

It was good to catch up. I'll see you again soon. Please don't text again, my daughter plays with my phone, and it would hard to explain. I'll speak next week x

Lucy looked at the text and immediately set aside any doubt. She decided she'd wait to hear from him. That she'd trust him. She called her Mum.

'Hi. That's me back. Yeah it was good. Yeah, went well. No problems. Do you want to walk back round with the kids, and we'll get some dinner together?'

Lucy threw her phone on her bed and head into the bathroom for a shower. Picking up the towel, she sniffed it to find Keith had clearly wiped his cock on the towel. Dirty bastard, she laughed, reminding herself not to text.

11

Week Three

Was there anything worse than that feeling? If the highs are so good yet the lows so bad, then it should be illegal. If it were a drug, it would be banned, or at least licensed. Dave surmised that Bryan Ferry was indeed right: Love is a drug and a pretty dangerous one at that.

It was that feeling that led Dave to start Romantics Anonymous. He wanted somewhere that those suffering the ill effects of romance, who found themselves addicted to their own romantic urges, or felt beaten down by the whole business, could begin their road to recovery. Now, each Monday, he chaired his group at the Trinity Community Outreach centre. But that required work. Each Monday evening was a rush and his commitments to his work at Scottish Spinsters, his wife Morag, their two sons and their dog, his favourite child by some margin, all fell by the wayside.

That week, he shifted back from his folding desk, before closing the blinds only just noticing it was already dark outside. He could hear the rest of the house rousing as he decided to ignore the call to sort dinner for the family. It's Morag's turn, he thought to himself, on account of him having made the last 4 square meals and walked Misty several times consecutively. The Melahuilish family division of labour always appeared to fall unfairly on Dave, he thought, as he looked over his notes for that night's meeting.

Ryan Alexander

Lucy Bruce

Derek Horn

Katrina O'Shaughnessy

Tony Sinclair

Stirling Wilson

And now Millie Singh

'Are you joining us?' bellowed Morag from the kitchen.

Dave pretended not to hear, on the basis that he was busy, and Morag should know that she'd already left it too late for his dinner. But on her second call of 'Dave!' he could remain silent no longer.

'What?' he retorted resolutely maintaining his stubborn rejection of kindness, and finishing that week's agenda instead.

Dave typed out his signature on every email fully, reassuring members that they had his details in case of emergency. As he hit send he heard his cue to, safely, head into the kitchen as Morag and the kids trooped off upstairs after their meal. Dave headed through to pick over the leftovers for him and Misty, only to be greeted by a full meal plated up for him. Maybe he would have time, he thought.

He still divided it up between Misty's bowl and his plate before zapping it in the microwave for a minute, trying to resuscitate a lukewarm chicken pie on full power in as little time as possible. As he carried the plate to the table testing for warmth, only to simultaneously be disappointed by the coldness of the middle and then burn his tongue on the filling nearest the crust.

Just as he was polishing it off, Morag came back downstairs. 'Thanks for dinner' he announced – completely at odds with his earlier retort.

'No problem,' replied Morag, clearly delighted that she was right again.

'Is that you heading off?'

'Yes, thanks dear,'

He shouted up to his boys as he departed, then dropped to his knees to cuddle Misty fully. 'How was your dinner?

Don't worry - I'll take you out for a walk as soon as I get back,' he whispered. and kissed her on the nose. Dave sat in his car – service overdue and oil change needed; he was reminded immediately after sliding the keys into the ignition. Next week, he thought to himself and drove off at pace, drumming along to The Pet Shop Boys as he weaved through Suburbia.

Dave parked up at the Trinity Outreach Centre and could see Ryan Alexander already waiting. Ryan had been managing his romance addiction for a few months, and Dave had resisted his offers to help as much as possible, Ryan had that needy vibe about him which Dave could ill afford outside the group setting. Still, no matter how many times he said he was fine, that didn't stop Ryan showing up early.

'Hallo Daaavve,' Ryan called as he makes his way to the entrance, like that League of Gentlemen character they both knew from the late 90s. Dave had long since tired of the reference.

'Hello Ryan,', his 'your early tonight' laced with passive aggression.

The Trinity Hall was formerly a grand building, built courtesy of Andrew Carnegie's funds in the 1900s – originally a library and now a home to several groups and managed by the local council. Varied attempts at modernisation hadn't been kind to the aesthetics of the place. The ramp to the entrance put off more visitors than it catered for. Dave's booking started 30 minutes before the start time, but it was already 10 past and the Karate Class were still in the hall. Dave hovered outside, peering into the windows trying to make eye contact with sensei Jamieson.

'Just go in Dave,' encouraged Ryan with a shove to Dave's back, 'It's over time.'

The force of Ryan's nudge sent Dave stumbling and apologising through the swinging door.

'Sorry - is that the time? Already?' enquired sensei Jamieson between screams of 'oosh' followed by a 'woocha.' He then adopted a prayer stance.

'Class dismissed.'

The karate class students picked up their kit and a stream of budding ninjas hurried by Dave and Ryan. sensei Jamieson waved silently as he left last. Exasperated, Dave passed on the notion to remind him of the time for his booking on the basis that sensei Jamieson once described how his pressure punches could rupture a man's spleen. Instead he began laying out the plastic chairs in a circle of trust.

* * *

'Hello everyone and well done each of you for making it along again tonight. It's so good to see some of our new members returning and some regular faces again. Tonight, we will continue on our theme of personal rights and how we must remember to maintain these rights and safeguard ourselves in the face of romance. And, in the usual manner, let's start with a quick check in, if that's okay?'

Dave turned to his right and invited Lucy to make a start with her check in.

Lucy was telling everyone how she'd met a guy she'd been involved with previously and how she'd missed her new start at the Samaritans shop she'd been trying to get involved with. She was telling everyone how magical it had been before revealing that he'd asked her not to text him until he'd heard from her. Dave didn't have the heart to tell her, but Jack did.

'Sounds like he's still married'

Jack surmised as he leaned back on his chair.

'Jack could you please wait till check-in's are over,'

Dave tried intervening, but Jack wasn't for letting it lie, appealing around the room for support in opening Lucy's eyes to the painfully obvious.

'Does anyone else think so? C'mon?'

The room looked around nervously, unanimously they mostly started nodding in unison. Lucy flushed red.

Katrina pitched in.

'Did you discuss his relationship, what did he say?'

Lucy replied triumphantly that he was separated from his wife after a long time. That they had still been sharing a house whilst they tried to sell it but there hadn't been much interest, so it'd been awkward and difficult for him. He was taking his time to meet someone new and didn't expect them to pick things back up where they'd left off. 'Last time his wife had found his texts, she told the group, 'and I'd replied pretending I was his mate joking around after he called me from the bathroom asking if I would help him. His kids were too young to handle a breakup' she added. 'But obviously that's changed.'

Jack was becoming surprisingly animated.

'He's a liar. Lucy, you need to get him tae fuck,'

Dave intervened carefully.

'Thanks Jack. Lucy maybe you could wait till he's text again and you can arrange to chat through?'

He could see that Lucy was clearly troubled by the exchange. She furtively looked around the room.

'I think I've been taken for a mug. Have I been a mug?'

Ryan leaned forward, looking to help resolve the awkward tension in Lucy's realisation. 'You're fine, Lucy , its maybe all above board. Worth being careful and as Dave suggests chat through with him the next time you are both speaking.'

Dave reluctantly accepted Ryan's support in attempting to calm Lucy down. She was obviously being strung along but she needed to work that out for herself, largely.

'Be careful and remember your personal rights. You are allowed to ask questions. Maybe you could revisit the voluntary job and see if things have calmed down after Saturday and maybe try and reapply there. I'm sure you'd be a great help to them.'

Dave watched as Lucy mentally took note. Watching to make sure she was fine before moving onto Tony, who'd been quiet thus far.

Tony was in full flow. Telling everyone how we'd finally seen his daughters this weekend but suggesting that they'd been there for money rather than anything else. And when he'd dropped them off, there'd been a car in the drive, and a new man in the kitchen he'd paid for.

'I'm no worried about her, I mean, she's been ruined for every other man if you know what I mean. All I'm fucking worried about is ma lassies being there. In that house. All my girls and him. I mean he had the look of a beast hinging about him, plus it's no as if she's anything special these days. So, you've got to question his motives. See ma logic? If he's playing the long game, then he's picked the wrong wan. I'll chop it off and ram it in his gub. Leave him smoking his ain beef like the perverted cunt he is.'

Dave thanked Tony for sharing and encouraged him to keep control of his emotions, reminding him that his wife would have the kid's best interests at heart. But Tony was desperate to have the last word on the matter.

'Thanks Dave. I am calm, but staying vigilant. Canny be too careful these days. Plenty benders and deviants kicking about in all walks of life these days.'

Dave took a deep breath, hoping rather than expecting that Tony might listen to his advice. He was pleased to see Millie back, if nothing else she was well spoken and one of the first new, new members he'd had join for over a month. She was, again, immaculately turned out. Dave wondered what she did for a living, he stopped pondering and asked her to check-in with the group. As she took a breath, Dave noticed Katrina shuffle forward on her seat as if she were getting the popcorn out.

Millie began describing her circumstances, how she'd recently come out of a long-term relationship and was back living with her parents whilst her partner was still trying to resolve things. Dave thought that this boy, her ex, sounded like a right piece of work. She had tried blocking his number, but he was then withholding his number and generally playing every control freak card in the deck. Dave could see that Millie was worried that she'd succumb to his efforts, she seemed like the type to maintain the status quo rather than cause a scene. But Dave had seen too many broken hearts in this world, too many dreams that had been broken in two.

'That sounds tough Millie. Remember that romance can be an issue for everyone, your ex may have an issue himself and responding and encouraging his behaviour will not only help increase the likelihood of a return to a negative situation for you, it may be also affecting them'.

He watched as his summary struck a chord, but she seemed to retreat into herself. With seemingly nothing more to say, Dave thanked her before moving onto Katrina. And, as expected, Katrina ran over the same story she did every other week. How she moved over from Ireland after a holiday romance and the guy left her and how she's on top of her romantic leanings. Any help to anyone else she could be she was there to help. Blah, blah, blah. Dave was convinced she just came along to hear other's stories. He smiled and thanked her for the support.

Dave looked over at Derek. Derek was deep in thought, car keys, folder and pen laid in front of him. Suited and booted as ever. Dave wondered if he'd ever seen Derek not in a suit, he honestly couldn't remember. He listened as Derek regaled the reasons behind his breakup and provided the group with an update in the shape of his attempt to win back Patricia with surprise trip to Paris, which he was amazed hadn't been taken up. No one else appeared to be as surprised.

'Thanks Derek. Can you see why she mightn't have accepted the offer?'

'It was 5-star accommodation, business class travel. I can't believe she didn't see the effort I was making.'

Dave could see Katrina was shaking her head and getting ready to speak.

'I think you need to resolve what happened with her finding you in Manchester first Derek,'

Dave thanked Katrina for her input. He didn't mean it though. He went on to ask Derek if he could see what had happened, pointing out that he had tried to fix a situation broken by romance with new romance, without having yet repaired the damage done by his infidelity.

Derek was still unconvinced.

'That's all well and good. But she is still living under my roof, still enjoying the privileges of my lifestyle. That's what she likes...'

'Or is it that she loves you, that keeps her there and she'd like a resolution to her upset and broken trust. Rather than romance or more of your using your wealth to paper over the cracks'

Dave watched Derek struggle to accept the realisation that his bank balance couldn't buy what he wanted. Derek sat back and scoffed, shaking his head as he laughed off any attempts at reasoning with himself. Derek then looked down at his feet.

'Maybe you do have a point. I do love her. I'll try. Thank you all for listening, as well as the suggested advice. It is warmly appreciated'.

Dave was pleased. He could see Derek still thinking over his approach whilst he moved onto Stirling. Stirling was telling everyone how he was prepared to be moving in a different direction, more accepting that him and Sarah's relationship could be over. Dave wasn't sure how much this was delivered for Millie's benefit rather than a true reflection of where Stirling was at.

Dave looked over at his friend Jack. Trying not to laugh as he asked for his check-in, having already received a lengthy tirade over the phone from Jack during the week, who'd found out that his boss, John, and Sonia his recent heartbreak, and Deirdre, the landlady they'd had a threesome with, were now all in a polygamous relationship together.

Jack described how his boss, Stevie, had raced down to Scarborough not long after he'd given him the details about Deidre's hotel. He'd then found them and joined them on a night out and, after a few days together, they were now happily involved in a three-way relationship. Fast forward a few days and they are now opening a swinger's night together in Blackpool called Trapeze, a fresh start for all parties with Deirdre selling the hotel in Scarborough.

'Upshot then being with Stevie travelling away I've been promoted to operations manager at the Timber Yard.'

Dave was amazed at his friend's ability to still feel aggrieved despite this being a recovery of fortunes of gargantuan proportions given the initial outlook.

'Well life does work in mysterious ways,' said Dave.

'And congratulations on the promotion. What are your own feelings at the moment regarding romance?'

Jack had his hands up, palm facing forward, as he replied.

'I'm over it all, Dave. A close shave and now back on the wagon, so to speak.'

As he handed over to Ryan, Dave wondered to himself how long that might last. He glanced up at the ceiling as Ryan described, in some detail, the two main love interests in his life. Basically, he'd been the recipient of 'it's not you it's me' on both occasions, the main reason being suggested was his being too nice. He'd heard it before, and Ryan was obviously annoying, but Dave felt sorry for him when he described feeling crushed.

'Were you together long?' he asked, already knowing the answer. but still surprised to hear it had been just over 5 weeks and that Ryan thought that she was the 'one.'

There were a few raised eyebrows around the room. As Dave pressed on.

'When was this, Ryan? How are you feeling now?'

'2 years, 1 month and 13 days ago today. I'm getting there. She's married now, to a guy called Alan and they have a baby. I just can't stop thinking about what could have been.'

Dave couldn't believe that Ryan was still counting the days since. He was going to have to try and talk him round to letting that go, thinking it was a tad unhealthy. He asked about the other relationship he had mentioned.

'Susan? 55 days we were together, I had bought an engagement ring and had it in my hand as I proposed before she kissed my head and walked off. After she walked away, I stood there on the sand, just staring at the ring. It was supposed to be perfect - her birthstone, pink for October, everything she loved. But it felt like a weight in my hand, a reminder of how I'd misjudged everything. So, I threw it as far as I could. Watched it disappear into the waves.'

The girls in the room swooned. Katrina mostly.

'Aww. Ryan, that's lovely.'

Ryan was despondent.

'That's my problem thou being too nice, apparently.'

Dave was taking a note to revisit some sessions for Ryan's benefit. As he lay down his notepad, he reassured Ryan that it was never a case of being too nice, but probably allowing romance to cloud his judgement.

He looked around the room having finished check-ins for the week.

'We'll be looking at attachment styles and hopefully these can help us all understand why some of us look for signs of commitment in the coming weeks. Last week we began looking at personal rights. Can anyone remember the personal rights we discussed?'

Stirling enquired first.

'Is it the right to party?' before chuckling away to himself. Reaching out for a high five from Jack, which Jack soundly delivered.

Dave was unmoved by Stirling's rapier wit.

'No, Stirling. Anyone else?'

Lucy raised her hand.

'The right to say no' pronounced Lucy, pleased with herself.

'That is right, we all have the right to say no, in any situation and in anywhere in life and no matter how much anyone may want to persuade you otherwise. You always have the right to say no.'

Dave stood up and pulled a pen from the side of the white board on the wall before announcing,

'This week we'll begin by looking at some of the remaining personal rights starting with...'

1. To say that you don't know.

Dave stepped back from the white board.

'Can anyone tell me where it's important to protect your right to say you don't know.'

Derek raised his hand.

'When asked when your wife might actually be ready to leave on an evening?'

'Yip, that could be one.' answered Dave before looking to Lucy.

'It's important to say you don't know if someone asks if you love them'

'Great example' Dave confirmed happily, delighted that they were now getting into the topic.

'It is really important to remember you have the right to say you don't know when it comes to any personal feelings.'

Derek looks pensive before raising his hand again.

'So. Bear with me. I'm just thinking, when Patricia says she doesn't know if she'll ever get over what happened, that's okay?'

Dave took his time to respond to that one.

'Yes, Derek, she absolutely has the right to say she doesn't know if she'll ever get over what happened and it's important that you remember she has that right.'

'Surely, she must know, deep down.'

Dave took even longer with this response.

'In your opinion Derek, she maybe does know but she's very much entitled to say she doesn't know.'

The rest of the room sat thoughtfully as Dave uncapped his pen.

'Which takes us nicely onto our next two personal rights.'

Dave writes on the board below his first listing, announcing each as he does.

2.To have your own opinion.

And then followed that up with:

3.To express your own opinion.

'Can anyone think of a time in a relationship where it's important to remember you have your own opinion?'

'When meeting someone new?'

asked Katrina before confidently continuing.

'It's important to make your own opinion whether they are good for you or not, despite anyone else's suggestions.'

'That's correct,' said Dave.

'It's important to have and maintain your own opinion regards compatibility with a potential partner. That is a great example, thanks Katrina. Anybody else have something? Think of a time where it's important to remember we have the right to have our own opinion.'

This time he looks around the room and tries to catch the eye of some of the lesser involved members. Jack raised his hand.

'I've been thinking back to that hotel bar in Scarborough, and with what's happened with Stevie, Sonia, and Deirdre. I mean I thought it was obvious I'd be up for it, but if I'd only just said'

Dave continued nodding with a wry smile on his face

'That's right Jack, it would have been an opportunity to express your feelings then. Why do you think it would have been important to express your feelings then?'

'I just keep thinking maybe they didn't realise. It would have removed all doubt if I'd just said. I could have been running a swingers hotel with the pair of them!'

'That's correct, expressing your feelings can help remove any doubt where our true wants or opinions aren't clear. Miscommunication is a common result of romance clouding any situation, and can lead to conflicting opinions which, if unexpressed, can lead to further problems.'

Jack then threw a grenade, his eyes aimed at Dave but his words landing squarely at Lucy's feet.

'Like whether you are married or not.'

Dave glanced at his watch and confirmed they'd already run over. He called the week to a close, thanked everyone for coming, and, as the chairs scraped back into position and the group began to disperse, he stopped Lucy briefly at the door.

'You alright?' he asked, his tone gentle but searching.

'Fine, thanks,' she replied, her words clipped, her eyes downcast. She hurried out without looking back.

As the rest of the group filtered out, Dave gathered his notes and lingered in the now-quiet room. The tension Jack had unleashed still hung in the air, an unwelcome echo that refused to fade. He turned to the whiteboard, rereading the rights they had discussed, each written in his careful, deliberate hand. He wondered if Lucy was replaying Jack's words in her mind as she walked out into the cold night.

'Like whether you are married or not.'

Jack's offhand remark had landed with all the subtlety of a brick in the face, shattering the tentative composure Lucy had worked so hard to maintain. Dave sighed. The group wasn't always kind....some weeks, it was a battlefield where fragile egos and unspoken truths collided. But that was part of its messy charm, wasn't it? Growth didn't come without discomfort. Still, this moment felt more cruel than constructive.

He couldn't shake the uneasy thought that Lucy might not come back next week. Jack, for all his bravado, likely wouldn't give it a second thought, but Dave knew better. He also wondered, with no small amount of exasperation, how much of his own truth Jack was avoiding. The man had a way of shining a light on everyone else while keeping his own shadows firmly in place.

The group wasn't perfect. Far from it. But it was all Dave had to offer... a space to lay it all bare, even if it hurt. And for most of them, it seemed to be just enough.

By the door, Katrina and Ryan lingered, their conversation hushed but intense. Dave caught the fiery determination in Katrina's posture, her phone already out and her fingers flying across the screen. Whatever she had in mind, Dave wasn't sure he wanted to know. With a final sigh, he flipped the light switch, leaving the tension behind in the shadows of the empty room.

* * *

'So what did you do with the ring?'

'After I watched her walking off, I dusted the sand off my knees and walked to the edge of the water before I threw it as far as I could.'

'What?' Katrina said, completely incredulous. Waving her red hair out like a red flag, before gathering it back and tying it up between both hands. She looked serious, she leaned into Ryan.

'When was this?' she demanded.

'Just over a year ago now, 372 days to be precise. I figured it was a lost cause and if she didn't want it or me, it was best in the sea.'

'Have you never thought about going out and looking for it?'

'I couldn't even look at it. The pain was too hard, I'm glad it's gone. '

'How much was the ring Ryan?

'Thirteen thousand pounds from Asterria,' confirmed Ryan.

'£13,000!' Katrina retorted, clearly amazed both at Ryan's stupidity and relaxed attitude at both the financial loss and lack of remorse.

'Give me your number' announced Katrina abruptly whilst producing her phone.

'No texts or that, we're not pals suddenly because you've been an eejit and flung your thirteen grand ring in the Forth, but I've got a friend that does beach combing and treasure hunting. I think she might be able to help get you reconnected with your engagement ring.'

Ryan was still bemused by her keenness to help and still wasn't sure if he wanted to find it but he gratefully accepted anyway.

'Let me know what she says!'

12

Diamonds

Lucy walked past Katrina and Ryan and waved off a quick goodbye to both as she got into her car.

She sat there for a minute, then another convincing herself that Keith was being honest with her this time. She made herself defiant, the group didn't know her Keith, not like she did. She wanted to show them all that she wasn't being stupid, not this time. Eventually, she pulled out her phone, and scrolled through the numbers till she found Keith. She began typing 'can we talk when you are free? Xxx' But it didn't feel right. She deleted the last two kisses and paused for another minute, staring at the message. No. She deleted. 'Hey Handsome,' she wrote, 'it would be good to catch up soon. X hits send and hurriedly stuffs the phone in her pocket, before starting the car. I'll show them she thought to herself, remembering to wave to Dave, already checking for a reply to her text.

'Hello, that's me home.'

Lucy pulled the door quietly behind her as Ellie and Archie came running to the door. The smell of Vosene shampoo and their fresh pyjamas filling her up as she held them both in a big cuddle.

'Give me a minute' she laughed before removing her jacket and hung it up by the front door.

Her Mum, Janet, came through into the hall behind them.

'How did you get on this week?'

'All good' responded Lucy, smiling widely.

'I've got these two angels and what else could anyone else want in life?'

Janet smiled back at Lucy.

'Good. Well I'm off up the road to catch up on Coronation Street, these two have had me watching Squid Games. How can you let them watch that violence?'

Lucy turned on her sternest Mum Voice.

'What did I tell you two?'

'Soooooorrry' they choroused sheepishly.

'Have they been winding me up, again?' asked Janet.

'I'd already told them they were both too young to be watching it.'

Lucy confirmed.

'But everyone at school has watched it all already, it's not fair.'

Archie tried to remonstrate as slunk back towards the stairs.

Janet reached around Lucy and grabbed her coat before she kissed Archie and Ellie on their heads and grabbed a quick hug from her daughter.

'Angels right enough.' She quipped as she headed back for Coronation Street and someone else's drama.

Lucy ushered both kids into their rooms and their pyjamas before running a shower for herself. 'You can have 10 minutes on your iPad and then I'll be through to say goodnight – NO squid games!.'

'Okay' both agreed grudgingly.

Lucy looked in the mirror as she waited on her shower warming. Pulling one breast up and flapping it back down, she wondered if Keith did find her attractive at all or if it was just the lure of a 'bit strange' that did it for him. She jumped in the shower after checking her phone, again. Still no texts.

The next morning, she checked her phone. One text, received at 6:48am, it was him.

Hey babe. Catch you later today about 10am? X

No problem Handsome. Speak soon. X

She dragged herself out of bed, before hollering through to the kids, without breaking stride,

'Time for school guys'

She laid out breakfast for the kids, on autopilot, before sitting down for a coffee as she signed off a permission slip so that Archie could watch 'The BFG' . The irony not lost on her that most of the kids in his class had already watched Squid Games without their parents' knowledge but the same kids needed a note of confirmation in case the big friendly giant offended them.

Archie and Ellie finished off their breakfast before she gathered up their dishes, before fixing Ellie's hair and sending them off to school. She used to walk them to school but had got tired of trying to keep up with all the yummy Mummy's and their perfect lives. Now she'd normally grab a few hours social media me time before rising at about lunch, but today she had plans.

'Have a good day, don't slam the –' The door clattered shut cutting her off.

She jumped in the shower and quickly shaved her legs, even extending to a quick tidy of her lady garden. Not a full Brazilian, but she no longer had a bush extending out like Diana Ross in the Supremes. She kicked the stray hairs down the plug hole and wrapped a towel around her head.

Sitting at her dressing room table she pulled her face from side to side. The years hadn't been kind, she thought, as she got to work on rolling them back. Half an hour or so passed and Lucy felt passable, she'd tided the hallway, bedroom, and kitchen - on the basis that these might be the only three rooms Keith should see. Just as she sat down, her phone started ringing. It was Keith.

She composed herself.

'Hello handsome,' she purred.

'Hey Babe,' he responded eagerly. 'How you doing?' What have you been up to?'

'Not much,' she replied,

'I'm not long out the shower. Lady of leisure today, kids at school so I'm just about to make a start on some housework.'

'Lady of leisure. Not bad for some. How about I pop over and give you a hand?'

'With my housework? Will that just be making the bed?' She flirted.

'Well have to make a mess of it first' responded Keith.

'I'll be over soon.'

Lucy was delighted all her effort hadn't been in vain. It seemed like an eternity passed when finally, the doorbell chimed 'Under the Sea.' It really was embarrassing; she took a mental note to change it.

Keith brushed in, looking smart in his shirt and tie.

'Off somewhere nice?'

'How do you mean?', enquired Keith.

'Suited and booted today?'

'Oh, I managed to get a few hours away from work. When I'd seen your text, I just thought that was perfect.'

The feeling of last night's group piling in on her resurfaced. Lucy could feel she was about to ask the question, the question she didn't want to ask.

'Keith, can I ask you something?'

'Yes babe',' answered Keith.

Already unbuttoning his shirt and loosening his tie.

'Are you seeing anyone else?'

Keith seemed surprised at her question.

'No one else apart from you and the wife.'

Lucy was crestfallen. She felt his words hit her in the gut, like a sucker punch had caught her off guard. She had to retaliate. She recoiled and tried again, this time hoping for a different response.

'You're married?'

'Yeah' said Keith.

'Not that should matter to you, I'm not cheating on you'. He laughed.

A carefree laugh. So flippant in its execution that he continued undressing. Lucy stood up from the kitchen table.

'Can you please leave?'

Keith paused, his shirt open and one shoe off.

'You what?'

'You want me to leave? Are you mad?'

'I've asked you to leave so now you can just fuck off, you cheating scum bag.'

Keith didn't even flinch. Shrugged his shoulders before he dropped to tie his laces.

'Alright, if that's the way you're going to be, then fine but don't think there will be a long line waiting behind me, you should take every chance you can get!'

'That's fine, you can go back to your poor wife – I feel sorry for her.'

'She's not a single mum so probably not needing your pity. Eh?'

'Just shut the door on your way out, please. You disgust me'

Keith slammed the door shut and the letter box clattered. Lucy had anticipated the thud of the door, and the clatter, but she still winced as they both rattled through her.

She took this as a sign to give up on her brave face as she slumped on the sofa and got angry at her own stupidity, and even angrier at his flippant response. As if she shouldn't have expected any better than a quick knee tremble behind his wife's back.

Lucy sat replaying every second that had just unfolded in her mind, perfecting her responses and re-editing every scene. Eventually yelling 'Bastard!', now that she had a million better ways to tell him to fuck off. She got up to make herself tea.

She pulled the dishes out of the washing machine and put them back in the sink. Wiping her tears intermittently with the top of her arm as she washed and rinsed a full rack of plates and cups. The foolish shame drenched her as she imagined sitting in her group next week, admitting to everyone how obviously wrong she'd been, again.

How could he just bounce out without a seconds thought.

It was him that was in the wrong.

It was him that should feel ashamed.

It was him that was the cheat.

Lucy turned on the kettle and stood transfixed as it boiled. Not even noticing as the steam bellowed and the switch clicked off. Keith wasn't to have heard the end of this, not this time. Keith would feel this hurt.

13

Treasure Seekers

Ryan was looking in the mirror, unsure about how to dress for a date, which may not be a date. In fact, it was definitely not a date. He said it out loud in the mirror, 'This is not a date,' and stared at himself just long enough to let the message sink in.

Content that he'd had a word with himself, he went back to switching between his good jeans and his previously good jeans. The debate here was that his good jeans were normally reserved for going out. But then again, he was going out. But then again, again, he was going out to search for a ring with a woman who he fancied but didn't want to fall in love with. He opted for the good jeans anyway, based on the hope that, because Katrina never knew his good jeans from his old jeans, she'd hopefully just assume that he always wore good jeans. He pulled on a beige jumper over his navy shirt and laced up his Timberland moccasins before discarding them in favour of his old caterpillar boots. These boots were reserved for walks only. He was satisfied that this was the right level of keenness for his planned activity.

It was a short drive to South Queensferry. He weaved along the cobbled road and through the High Street, parking up alongside Hawes Pier. He noticed Katrina stood with, who he assumed to be, her friend Agnes, on account of her holding a metal detector and shovel. He made the job of parking immensely more difficult by attempting to wave midway through. He looked in the rear-view mirror and confirmed the flushed feeling in his cheeks, before he noticed that his giddy excitement already had his heart racing. He stared for a second in the mirror, took a deep breath and gave himself another quick word. 'Platonic' he said out loud, before he opened the car door.

The wind caught Ryan by surprise and he had to catch both sides of his spray-away jacket in order to zip it up before he walked towards Katrina and her metal-detecting friend. He faced the wind head on trying to soften the blush of his interest as he approached them.

'Bit breezy,' he offered, both hands thrust into his jacket.

'Nice fresh sea air,' countered Katrina as she introduced her friend Agnes. 'This is Ryan, the eejit with the ring I was telling you about.'

Agnes offered out her hand, which Ryan shook vigorously, thanking her profusely for coming along.

Agnes opted to shoe gaze throughout Katrina's introduction and Ryan's warm welcome. Only briefly peeking up to flash eye contact when her name was mentioned. Ryan thought she looked like Daphne, from Scooby Doo, had gone hiking for the day. He too found himself staring at her boots before he looked up and back at Katrina. And when he did, he already knew his fate.

Katrina was flushed with confidence; her skin illuminated against the shards of sun breaking through the clouds. She was beautiful, thought Ryan. Her soft accent trilled over his ears like a harp being strummed. He felt himself blissfully daydreaming before her tone changed and brought him back to reality.

'Is this where you did it then?'

Ryan stood perplexed. 'Did what?'

'Threw the fecking ring in the sea. Were you stood here when you chucked it?' Even then, it was still harp song.

Ryan was immediately embarrassed and set about apologising and correcting himself. 'Yes, well, it was here but down on the beach.'

Agnes spoke up from behind her hood. 'How many yards out?'

Ryan didn't know a yard from his foot, but rather than asking for clarification it only prompted him to guess, not wanting to chalk up points on his man licence. 'It was about 50 yards along that way, right at the edge of the water.'

Scooby's pal just looked at him. 'So, the tide was out, was it?'

Ryan was as out of his depth, almost as far as his yardage.

Agnes continued, 'Cos it's only 40 yards to the tide just now.'

Ryan tried to clarify 'You see, I went right down to the beach, stood right next to the water and threw it in as far as I could.'

'So was the tide in or out?' Agnes persisted.

Ryan hadn't realised the Forth was tidal; he had no idea. He figured it was a river, but confirmed it was out which, in turn, Agnes confirmed was good. There was more chance it had been brought inland. She picked up her metal detector and shovel, then set off down the steps towards the beach.

Katrina caught Ryan's eye excitedly.

'See, Ryan. What did I tell you? There's a good chance it's been brought inland.'

Katrina repeated Agnes' statement more confidently before she nudged him to follow her.

Ryan didn't share this confidence, primarily on the basis that he didn't know his tidal from his yardage.

Ryan and Katrina walked behind Agnes whilst she confirmed Ryan's proximity to his throwing point, even getting him to demonstrate his throwing style. Agnes was deep in thought. Soon enough, she was off scanning the beach while her detector whizzed and beeped. Ryan decided it sounded like a Geiger counter; Katrina had asked if he'd been worried about radiation. All he could think about was how she radiated. He watched her as her red hair jostled and bounced in the wind, while gulls hee-hawed themselves at his same old sappy antics in the background.

Suddenly, he snapped himself out of it and the two of them noticed Agnes was digging away having abandoned her detector on the sand.

'Come on, Ryan,' called Katrina as she ran over to check her friend's find. Ryan tried to match her enthusiasm, jogging with her over to Agnes.

Agnes was busy digging and sifting through the sand. She studiously sifted through every grain as Katrina and Ryan watched on.

'I'm assuming there's all manner of stuff that gets washed up on the beach.

What's the best thing you've ever found Agnes?'

Asked Ryan, who had felt a little helpless stood watching.

Agnes clearly heard him but tried not to respond. She instead continued to scan the pile of sand she had dug, meticulously searching through whilst avoiding any interruption.

'The tides going to be coming in soon,' she shouted over her shoulder, 'we'll get on quicker if one of you does some of the digging.'

Ryan and Katrina shared a look like they'd been chastened by a schoolteacher. Ryan picked up the abandoned spade and began to dig where Agnes had probed. As he heaped up piles of sand, Agnes probed further through each of them.

'There it is,' yelled Katrina, as she caught a glimpse of shimmering metal. Leaning in close to look over Agnes's shoulder. Ryan dropped the spade and joined Kat who was watching Agnes excitedly. Katrina and Ryan were now huddled over the mound of sand and both watching for a glimpse of the find which Agnes had uncovered.

Agnes finally picked up the object and rubbed it slightly between her gloved fingers. 'An old ten pence' she announced defeatedly, tossing it aside before she continued her scanning of the beach. Katrina picked it up and presented it to Ryan, they were both significantly more impressed with their find than Agnes had been.

'Look at this' exclaimed Katrina. Ryan took the opportunity to squeeze in close and look up at the coin she held in front of her. Taking the time to watch her studying the coin purposefully.

'It's from 1982, that's the year I was born. Must be lucky!'

Ryan was still watching Katrina's smiling face closely, thinking to himself how young she looked for being in her 40s. He couldn't believe she was nearly ten years older than himself. That only added to her appeal for Ryan. He took the coin from her and advised he'd clean it up, as he slipped it into his pocket.

This process went on for hours: Agnes detecting, Ryan occasionally digging, Katrina getting excited and then attempting to capture Ryan's enthusiasm for the various bits of tat they'd unearthed – in between Geiger bleets, she'd ask Ryan to pick up rocks that they'd incorrectly detected so that she could keep them in her garden. Ryan wrote his name in the sand and then Katrina came and kicked it over, giggling to herself. Ryan responded by writing her name in the sand, followed by 'loves Agnes'.

'Quick,' Katrina laughed, trying to hush herself at the same time, 'clean it up before she sees it. We'll be getting another row.'

Agnes called them over again and they both rushed over. Ryan began digging. 'A bullet,' announced Agnes before tossing it aside. Katrina studied it, before washing it in the sea.

'Do you think these are pirate's bullets, Ryan?'

Ryan wasn't sure in the slightest, but he was happy to play along. 'Here, you could be right. Maybe there was a feud as they approached Blackness Castle and the pirates had to bury their treasure as the boat sank.'

Katrina looked thrilled by the fantasy mystery of their find.

'Musket's sticking over the edge of the boat as they hurriedly dragged their bounty to safety,' she added. 'And then leaving under cover of darkness, only to never return.....'

'We'll find it, the treasure, I mean,' confirmed Ryan, 'and Susan's ring.'

'It's not Susan's ring, Ryan; It's your ring. It's you that paid for the bloody thing,'

Ryan apologised.

Katrina told him not too.

He apologised for apologising.

Agnes called them over again, and Katrina grabbed the shovel. 'I'll go. You tidy up your beach graffiti,' she smiled.

Ryan laughed as he kicked over the sand and watched as they both scanned and dug excitedly. He looked up at the High Street and over the bridges. It wasn't a bad spot, he thought to himself. Katrina looked at home on the beach. She seemed like the type that went for walks on the sand. He could be like that too, he thought, kicking the sand off his boots. He laughed at himself and gave himself yet another warning. Just then, he heard Katrina yelp and looked up. Agnes had discarded her metal detector. He made his way over, trying not to get too excited, but he couldn't help himself from calling over and over again, 'What is it?'

Katrina was holding aloft another bullet.

'We're getting closer to the treasure,' She announced, beaming completely at odds with Agnes's demeanour. She packed up her shovel and switched off her detector.

'Tides in,' she grumbled,

'we'll need to finish up.'

Ryan was disappointed; not that they hadn't found Susan's ring, just that it was over.

The three of them walked across the beach, the sound of the sea lapping behind them. With a good session of detecting finished, Agnes seemed a lot more content with herself.

'I once found a fellas wedding ring on a beach across the water,' she said and pointed over towards Fife. Finally answering Ryan's earlier question.

Agnes explained that she'd been interviewed by the local paper after it, and then it'd been picked up by some TV outlets. She'd become a bit of a thing in the metal-detecting world.

'Well we'll just need to come back and try again, if it's going to catapult you to stardom,' suggested Katrina.

Agnes had already kicked off her socks and was changing her shoes whilst sat in her estate boot open wide. Ryan offered them both a coffee for their help, but Agnes needed to get back for her cats.

Katrina, however, accepted Ryan's offer.

They headed into the pub at Hawes Pier and picked a quiet seat by the window. The Hawes Inn was a traditional pub with a roaring log fire. Katrina emptied their bounty onto the table and counted it out in front of Ryan, who had cupped his hands to help funnel it safely into the middle of their table. Katrina began sorting and counting out aloud.

'Three pirates' bullets, two pound coins, three nails, one allen key and one earing.'

The pair of them looked at the collection of scrap piled on the table as if it really was treasure. They were both delighted with themselves. The waiter brought over two coffees, which Ryan paid for. Both of them sat for a second as Ryan frantically thought of what to say next. Katrina took a sip of her coffee and then leaned back to look out of the window.

Ryan suddenly remembered and produced the ten pence coin from his pocket.

'Aren't you forgetting something? Asked Ryan triumphantly.

'My lucky coin!' Katrina snapped it from his hand and laid it alongside the rest of their bounty. Making sure it was date and queen side up, before she smiled again at their haul, now complete.

'That was great fun' she said, turning her attention back to Ryan.

'It's a shame Agnes won't be able to help us out again. She's got a few weeks of assignments already booked up'

Ryan's heart sank. He took a drink of his coffee whilst he tried to hide the full enormity of his disappointment.

'That is a shame' He finally added.

Katrina hadn't looked up from their collection of materials before she continued...

'She did say that she had a spare detector I could pick up.'

A smile flickered across Ryan's face before Katrina continued coolly.

'If you think we could behave ourselves without her taking charge that is' she laughed.

Ryan was quick to seize the opportunity. Immediately giving himself a pinch for his keenness.

'Brilliant!' He blurted out before stifling himself slightly.

'That would be great,' he then settled for, forgetting his earlier response was audible.

Katrina smiled and nodded affirmatively.

'I'll let Agnes know that I'll collect it. Sure, we can pick up where we've left off today'

Ryan watched as Kat took another drink of her coffee, shook her hair back and then gathered it up before letting it all fall back on her shoulders. Ryan was mesmerised but confident his eager outburst hadn't fully unmasked his true feelings. He had steadily policed his internal thoughts, immediately discounted every single suggested question that his smitten brain conjured for him.

Each remained unasked and Ryan was pretty sure he hadn't been too much already. But, for all his iron will, he took a relaxed sip of his coffee and burnt his lip, and his attempts to style it out without letting off a yelp, only caused him to spill coffee on his good jeans which seeped through and burnt his thigh. Somehow, though, she hadn't seemed to notice and instead kept chatting about where they'd start next week and what they'd do if they found the pirate's treasure.

'One guy found an ancient golden necklace worth a million pounds, in Stirling!! That'll do me' she said confidently as she tipped up the last of her coffee.

'Time for another?' offered Ryan.

Katrina politely declined, insisting that her two cats would be missing her as well.

For a moment, Ryan was disappointed, but when he stood up it was washed away by the relief that his jacket covered the offending mark on his jeans. Katrina collected up their treasure and brushed it into a carrier bag she had in her pocket. He thanked the waiter, who returned to collect their cups and then held the door open as they left. Even outside, Katrina was still talking about what they might find as she turned towards the walk for her car.

'I can run you along, if you like?' Ryan offered.

Katrina insisted that it was just a minute's walk before they arranged to catch up at the next meeting to make arrangements for the following weekend's ring hunt.

Ryan made his way back to his car and unzipped his jacket before placing it in the back seat. He looked along towards Katrina, hoping to give her a last wave, but she wasn't for turning. He settled into the car and caught his smile in the rear-view mirror. This hadn't gone to plan.

14

Week Four

Stirling's Golf GTI was a statement, despite the fact it's achingly bad for his back. He looked up at the Trinity Outreach building and locked his car as he strode towards the door, satisfied with both the clunk and the flash of the lights. He was even more pleased to catch up with Millie as she made her way to the door. He quickened his pace just enough so that he could hold the door open for her arrival. 'Alright there,' he said, but felt himself trying not to cringe, already frustrated with himself for his lack of vocabulary.

'Hi' Millie stifled back to him, obviously guarded.

'You alright there, doll?' He enquired further, thinking to himself she looked shaken. Just at that a blue Subaru hurled out of the car park. 'Prick,' summarised Stirling.

'You're right there' Millie confirmed.

'Do you know them?'

'Yes,' confirmed Millie. 'That is my charming ex.'

Stirling beckoned Millie inside before he stepped out from the door and looked up and down the street. 'Looks like he's away, he causing you grief hen?'

'Not really' replied Millie. 'It's all getting a bit tedious to be honest.'

'Well, if you need any help, just ask, don't think you need to be dealing with idiots like that yourself.'

'Thanks' smiled Millie as they made their way along the corridor. By the time they'd made it down the corridor, they found they were last to arrive. Dave welcomed them both with a wide smile.

'Hi Guys, hope you're all well – take a seat.' Millie picked up her usual spot next to Katrina whilst Stirling took the seat immediately to Dave's right. Dave Melahuish has already kicked off proceedings, but he recapped for the latecomers.

* * *

Stirling updated the room with what Dave felt was the typical dying embers of a relationship, with the more positive aspects aimed at Millie, Dave turned to his newest member for an update.

'Good evening, Millie, are you okay to share with the group this week?'

Millie gave out a bit of a sigh before addressing the room 'I can well and truly say I have noticed I definitely need some help this week'

Dave sat back as some of the other members of the group gave her a quick round of support and congratulations. 'Well done, Millie,' summarised Dave, watching as Katrina touched Millie's elbow.

'My ex-boyfriend, Stevie, has been sending me gifts and we'd had a few chats where I couldn't quite hurt him and found myself just talking away, trying to be kind to him. I know that he's hurt and I do love him but I'm just not in love with him, not after everything that has happened' She paused.

Dave felt inclined to fill the space, uncomfortable with the silence. He was relieved when she started again.

'It was my Dad, really. I couldn't let him down after he'd seen how hurt I'd been afterwards. I didn't want him to worry about me being so weak to succumb to a pair of Louboutins and a new handbag. I couldn't disappoint him by being so weak … but I wanted to. So, anyway, I text Stevie and told him that it was totally over and asked him to stop calling. After that there was just silence, but I knew it wasn't over. A few times I'd had a feeling someone was watching me and well tonight I confirmed it, he's been following me – out in the car park, he confronted me.'

Dave was quick to react. 'Here?' he asked, appalled at the suggestion that his place of romantic safety and the circle of trust could be threatened.

Stirling picked up the reply, on Millie's behalf. 'Aye, right out there Dave. I checked though, he's well clear. Blue Subaru, drug dealer's car. Nice motor though.'

Dave watched as Millie winced at the summary, thinking Stirling was probably on the button; A blue Subaru was definitely a drug dealers car. He was still a bit annoyed at how quickly he'd reacted to the suggested threat. He deliberately took a breath. 'What happened next Millie, are you okay?.'

He watched as Millie fiddled with the straps of her bag and assured him, she was fine. Told everyone how she told him again it was over, and he had shouted back that it wasn't over for him, before speeding off.

Stirling stepped in again. 'That's when I arrived, he just left the car park as I was getting out the car. I told her, didn't ah? Don't let him get to you, you aren't dealing with this alone.

Dave smiled thinking of course Stirling had to clarify that this had all happened before he arrived, he was clearly shaping up as her wannabe knight in shining armour. Dave didn't think this would be a bad thing, he was a good lad, whilst this boy Stevie was obviously a piece of work. He looked over at Millie again who was still fiddling with her bag straps. He wanted to round up a posse from the group and collectively hunt this Stevie down, fast forward weeks of grief for Millie. He was biting his lip, as he always did, remembering what he always told himself. Let it work out, Dave, don't get involved. Romantics Anonymous is about guiding and enlightenment. He silently agreed with the voice in his head.

'Thanks Stirling and thanks for sharing, Millie. We are all here for you and it sounds like you have had a difficult week. You have made some difficult decisions. Identifying our problems with romance and then stepping back from them is one of life's most difficult abstentions. Well done you.'

Next up was Derek. Dave hadn't ever really scratched the surface with Derek. He clearly thought himself a level above the remainder of the group. Public school had robbed him off an imposter syndrome which affected most of the other members.

'I'd had a think over some of the areas we covered last week and I'm accepting I have an opinion and that Patricia has hers. I think my expectations have reached petra deorsum, but it does feel better now that we seem to be encroaching upon an upward curve and we are talking tentatively. I'm biding my time for now. All in all, no worse than it was last week and potentially a trifle better'

Dave was delighted when Katrina asked for a Latin translation, despite him making a face to suggest he already knew.

'My apologies dear. I always felt that the Latin interpretation rolled off the tongue better. It translates as rock bottom, and as a result the only way is up'

Jack enquired if that wasn't one from the philosopher Yazz of the plastic population. Dave chuckled to himself as it sailed over Derek's head. Dave winked knowingly at Jack who was still delighted with himself.

Dave turned around to see Lucy sat next to Derek. She had been quiet so far. Dave felt like he already knew what was coming, he asked tentatively if she was okay to share. He watched her as she took a deep breath. She already looked defeated.

'Well, firstly, I have to say thanks to those of you who helped me face the truth.' A grunt caught in her throat as the tears she'd been holding back burst out. 'Turns out you were right; Keith was married, and I was just being a mug again.'

Jack got up to give Lucy a hug – which she accepted gratefully.

Katrina spoke up too. 'His wife is the mug Lucy, not you, don't you worry girl'

With that, she managed to compose herself a bit. 'Sorry that I was being stupid, I'm just so upset with myself.' She calmed down further before continuing, again. 'He was so blasé when I asked about her, I just couldn't believe it.'

Dave tried to think what to say, but was forced to keep erasing the flashing 'we told you so' light that was blinking furiously in his frontal lobe. Lucy was still sobbing, repeating that she was feeling stupid. Stupid and used. Dave caught a thought and went with it. 'You were conned by a romantic notion Lucy. That is why we are all here, it doesn't make any one of us stupid. We are all survivors and no matter how many times we fall we get back up and well done you for coming back. It would have been easier to walk away and not come back but you are here. You are not stupid. Keith though, definitely.'

The rest of the group were encouraging her too, finally some of it seemed to hit home. Lucy wiped her tears 'Never again', she confirmed. 'I'm a non-practicing lesbian from now on.'

Dave thanked her for her update as the rest of the group continued to wish her well and congratulate her for getting over Keith.

Scanning the room, he noticed Jack who looked as though he was probably still thinking about lesbians practicing. Dave interrupted his thoughts to ask for his check-in. Jack updated the group that his estranged love interest, Sonia and her lesbian lover and her husband had now setup a swinger's website as well as their swinger's hotel in Blackpool. Jack had suggested that the guys at work had been looking at it, which Dave knew only too well meant that Jack was all over it.

Dave joined the group in a collective sigh of relief when Lucy joked, through a bubble of tears and snot, that she'd like to have a play in their pleasure beach.

Dave raised his hand in acknowledgment but encouraged Jack to continue. 'And how are you feeling about this, Jack?' Almost baiting him to share more.

Jack had missed his track entirely, revealing his own key interest 'What the website or the hotel?' He asked almost innocently.

Dave clarified that he was actually meaning Sonia and her new romantic interests before Jack went on to explain that he'd registered with the website already. And then, subsequently, not slept for two nights whilst watching couples fucking, woman cavorting in lingerie as well as reading through various looking to meet posts. Finally, he confirmed he had two meets lined up, as well as a swinger's party on Saturday.

Dave was trying to get Jack back on theme, and asked if this all might be an effort to re-engage with Sonia, secretly hoping she might see him and rekindle their romance.

Jack sprung to life.

'No chance! She's down in Blackpool, and ma search radius is only 30 miles. I'm maybe on madshaggers.com but I'm no mental. You seen the price of petrol?'

Dave reminded Jack to keep his romantic feelings and notions in check. And tried to change the subject by asking about his recent promotion.

'Not too bad, phoned in sick on Friday but I hadn't slept as I was up all night on that website, but I was back in today. Going well. Thanks Dave'

Next up was Tony, who before Dave even turned to him was already apologising as he typed on his phone, explaining that kind of website was maybe just the place for him. 'You see. I've always struggled with a wandering eye as well as the occasional wandering hand Dave, these days more wi the reaction you get than anything. Bints crying rape the minute you hold a door open for them and glance at their tits. I'm gonna have a wee looky see.'

Dave watched the woman in the room recoil at Tony. Tony had a manner that oozed sleaze and too long a lingering look on the female members of the group. The old creep gave Jack a thumbs up and finally gave Dave his attention, stuffing his phone back into his pocket triumphantly.

'The past few weeks my daughters have been coming over and, when I'd dropped them off, I'd been bothered by this deviant that's pumping my ex. I've been asking the girls about him, but they've only managed to confirm his name is John and he's a divorcee. I can see him getting a 6am interruption to his travel to work wan morning, just to remind him what he's mixed up with here'

Dave couldn't but help think that Tony was judging this new guy by his standards, thinking Tony would have his eyes all over somebody else's teenage lassies, but it felt like the kind of input he was happy to keep to himself. Instead, he went for a far more diplomatic approach. 'You've got to develop confidence in people Tony and start from a position of trust or even halfway there, you can't judge someone unfairly and treat them guilty at the outset.'

Tony was trying to respond but Dave continued.

'You have every right to be guarded but you'll need to remember you can't control someone else's emotions or actions'

'I'm trying Dave, it's just sometimes you get a gut feeling for some cunt. John looks like a wrong un. It's bursting my heid, am out myself this weekend and hopefully that takes my mind of things. I might bump into one of you lucky ladies. Let me know if you've had a few wines and needing a good see-ing to.'

Every woman in the room stared at the ground whilst Tony looked around hopefully.

Dave moved onto Ryan without saying any more. 'My week's been good Dave nothing significant to report, went to South Queensferry with Katrina and her friend Agnes who does beach combing. We've been looking for Susan's engagement ring, the one I mentioned last week'

Dave raises his eyebrows, more so that Katrina had actually got involved, but again tried to regain his most discreet possible face. 'Thanks Ryan, and any success?'

'Not yet. But it's really interesting: Agnes has a metal detector and a great track record in detecting long lost items. She found a guy's wedding ring, who had been swimming in the sea off the coast of Burntisland. No luck yet but we're going to keep trying.'

'£13,000 is a lot of money,' Katrina said, making it painfully clear to the group her motivations for all this. 'And we've all already lost too much through romance. It would be good to win one back from its clutches, so to speak.'

15

FIFA

Jack plugged in his controller and sat back on the extra chair which Paul had brought in from the kitchen. Paul looked over to Stirling. 'Brung his own fitba bits, means business. Bit of a shark this boy?'

Stirling laughed from the sofa. Another of his friends Gary was sat defeated, rolling a joint as a penalty for taking a three-nil tanking from Paul.

'He likes to think he is, but my money's on you, he's on away turf This is a home game for you.'

Paul was providing his own commentary as the game kicked off, acoustically backing his confidence. Stirling was talking with Gary who'd now sparked the joint.

'How's things going with the ex? Settled down any?' Gary asked between his first draws.

Stirling shook his head. 'It's like one step forward five steps back, man. I couldn't tell you. She seems to float from one day to the next and change her mind completely. I knew I'd fucked up. Leaving lines on the coffee table was a big mistake. I knew that, I never did it intentionally but then sending her a picture of that burds fanny was a disaster.'

Paul was shouting at the telly before Jack slid off the chair onto a knee slide 'Beautiful' he crowed as he savoured the replay from each angle.

'Get on with the fucking game,' Paul growled, trying desperately to find a skip button he hadn't yet discovered.

'So what's your thinking, are you gonna get it back together? Gary asked.

Stirling opened his eyes wide as he took a draw of the joint. 'I fucking hope so. See this paying for a flat and maintenance is a tough gig. I've already nearly maxxed one credit card and I've still got Amsterdam to come. Are you still coming?'

'Aye man, deffo.'

Gary didn't look or sound convincing.

Stirling looked up at Paul.

'You still going?'

Paul was angrily battling buttons as if trying to accentuate the digital instructions with his own analogue anger.

'Fuuucckk sake,' he shouted, before turning to Stirling.

'What the fuck is it?'

Stirling looked up to see Jack pulling his hoody up over his head and running around the room.

'Have a look at that, eyeball Paul!'

Stirling shrugged his shoulders before joining in.

'On your home set up tae, Paulo. Are you taking that?'

Paul was blaming his team selection and changing settings and players as if he was some sort of sofa Guardiola. He turned back to Stirling.

'Aye I'm still going, man. Amshterdam shun, canny wait. First I'm beating this cunt.'

'Mon' he added, nodding to Jack before he kicked off nonchalantly.

Stirling tried to pass the joint to Jack, but he protested that he was playing a game, ducking out of the way of the ashtray as he continued with his defence. He only halted his resistance when Paul broke into a cheer.

'The comeback is on' Paul piped up, whilst Jack paused and dragged heavily on the joint.

'I'm about to get busy, motherfucker,' he exclaimed, passing the joint over to Paul as they took an impromptu break.

Jack asked Stirling how he was getting on with the Asian burd from the groups, and Gary seized on this announcement immediately.

'Suck you long time. Amewican GI'

Stirling blushed briefly before telling them both to fuck up.

'She's no fucking Chinese or that. Middle Eastern, I think.'

'Indian, actually,' Jack corrected him.

'An Indian bird,' Paul's face lit up. But Gary was puzzled.

'Do they no drink or smoke or that. Letterbox and that, fully masked up.'

Stirling was back smoking a joint, but after holding his draw in gave him an answer on the exhale.

'Nah man, she's sound, like. I think that's Muslims you're thinking about. I don't know.'

Paul passed the joint back to Gary and picked up his controller again, before announcing 'She's Sikh. ... Sikh of that fucking lanky cunt stalking her.'

Stirling bristled as he accepted the joint from Gary.

'Well, whatever she is, she's braw and she's a nice person. And, if things aren't working out with Sarah then I need to be looking at my options.'

Jack was laughing as Paul's controller flew into the middle of the room.

'Penalty! Should be a red card too, that by the way.'

Jack turned his back to Paul, who picked up his controller and tried to get a look at the direction of Jack's fingers. Jack peered over his shoulder at the telly as he sent Paul's keeper the wrong way. Jack held up three fingers as he announced the score to the room. 'You can quit now if you want, pal? Nae point prolonging the pain.'

'Fuck that' countered Paul as he began frantically playing against the clock. He was utterly dejected as the referee blew the whistle.

'Fuck sake, shark, man, that's what you are.' Jack pushed the rolling tray towards Paul's direction, but he stormed off into the kitchen before even laying hands on a rizla.

'Anybody wanting a beer?'

Jack looked over at Stirling.

'You up for a beating tae?'

Stirling thought about it for a second before neglecting to give Jack the opportunity to build on his success. Paul was the best FIFA player he knew until now.

'You'll wait for another day, big chap,' said Jack, knowing one day he'd have the pleasure of absolutely pumping Stirling. 'I don't want to ruin your good mood.'

Paul came back in with four cans of Tennent's lager and handed them around the room. Gary started talking about some South Korean film. Jack was asking Stirling about Millie again.

'So you think you're in there then big man?'

Stirling settled onto his seat before admitting,

'I don't know. She has this mental ex-boyfriend who's always popping up. Plus, if I can patch things up with Sarah then, well that's option A'

Jack was nodding along as he opened his can. 'Cheers Paul.'

Stirling looked at the rolling tray on the floor in front of Paul before looking up at him.

'Have you hurt your fingers trying to wrestle that controller there?'

Paul looked at him blankly, 'Naw.'

'Get rolling that joint then.' Gary laughed along, as Stirling interrupted himself.

'Wait a minute. Jack, tell them about that mad website you found.'

Jack started laughing before bringing out his phone.

'Wait till I tell you about this boys. It's called madshaggers.com; page after page of burds wanting the boaby. Hunners of them, videos, pictures. All of them, it's pure filth.'

Gary grabbed at his phone with a look of long-since-shagged hunger in his eyes.

'Let me see, what's the address?'

Jack held him off with one hand, and lifted the phone above his head and out of reach.

'Calm down, wee baws. I'll give you it. I'm just no wanting any of you's looking at my cock and balls. Here you go, it's www.madshaggers.com. Unbelievable Jeff.'

At that Paul's wife came down the stairs. They all returned to the game sheepishly. Jack hurried his phone into his pocket.

'What are you's burning in here?' she asked.

Paul reassured her it was merely the Cali blunt weed shit before they all started a fit of the giggles.

'Aye, very funny,' announced Paul's wife before checking in with Stirling.

'How you getting on Stirling? You and Sarah still separated? Kayleigh getting on okay?'

Stirling knew already that she knew exactly what was going on. He took the opportunity to give her the soundbite to feedback to Sarah.

'It's really tough, hen. But I'm getting there. Gave up the gear and just trying to prove to her that I have learned my lesson.

Paul's wife smiled. 'That's great, wanting to have a word with him whilst you're at it.' nodding in Paul's direction.

Paul held out his hands open palmed in an impassioned plea of defence before ushering her away with,

'We've got stuff to plan for our trip away.'

She looked furious. 'Still think you're going to Amsterdam, do you?' before she about turned and headed off, back up the stairs.

Paul shrugged off her suggestion, obviously rattled. Before announcing that he'd definitely be fucking going.

Gary picked up the controller from his feet and looked towards Jack. 'You taking challengers champ?'

16

Tony's Story

Tony worked in the warehouse at Atholl Safety checking in parcels as they arrived off the vans at goods inwards. He'd been there 15 years since he got made redundant at the jeans factory in Camelon. Since his divorce, he'd began socialising with some of his younger work colleagues. It was a Friday afternoon and he'd decided they were hitting the town. He grabbed his 12th coffee of the day as he's talked to Barry who worked in the office.

'Is that Claire in today?'

'She is that,' Tony replied, Barry knowing already where Tony was leading to. 'I'd have her locked up in my flat till the council came about the smell'

Barry laughed along but Tony's reputation as a sleaze didn't take much to confirm as Claire bounded through the door. 'Hiya Boys. Friday at last! You's up to much this weekend?'

Tony looked her up and down. 'Me and Bazza are hitting the town, you're welcome to join us if you like?'

'Nah, Tony, my husband wouldn't be too happy with that now would he – hitting the town with you two studs!'

Tony laughed along, taking a minute to compose himself as he stared at her ample bosom. 'Well, the offers there if you get an opening.'

'I'll bear that in mind,' laughed Claire as she headed back into the office.

As the door closed, Tony continued, 'Like a shit house door in a gale.' Barry nervously chuckled along before changing the subject. 'Right Tony, I'll get you at The Star and Garter before the 8pm train?'

Tony nodded. 'Bang on Bazza, see you then.'

He finished his coffee, checked his watch, and decided it was time enough to give his hands a good wash and get packed up for the weekend. He picked up his phone and jacket out the locker before making his way through to the main exit. A group of the telesales staff were leaving, and he held the door open for them, leaving just close enough a gap for them to pass without brushing against him.

'After you ladies.'

Each one slunk past him awkwardly as he pulled the door closed and began his walk up the road.

* * *

When Tony arrived in the pub. Barry was already at the bar.

'Pint, Tony?'

'Too right, son,' confirmed Tony, surveying the room.

'Have you eaten?' asked Barry, producing a fresh pint from the barman.

'Eating's cheating'

Barry chuckled again. 'There's a train at 8 o'clock. If we're quick with these we can still make it.'

'Couple of chasers for the journey then?' Tony asked for two jaeger bombs, which him and Barry polished off before settling down to their pints.

'Look at that.' Tony pointed over to a group of younger women who appeared to be making the beginnings of a hen night.

'Begging for it'.

Barry was uncomfortable, sat there with him leering, and was relieved when he eventually broke off his stare.

'What's the plan tonight then Bazza?' Whaurs the best fanny through here?' asked Tony.

Barry had no answer for him. He settled on, 'The night is young, Tony' before finishing up his pint. Let's go we'll make that train.'

* * *

The train only took twenty minutes before it was time for them to disembark. Tony pointed out a male couple further along the platform. 'Look at that man, does that no turn your stomach?' Barry had no idea what Tony was even talking about. 'They fucking bufties, jobby jabbers, man it's no right Bazza.'

All Barry could do was laugh it off.

'Each to their own man, but it's no for me.

'If god had meant for guys to be fucking each other's erses he wouldn't have given burds a fanny am a right?'

Barry's discomfort was obvious.

'Right you are, Tony. C'mon let's get heading'.

Waverley Station was still busy with office commuters rushing home after a few after-work drinks in the pub, and they jostled for position with those who were now fully embarking on their big night out. They made their way up the stairs. Tony sparked a cigarette as they cleared the last few steps and emerged onto Market Street. He took a draw and tutted as the couple he'd seen in the train station made their way past them again. Tony nodded towards the sport bar opposite the train station.

'Quick pint in here?' He offered, before presumptuously striding off in that direction.

Baz accepted and followed Tony's stride. Tony held the door open for a couple of girls who were making their way in as he looked them up and down before winking at Barry.

The bar had a dangerous mix of those who'd come out mixing with those that were out – out, as well as those that hadn't meant to be out but were now fuelled on gin, cheap lager and the sniff of a workplace romance. Tony was in his element here, the potential mix of toxicity already fuelling his excitement.

They finished their pints before agreeing on another couple, this time with shots. Tony left Baz at their table as he strategically delivered himself to the bar adjacent to the girls he'd held the door open for earlier. He ordered his pints and offered them the chance to join him and Barry with a few shots.

'Lesbian bints,' Tony summarised as he deftly delivered their drinks back to the table. Motioning Baz his beer as he swiftly polished off his shot.

'Time to get heading from here?' Barry suggested.

Tony agreed, but only after surveying the bar with one last scan.

They made their way up the hill towards the royal mile. They stopped off for another pint, and were almost immediately disappointed to see that many of those that had come out-out were now either catching up with their senses or had run out of steam. All that was left was the Friday crowd. Tony wasn't one to hide his disappointment.

'Fucking shite in here, Bazza. Full eh auld desperate cunts and teenagers.'

Baz looked like he'd seen enough too. Quickly polishing off another pint before Tony nudged them towards the door.

'Mon. Cab Vol. At least there will be some fucking fanny there. Oota this shitehole.'

They sloped down off the Royal Mile and eventually nodded to a couple of doormen as they made their way into Cabaret Voltaire. Tony's face lit up as the hen night they'd seen earlier appeared to be in attendance.

'Now we're talking, Barry lad. Head up that way,' he pointed, ignoring the table Barry had picked in favour of the standing area adjacent to the hen party. Even from a distance, Tony eyed up several of the young women in attendance. And when they took their place in the standing area, each time one of the girls went to the bar he tried to strike up a conversation, but it was way too loud for small talk.

Frustrated he turned to Barry. 'Canny hear yourself get a fucking hard on in here.'

Barry had seen enough. Tony's desperate lunges were becoming increasingly bold and, despite the noise, he could see groups across the club pointing their way accusatively.

'I'm thinking about calling it a night,' said Barry before zipping up his coat, not waiting for Tony's protestations.

Tony was shocked. 'It's only 11 o'clock man, the night is young.' Barry was already focused on escaping Tony's mating dance via the last train back to

Linlithgow. Tony's offer of paying for a taxi back later was not the tempting offer he'd intended.

Despite Barry's departure Tony was determined to stay on. 'See you later you lightweight,' he shouted after him. 'I'll make up for your lack of shagging ya wee bender – keep up the good name of us Lithage boys!'

Barry shook his head and then patted his colleague goodbye. 'Have a good one,' Barry smiled. Relieved to be disassociating himself with the drunken menace that was Tony.

* * *

Tony checked his phone, waiting for the clock to turn half past and the last train back to Linlithgow to roll out of Edinburgh with Barry on it. Once it turned 11.31, Tony slipped out past the bouncers and made his way back towards the city centre. Setting off down Leith Walk, he only has one destination in mind, but tried to carry himself in such a way that no one would ever guess it. His swagger got all the stronger, and his pigeon chest puffed out straining the top buttons on his shirt.

Making his way in, he nodded to a few regulars as he took his jacket into the cloakroom.

'Hi, Tony, long time no see' declared the blonde-haired attendant.

'Good to see you again tae. Busy tonight.' Tony smiled broadly as he made his way onto the packed dance floor. It wasn't long before he was dancing up close, rubbing, and grinding himself against anyone who got close enough, as they danced along to garish disco. Tony was already happier with the music. Finally, he thought, something you can move to. And hear yourself think.

'You come here often,' he asked as he's ground his crotch up against a pair of leather jeans on the dance floor.

'Not as often as you could cum there if you want,' replied his dance partner as they pressed back on Tony's eager crotch. 'Do you want to grab a drink?

Tony ordered two pints and two shots, and they both sat down at the bar.

'What's your name then?' smiled Tony.

'Kevin,' his drinking partner replied. 'I recognise you. You're Tony, aren't you?'

'That's right. Tony it is. Well remembered.'

'What can I say,' replied Kevin. 'I'm a sucker for a big hairy bear,' he said, and reached over to Tony's bulging crotch. 'Do you want to head somewhere a bit quieter?'

'Where you thinking,' asked Tony.

'My flat isn't far,' Kevin replied, as he drank up and encouraged Tony to do the same with a finger on the end of his glass. Tony's eyes fixated on Kevin's leather jeans as he pushed their empty pints towards the barman and downed both shots, 'c'mon big boy' slapping Kevin's backside as they left the bar, 'let's get putting that to good use.'

As they left the club, Tony groped Kevin's leather clad bottom and leered into his ear.

'Do you want me breed you, claim that tight hole as mine this time'

Kevin pushed Tony off, taking his hand before encouraging him playfully. Coyly suggested that he could if he plays his cards right.

Tony abruptly drops Kevin's hand and steps into a shop doorway. Panic had struck.

'Fuck sake. Stand right there. Fucking, eh. Stand fucking there!'

Kevin wasn't entirely sure what was adrift as he stood motionless and faced Tony.

'What's up big boy. You okay?' asked Kevin, still puzzled.

Tony ducked down to try and hide behind Kevin's frame, like a walrus trying to hide behind a rhino. He stumbled back into the doorway then fell flat on his backside, drink had clearly got the better of his balance as he lurched like an ocean liner. Kevin leaned over to help him. Tony pushed his hand away.

'Just a fucking minute. Stay right fucking there!' Tony commanded.

Tony stared through the gap between Kevin's arm and his body, watching a crowd pass immediately behind his human shield. Unwittingly nodding a customary 'alright' as he caught someone's eye. He turned away immediately and ushered Kevin behind him as he lumbered back to his feet.

Tony marched directly ahead, in the opposite direction of the group just passed. Kevin trailed behind him, somewhat bemused.

'Is he still looking?' asked Tony, still panicked. Now talking to Kevin in hushed tones over his shoulder.

Kevin turned around unsure who to look for before he guessed it was fine and shrugged that they'd passed. Tony uncomfortably joined Kevin's side, after he continued to nervously check over his shoulder. He only relaxed marginally after they lost sight of the group entirely.

'Sakes. That was a bit close for comfort. I know one of the boys in that group' confirmed Tony. 'Do you think he seen us?'

Kevin assured Tony they'd be alone soon as he buzzed open the door to his flat. He held the door open for Tony who dutifully felt him up as he made his way into the close.

17

Week Five

Dave had already relayed Jack's apologies and welcomed this week's attendees along to their RA meeting, and Lucy was well into the story of her first week as a non-practicing lesbian. She had been back in touch with the Samaritans regarding her volunteer work. She'd had another embarrassing incident though, which she didn't want to share with the group initially. Judging by her tone, Dave though it couldn't be anything too dramatic. At least not compared to her last few weeks.

'Go on, go on' Katrina rallied, pressing her to continue.

Lucy shook off her reluctance and started with her story. 'Well. As a newly non practicing lesbian I was sat quietly by myself on Saturday night whilst the kids were in their rooms and thought I might have an opportunity to have some time to myself.' Lucy made a face like she was relaying a secret message.

The group sat watching blank faced until she repeated,

'Some time to myself,' but with additional emphasis, as if she was checking they all knew what she was alluding too. They were soon, mostly, on the same page. Lucy then described her dismay when her hopes were dashed when she reached into the drawer on her bedside table to discover it was gone.

Ryan, however, had not been on the same page. 'Sorry, what was gone?'

Katrina issued him with an answer in rapier time, clearly disappointed with his slow uptake. 'Her vibrator, Ryan'

Ryan shrunk back into his seat.

Lucy picked up with her story again. First describing how she'd ventured into her son's room only to be greeted by his annoyance at her disturbing his gaming time. Sliding off one ear of his headphones to then satisfactorily respond "No!" – when asked if he'd been in Mummy's room.

Lucy then nervously ventured into her daughter, Ellie's room.

'"Hi Ellie," I said,

"have you maybe been in Mummy's room recently?"

"Yes," she answered.

"And maybe have you taken something from Mummy's drawer." Again, "Yes," she answered.

"I've got your microphone."

And she produced the thing, complete with cable, from her box of toys'

The room erupted in laughter. As Lucy blushed.

'It gets worse though. When I had asked her what she was doing with it? She'd told me she'd been singing along with videos on TikTok. Oh my god, my heart sank. Can you imagine the Mum's at the school gates whispering about that one? Or worse her friends. I'd imagined how many thousands of people might have seen her singing into my embarrassingly large vibrator'

Dave was laughing along, pretty sure Jack would have loved to be hearing about Lucy's vibrator. He thought he'd best show some concern, asking if she'd managed to remove the videos. Lucy confirmed that there had been only two and it was just her friends who'd liked them, they only had single digit views, which she had hoped was only other innocent viewers who'd made the same assumption as Ellie.

Katrina was trying to stifle her giggles, eventually managing to ask what she'd told her. Lucy described how she quietly closed the door and sat next to her on the bed asking if they could have a chat about Mummy's microphone. The chat hadn't lasted long before Ellie asked her if this was a 'sex thing,' which Lucy confirmed to her, quietly. Ellie, clearly disgusted, decided that she was never going into Mummy's room again.

Tony was sat eagerly listening. 'Did you manage to have a wank then?'

'Surprisingly, Tony, the notion had kind of left me. The thought that Ellie might have been trending on TikTok singing into my vibrator had really killed the mood for me.'

Lucy made a face at Dave which he replied with. Tony looked as if nothing would put him off a wank.

Stirling went next, and was still going on about attempting to build bridges with his ex, whilst preparing for what he described as 'jet lag' from his pending trip to Amsterdam.

Next with her check-in was Millie, immaculately turned out as ever. She was still having problems with her ex-partner, Stevie, who'd turned up at the Adler and Stevenson office unannounced with flowers for her. Dave thought to himself that she was wavering from her previous state of solid resistance, despite her describing him as a menace, a real menace. Dave was asking how she felt about his unexpected appearance.

Millie looked around the room and paused for a second before she spoke. Brushing her hair back before she started. 'Actually. I felt, for a split second, like I was impressed that he walked and left the flowers and never caused a scene. I honestly thought maybe, just maybe.'

Dave leaned forward on his chair trying to silence the disparaging voice in his head. Luckily, he wasn't required to voice anything as Millie continued,

'Mr. Adler had brought me over a lovely vase, and I'd left them in my desk. Mr. Adler even described him as a handsome young man, and I had a bit of a skip in my step.... until I got into the car park and there he was waiting by my car.

He went off on one straight away. Asking where the flowers had gone. Ranting on and on again. Full of threats. I brushed past him and told him to forget it and to stop harassing me, that I'd put his flowers in the bin and that he needed to get help.'

Dave was quite pleased that Stevie had already fucked up. Millie carried on explaining that he then followed her home for a large part of the journey home, tailgating and then driving alongside her. He only relented when she turned into the street where her Mum and Dad lived.

What a wee shite bag this clown was, Dave thought to himself. He sat quietly watching as Millie continued to describe the problems, she was having with him. Withheld numbers, fake social media accounts. Only when she started to get emotional did Dave step in.

'You're doing great Millie. Remember your personal rights and remember you have a right to make your own opinions but more importantly please remember that you don't need to put up with any harassment like that. Not from him, and not from anyone.'

Katrina piped up as well. 'Absolutely. Dicks like that should be locked up. You're doing the right thing Millie, steer well clear. You okay, babe?'

Millie reassured Katrina that she was fine before she responded to Dave

'My Mum and Dad have been saying the same, they've been telling me to contact the police. If it happens again or escalates further, I will.'

Out of the corner of his eye, Dave could see that Stirling was clearly annoyed, and desperate to get on his white charger and sort it all out for her. After a wee cough to grab Millie's attention, Stirling offered to chaperon her to work and back.

Millie looked around the room, before offering a 'Thanks' to all. She'd stopped fiddling with her bag this week, which Dave saw as a sign of progress. But he didn't think that he'd heard the last of Stevie and urged her to be careful.

His attention moved towards Tony who appeared to be deep in thought, and Dave couldn't put that down solely to the talk of wanking. Earlier, when they'd been laying out the chairs before the meeting, Tony had turned to Dave and asked why it was called the circle of trust. Dave was shocked, never having thought of Tony as a curious kind.

'Because that is what we have Tony, a circle where we support and trust each other. It's the foundation of our group.'

He'd nodded, but it seemed as if he wasn't even listening. The same silence hung over him now.

It was only after a slightly louder call of his name, that Tony stirred and apologised for his mental absence.

'Sorry Dave. My week was good, night on the tiles at the weekend and got lucky but nothing serious, just the way I like it!'

Stirling quickly seized on Tony's update. 'Were you out in Edinburgh.'

The colour seemed to drain from his face as Tony confirmed that aye, he had indeed been out in Edinburgh. 'I was that wee man. Cabaret Voltaire for a bit, few pubs, and clubs. You know me chasing the fanny – or rather the fanny chasing me. Some of they Edinburgh burds really can't get enough of a real man. Woke up in some middens flat and let myself out before she woke up. I'm no looking for breakfast in bed, just a quick fish supper'

'Aye, where did you pick her up?' Stirling asked. The questions and answers pinged back and forward, with Stirling trying to wring every bit of information about what particular pubs he'd drank in, how much they'd had, and who had been with him. And it was clearly getting to Tony.

Dave noticed Tony getting a bit agitated by Stirling's questioning. Snappily suggesting that his accompaniment would have been Barry from his work and that he was a bit of a lightweight.

'Yeah, I'm normally out till day light but sometimes you've got to look out for the young team. That would have been me taking him back for his taxi, he didn't fancy sloppy seconds, after yer auld Da, gave him the option thou. I'm sure she'd have took it, they all love a threesome. Don't they?' Tony chuckled away whilst looking around the room.

No one else was laughing.

Dave felt uncomfortable watching him and decided to step in. 'You should maybe help Stirling and his mates out in Amsterdam Tony, maybe learn a few moves from a veteran?'

Dave watched Tony take his lifeboat eagerly. Muttering under his breath something about the young team these days. Dave thought Stirling was looking pleased with himself, which was just all a bit strange. He brushed it off before asking if Derek could check in with the group.

Derek confirmed that things had been steadily improving and that he was continuing to use some of the more recent group learnings to help reach some common ground with Patricia. He seemed to actually be coming to the realisation that it wasn't all about money. He signed off with 'Excelsior,' before immediately explaining to the group what it meant. 'Onwards and Upwards. Folks.'

Then it was Ryan, who to run through the full background of his time at Romantics Anonymous even though they all knew he had something new to say. Even Millie was clearly tired of the same thing each week from him, and was staring up into the ceiling tiles. Finally, Ryan got onto his week's beach combing with Katrina.

'Well. Agnes couldn't make it but both me and Katrina went along and scoured the beach and rock pools for Susan's engagement ring. We didn't find it, but we did find a few more old coins as well as a lot bullets, which is a bit weird. We slightly missed the tide times this week, so it was really a race to get through the full area we planned to cover but we got there.'

It was the most animated Dave had seen Ryan in a long time. Dave thanked him for his update before checking if Katrina had anything to add, not expecting much.

Katrina started off with her usual diatribe of watching the perils of romance and describing how well versed she was now in avoiding them. Dave watched as Tony stifled a yawn, his cheek quivering and lip twitching as he failed miserably. Suddenly Katrina appeared to spring into life, as if breaking the chains of her usual churned out response. As loudly as her southern Irish accent could carry, she was on her soapbox. 'As my friend Ryan has described we'd been beach combing and it really would be a fantastic wrong to right by returning RYAN's ring to him and not have this Susan's name attached to the lost ring or Ryan's hurt any longer'

Dave was a bit taken aback. So apparently was Katrina, who recoiled back into her usual seated position before adding, this time much more quietly, 'Apart from that I've been doing a bit of drawing, which was an old hobby of mine and I've found that really helps. Very therapeutic. Just wee sketches. I used to paint a bit, just watercolours mainly. I was supposed to go to art college but came over here and well never took it back up.'

Dave wasn't sure if this was the same woman. He was so taken aback he almost forgot to pick up the next section so then hurriedly issued a thanks to everyone for sharing before adding.

'It would be good to see some of your work one-week Katrina; art can be a great source of therapy.' Katrina shuffled her legs close together and smiled at Dave in response. He found this unnerving; a pleasant change, but unnerving none the less.

18

Late Call Offs

Stirling had woken up in a strange hotel room. He got that instant feeling that he might be in trouble when he picked up his phone from the bedside table, 10am, and the memories started hitting him like a barrage. The races, singing in the karaoke, the strange chat with an Irish guy in the bar and then smoking a joint outside, walking home, bursting for a pish. Getting to the hotel and remembering where the toilet was, getting there and realising it was the kitchen, but it was too late as soon as his feet hit that tiled floor his drunken brain had activated pish mode. He remembered switching the stream to his suede desert boot to dampen the splashing sound. Relieved, he had squelched upstairs to his room, leaving one wet footprint behind him.

Amsterdam – the memory hit him like a thunderbolt. He was heading to Amsterdam at 4pm today and was in a hotel room in Perth. He stretched and scrolled through his phone. He'd been googling Millie Singh when he came back to his room but thankfully not text or phoned anyone whilst he was out of it. He decided to phone Sarah.

'Hallo, aye no bad, no nae winners, turned into a late one. Karaoke? Aye, you know me too well. How's the wee one? Good stuff. Are you still alright to take us to the airport? Sound, 4 o'clock. See you. cheers'

He dropped his phone on the bed and looked down at the pile of clothes on the hotel floor, which looked like someone had been vaporized. He picked up his desert boots, one was covered in beer splashes and mud, while the other, the one soaked which he assumed had been soaked in pish, looked brand new. Impressed, he decided he must remember to pish on the other boot sometime. He packed every garment into an Asda bag and flung it into his case. He skipped breakfast before heading out of the hotel, relieved to see that his single footprints had dried away, slipping his key card in a box at reception. There was no way he could even risk getting questioned about his massive drunken pish in their kitchen.

Walking to the train station, his phone pinged. It was Gary. 'Sorry for the late notice, Stirling, but I can't go to Amsterdam today; work drama.'

Stirling shouted, 'fuck sake' before volleying his case in the street. Regaining his still drunk and limited composure, but still shaking his head, he decided to phone Paul.

'Alright man?'

'No too well man. I'm struggling, I've been up all-night shitting. I think I'm going to have to go to the hospital.'

Stirling could have thrown the phone into the road. 'Whit? For the shits?'

'Aye man. It's bad, All night. Every time I stand up, I need to shit again.'

'Take some Imodium ya blouse and you'll be fine. We're flying to Amsterdam in 5 hours.'

'I wish I could man. I canny no like this, it'll kill me.'

Stirling was moments from unloading a torrent of cunts and bastards at Paul, but composed himself again, realising just how much of a dick he was being. Still though, he was not convinced Paul hadn't just created a story to avoid a session, and the wrath of his Mrs. it wouldn't be the first time. But what could he do?

He put in a video call to Shaun and Al. They both picked up immediately.

'You look rough as fuck,' started Shaun, and Al obviously agreed.

'Aye very good, I canny mind much last night. Apart from pishing on the kitchen floor.'

Did you get any winners?' asked Al, still laughing.

Stirling paused before remembering he actually did, all day backing George Elliot's horses had given him a return. He looked in his wallet and he had what he thought was about £500 in crumpled notes. Stirling pulled out the notes and dropped his case before fanning the handful of notes in front of his phone. 'Did that boys, loadsa money! Anyway, they two fannies have pulled out.'

'What?' replied Shaun. 'Aye man, Paul's no well and Gary's now working.

'Fuck sake,' said Al. 'What we gonny dae?'

Stirling jumped on his question immediately. 'Well, they're no getting their money back, do either of you know any cunt that would go today?'

Both were shaking their head. Silence rang out between the three of them as they thought of and immediately discounted potential replacements. Stirling realised he was still stood at the station doors and rummaged through his wallet for his ticket. Just then, an idea hit him. It was a drunk one, but it was an idea.

'I'll phone ye's back, I need to get this train or I'll no be there either.'

* * *

Sarah turned up about 3:45pm. Stirling pulled his case together

'Alright?' Sarah asked as he closed the boot and jumped in the front seat.

'Aye, no bad,' Stirling replied, trying his best to mean it. Sarah had arrived at 3.45, and that had only left him half an hour to shower and repack his case with a change of jeans, two shirts, a toiletries bag, a phone charger and 5 cans of lager. 'Here, you'll never guess who cancelled?'

Sarah laughed.

'Let me think, it must be Paul ... in fact, Paul or Gary?'

'Bingo,' replied Stirling. 'Both of them, this morning'

'What happened this time?'

'Gary's having to work and Paul's got the super shits, going to hospital apparently. Full of shit, mare like.'

Sarah smiled. 'Oh well, it'll be good just the three of you, more room in that executive suite you've booked.' Sarah was referring to the five-bed dorm in the hostel that was waiting for them.

'No really,' replied Stirling.

'There were quick contract talks and I've moved before the transfer window banged shut.'

'Really? Who's going now?'

'You'll maybe know Jack Stewart, stays in Tamfourhill?' Sarah shrugged her shoulders.

'And Tony is from Linlithgow, I canny mind his second name., Sinclair, that's it,' confirmed Stirling, chuffed with himself.

'It's all right I've got their addresses, fire round and pick up Shaun and Al first, I told Al we'd get him first.'

One by one, Sarah stopped and picked up the excited travellers, and Stirling greeted them with a can of lager. Each maintained a discrete edge to their anticipation of Amsterdam's offering, both of the flesh and the beak; Guy code was closely observed. They all exchanged welcomes with Jack as he entered the back seat. Jack knew Shaun from a concert they'd been at years ago. Then, finally, Sarah pulled up outside Tony's flat.

Tony emerged from the flat like a released prisoner. Black leather jacket, stonewash jeans and a black Head holdall.

Al clocked his new travel partner immediately.

'What's he got in the bag? A bottle of brut and four cans of Skol,'

'He looks like he'd drink them all, tae,' Shaun joined in. The hilarity stifled as Tony slid open the door.

'Alright troops, I'm looking forward to this.'

'Tony,' exclaimed Jack, 'what's happening sir, I never realised you were coming?'

Tony shook his hand firmly and nodded towards Stirling. 'Did he no let on likesy?'

'Didn't want to ruin the surprise,' replied Stirling sitting in front, avoiding Sarah's look, which he knew would have several questions. He introduced Tony to everyone, and handed him his can. Everyone received a nod, apart from Sarah who Tony took the opportunity to confirm was still single before winking at Jack.

* * *

They arrived at the airport, and each said their goodbyes to Sarah who yelled to them to have a good time as she sped off. Once she was definitively out of sight, Stirling pulled them all-round like a scout master. Jack pulled out £50 and thrust it into Stirling's pocket.

'Here,' he said, 'before we get started.' This prompted Tony to do the same, pulling out a wallet which looked like it originally had leather in the 80's.

'Are you sure that's all your wanting, big man?'

'Aye man,' Stirling confirmed. 'It was just for the change of name on the flights, I've text each of you your boarding passes for the way out'

'Sound' replied Tony 'drinks are on me then. Just make sure I don't fall asleep, I'm always falling asleep when I'm on the lash.'

But Al quickly stepped up. 'Eh, listen boys, I've got something for us at the airport.'

'What do you mean' asked Stirling.

'Some chico.'

'At the airport, are you fucking mad? We canny take cocaine into the airport!' Stirling was already dreading the idea of having to take everything Al might have packed for the weekend before they even got on the plane.

'No, this airport, ya fud,' Al corrected, 'at the other side: Schiphol. I've got an Albanian boy picking us up, he can get us as much gear as we want... and take us to the digs.'

Jack, Shaun, and Stirling started celebrating like they'd won the lottery. Tony was too, but clearly didn't know what he was celebrating.

'Amsterdam taxis are the best taxis in the world eh boys,' he chipped in.

Alan just looked at Tony, bemused, 'aye pal, best taxis in the world'.

'Right troops whatever happens in Amsterdam, stays in Amsterdam' announced Stirling as they made their way into the airport. 2 hours later, after being warned to keep it down in the Wetherspoons, they finally get on the plane, and Tony's told Shaun how he'd shagged an air stewardess before. He told him that he'd had piles and couldn't sit on the seat so stood beside her on a flight back from Portugal one year. Ended up humping her behind a curtain. Shaun already knew Tony talked some amount of shite.

19

Stirling to Amsterdam Night One

The taxi drivers English, Dutch and Albanian were all better than Stirling's. 'So, you guys want some good drugs yeah?'

'100%,' confirmed Stirling before Tony shouted from the back, 'And some pussy!'

The taxi driver confirmed they were in right place.

'I can get you whatever you want but no pussy, the red light girls will sort that for you. What drugs are you guys after. Ecstasy, Cocaine?'

Stirling adopted a more serious tone as he replied.

'Cocaine'

They quickly started counting out Euros in the backseat of the car before Stirling remembered he had his winnings in his pocket. '2 for me,' shouted Shaun, before Jack added 'I'll have one.' Al held up 2 fingers and watched Stirling take note in the mirror.

'What are we getting?' Tony asked, dumbfounded, and unwilling to commit to a number.

Al explained in one word: 'Ching.'

'I've never had ching before, but fuck it, I'll have one too.'

Stirling counted, 2, 4, 5, 6 – 11. How much for 11 gram?'

Al's shook his head. Shaun leant forward and asked if Stirling could count, before helping him '2 for me, 2 for Al, 1 each for they two... and you want 5?'

'That's right,' confirmed Stirling. 'How much?' he asked the taxi driver, half hoping he'd say he didn't have 11. The taxi driver pulled out a tray of about 120 bags and counted out 11.

'650 Euros, 65 euros per bag.'

Stirling countered this rapid. '500 euro'

The taxi driver's quick agreement immediately confirming to Stirling that he'd poorly negotiated.

'And the taxi journey included?' he suggested, before reaching out his hand.

The taxi driver shook his hand and Stirling picked up the bags before handing them back to Al and Shaun in the middle row.

'There we go boys.'

Shaun and Al were chopping out lines within seconds. Stirling couldny believe their audacity, 'Can you's no wait ten minutes?'

'Fuck that,' said Shaun. 'What if it's shite?'

'It's no shite' confirmed Al, tilting his head back as he savoured the acrid drop of his first line which slipped through his nose and tingled the back of his throat satisfyingly.

'That's the fucking real deal there.' he confirmed like a connoisseur of fine wines.

Shaun sniffed up his first line and quickly nodded in agreement. Ten minutes later he was leaning forward in his seat, sat perched between Stirling and the taxi driver conducting conversation between their heads as if he was umpiring a tennis match. Telling the driver how he should be running bus trips from the airport.

'That's yer fucking tip there big yin. Bus trips, am telling you - you'd be fucking rolling in it'

* * *

4 hours later they were still in the room, with twelve lines neatly chopped out on the bathroom shelf. The room itself looked like a prison cell: no TV, a locker each for their clothes, one small towel each and not even a bar of soap in the bathroom. The small window had been left open, in an attempt to shift

the unmistakable smell of stale smoked grass. As a result, the room was as cold as it was outside. They never noticed thou, as they were all buzzing on arrival excitement as well as the immediate hit of several lines of gear each. Jack had the tinny trill of music blaring from his iPhone. Stirling was getting pensive.

'Right boys look at the time, we need to get out and about – we canny sit about here for two days!'

'He's right' said Shaun, 'let's get out this room.'

They all started packing up before having another 45-minute debate about how much cocaine they should bring before they settled on one bag and one further line each for the road, leaving the rest in the room. Jack remembered to freshen up with a spray, and was delighted with himself for remembering his social etiquette before sharing his wisdom around the room. Everybody gratefully accepted. Shaun then remembered he had some chewing gum, and shared that around the room as well.

Satisfied that they were now in showroom condition. The five of them made their way down the stair, and congratulated Stirling on his organising as well as Al for his international drug links. Eyes out on stalks, chewing like mental, reeking of lynx Africa but feeling on top of the world. Shaun hailed them an Uber, delighted he could select a 5-seater for the journey.

'This uber is the future man.'

Tony's told Al that 'Amsterdam hostels are the best in the world. Better than anywhere in the world' while Stirling surveyed the reception. It was busy with backpackers and tourists. Shaun shouted out 'that's the taxi here' and they all trailed out, feeling like they were on the set of a movie. They squeezed into the car before Stirling asked Shaun where there headed.

'Red light district,' confirmed Shaun, and the car erupted in a cheer.

'I fucking love this city!' yelled out Jack.

'Best city in the world' Said Tony.

By the time they arrived in the red light district it was already 2am. They found a pub and ordered up 5 large beers. Jack noticed that they are the only folk in the full pub with full actual pints. Within 15 minutes Tony was up getting another round in and Stirling was lining up a few patsy clines in the toilet.

Soon, they got onto the subject of Romantics Anonymous.

'So, what's this bird like that he fancies, Jack?' asks Shaun.

Jack start laughing 'Millie!.'

'That's it,' says Shaun, 'never shuts up about her. Is she braw?'

Jack screwed up his face in confirmation before adding,

'She's tidy like. Ae Tony?'

Tony was staring around the pub like a man possessed.

'What was that,' he asked, no even breaking his stare.

'Millie, the bird that Stirling fancies, what's she like?' repeated Jack.

'What a body, I'd let her shite on my chist.'

Stirling returned from the toilet.

'Quick, disabled toilet, there's another four laid out.'

Tony headed to the toilet while Shaun continued,

'We were just talking about your bit Shereen Nanjiani, big man. Jack was saying she's fine like.'

Stirling was unabashed. 'Totally, what a body on her'

Alan took his cue and headed to the toilet as Tony picked up the conversation from before he left.

'So who do you fancy in the group then Jack?'

Jack wasn't sure if he wanted to divulge but the cocaine had him talking more than he could even filter.

'Lucy is a bit of me, filthy – I can tell.'

'You think?' asked Tony, surprised.

'Oh, aye man, she's no had a couple of weans cos she doesny like the boaby plus did you hear her the other night there, she's a dirty.'

Tony was still weighing up the female members of the group when Shaun intervened.

'Right, so you three all go to a group to help with your problems with romance and you's are here in the shagging capital of Europe taking about burds in that same group that you's want to ride. You's are mental!'

Tony, Stirling, and Jack were still defending themselves when Al returned from the toilet.

'Were they three all for me?'

Stirling's laughed even louder.

'Naw man, one each ya greedy cunt look at you.' Flakes of white powder were dropping off Al's nose. 'You couldn't get anymare up there?'

'Ah well, we've not all got massive hooters like you big man.' Countered Al.

'Right, where are these hookers?'

They all drank up and headed out into the street.

* * *

'We going in then' Jack nudged Al.

They'd been circling the red-light district in amazement, passing window after window, the red lights lighting up the cold night and shimmering in the reflection of the canal. There was still a buzz in the air as they survey the best of Amsterdam's late-night offerings. Each window enticing their drunken lust with a tempting wink or a partial opening of a door. But then, one African girl had decided to be a bit bolder and chapped on the window with a hair comb and announced, 'I do the two of you for 60 euros,' to Jack and Al.

'Mon then,' replied Al as they awkwardly slipped open the door. She whipped the curtain closed behind the two of them.

Two minutes later the both of them were naked as the she stripped off suggestively and stepped over to the two of them. Al was captivated by her pink pussy whilst Jack immediately began feeling her breasts when she confirmed abruptly, '60 euro suck and fuck. Money first.'

Al got his wallet out of his folded jeans and pulled out 3 twenties, then winked to Jack to not worry about his. She slipped the money under her mattress and dropped to her knees. She sucked Jacks' cock expertly. As Jack struggled to contain himself, he glanced over to Al who was wanking furiously and started laughing.

'What the fuck are you daen?'

Al started laughing back.

'I canny fucking get it up man. That fucking gear, I'm fucked.'

'You'll be fine when she's sucking you, man.' He looked back at her, and she bent over and guided Jack into her pink wanton pussy. Jack grunted as he fucked her and started pumping furiously. But Al was still wanking like mad when Jack turned to him.

'Will you fuck off with that man, you're putting me off,'

'Don't worry I'm no looking at you, I'm watching her.'

'Fucking stop it for two minutes man, you can start again when I'm done.'

Al looked pensive as he dropped his semi and looked out the gap in the curtains, still listening as Jack blurted out 'you're gorgeous' when he buckled and came. He started watching again and got back to working on his hard-on as she slipped out from under Jack, having removed his condom tied it, deposited it in the bin and washed her hands before she then dropped to her knees in front of Alan.

His limp dick sat there in her mouth as she began sucking on it. Al stared at her, trying to fuck her mouth as he desperately tried to gain purchase on his semi. He never even noticed Jack collecting his jeans but felt him patting him on the back and encouraging him.

'Get in there, big yin.'

She lay back on the single bed and asked Al to fuck her, but Al couldn't believe his bad luck.

'Where you going, I about fucking had it there,' he said, and started wanking his semi erect cock again. He leant over her as he tried to contort and control his efforts, utilising his thumb as a makeshift splint. Eventually he slipped off and licked her pussy whilst wanking again, before shuddering to a very brief halt and immediately rising to his feet and getting dressed, surprised at how much he'd been sweating, wiping a deposit of cum on her red curtains. He hurriedly left the small room and joined the waiting crowd who cheered as he returned.

'Did you get on better without me?' asked Jack, smirking.

'Ha-ha, ya dirty bastard' congratulated Stirling as they returned on their weave around the red-light district. 'It's 5am boys,' advised Al as the realisation dawned on the group that there first night was over.

'Let's get back to the digs.'

20

Stirling to Amsterdam Night Two

When they got back to the digs they were already laying out breakfast. But none of them were hungry. Stirling's stomach felt about the size of a roasted peanut. Tony, however, sat down and subsequently began troughing through a full buffet continental style breakfast. Everyone else passed as they made there way upstairs.

One pre-bed line became two and then became three, as Jack, Al, Stirling, and Shaun chatted away through the wee small and bigger hours, early morning becoming late morning before Tony cane stumbling in.

'Where the fuck have you been?' asked Al, who'd already had more than a few questions about Tony.

'I got smoking joints with two French birds outside and stopped a boy getting stabbed,' advised an animated Tony, telling them he intervened by producing a half smoked joint and telling the pair of them to 'chill out and have a smoke of this.'

'Nae chance man, you're a fucking legend, sir.' Jack put on Buffalo Soldier, and they all started singing about Alfredo Morelos, apart from Tony who climbed into bed and within 10 minutes was snoring heavily.

'Fucking hell that cunt sounds like a buffalo' said Jack.

'How can the fucker sleep? I'm jealous.'

Al agreed before asking where they found this cunt.

'He's no wired up properly.'

They all agreed before climbing into their bunks, none of them sleeping apart from Tony intermittently either snoring, farting or stretching. Four hours of this followed before Stirling declared to the room. 'I could go hame, I reckon I've got two options: ching and beer straight through or hame.'

Al agreed, rising from his bed.

'Fuck this'

Jack was not yet happy to get involved, clearly unsure if he could survive another night like the one before on zero sleep, but the sound of Shaun shitting in the toilet, flushing and then his yelps as the cold water of the shower hit him forced the weary straggler up and awake.

Five minutes later Shaun emerged from the shower,

'That showers got two temperatures: fucking Baltic or molten lava.'

'Feel better though?' enquired Jack, almost pleadingly.

'Aye,' confirmed Shaun, before doing a quick shadow box,

'ready for round 2,'

* * *

Shaun, Stirling, Jack, and Al were all dressed and showered by the time Tony woke up and immediately crackled into life. 'Good sleep that, you boys up and about already? Wait five minutes,' he said, and bundled himself into the shower. Each of them listening as he took his turn on shower roulette and started singing.

Stirling looked round at the other three. 'Line?'

Unanimously they nodded in agreement.

'Much have we got left?' asked Al. All four of them start producing empty bags. 7 empty bags and 3 ½ bags left.

'Fuck sake,' said Stirling, amazed. 'What the fuck did we do?'

'Snorted it' summarised Shaun.

Tony came through from the shower, pulled on the same stonewash jeans from yesterday but rolled out a new white T-shirt and sprayed a liberal amount of deodorant indiscriminately around his person. 'What's the plan the day boys?' he asked eagerly.

'Gear and beer, then fuck knows and that' announced Shaun.

'Good stuff, let's do it.'

The five of them headed into town, a shadow of their yesterday selves. The cocaine seemed to have lost its magic and rather than catapulting them to a hundred miles an hour, it now kept them ticking over at walking pace.

They toured round a few bars, amazed as their second day appeared to be dripping away from them. After several beers and the bulk of the remaining ching they were almost back on an even keel, and walked from bar to bar, taking in the general buzz of Amsterdam's weekend nightlife.

Soon, they stumbled across a smart shop which had aroused Jack's interest.

'This is what we need boys.'

He pointed up at the window: Mexican magic mushrooms and LSD tabs. There wasn't a lot of enthusiasm.

'We're fucked anyway,' said Jack, going into full pitch mode. 'We're kicking about here like zombies. The cocaine lasts about half a step and I'm needing mare It's our last night in Amsterdam, we might as well get out our tree and see where it takes us.'

Jack found an unexpected ally in the shape of Shaun, who pipes in that they do only have one gram of ching left between them.

One by one they succumbed to Jack's plan. Jack soon returned with 3 boxes of Mexican magic mushrooms and 5 acid tabs.

They found a bar with a seating area outside; a waitress came over and took an order for drinks. They ordered 5 half pints, now accustomed to a more European drinking pace. Jack started sharing out the acids, first, and then the mushrooms. Each of them took half an acid, apart from Jack who took the last tab, washing it down with a Heineken. Then they started popping open the plastic boxes of mushrooms. Each of them tried chewing, swallowing, gulping, and eating them. None of them went down easily.

Half an hour later they all looked like they'd barely survived a bush tucker trial.

Jack's eyes were like dartboards, and he announced they should go for a walk. Without saying a word, they all agreed, and walked off before the waitress caught up with them to ask them to pay their bill. Stirling argued that he'd already paid for them, in the street, before they all returned to the table.

'I paid using a 50 euro note' he stressed, positively confirming. He opened his wallet and pointed inside.

'It's now gone.'

The waitress retrieved her manager as the five of them looked at each other: Stirling, still adamant, the other four puzzled, not knowing if this was even happening. At that, Stirling produced a 50 euro note from his back pocket, just as the waitress and her manager returned to the table. The other four fell about laughing as Stirling tried to explain himself, but while the others laughed the bar manager was clearly not happy. Still, the gravity of his upset was not felt by the group who were now happily tripping out their head.

Jack was still replaying what had happened and giggling to himself.

'When you pulled that 50 out man, your face just dropped.'

Even though the bar manager continued to rant away in Stirling's ear, he placed her on mute whilst explaining that the 50 had almost certainly disappeared and then reappeared magically in his pocket.

Once settled up at the bar, and the manager had shouted herself sore, the five of them walked through the lanes and canals trying to find their way back to the hostel, recognising parts and then forgetting them as soon as they had passed. It started raining heavily suddenly, which heightened the need to accelerate the pace of this aimless journey back to the hostel. Soon enough, paranoia set in across the 5 of them like a contagion and without speaking they somehow zeroed in on a route home, and walked silently to the hostel. Individually they were shaking off phantom followers and avoiding big faces watching them, feeling like aliens. Unwelcome aliens at that.

It was dark before they got back into the room.

'What time is it?' asked Tony.

'Back of one big man' responded Jack, Al follows up with a 'bedtime.' Leaving no time for negotiation.

All five of them make it into the room, still drenched in paranoia with the starting's of a horrific come down already taken hold. They were all silent.

Stirling was in his bed. Under the covers, tossing and turning. Intermittently trying to work out puzzles of nothing in his brain before thinking over everything in his life to this point. Wondering if he was even worth anything to anyone in this life; For Millie, for his ex, even for Kayleigh. Catching brief hallucinations out the corner of his mind and turning away rather than facing them become reality. It was then it first started.... the noise of someone wanking in the room, steadily clapping away at themselves. Stirling tried hard not to think inside each of their heads. Fighting off visions of each of their fantasies. Focusing instead on the street noise outside.

Minutes turn into hours and eventually the noise in the street dissipated to silence, all he could hear was the unmistakable sound of his fellow travelers lengthy comedown wank. He tried, unsuccessfully. to somehow rewire his own hearing, his pal's grubby fantasies now flashing temporarily in his frontal lobe to accompany the rhythmic slap of their self indulgence. He was convinced that it was Tony, hours later it was still Tony. Stirling blocked out images of Tony with the man he'd seen him with, flicking between channels in his brain and not liking any of them. Continually being brought back the room and returning to Tony's wank. It was 100% Tony. He couldn't sleep and his flight was in four hours.

Out of nowhere Tony sat bolt upright.

'Fucking hell Stirling. Will you finish your fucking wank – get your Shilpa Poppadom ride finished and give us all peace!'

Stirling was immediately embarrassed but then felt a surge of defensive anger in one big rush... he responded with 8 hours of come down venom.

'Me!? Me!? Fuck you ya dirty auld poofter cunt. Who the fuck do you think you are talking to? You should finish wanking over your big boyfriend with the leather trousers. Fucking cunt.' Still smarting he signed off:

'Aye we all ken your secret ya bender.'

Silence filled the room, just the sound of a wet flag flapping in the wind outside their window.

Neither of them had been wanking.

The sound of the wet hotel flag flapping in the wind was now their only accompaniment. Each of them pretending to sleep, no one able to make the tension feel any better. Stirling checked his phone and then broke the silence by confirming it was 8am, and they needed to be in the airport by ten.

'I've messaged you all your boarding passes'. He announced, sparingly using words as if they were a tapped resource. Before he made his way through to the bathroom.

He stood in the shower, this time dealing with the temperature switches silently. When he returned to the room. Tony didn't speak; he jumped down from the top bunk and headed into the shower himself – returning an alright to Jack as he caught his eye on the way. The tension dropped as the shower started.

'Fuck sake Stirling' said Shaun 'what did you go and say that for, the big daft cunt is all right.'

'It's true' replied Stirling,

'aye I know but c'mon man' countered Shaun.

Jacks going for a different tact,

'I definitely thought it was you wanking.'

'I'm still annoyed I actually thought I was hearing you's wanking for hours last night and it was a fucking flag' laughed Al.

The tension returned as Tony come back in from the shower and dressed himself silently, packed up his stuff and moved to depart.

Shaun tried to intervene.

'Hey big man, Tony, don't go we've got a taxi coming in a bit.'

Tony opened the door and walked off without saying a word. Shaun urged Stirling to go and follow him but Stirling was having none of it.

'He's a big boy, he's got his ticket.'

The four of them sat at departures at Schiphol airport whilst there was no sign of Tony. The gate got called and the four of them stood at the departure gate as they then announced his name over the tannoid. The gate staff advise he's not been through security and their flight must leave. They boarded the plane minus a Tony.

21

Nothing to declare

It was Monday evening and neither Jack nor Stirling had heard from Tony yet. As a result they had agreed to arrive early and watch out for him.

'Still no word?' asked Jack,

'Nothing' replied Stirling, swiping his phone back to life and scrolling through his many attempts to show him.

'I've tried texting and phoning loads but nothing, the ring tone has changed back to normal so I'm assuming he's back, somewhere.'

'Poor cunt,' summarised Jack. 'How did you know, that he was gay like - I'd never have guessed.'

'I'd had an inkling, but it was the other week in Edinburgh when he was out. I'd seen him walking up Leith Walk with a big fella with the leather jeans and all that. I knew he'd clocked me, but he tried to duck down and avoid being noticed. Not that I'd mind like. I just didn't like what he'd said to me. I don't mind if anybody's black, green, gay or a big raging tranny. I play with cock every day.' Jack looked up at Stirling in surprise.

'Just my own likes,' Stirling grinned.

'Still, wish I had said something or caught up with him before we left, but my head was full of mince. I'm blaming the gear.'

Jack and Stirling were still stood discussing Tony's potential whereabouts when Ryan's car arrived. Stirling looks over at Jack.

'That's Ryan here. What are we going to say?'

Jack was watching Ryan park up his car whilst Stirling continued.

'What will we say Jack? We canny tell everybody he's went rogue after I called him out for being in the closet. Can we?'

Jack was still silent, watching over at the horizon. Eventually buying time.

'Just stall him the now. Give it another five and then we'll speak to Dave when he gets here'

Ryan bounced over to them excitedly.

'Hi Guys. You're early tonight, are you heading in?' Stirling was still looking beyond Ryan at every passing car leaving Jack to respond.

'No yet, Ryan, we're waiting for Tony. You haven't heard from him, have you?'

Ryan looked puzzled as to why they'd be looking so eagerly for Tony. 'Not since last Monday guys. Sorry. Is Dave here?'

'No yet,' Stirling answered, 'but I think that's his motor.'

* * *

Dave was pulling into the Trinity car park when he spotted not just Ryan, but Ryan accompanied by both Stirling and Jack. He checked the clock on his car and his phone, before confirming to himself, yup, definitely early.

He parked up and locked the car before making his way over to the gang waiting. Jack and Stirling were quick to approach him first.

'Hi Dave,' Stirling fired in, 'you okay? Have you heard from Tony?'

Dave was not sure how to react at first. He struggled to make the connection between the two in front of him and Tony's not coming tonight. Regardless, Dave confirmed he was not coming along that week but he'd be back next week. He'd had a weekend away and was not long back.

'What a fucking relief. Have you spoke to him?'

Dave never answered, immediately suspecting something was amiss.

'What's going on guys?'

'It's a long story,' said Stirling as the three of them walked towards Ryan who was waiting at the door. 'Short version is Tony came with us to Amsterdam, but we hadn't seen him since yesterday morning and we were getting a wee bit worried.'

'Well, he's definitely home now, so no need to worry.'

'Hello Ryan!' Dave offered, much friendlier with an audience.

'Hallo Dave' replied Ryan, prompting both Jack and Stirling to repeat their own versions of the same.

'Hallo Dave', 'Hallo Dave'

It wasn't two minutes before Sensei Jamieson called his class to a halt and they all shuffled into single file and left the hall. Dave held the door open. Sensei Jamieson bustled out at the back of them, nodded to Dave and then stared at Stirling and Jack, paused in silence, and then continued to the door. Before he left, he turned and looked back at the pair of them once more.

The two of them sat puzzled.

'What's with Chuck Norris?'

'I dunno,' giggled Stirling nervously, 'but he's no happy with you'

'Me?' asked Jack, 'I thought he was looking at you.'

The rest of the group arrived in ones and twos before Millie and Katrina arrived last. Stirling was delighted when Millie chose to sit next to him ahead of a seat next to Derek. Her and Katrina were exchanging niceties as usual, when she lay down her bag and turned to Stirling.

'Survive then?

'Barely,' replied Stirling, 'well worth it though, I think.'

'I didn't think you'd make it tonight' smiled Millie.

'Would you have been disappointed?'

'Obviously' giggled Millie 'Disappointed not to hear about your exploits!'

Stirling nudged Jack who leaned over and whispered I love you's into Stirling's ear.

22

Week Six

Dave sat back in his seat, still trying to decipher what had happened with Tony, whilst Jack run through a severely edited version of events that unfolded in Amsterdam. Dave knew Jack too well to think this was the full story and was still smarting from the realisation that his opportunities to be involved with the full unedited version had long since sailed and now even Tony was ahead of him in that particular pecking order.

Dave quipped that he didn't realise that Stirling was arranging a field trip before Millie joined in, following Dave's cue

'Yeah where were our invites' tapping Katrina's knee as if to tag her into the fight.

'Not really my scene anyway' Katrina added, tossing her hair with mock offence.

Dave waited as Stirling justified the inclusion of Tony and Jack, suggesting that he didn't think the girls would be ready at half an hours' notice, protesting that he had late call offs that day. Finally, when the excuses were over, Stirling ran through his own heavily redacted summary of their Amsterdam trip.

Dave looked over to Jack knowingly who started laughing before reminding Stirling (and Dave) that...

'What happens in Amsterdam stays in Amsterdam.'

Dave congratulated them both for making it back in one piece before poignantly adding that they'd done better than Tony in that respect, watching as they both looked towards the floor before Dave spoke with Millie next. What had happened between them and Tony was still gnawing at him as Millie pulled forward her seat and began summarising her week between groups.

'This week I've felt a lot stronger than I have done for a long time. I've become more determined with my recent life choices. Particularly regards Stevie. I mean, he still gets in touch every few days, telling me he's turned a corner, that he's invested in new ventures and that he's getting help for his own challenges blah, blah, blah. To be honest, though, I feel like I've heard all this before. And it's now a case of too little too late for us as a couple. I really do hope that he makes progress with all the things he's mentioned. I do want him to be well despite everything else.'

Dave noticed that Millie was nodding throughout her check-in, as if to convince both herself and the rest of the group. He wasn't fully buying it, not yet anyway, Millie seemed too nice to stick to her guns. Millie seemed like such a people pleaser that she'd find it impossible not to be worn down... .eventually. And this Stevie sounded persistent, nobody's THAT persistent when they don't think they have a chance.

Nevertheless, he found himself nodding back in agreement and smiling as she continued. Willing and wanting her, and him, to believe what she was saying.

'I've been throwing myself into my work. Mr Adler wants me to launch some of my designs in the coming weeks. I'll be the first to have a proper launch, at this stage in my career. Mr Adler thinks that I have a real talent. He said that my work is better than 95% of the designs he sees each day ... and he sees a lot!'

'That's great Millie, well done you. Sounds like you're focussing on the positive influences in your life. Keep it up!' Dave encouraged her.

He wanted to tell her to change her number, delete her socials and never speak to Stevie again. But she needed to get that realisation herself. He'd seen this same situation play out so many times before.

Millie nodded again and smiled back at Dave, looking relieved that her check-in was over. Dave flicked his attention onto Lucy who'd not had much to report other than her kids, the volunteer shifts, and her continued path of non-practicing lesbianism. He caught both Stirling and Jack exchanging nods and winks as she did.

Dave turned to Derek next, who seemed buoyant. As he checked in with the group, he explained how he had been doing a lot of soul searching, and was now finding that the groups had been helping with his approach to his estranged wife and allowing them both the opportunity to converse. Dave could sense that Derek was building to a big reveal before he cleared his throat.

'And the latest update from me is that I'm leaving the rat race, I'm selling the company and going to retire. I've made enough money for myself and Patricia to live out what we want in life and, well, as soon as I can find a buyer that'll be me; a man of leisure and with time to think on what I can do with my resources. It's a different feeling thinking of these as a finite resource, however much it may be. '

Dave was amazed at Derek's ability to lose the support of the room, even when making big life choices. Even without trying he lorded it. Dave reminded himself that's what he was there for before congratulating Derek and delving more into what had happened.

'A few weeks back David you were talking about our personal rights, and I'd got to thinking about Patricia's, as opposed to my own, and how I didn't respect them. I'd never given Patricia too much of an opportunity to express them and hoped that I could blind her by my wealth. After talking, for a long, long time it eventually became apparent that Patricia's probably the only person that doesn't want my money, she actually hates it. I know it sounds frightfully bizarre, but I'd always put myself under pressure to give her what I thought she wanted, and it turns out I was wrong.'

'That's sounding like the result of a lot of soul-searching Derek,' Dave said, as if he was delighted by this development.

'You're right David and believe it or not, I found one.'

This struck a chord with the group, probably a bit too much, as they first laughed before one by one joining in with a spontaneous round of congratulations. Derek thanked the room and waved off the attention.

'Hello Ryan,' Dave said.

'Hallo Dave.'

Dave rolled his eyes before insisting that Ryan go on, despite his better judgement.

'Still pleased that I've managed to resist the temptation to embark on the search for romance after having been burned heavily twice. I now find myself safely at a distance from romance and not really at any risk. I feel that I'm almost a veteran of this group and I'd like to think my experiences can help warn off others as well as serve as a reminder. Regards my week, again myself and Katrina went looking for my ring along the beach.

'Hallelujah! He's said it. Do you all realise that's the first time he's ever called that fecking ring anything other than Susan's ring?' said Katrina. Way more pleased with this development than Dave had expected.

'You're right!' said Ryan, elatedly.

Dave had missed the reference to the ring entirely, his mind having floated back to Tony's potential whereabouts. He was surprised by Katrina's avid attention. Dave decided he'd ask how the ring search was going.

Ryan duly provided an update.

'Still nothing Dave. We've moved along towards Hawes Pier thinking that maybe the tide could have washed it along. You never know though – there's maybe a crab side stepping about with some serious bling anywhere along the Forth.'

Dave was nodding along, in order to confirm his full attention. He suggested that the exercise mightn't find the ring but provide a lot of other benefits as a result.

Katrina was also nodding in agreement.

'That's right Dave. He's done brilliant and he's not even told you what we did find! C'mon Ryan share with the guys?'

Dave stared at Katrina, thinking 'thanks for confirming' sarcastically whilst Ryan prepared for his next installment. 'Oh yeah,' he said, rising to Katrina's encouragement, 'I nearly forgot. Well just as we moved along, I found an old crown coin, one with Queen Victoria on it from 1897. It's huge.

Probably worth about £50 to a collector'

Katrina looked ecstatic. Like a proud mother. Dave slightly less so. Nevertheless, he felt obliged to join in with their enthusiasm. 'Wow! That's great Ryan, are they not large coins?'

Ryan was already riffling through his pockets.

'They are that, Dave. I've brought it with me, wait till you see it.'

Ryan reached into his pocket and pulled out a pristine white handkerchief and unwrapped his shiny silver coin.

'I've cleaned it up and gave it a shine,' he said proudly before passing it around the room. Each member of the group provided the same amount of strained effort as they passed Ryan's crown around the circle of trust.

'Some size right enough,' said Jack before passing it onto Millie. Millie looked as if she had held it for what she felt like was an appropriate amount of time before passing it onto Katrina who, was still smiling maniacally as she relayed it onto Lucy with additional commentary.

Dave felt obliged to comment further, given their obvious delight. 'How did you clean it up Ryan?'

'You'll never believe this! Brown sauce and Mr. Sheen did the trick,' he said, grinning ear to ear as he collected the coin off Derek, wrapped it back up in his white handkerchief and nestled it back safely into his pocket.

Katrina was still glowing with pride. Dave continued around onto Katrina, asking if she too had brought treasure with her, all while wondering to himself how this had descended into a show and tell.

'I did help find it! I located it and Ryan did the digging. It was a bit of a fight to get it out but he got their eventually. We had a coffee in Orocco Pier afterwards to celebrate.' Dave was beginning to think Katrina's interest in the full search was actually genuine, watching her talk over the finer details animatedly.

Stirling was impressed too.

'Orocco Pier? You'll need to find a few more crowns if that's where you're getting your coffees!'

Katrina seemed to almost catch herself as she then reverted to her usual incantation of managing romance and describing how long she'd been coming along as well as how keen she was to help pass on her knowledge to other members. Dave didn't think he'd ever heard Katrina so thankful or indeed speak for as long. He was almost impressed.

With that, catch ups were over and Dave proceeded to pick up his pens and push back the white board from behind his chair.

'I know Tony isn't with us this week, but I'll pick up with him regards these two remaining personal rights, if that's okay with everyone else?'

The other members of the group all nodded in agreement. Dave turned to the board and began to write:

1. To choose how you spend your time.
2. To make mistakes'

He recapped his pens and sat back down in his seat before asking around the room.

'Can anyone recognise these personal rights and think how we may have evidenced them in our weeks that have passed or how we could have used them?'

Stirling raised his hand.

'I chose to spend my time in Amsterdam after a day at Perth races and that was a big mistake!'

And Jack decided to add to Stirling's theme.

'I decided to accept a last-minute invitation to a trip to Amsterdam and magic mushrooms were a huge mistake!'

The chilly defensiveness, that had surrounded the pair thus far, had clearly dropped when Stirling and Jack began to reflect on some of their weekend highlights.

'Remember me with that 50 euro note, aww man, the bar manager wanted to kill me ae?'

'I can think of a mistake I made, 2 for 1. Al watching me, nut, big mistake.'

Dave cut their reminiscence short.

'I'm expecting a few mistakes were made in Amsterdam last weekend, Anybody else?'

Derek sat bolt upright before announcing,

'Do you know what I've decided?'

Dave encouraged him to go ahead.

'That I'm going to ask Patricia to come do the Route 66 tour in a campervan with me. It'll be a top of the range model, you know? We're not talking about a gypsy's caravan here.

'I didn't imagine you would, Derek.' Dave said,

'But that's sounding like a great example of how you can choose to spend your time. And if it's a mistake, then it's your mistake to make.

But already, after just the mention of gypsies, Dave realised he'd lost Stirling and Jack to their impressions of bare knuckle boxers they'd seen online, and Dave was fighting over them to be heard. Jack was in full Paddy Doherty mode as if he were calling out Tommy Fury on TikTok 'You Stirling Hamilton. With your double town name. I'm gonna fight you and your Mammy. Mammy Hamilton I'm coming for you. I'm gonna ruin you, your caravan, and your big baby boy Stirling.'

Dave gave him a stern look, as did everyone else in the circle but Stirling, and eventually he got the message and shut up as Katrina piped up and offered Derek some congratulations too.

'Ignore that pair, Derek. It's really a lovely sentiment.'

Dave glanced at the clock, thinking the night had settled into its usual rhythm of banter and bravado. He should have known better. This group had a way of taking left turns into places he wasn't prepared to go. He asked if anyone could think of any mistakes they'd made.

There was a nervous ripple of laughter as the group mulled over a million examples before Lucy sheepishly put her hand up.

'Carry on,' says Dave, 'you don't need to look for permission.'

Lucy began to explain, 'Well I'm thinking this one is pretty bad, but I've been hurting and well, I think it's gone a bit far.'

Dave thought this sounded ominous.

The rest of the group had quietened to a hush and were now mostly on the edge of their seats. Dave watched Lucy as she rubbed her face and then rested her chin on her palm, she looked around the room and then closed her eyes as she shook her head. She took a deep breath, crossed her arms, and then leaned forward. She tentatively began to explain her mistake...

'Well, you know how I met that guy Keith a few weeks back...'

'Prick,' snapped Jack,

Dave thought this was pretty hypocritical, given Jack's history, but let it slide. 'Thanks, Jack. Go on, Lucy.'

Lucy's voice wavered as she began....

'I told him I was late.'

The group stilled. Lucy's face flushed as she continued, her words tumbling out in fragments.

'He started panicking, telling me to... to get rid of it. That's when I snapped. I told him I couldn't, that... that it might be the only chance for a kidney donor if one of my kids ever needed it.'

Katrina leaned forward, eyebrows raised. 'Wait.....are you?'

Lucy shook her head, crimson with shame.

'No. I just... I wanted to make him squirm. Just for a bit.'

Dave glanced at Stirling, who shook his head in disbelief. Jack's wide eyes darted between Lucy and Dave, as if trying to gauge whether this was still real life. The room felt charged, teetering on the edge of judgment and fascination.

Lucy's voice cracked.

'It just... spiraled. He called me. He was being awful. Rude, demanding I do something about it. And I was angry. I told him I couldn't because...' She paused, hands trembling.

'Because if one of my kids ever needed a transplant, I couldn't live with myself if I... if I didn't give them a chance.'

Dave's mind reeled. The level of detail in Lucy's lie was almost as shocking as its implications. It wasn't just a simple story. It was twisted and meticulous, the kind of fabrication that grew its own life. He tried to focus, but his thoughts buzzed with disbelief.

Lucy's voice cracked as she pressed on. 'He started panicking about what he'd tell his wife and kids. He said his wife would never forgive him this time. And I just... I told him I didn't care about his wife. I said I was having

141

his baby and he'd have to support it. It just kept getting worse.'

The group was on the edge of their seats, watching the story unfold like a car crash they couldn't turn away from.

Dave exhaled slowly, willing his voice to stay measured. 'Lucy, you've made a mistake. That's your right and we all have the right to make mistakes. You've been brave to share this. But now, I think you're looking for support to figure out what to do next. Is that fair?'

Lucy nodded, tears streaking her face.

'I do, Dave, I really do. I tried to stop, but it just kept snowballing. A few days ago, I told him I'd been rushed into the hospital. I said I'd had an ectopic pregnancy. And... I could tell he was relieved. That made me furious all over again.'

She sniffled, wiping at her eyes. 'I told him my brother had to come home on emergency leave from the army to take care of my kids while I was in the hospital. I said he knew everything and wanted to talk to Keith.'

Katrina groaned, burying her head in her hands. 'Lucy... do you even *have* a brother?'

Lucy shook her head again, fresh tears falling.

Dave pinched the bridge of his nose.

'Where does this stand now?'

Lucy took a shuddering breath.

'I told him I was still in the hospital. That my brother was furious and ready to tell Keith's wife everything unless I convinced him not to. I even... I got a second SIM card from Tesco. I've been texting him as my brother.'

The room was silent. Jack stood abruptly, shaking his head like he couldn't believe what he was about to do.

'Give me the SIM card.'

Lucy hesitated, then handed it over. Jack inspected it, then turned to Katrina. 'I need your earring.'

'What?'

'Just... trust me.'

With surprising deftness, Jack popped the SIM card into his phone, muttering under his breath. After a moment, he began typing furiously.

'Right. Here's what we're sending. Everyone ready?'

He cleared his throat and read aloud as he typed:

Lucy has called me and begged me not to cause you harm. She doesn't want me to tell your wife, and she won't let me lay a finger on you. Consider yourself lucky – this time. Your poor wife doesn't deserve this. But if you come near my sister again, I won't hesitate. Understood?

The room was utterly still. A moment later, Jack's phone buzzed. He read the reply aloud, his voice heavy with disdain:

'Sorry, thanks, and understood.'

Jack swapped the SIM card back into Lucy's phone and handed it over without ceremony.

'There. Sorted. Keith's a prick.'

Dave blinked, simultaneously stunned and impressed. The group looked at Jack with something bordering on reverence. Lucy, sobbing and profusely thankful, tried to express her gratitude, but Jack waved her off.

'I said, he's a prick. Don't text him again.'

Dave cleared his throat, regaining his footing. 'Thank you for sharing, Lucy, and thank you, Jack, for helping resolve this. Lucy, this is a lesson in how romance, especially when it goes unrequited, can push us to places we never thought we'd go. Mistakes happen, but how we handle them is what matters. You've taken a step tonight, and that's something to build on.'

The group offered Lucy reluctant murmurs of encouragement. As the room began to disperse, the weight of what had just unfolded lingered in the air. Dave stacked the chairs in silence, Katrina giving Lucy a comforting hug while making *can you believe this?* eyes at everyone else.

Dave sighed. The dangers of romance right enough, he thought to himself. Some nights, this group felt more like a minefield than a safe space.

23

Week Seven

Dave watched Derek park up in the disabled space and then muster a fake jog as he held the door for him.

'Good evening, David. Are you well?' asked Derek.

'Not too bad, thanks. How are you doing?' answered Dave.

'Actually good – I think?' came Derek's uncertain reply.

Dave was already looking around the waiting area, perturbed by a figure waiting outside the hall, but carried on the conversation out of politeness. 'Well let's see what we can do with that element of doubt.'

As Derek took a seat, Dave addressed the mysterious man.

'Sensei Jamieson?' he asked tentatively, realising he'd never seen Kevin out of his kung-fu whites and black belt. Still, his intimidating frame and smooth, bald head were fairly distinctive.

'That's right,' said Sensei Jamieson commandingly.

'Is there a fella called Stirling comes here?'

Dave was a wee bit unnerved, reminding Sensei Jamieson of his group's anonymity.

'Sorry Kevin, I couldn't confirm that, even if I wanted to.'

It seemed to be the response Kevin was expecting, since before Dave had finished, he had already moved on to question Derek. 'Are you Stirling?'

Derek pointed to himself. 'Me? Stirling? No. I'm Derek. Can I help you at all?'

It was time Dave intervened.

'Thanks Derek, we can make our way into the hall now,' he said, attempting to usher Derek away from Sensei Jamieson.

'You can actually,' replied Kevin, growing increasingly animated. 'Would you know where I'd find a man called Stirling?'

Dave interjected, 'Kevin, can you please leave my members alone?'

But Derek was already in the middle of his reply

'I can't help you, Mr. I suggest you calm yourself down a tad,' he said, making his way into the hall.

Dave hung back while Derek lingered in the empty room. At that moment, Lucy arrived and brushed past Dave and Sensei Jamieson, joining Derek in the hall.

'What's going on there?' she asked Derek, both now hovering in the middle of the hall.

'The guy from the kung-fu club, I think, is looking for Stirling... and he's not very happy,' replied Derek.

'Christ, Stirling could have picked a better fight than this one!'

As Ryan entered, swishing through the main door, Kevin was up like a shot. 'Stirling?'

Before Dave got a chance to interrupt him, Ryan opened his mouth and replied, 'No he's just coming. Is everything okay?'

'Ryannnn!' shouted Dave, following the agitated Kevin into the car park.

Ryan wandered into the room, looking at the others with a confused expression on his face.

'What did I say, what's going on?' he asked, palms open wide.

Lucy piped up, 'Kung-fu Guy is after Stirling.'

Derek instructed Ryan to follow him out back to the car park. On arriving, they saw Dave trying to persuade Kevin to leave, just as Stirling was walking towards them.

Stirling beeped his car closed, approaching Dave.

'All good, pal?'

Dave didn't respond; he was too focused on the Sensei.

'Dave. You okay?' Stirling pressed further.

By this point, Sensei Jamieson was even more animated.

'That's him, is that him? That's him.'

He pushed Dave aside before marching up to Stirling.

'You Stirling?' Kevin demanded, convinced this was the man he'd been looking for.

Stirling took a step back, spreading his keys through his fist in his pocket before replying, 'Aye it is, and what the fuck are you wanting?'

'It's you, is it? Think you're some kind of wise guy? I'm going to kill you with my bare hands.' Yelled Sensei Jamieson.

Sensei Jamieson's martial stance looked intimidating, but to Dave, the whole scene had the air of a bad action movie. He stepped in anyway, someone had to be the adult here.

'Can everyone please head into the hall?'

Stirling wasn't ready to back down.

'Is that right, pal? Dave, you crack on, I'll be in in a minute when I'm done with Bruce Lee here.'

With that, Kevin ran towards Stirling whose defence folded the moment he made contact. Kevin overpowered him with a series of rapid punches to the ribs and kicks to the legs, bringing Stirling down.

Both Derek and Ryan ran over to assist Dave with breaking up the bout, but it was a futile intervention. As Dave helped Stirling to his feet, Stirling continued shouting abuse at Kevin and tried to attack him once more.

Dave saw the need for a new approach.

'What's going on Stirling?'

'You tell me, Dave. Who is this fucking joker?'

'This is Sensei Jamieson, he runs the class before ours.'

'Sensei *who*? I've no idea who the fuck he is, but I'll be sending him back to Cobra fucking Kai with his tail between his legs if he doesn't fuck off.'

Stirling circled Ryan and Derek, half trying to avoid his assailant while trying to seem like the aggressor. Stirling side-stepped Ryan and attempted a rangy hook at Kevin, who responded by cracking the back of Stirling's arm and kicking him in the ribs. Stirling deflated on impact as the group rushed around them both, now supported by Katrina who'd approached from her car.

'Get off him you bully,' she shouted while trying to fend off Kevin, who now had Stirling in a head lock, proudly torturing his captive.

Just then, Tony's car skidded into the car park, and with the engine still running, he leapt out the car, shouting 'Kevin!'.

He managed to wrestle Sensei Jamieson off Stirling, who fell back, trying desperately to catch his breath. Tony started yelling at Sensei Jamieson as Katrina helped Stirling back to his feet.

'I told you to leave it Kevin, ya radge cunt. I told you that I would fucking speak to him myself,'

Kevin, looking suitably chastened, adopted a more apologetic tone. 'After the way he hurt you, the way he left you alone?'

Tony's quieter approach seemed to appease the kung-fu master. 'Yes, I told you I would deal with it, and he didn't leave me on my own. I didn't want to speak to any cunt.'

Kevin now had Ryan and Derek on either side of him, with Dave offering an additional layer of protection beyond Tony and before Stirling. Dave felt like it was time to get to the bottom of the situation, seeing as they were, by now, running ten minutes late.

'Is everyone calm now?' Dave asked, keen to move people along.

Tony walked over with Kevin towards the perimeter of the car park as Dave rounded everyone else up and checked on Stirling who was still being tended to by Katrina.

'Alright everyone, into the hall please.'

The group all slowly wander inside, almost sad the party's over. Katrina took Stirling into the gents' toilets to clean him up as Dave hurriedly pulled out the chairs and hastily arranged them into the circle of trust, before encouraging everyone to take a seat, eager to put the events of the last fifteen minutes behind them.

Before long Stirling made his entrance, and Dave glanced up at him.

'How are you Stirling?' he asked, as Stirling took his seat, still flanked by his amateur nurse.

'I'll survive, Dave. I just couldn't get a proper hit at him. What was his problem?'

Derek piped up, 'After Tony pulled him away, they both stood talking for a while. We stood by in case he tried attacking you again, but he seemed to know Tony – he was telling Tony that you'd hurt him?'

Stirling appeared to blush before immediately closing up.

Jack appeared to have made the connection, summarising his thoughts aloud for the group's benefit with just two words.

'Fuck's sake!'

Stirling looked up at Jack. 'Exactly what I was thinking.'

Jack started laughing to himself as the rest of the group sat bemused. Dave was equally confused, but keen to draw a veil over the fight, he took a breath and began to speak.

But then a frustrated Derek interjects, 'Is that really how we're leaving it? The black belt from the other group attacks one of us and we just leave it there. Are you okay Stirling?'

Stirling raised his hand with a wince and replied,

'I think I know what's went on tonight Derek, but I'm no really at liberty to say. I think that might be why this all started – me and my big mouth.'

'I think Stirling's right,' said Jack. 'I've got a feeling something said in Amsterdam might have upset Tony, and that this was connected.'

The rest of the group were trying to keep pace with the unfolding events, but no one appeared to have made sense of it yet, though Millie had a good go.

'So did you guys meet Sensei Jamieson when you were in Amsterdam?'

Stirling shook his head, as Jack replied,

'No, we never bumped into Sensei Jamieson.'

Jack's answer obviously hadn't helped Millie so she persisted.

'So why would he be upset by what Stirling said to him then?'

Stirling raised his hand to Jack, as if to tell him to stop, but Jack continued, 'Tony was upset before we left and didn't come back with us.'

Dave's brain was working overtime, but there were just too many blanks for him to make sense of it.

Unperturbed, Derek picked up the questioning again, on behalf of the group.

'Sensei Jamieson was upset about how Stirling had upset Tony?'

'Correct,' replied Jack, who was now desperate to bring everyone up to speed.

At that, the hall door slid open and Tony popped his head around it.

'Room for a wee one?' he asked sheepishly.

'Of course Tony, come and grab a seat,'.

Tony made his way to the remaining seat before looking around the room, which was deathly silent.

Dave tried to bring things back under control.

'Ok, can we please proceed with check-ins? Millie, are you okay to go first this week?

Dave watched Stirling, Jack, and Tony closely while Millie checked in. He could tell there was something simmering between the three of them, and a result, he was only half-listening as Millie ran through her check-in. He'd grasped enough to realise she was still resisting Stevie's overtures before she finished, letting everyone know she had a pending launch event at Adler and Stevenson.

Dave asked when this was, and she was delighted to elaborate.

'Three and a bit weeks Dave. It's a great opportunity for me. I've been mainly focused on that recently. I've got invites for each of you, in my bag, I mean, if any of you'd like to come. You don't have to, but I just wanted to say thanks and I could do with the support.'

Dave was still keeping an eye on the tension between Tony, Stirling and Jack as he responded,

'That's really good Millie. If you want to pass them around, I'm sure a few of us will make it along. And with your previous partner, how's things been progressing there?

Millie's enthusiasm visibly drained from her.

'He's a nightmare, Dave. He's always ringing and texting. It's gone from romantic indulgence to threats and abuse. I'm now getting locked out of my social media accounts which I'm assuming is down to him, but I can't prove it.'

Dave encouraged her to ring the police and make sure she had these instances logged, going on to explain how she could contact them discreetly in an emergency situation.

Millie handed out her invites to the group before Katrina began her weekly check-in. Dave watched as the group all gratefully accepted the invitations whilst Katrina ran through her regular repertoire, before telling everyone about her ongoing ring searches with Ryan. Dave thanked her for her check-in before finally moving to Stirling.

He said he had been busy with work but was spending a lot more time with his daughter. He also acknowledged that tonight hadn't really gone to plan, but that it was probably deserved. Dave thought he was looking a bit remorseful which, given the circumstances, he felt was uncalled for. He decided to call it out.

'Okay Stirling, that's good that you're getting a lot of time with your daughter and a few outings with work. Thanks for sharing. I'm still not entirely sure what went on tonight but I'm sure there's no excuse for physical violence. I'd also like to apologise to the group as this should be a safe space for you all. I'll make enquiries with the council regarding some additional security – I'm assuming Sensei Jamieson used his hall pass, which I might have to report. Anyway, apologies all. Lucy, are you able to check-in with the group this week?'

She did so, telling the group how she was getting her kids haircuts ready for school photos, which was always a drama Dave had been keen to avoid himself. She'd dropped her non-practicing lesbian mantra in return for, 'I'm still off the market in that respect but dipping my toe in the water physically,' as she coyly looked over at Jack.

Dave thanked Lucy for her check-in, before looking back over at Jack who tried to plead innocence with a combined effort of his hands and eyes. Dave knew better, though. He glanced over at Tony again, who seemed eager to get some point across. Dave leaned back on his chair, noticing that Stirling wasn't nearly as keen to hear it.

'Tony, are you able to share with the group this week?' Dave asked.

Tony launched into his spiel.

'Firstly, I'd like to thank Stirling, you're a right wide lanky cunt. Ah'm supposing that was your plan all along. What was wrong were you want me to ride you? Gagging for a bit of daddy cock, were you? Want me to bend you over and bring you down to size? Couldn't help yourself, could ye?'

Dave, perplexed, looked up at Stirling who replied without hesitation.

'Look Tony, I'm sorry everything turned out the way it did but naw, I'm no looking for you to ride me.'

But Tony wasn't letting go.

'Are you sure? Cos I can stand the smell if you can stand the pain. Help open up your tight wee arse to some man-love. Is that what ye were after?'

Dave winced at Tony's phrasing, still not entirely sure where this had come from or was going, as Stirling geared up to reply.

'Look Tony, I've no problem with what way anybody wants to roll. I play with cock every day, but just my own big chap. That's no what I like, no problem with what you're after for yourself though. As I said I'm sorry for what happened, I shouldn't have said anything.'

Realisation slowly dawned on Dave.

'That's right Stirling, you're only after wee Millie,' Tony said.

'But like us, you two won't be riding either. She likes a real man, no a jumped-up prick like you. Jumping about dressed like a casual, mare chance of you sleeping with a casual than actually stepping up.'

Stirling shook his head and held up his hands.

Dave decided to step in, asking Tony to refrain from personal insults and the continued use of profanity.

Tony wasn't finished.

'Out of line? You think so. Ah forgot you like private personal business getting aired better, don't you. That's what we're here for and if we're all being honest then I'll start. I'm a poofter, a big bender, a bent shot, arse bandit, raging homo, a big hairy-arsed fucking faggot, a nancy boy. You happy now?'

Dave didn't appreciate Tony's tone, but didn't want to miss what was being said.

Just then, Jack stepped in to respond.

'Do you know what Tony, I am. Happy you're being honest with everyone else and yourself. Because, see, in the past it's been uncomfortable being round you whilst you threw out your bullshit about shagging women and being god's gift to the ladies. We all knew that was a load of shite.'

Tony stalled at Jack's honest rebuff.

Katrina thanked Tony for his share, telling him it was incredibly brave and congratulated him.

Tony responded in his usual fashion.

'Thanks Katrina. Don't worry hen, if you ever need some attention, just you turn around and I'll treat you like a man.'

Katrina declined his generous offer.

By this point, Dave had collected himself and connected the dots. He first thanked Tony for his very personal share, before asking about Sensei Jamieson's part in tonight's earlier skirmish.

Dave watched Tony deliberate over his answer.

'Wur shagging. Well, I'm shagging him to be exact... but sometimes I give him a blow job.'

Dave hadn't been involved in a 'coming out ceremony' before, but if he had ever imagined one, he might have anticipated a more eloquent affair. Regardless, Dave started clapping and the rest of the circle joined in, eventually raising to their feet. Jack made his way over to Tony and shook his hand before breaking into a full hug. Derek made his way over and shook his hand with vigorous congratulations. One by one, the group all embraced Tony, though the male members were careful not to linger. Stirling made it over last – Tony accepted his congratulations while also suggesting that Stirling would be next to come out.

Dave felt more at ease, knowing the full situation. Relaxing back into his chair, he surmised, 'Well that's going to take some beating.'

'Another beating? Kevin back for another go at Stirling?' suggested Jack.

The room broke into relieved laughter, even the suitably humbled Stirling.

Derek began his check-in and let everyone know that he'd started proceedings to sell his shares in the business, while Patricia had not only agreed for them to get back together, but had also agreed to join him on a tour of the famous Route 66 across America in a Winnebago.

Dave, still reeling from tonight's events, found himself struggling to give these various breakthroughs the attention they deserved. He pushed himself to an almost-credible 'Wow!' before continuing, 'this certainly is a week for announcements. Derek, how did all this come about?'

Derek was clearly happy to be given the floor.

'I will be glad to do so, David. We had a few discussions, and I was honest. We'd spoken a lot about our personal rights over the past few weeks here, and I'd began to realise that Patricia had hers and I had my own. From there I began to think about what motivated me to act the way I had.'

'Anyway, this prompted a bit of a heart-to-heart, and it transpires I was trying to impress Patricia and... she was already impressed. And when I felt she didn't want me or what I was offering I, shamefully, sought solace somewhere else, with someone else. It was my own foolish ego. We're going to live and enjoy life, put our faith in one another and throw caution to the wind.'

Much as he wanted to be, Dave wasn't entirely convinced. He wondered to himself whether Derek believed what he was saying or had been coming along long enough to learn what to say. He thanked Derek for the update and remarked on what an amazing night it had been again – not forty-five minutes earlier he was breaking up a fight in the car park, and now he presided over two of his group sharing some real breakthroughs in their romantic lives.

Ryan ran through a quick summary of Tony and Derek's announcements while suggesting his own would pale in comparison. Dave agreed, because they did. He'd still been looking for a ring in South Queensferry and was still digging up coins and old bullets. With that, Dave spun around to face Jack, last this week in the circle of trust, before asking him for his check-in.

Jack appeared reluctant to share given the evening's more exciting revelations, but Dave encouraged him to go on, reminding him that everyone was on a different path. He instantly regretted encouraging him when he began.

'No problem, Dave. Well, you'll maybe remember a few weeks ago I joined a website called Mad Shaggers. Well, this week I'd went on what they call a social, in fact two socials, and then a party. It's been quite a week.'

Dave remarked on how positive this sounded, before asking how a social worked. Jack was delighted to explain.

'Well Dave, they were a bit like a date – like a date but no a date. Like a date where you want to check that someone is who they say they are and, err, if you still want to have sex with them ... and if they still want to have sex with you, then you go for it.'

Dave thought Lucy seemed to have more than a passing interest as she asked Jack if it happened there and then.

He went on to describe to her that he would then organise another meeting somewhere else that wasn't public, where he could follow up on the confirmatory social that had already taken place.

Jack went back to describe how his two socials had worked out with two different women. He'd met one for a coffee and one for lunch, and for no particular reason Jack had gone home to change his shirt in between.

Dave was curious. 'Why did you change, Jack?'

Jack took to the centre stage with his response.

'Honestly, Dave – see I was worried about getting recognised by one or the other so thought it was a bit like a disguise. I dunno why just thought it felt a bit wrong – anyway the second one was just a coffee, but it went well so she invited me to a party on Friday night. I was delighted – all afternoon I was like a dog with two cocks, running about all excited. Party was in Hamilton so I had to get a couple of trains through. I got ready and got a carry-out from the shop up the road, had a few cans and bought a few extra for the fridge, as well as a bottle of Jack D and some cola. Jumped on the train and had a few cans on the way through, you know for a bit of Dutch courage.

I text her on the train, and she told me to ring the bell three times when I got there - said the party had started already. I wasn't keen on just walking into someone's hoose, so I did as she asked. Rang the bell, and when she opened the door... Jesus, Dave; black stockings, basque, thigh-high boots, and this lacy mini-skirt thing that barely existed. No wonder she didn't want to hang around answering the door!

She ushered me in, took my carryout, and asked, 'What's this for?' I told her the fridge. She shrugged and pointed me towards the living room and upstairs, saying there were people everywhere. The living room? Two women, stark naked, sharing a dildo on the floor while a fat guy sat wanking on the armchair. Classy.

I headed upstairs, opened one door, and there she was Fiona, the stockings lassie, bent over the bed while two guys stood behind her, all cocks out and a camera filming the lot. Disco ball spinning overhead. Like an X-rated Studio 54.

I closed the door quick and tried the next one. Guy on the bed getting a blowjob, another lassie behind him with a strap-on going to town. At this point, I clocked her, it was the other lassie I'd had lunch with earlier in the week! I said, 'It's yerself!' and she lit up, came over, and next thing I know, we're on the bed going at it while the others kept doing their thing. But it started getting a bit weird, hands coming out of nowhere to touch her tits mid-shag. Too much for me, so I grabbed my carryout from the fridge and headed for the door. Waved to the fat guy in the armchair, still wanking by the way, just so someone knew I was gone.

Train back home, finished my cans, got chips with curry sauce and cheese from the Eastern Promise, and made it back in time for *Match of the Day*.'

'Ok Jack, thanks for sharing,' said Dave, dumbfounded.

The rest of the room were silently awestruck.

Dave didn't know what else to say, or even where to start. He asked if he had any more socials or parties lined up.

'Probably Dave. I'd rather suss out my bearings a bit more, now I know what I'm going into, make sure it was all to my liking. I'd have preferred to have had a bit of a bevvy and some chat but it wasn't like any other party I've been to before. I think I maybe bailed a bit early.'

Dave remembered why they were all here and clung onto it, asking Jack if there had been any romantic leanings towards Fiona or his other 'social meet.' Jack confirmed there had been none – 'strictly come shagging' was his mantra in this regard as he struggled to remember the other girl's name.

Dave couldn't follow that. He closed the check-ins and thanked everyone for their participation in what had been a busy week. He wrote the attach-ment styles he intended to cover on the white board and asked the group to give them some thought over the week ahead before describing them briefly.

1. Anxious (also referred to as Preoccupied)
2. Disorganised (also referred to as Fearful-Avoidant)
3. Avoidant (also referred to as Dismissive)
4. Secure

Dave flipped the cap back on his pen and turned to face the group.

'That's us this week. Thanks very much, everyone. Derek, I hope you have a lovely trip with Patricia. Stirling, hope you are feeling better soon. Tony, thanks for your share and everyone, well done for your continued commitment to battling the issues associated with romance in your life. It's tough but with each other's support I'm sure you'll all continue to make progress. Have a good week.'

Lucy made a beeline for Jack after she packed up her bag before casually sidling up to him on the way out.

'What a week that was!' she said.

'You're no joking there, Lucy. I thought Stirling was for it at the start... can't believe how it's all turned out.'

'I meant for you,' she replied.

Jack laughed as he remembered the whole episode.

'Yeah, it was a strange old Saturday night, that's for sure.'

He held the door open for Lucy as they made their way outside.

'I might have to have a look at that website myself,' Lucy said, expecting that she'd surprise Jack but instead, he took it in his stride.

'I thought you might,' he said, laughing, before making his way to his car.

'If you do sign up, look out for me – my profile is silverfox71.'

Lucy waved him off as he drove away, before climbing into her car. She paused to let Katrina pass, giving her a friendly wave, before waving goodnight to Tony and Kevin who were now deep in conversation at the gates.

Dave lingered by the door, watching Tony and Kevin laugh at the gate. Derek's joy, Tony's courage, Stirling's bruised pride; it had been a night of breakthroughs. He hoped they'd hold onto the progress they'd made. Romance might be messy, but tonight, it felt like they were all moving forward.

24

A Jimmy Riddle

Katrina sat in her car and sighed. She could feel the end of her time at Romantics Anonymous drawing near, and she wasn't sure how to feel about it. Would she miss her role as the spurned holiday romance? Or would she finally let go of the identity she'd clung to for so long? Shaking her head, she slid the car into gear and pulled out of the car park, her thoughts swirling.

By the time she arrived home, her movements were automatic. She unlocked the door, greeted her cats, Dana and Sounness, and set down their food bowls. Dana was named after the Irish Eurovision winner; Sounness, after Jimmy's beloved Rangers player-manager. The contrasting names were a bittersweet reminder of the life she'd built with Jimmy, even in his absence.

She glanced at her latest painting, a vibrant depiction of St. Stephen's Green, and felt the familiar pang of regret. It was a place she and Jimmy had planned to visit together but never did. Her art was a lifeline during his imprisonment, filling the void his absence had left.

Katrina settled onto the sofa and poured herself a glass of wine, memories tugging her back to the start of their story: a love affair born under the neon glow of Ayia Napa. She smiled faintly, recalling the night she'd met Jimmy, his cheeky charm and the ridiculous way he'd defended his... manhood. 'Say what you want, doll,' he'd declared, 'but *that's* my best feature!'

He'd proven his point, of course, and from that moment, they were inseparable. Until they weren't.

Jimmy's departure from Cyprus had marked the beginning of something both magical and doomed. The late-night phone calls, the playful exchange of cultural gifts, her Taytos and Club Orange for his Irn Bru and caramel wafers, had kept them connected across the miles. But even as they dreamed of a future together, Katrina had known deep down she might never make the leap.

When she finally packed her bags for Edinburgh, her mother, Siobhan, had been supportive. A trailblazer in her own right, Siobhan had weathered her own storms of love and judgment, and she believed in Katrina's decision. Katrina arrived to find Jimmy waiting at the airport, his infectious humor on full display with a handwritten sign that read "O'Shaughnessy" in orange, complete with a Union Jack. She laughed as he swept her into his arms.

For those first few days, everything was perfect. But Falkirk was small, and people talked. Katrina couldn't help but replay that fateful night at the nightclub... how her friendly conversation with the wrong person had set everything in motion. She wished she'd stayed in with Jimmy like he'd wanted. Wished she could take it all back.

The morning after, the banging on the door had jolted her awake. Jimmy's arms tightened around her protectively as officers stormed in and arrested them both. She could still see his face as he tried to shield her from the worst of it, insisting she was innocent. But his confession sealed his fate. Leaving him at the station after she was released, she could still see him stood in his handcuffs smiling as she walked free, shouting over to ask if she'd met Vinegar Tits in there. She'd laughed through her tears then and then almost every visiting hour since.

The court hearings had been excruciating. While Jimmy's friends were divided on who was to blame, Katrina knew the whispers among the wives and girlfriends had one real culprit: the Fenian tart was the reason he was behind bars.

For eleven years, she'd visited Jimmy faithfully, keeping their life alive through paintings, photographs, and the cats he named from his prison cell. Yet as much as she'd clung to him, she had also leaned on others.

Romantics Anonymous had become her sanctuary, a place where she could share the story she'd polished over the years, one that painted her as the jilted singleton.

Katrina took another sip of wine, her thoughts flickering to the group. Would they understand when she stopped attending? She doubted Jimmy would approve of her staying, especially not her growing friendship with Ryan. It was unfair, really. Ryan, with his earnest efforts and kind smile, had become a bright spot in her week. But Jimmy's jealousy had been the spark that started the fire all those years ago. She wouldn't risk lighting it again.

Her phone buzzed on the coffee table, pulling her from her thoughts. She picked it up, hesitating before opening her messages. Finally, she scrolled to Lucy's number and typed out an invitation to meet for coffee. She owed Lucy an explanation, at least. As for Ryan... she'd have to ghost him, for Jimmy's sake.

The lump in her throat grew as she set the phone down. Eleven years. That's how long they'd spent more time in a prison visiting room than anywhere else. How could they go back to normal after that? Did she even know what "normal" looked like anymore?

Sounness leapt onto the sofa and curled up beside her, purring softly. Katrina stroked his fur absently, her gaze unfocused. She couldn't let herself imagine Jimmy back home, not yet. But the truth was, no matter how much she tried to prepare herself, she had no idea what the next chapter of their story would bring.

For now, all she could do was finish her wine, snuggle her cats, and hope that, after all this time, she was still the Katrina Jimmy wanted and needed her to be.

25

Week Eight

Dave was just saying his goodbyes to Misty as Morag called through from the front room.

'Dave, do you think we can have a chat when you get back?'

He appeared in the door frame. 'A chat?' he enquired, not too keen on the ambiguous nature of the request.

'Yes. I've been thinking we could be looking at our future and I've a few ideas what we could do when we get your share options through from Scottish Spinsters.'

Dave had been quietly excited by the prospect, but hadn't wanted to get ahead of himself. 'I've been thinking along the same lines. Absolutely, I'll catch up with you when I get back.'

He shouted up to the boys to be good for their mother, and then dropped to his knees to ruffle Misty's fur, pecking her on her wet nose and promising he'd be back soon.

Getting in the car and turning on the stereo, the sound of Wet, Wet, Wet reverberated around Dave as he ignored the reminders for a service and oil pressure popping up on the dashboard.

Pulling into the car park outside the Trinity building and heading inside, he was almost pleased to see Ryan, until he's greeted by his customary 'Hallo Dave.' He noticed that sensei Jamieson was back in his usual role with the kung fu class, rather than interrogating members of his group – natural order had been restored.

Sensei Jamieson called his class to a halt and the group departed in single file. He bowed his head and addressed Dave.

'About last week, Dave...'

But Dave didn't need to hear any explanation, and cut him short. 'As long as we don't see a repeat, I think we can all move on.'

Sensei Jamieson adopted his usual unapologetic stance, leaving Dave to the hall. Dave and Ryan proceeded to lay out the plastic chairs in the customary circle of trust. Ryan was making small talk, but Dave could tell he was tense.

'Is everything OK?' he asked, laying out the last two chairs simultaneously.

'It's been a funny week, Dave. I missed metal-detecting with Katrina, which I don't think she was happy about. I'm a bit nervous about seeing her tonight but I tried to explain myself; it was all a bit late notice.'

'It'll be fine, Ryan. Katrina is trying to help you and has been really upbeat lately. I'm sure she'll understand.'

Millie and Stirling were the next members to arrive, both deep in conversation. Dave could hear Millie telling Stirling all about her designs for her forthcoming launch event. Stirling trying his best to pretend he knew what she was talking about.

Tony arrived next, followed by Jack and then Lucy, who took their seats just before Katrina entered. She didn't look happy and made her way to sit next to Millie, studiously ignoring Ryan.

Dave started the proceedings by reminding everyone that Derek was off on his tour. Before he acknowledged his relief that things started more calmly this week. He looked over to Stirling who was still sporting a black eye, whilst Tony offered a defiant glance in response.

'We'll start of by completing our usual check-ins and then we'll be looking into attachment styles this week, and how these can impact our decision-making in life, particularly regarding romance.'

Dave turned to his left and asked Millie to begin the week's check-in process. She took the opportunity to remind everyone of her ongoing troubles with Stevie, as well as her forthcoming launch event. Dave was quick to reassure her that there would be at least two of them attending as he'd offered to drive, and Stirling had volunteered to keep Dave company on the way through. Dave insinuated this was some sort of obligatory chore but was actually happy to not be arriving on his own.

Millie turned to face Stirling, a massive smile on her face.

'Oh, are you coming too?'

'Of course, I am,' confirmed Stirling, before adding,

'I couldn't miss your big night.'

Dave watched while the pair of them flirted shamelessly, and Millie reminded them all again that they were welcome to come along.

Stirling checked in next, and mainly focused on updating everyone regarding his relationship with his daughter, Kayleigh. Stirling then went onto suggest, none too vaguely, that he'd met someone recently that he'd be interested in getting to know better but understood that they were both working through issues with relationships and that he was in no mad rush. Which then prompted Dave to ask if there was 'anyone in particular on the horizon?' Knowing only too well who he was referring to.

Stirling took a coy look at Millie who caught his glance out of the corner of her eye, before stuttering slightly. 'It's eh...very early days but sometimes it's just staring you right in the face.'

Dave wasn't convinced that Stirling stood a chance with Millie, but he was willing to be open-minded.

Jack was next to provide his week's update for the group.

'This week's been good – after my party escapades last week things have been a bit quieter but I'm still looking for more physical relationships rather than anything serious. Actually, I've been chatting to a new friend on Mad Shaggers and we seem to be very much on the same page!'

Dave reminded Jack that there was someone out there for everybody, but that he just had to be careful how to go about finding them. He tried to avoid looking over at Lucy, who blushed in confirmation of Dave's hunch.

Jack was quick to reassure Dave.

'Oh I'll be taking precautions, don't you worry. She's already proved herself fertile and I'm not looking for those types of complications!'

Dave clarified that he didn't mean sexual precautions, but that he was glad he was being sensible. He then took the opportunity to ask Lucy how she was.

Lucy still looked flustered, and stammered through the initial stages of her check-in. Her red cheeks slowly began to pale, before indirectly confirming that Jack needn't worry about any precautions for quite some time, as they were taking it slow.

Lucy and Jack then shared a lustful stare which Dave found more than a bit unsettling.

'Well thanks for sharing, Lucy. That's good to hear. Tony, how about your check-in?' Said Dave, quickly moving on to Tony for his latest update.

'Hello everyone. Well what a week it's been, turns out being honest about my gayness has been less dramatic than I'd thought. I've never had so much attention from the lassies at work, I should've done it years ago. Taking myself off the market has made Tony a wee bit unobtainable. Told Claire that I still held a candle for her and that if she ever wanted to try and convert me back, I'd let her have first shot. She's probably still thinking about it now, poor lassie. Apart from that, I've been out with Kevin a few times. It's a lot more straightforward getting a blow job when you can give one back. Honestly though, I still find it weird being out with guy who could burst fuck out of anyone but whimper like a wee bitch begging for my cock. It's like fucking Julian Clary on steroids. Anyway, I'm no really ready to tell the girls yet but getting a bit para about them finding out from someone.'

Dave paused before congratulating Tony for the progress he'd made, and then reminded him that he didn't need to broadcast his sexuality unless he felt comfortable doing so.

Tony thanked Dave for his advice before suggesting that Kevin had told him the same, and that he was all right for a 'big black belt bender.' Dave, pondering if a homosexual could be homophobic, then nodded towards Ryan who had been nervously looking over at Katrina for most of the night. From what he'd seen thus far, Dave hadn't yet seen her reciprocate.

Dave decided he had to put Ryan out of his misery, asking him to run through his check-in just as Tony finished.

'Thanks Dave and yes, happy to share with the group. This week was going well but it took a bit of a turn for the worse yesterday as I wasn't feeling well, and I had to miss my metal-detecting session with Katrina which I'd really been looking forward to.'

Katrina's face remained impassive.

Dave asked if Ryan was feeling better, which he was confirmed he was, when Katrina interrupted, still not looking his way.

'Funny that. Felt fine an hour before we were to meet and now fine again today. Well, that's just fine.' Katrina was using every pore to convey that things were anything but fine between them.

Ryan pleaded that he'd suddenly felt unwell and had given her as much notice as he could, but Katrina wasn't having any of it.

Dave hated to see Ryan so uncomfortable, and tried to support him. 'Ryan, you don't have to explain to anyone. You can make your own decisions, and if you're happy with them, then that should be good enough for anyone.' On the last word, he looked over at Katrina who caught his eye and glowered in return.

Ryan explained that he'd been out on Saturday and so headed out for a drive-thru KFC the next morning to make sure he was fighting fit. He'd eaten it quickly, as was his want, and then checked the time. He still had plenty of time to clean up the car, getting rid of the odd stray chicken bone and the stale, sweaty scent of the meal.

Katrina still didn't look his way, while the rest of the group all listened to his story intently.

'I nipped into the garage at Redding to give the car a bit of a spruce up. I got a packet of lemon wipes from the garage and cleaned all the dash and emptied out all the rubbish, put £2 in the vacuum machine and gave the car a once-over. I was on a roll. I tidied everything back together and thought I'll finish it off with a quick run through the car wash.

'I went back into the garage and bought a token for a diamond wash. Back in the car, I drove over to the car wash and punched in my code, rolled forward, and just as the brushes dropped and the shutter closed behind me...my stomach began to cramp up terribly.

'I was desperate. I was looking over at the garage store, trying to plan an emergency path to use immediately after the cycle finished, but the cramps got worse. I then started calculating whether I could stick my bum out the door, squirt out a deposit, and then quickly close it again. But the brush cycles were too quick. The cramps kept coming and coming and the pressing urgency to let it all go just got worse. The brushes went back and forth for what felt like an eternity. Eventually they stopped, and the dryer started to pass around the car. For a second, I thought I'd made it, but the moment I relaxed, the pressing urgency escaped from my guts and...I... well, you can guess what happened.

At first I just sat there in disbelief as the dryer finished it's cycle. Physically elated that the pain had been released, but mentally deflated by the thought of sitting there in my own filth, in my clean car, minutes before I was supposed to pick you up. Katrina... I then took a deep breath and called you, still sat there and I knew you weren't happy, but how could I tell you the truth?'

'When I got home, I parked outside my house, I tied my jacket around my waist, waddled into the house and went straight into the shower. It was probably the most degrading experience of my life, but I was mostly annoyed at missing our day out.'

Katrina's face had finally given up its stern stance and she was now crying with laughter. Fixing a tear with her small finger as she sat still giggling to herself.

'Ryan! You should have told me, I would have understood. Anyway, it's probably for the best, I don't think we're ever going to find that damn ring. We've looked everywhere.'

Ryan looked a bit crestfallen, even as the group reassured him. Jack told him (and the rest of the room), how, when he was on holiday once, he'd woken up and sprayed a misjudged fart all over the sheets as well as his then-girlfriend, so he really didn't have anything to worry about. He then shot an accusatory look at Katrina.

'Poor Ryan's sat in his own shite and you're giving him grief for no picking you up. Shocking!'

Dave thanked Ryan for his check-in and checked again that he was feeling okay, taking the opportunity to remind everyone where the toilets were.

Katrina's check-in was next, and she looked more approachable than she had all night. She said how she'd missed their treasure-hunting and now understood that Ryan had been unwell. She thanked him for clearing that up.

Jack seized on her unfortunate use of words. 'He couldn't leave it, could he? It would have been absolutely howling.'

Ryan protested, 'I've cleaned the car! I used Zoflora on the driver's seat... there weren't any solids, it was just liquid.'

Lucy proceeded to blow up her cheeks as if she were holding in a mouthful of sick.

Tony was still sitting quietly, before announcing, 'Fuck it,' and said he needed to tell them what happened to him this week. He looked at Dave for permission, who nodded in confirmation that he was fine to share (again) – he was interested to see where this was going.

Tony said that he'd been meaning to have a tidy-up downstairs but that he had been struggling to 'get to it proper' with a Bic razor. He'd spotted some Veet in Kevin's bathroom and, after studying the label, squatted on the bathroom floor as he smeared it over the crack of his arse, the cheeks and then his balls. He continued reading the label before sitting on the toilet to kill the suggested ten minute 'working time'.

At that point, his daughter phoned, which turned into a longer call than he anticipated, which he'd now regretted picking up as he couldn't tell her that he was sat on the toilet with Veet all over his arse and balls and desperately needing to attend to the burning sensation in his nether regions.

By the time he'd made a flimsy excuse to finish the call, everything was burning hot. He'd scraped some of the Veet off tentatively and began showering the rest away, only to reveal a burning red rash which seemed to be getting worse.

He made his way to the kitchen and scoured the freezer for ice before opting for the only alternative which was a bag of frozen vegetables. He quickly took a handful and applied them to the affected area. His fiery red balls and arse almost sizzling with relief as he did.

Unfortunately, it was at this point that Kevin had returned from shopping, to find a naked Tony on his kitchen floor, apparently pleasuring himself with frozen carrots.

The group were in hysterics as Tony recounted his story. Dave thanked him for the update before asking what made him share. Tony drew the connection between him and Ryan in the car wash – it was another warning about the pitfalls of modern entrapment.

'There's places you can be trapped and no even realise.'

Dave, trying desperately to get the image of Tony out of his head, thanked everyone for sharing before he recapped on the attachment styles they'd briefly looked at the week previous.

Dave stood up and noted these up on the white board again:

A secure attachment style.

An anxious-preoccupied attachment style

A dismissive-avoidant attachment style

A fearful-avoidant attachment style

Dave restored the cap to his pen, briefly noticing the vinegary smell of the ink, and returned to his seat. He started to explain that attachment styles were formed in childhood and followed us into our romantic partnerships later in life; that there wasn't a hard and fast description of any single person, but understanding what can make up our attachment style can really help us with understanding how and why we act in a particular way in a relationship.

Dave stood up and pointed toward the first term on the whiteboard: "Secure Attachment Style."

He turned to the group and began,

'Right, let's start with the gold standard, the one we all probably wish we had; or think we have. A *secure attachment style* is what you'd call the sweet spot. It's about balance: knowing how to let someone in without losing yourself in the process. People with this style aren't afraid of being alone, but they're not afraid of commitment either. They're upfront about what they want, and they expect the same in return. You could say they're confident in relationships, but not cocky. It's about being solid, steady, and able to talk things through without blowing things out of proportion.'

He scanned the room for reactions. Stirling's hand shot up.

'That's me, nae drama. Hate needy folk who disappear as soon as they get a partner.'

Dave allowed himself a half-smile.

'I'm not saying you're wrong, Stirling, but maybe let's keep that thought in mind when we look at the next one.' He tapped the board under "Anxious-Preoccupied Attachment Style."

'This one's a bit trickier. People with this style tend to overthink. They might get clingy or paranoid about their relationships, always looking for signs of trouble, even when there's none. It's not that they mean to create drama, but sometimes that anxiety can come out in ways that push their partner away, even if what they really want is closeness.'

Millie sat forward, arms crossed.

'Sounds like Stevie, down to a tee.'

Dave nodded but raised a finger.

'Maybe. But remember, understanding these styles isn't about excusing bad behavior. It's about figuring out what drives it, and deciding what we're willing to work through or walk away from.'

Millie leaned back, chewing on his words as he turned to the next term: "Dismissive-Avoidant Attachment Style."

Dave tapped the board again.

'Now, this one's almost the opposite of anxious-preoccupied. These folks avoid emotional entanglements like the plague. They'll keep busy with hobbies or work, anything that keeps them at arm's length from their partner. It's not always intentional, but it can come across as cold or distant. They like to feel independent, and sometimes they think they're better off keeping it that way.'

He paused, his eyes briefly flicking to Katrina, then quickly moved on before she could respond.

'And finally, we've got the wildcard: Fearful-Avoidant Attachment Style. This one's messy. People with this style want love, but they're terrified of it too. They're caught in a push-pull. They'll be all-in one minute, and then they'll pull back the next. It's chaos, really. They're scared of losing their partner, but they're also scared of losing themselves.'

Lucy raised her hand timidly.

'Yeah... that one's me. I always end up acting all psycho, pushing people away, and then freaking out when they leave.'

Dave offered a warm smile.

'Thanks for sharing, Lucy. And look, none of these are a life sentence. They're patterns, not prophecies. The point isn't to put ourselves, or anyone else, into a box. It's about figuring out what makes us tick and finding healthier ways to handle relationships.'

He took a step back from the board, looking around the room.

'So, here's the thing. Knowing your attachment style isn't just about understanding yourself. It's about understanding the people you're with. What makes them act the way they do, and how that meshes with your own patterns. It's not a magic wand, but it's a good starting point.'

Dave asked Ryan which grouping he thought was most relevant to him – the room unanimously agreeing with Ryan that he was probably sitting within the anxious pre-occupied style.

Only Tony hadn't really spoken much during this exercise, and so Dave asked him what his thoughts were.

'If yer saying these styles were created in childhood, then what? Is that my Maw and Da's fault that I've been a total fuck up. I dinnae think so. I think that's ma ain work, that wan. It's shite, man.'

Dave was sure that if he were a psychologist, he could pick apart Tony's character and probably rebuild him in a way that would help him see the world differently. But he wasn't. He concluded that the styles were something to think about, and if that anyone in the group had any real concerns about how their attachment style was affecting them in life, then it was good to understand this and then seek out further help.

Dave drew the meeting to a close with a sense of relief. It'd been harder work than he thought it should have been.

He began to pack up as the room began to empty, with everyone chatting away. Dave could tell when the group had been challenged emotionally - the chat was always directed between the group members rather than towards him. He wasn't upset.

26

Flat White

'Hello lovely, how are you? Sorry. Have you been waiting long?' announced Katrina as she arrived in Starbucks.

Lucy looked quite at home having come straight from the Samaritans, enjoying Katrina's double take as she proudly presented her badged polo shirt. 'It's fine Kat. I came straight from work. How are you? It's been a while, sorry... I mean outside RA, it's been a while. Are you doing okay?' asked Lucy.

'I am, thanks love. Let me get a coffee and we can have a proper catch up. Can I get you another?' said Kat, pointing to Lucy's cup as she folded her jacket over her scarf on her chair.

'Go on then, I'll have another caramel macchiato. Diabetes risk but well worth it,' she pushed her empty cup towards Katrina.

Katrina joined the queue and stood staring intently into Lucy's empty mug, studiously examining the ring marks of cream and caramel before wondering what exactly she was to be doing with the mug – she'd never had a refill before. She decided to discreetly discard the mug on the sugar stand as the queue moved along.

Ordering Starbucks always gave Katrina a mental challenge, as she refused to accept anything other than small, medium, or large in her vocabulary – tall, grande and venti could get to fuck.

Caitlyn, according to her name badge, was way too happy to help.

'Hi there. What can I get you?'

'Could I have a large caramel macchiato and a large cappuccino please?'

'To go?' responded Caitlyn, again, too cheerily.

'No, sitting in. Just over there' confirmed Katrina, contorting to somehow point through herself awkwardly.

'No problem. Take a seat and I'll bring them over.'

Katrina was impressed, returning to Lucy empty handed and eagerly sharing her small win, 'She's bringing them over,' as she took her seat.

'Oh, check you. Miss VIP.'

Katrina was only sat down a second before Caitlyn came over with their coffees, placing them down in front of them both with a broad smile and a 'thank you for waiting.'

Katrina threw Caitlyn a quick 'you're a star,' feeling it was deserved.

'Sooo, are your metal detecting trips back on after Ryan's car wash incident?' Lucy asked teasingly.

Katrina was delighted to start off on safe ground. 'Oh the poor soul. I was absolutely raging when he didn't appear, but you never expect someone to have shit themselves on the way,' she replied, still somewhat guardedly. 'I was thinking he should have made something else up. I know I totally would have.'

'Totally,' confirmed Lucy in an instant, taking a sip of her macchiato and enjoying its warmth as she continued, 'but I quite like that he didn't, you know.'

'Yeah, I don't think he's got a proper lie in him, Ryan – he's way too nice to carry one off,' agreed Katrina.

Lucy watched Katrina sit and ponder this for a second before she cut off her daydream. 'So, what's your big dilemma then, lovely?'

The question wasn't exactly welcomed by Katrina, even though she knew it was coming. 'Well, it's a long story and I just don't know where to start.'

Lucy was in her element; On the precipice of hearing fresh gossip – no better kind, she thought to herself. She tried to help Kat with some tentative encouragement. 'Is it man related?'

'It very much is, in fact its full-on man related.

'Oh, is it Ryan? Are you two getting close?' suggested Lucy hopefully.

Katrina recoiled, almost thrown off her admission. 'No, it's not Ryan,' she scoffed, worried that Lucy was picking up on her inner demons too eagerly. 'The truth is, it's my man,' she offered nervously, using her now empty coffee cup as a shield, grimacing as she felt her story begin to unfold.

'You see, when I first met Jimmy and came over from Ireland, he left me soon after... and I've been alone all this time. It just wasn't his choice.'

Lucy looked both interested and puzzled. 'So, you left him?' she asked.

'No, I never did and there lies my problem.'

Lucy was even more puzzled now. 'So you're still together then?' she asked, whilst her face suggested she didn't believe her own assertion.

Katrina slunk back into her chair before she looked up at the industrial light fixings, as if God, Mary, Joseph and the wee baby Jesus could all be hiding from view – it was now or never, she thought, and eventually blurted out her admission. 'Jimmy was taken from me. A week after I came over. He was arrested, he's been in prison and no, I never left him. I've never been with him for 11 years.... but I have seen him every week and I just don't know why I never told anyone.'

Lucy was open-mouthed. She decided to fill it with her coffee, conscious that Katrina was still watching her for a response. She held her cup there for a while, while thinking carefully about what to say next.

'So you've been waiting for Jimmy all this time?'

Katrina looked guilty. 'Yes, every visiting hour, every call available we've been in touch,' she replied, waiting for the next inevitable question from Lucy.

'What did he do?' she asked.

Katrina shuffled nervously in her seat, before they were interrupted by Caitlyn.

'Hi, Can I get you guys a top up?'

Katrina answered yes without even checking with Lucy, offering her broadest fake smile. Caitlyn shuffled off with their cups.

Katrina had a look around the room as if she was watching for undercover investigators trailing her, she then whispered her response. 'It sounds terrible, but he killed a man; he's been in prison for murder. It was a freak accident.'

Lucy sparked into life. 'You've been waiting 11 years for a murderer you were with for a WEEK?'

Katrina became defensive. 'He's not a murderer. He never meant to kill him.'

Lucy continued, 'Are you listening to yourself? Every single person in prison isn't guilty, they all say that!'

Katrina's eyes filled with tears and Lucy took this as a sign to back off, reaching into her pocket and bringing out a hanky. 'Here you go, lovely, sorry I'm just worried about you.'

'It's fine, it's fine,' Katrina assured her, thankfully accepting the hanky as she dabbed gently at both her eyes. She composed herself again and carried on. 'I know it was an accident as I was there, I was with him when it happened.'

Lucy was stunned. Meanwhile, Caitlyn had returned with their coffees and smiled profusely before offering each coffee to their intended recipient and then the card machine to follow.

Katrina was staring out of the window as Lucy ushered her coffee over to her. 'Are you okay? Look Kat, it's just a lot to take in but I'm sure you know what you are doing,' she said, pushing the coffee cup closer to her again. Lucy's gaze returned to the table, her eyes returning to focus on Katrina's bag, staring almost dreamlike at the gorgeous pink diamond ring sitting proudly in the exposed lining of her bag. Lucy did a double take, but there it was – a beautiful diamond ring. Before she could take another look, Katrina flipped up the bag and packed her purse back into it, sliding the bag back to her side.

Lucy paused pensively, waiting to see if Katrina had noticed her noticing the ring. But she continued as normal.

'Jimmy's parole application has been successful. He's getting out.'

Lucy was relieved; she wasn't ready to tackle the missing ring's existence in her bag just yet.

'Then you'll eventually get your Jimmy back?' Lucy asked optimistically.

'Yes, 3 weeks from now and I know I'm going to have to leave RA. I just wanted to tell you first; I've known you longer than anyone else and, well, I don't really have anyone else. When I moved over it was just me and Jimmy and, after a few years all his friends moved on, no one really wanted to be friends with Jimmy in the Jail, and I told everyone back in Ireland the same story. Since then it's been me, two cats and my visits and calls to Jimmy.'

Lucy watched as Katrina nervously checked her bag. 'And do you still love him Kat?' she enquired sincerely.

Katrina confirmed without hesitation, 'As much as the day I first arrived. I've lived every minute with him in prison and I feel like he was stolen away from me.'

Katrina was worried that she'd maybe dropped the ring, but didn't want to start a search and have to explain why she had it.

Lucy took a drink of her coffee and looked deep in thought – she was building up to a question and forming the words in her brain first. 'What about the guy who died, have you heard from them at all, do you know them?'

Katrina sighed and looked up before replying, 'His family and friends gave him a lot of abuse at the time, every so often I'd get his girlfriend abusing me or Jimmy on social media, a few times she messaged me. I remember seeing his parents at the court, his poor mum looked broken. They cheered when they announced the sentence, I just sat in a daze. I'd been here seven weeks when it went to court. I should have gone home but I couldn't leave Jimmy – the months rolled into years and eventually I just started telling people he'd left me, it was just easier than explaining all of this.'

'I can see that, what a mess to have arrived into. So, what's your plan for when he gets released?'

Katrina brightened up at the thought. 'I'm just going to hold him, hold him for as long as I've waited, and never let him go.'

'Would you not be better moving onto a new house somewhere, rather than back to his flat?'

Katrina was pleased that conversation was moving in a more positive direction. 'I didn't want to move on without him, and I still don't. I've saved a fortune living in that flat and we can move, I just want it to be something we do together. It's as if my life was on pause and now it's about to re-start, 11 years later.

'And you've never been with anyone else in all that time?' asked Lucy, almost in disbelief.

Katrina replied proudly 'Not even once, not even a thought. Since I met Jimmy, I've never wanted anyone else.'

'Wow,' Lucy replied without thinking, checking herself with a 'sorry' before adding, 'I hope he appreciates you and I hope it's all been worth it.'

Katrina was defiant. 'He still makes me feel like the only woman in his world, even from behind bars, even after all this time.'

Lucy finished off her coffee and placed the empty cup on the square napkin in front of her. Katrina was stirring at the remnants of hers. They sat in quiet for a moment.

Lucy looked at her watch and then looked again at Katrina. 'Anything else or is that you for today?' before laughing.

Katrina joined her in a laugh, releasing the nervous tension between them. 'That's me... for today anyway. Thanks for listening, I do really appreciate it.'

Lucy stood up, spread her arms wide and beckoned Katrina to come in for a hug. 'Listen, you'll be fine. You'll get your Jimmy back, and you can finally live the life you wanted to. Don't worry about anyone else, you've endured the worst. This is what you've been waiting for.'

Katrina began to cry and hugged Lucy tight 'Thanks Lucy, I think I needed to hear that.'

As they walked to the car park, Caitlyn shouted goodbye to the two of them as they left, looking over to her colleague, disparagingly. 'What are you meant to do to get a tip in here?'

Both Katrina and Lucy kissed each other goodbye, hugged again in the car park and then bid each other farewell. Katrina opened her car door and jumped in, placing her bag carefully on the passenger seat and then checking quickly – the ring was still there. Phew, she thought to herself.

Lucy, meanwhile, returned to her stunned silence, still fixated on how and why THAT ring was in Katrina's bag.

27

Daddy's Home

The stereo was blaring in Stirling's flat, as he was singing along in the shower to Lionel Ritchie at the top of his voice. He had decided he was on top form, and that he was finally going to make a go of it with Sarah. It feels good to do the right thing, he thought to himself.

Over the past few months they'd had a few close calls, and before that, Stirling faced a fairly acrimonious end to a sudden period of frenzied sex which found him laid on top of Sarah who began crying, such was her disappointment in herself. Unperturbed, Stirling had been trying his level best – even giving up the gear, as far as Sarah was aware, and also never turning up half cut to pick up Kayleigh, and stopping his relentless 'let's get back together' texts.

In short, he was a changed man.

He was putting on some Paco Rabanne Millions, on the basis that Sarah had remarked on it when he'd worn it last. He sat on the sofa and looked around, thinking to himself that he wasn't going to miss this flat. The four walls had been a constant reminder that he was on his own, particularly having listened to the family in the flat above thundering around on a Saturday morning as he suffered through another recovery. He picked up his phone and scrolled to texts from Sarah – their conversations had picked up and she'd even begun responding occasionally with two kisses again, after her having made a very conscious decision to withhold them.

Stirling looked again and noticed she'd texted. He grabbed himself a can of Irn Bru and began replying 'About 20 minutes xx' as she'd asked what time he was picking up Kayleigh.

Do you think we can talk for a bit when you pick her up? Xx'

Stirling stood up from the sofa, shimmied left and right and slotted an imaginary Adidas Tango into the top corner past the despairing arms of Peter Shilton.

'He shoots, he scores,' Stirling announced to the empty flat as he grabbed his keys and picked up his Stone Island jacket from the corner of his bedroom door, checking his hair in the mirror as he walked down the hall and pulled the door behind him.

Stirling whistled down the stairs, breaking into a jog as he approached the car. Pumping up the stereo and shades on, he drove up to Hallglen where Sarah was staying with her mum.

Parking the car outside in full view of the street, he made his way to the door. Kayleigh was at the window and he saw her blonde hair flash by as she ran to the door.

'Daddy,' she chirped as he picked her up and swung her around the garden.

'How have you been doing sweetheart? Has Mummy been good?' Stirling dropped this in for Sarah's benefit, as he could feel her eyes on him from the door.

He walked over, hand in hand with Kayleigh, to greet Sarah at the door.

'Someone's in a good mood.'

Stirling gave her a knowing look before crooning, 'that's because I'm seeing my two favourite ladies.'

Sarah laughed and shuffled Kayleigh's pink fairy bag to the door alongside an Asda bag for life. Stirling could see Sarah's mum peering unkindly out from behind the window; he couldn't wait to see her face when she found out Sarah and him were getting back together.

Stirling was hovering about the doorway, while Sarah kept looking at her watch. Stirling started to edge away, months of training to avoid being impetuous kicking in. He asked Kayleigh, 'Hey princess, are you going to give Mummy a kiss goodbye?'

Stirling picked up the bags and waited for Kayleigh to get into the car. Before he could stop himself, he blurted out, 'You can come with us if you want?'

She blushed, seeming flustered. 'No, it's your time together. I wouldn't want to intervene in your daddy/daughter time. Sunday?'

Stirling tried to hide his disappointment, both with himself and his knock back. He put on a big smile and picked Kayleigh up, making his way back to the car.

He drove off slowly, trying to clumsily extract a Sarah update from Kayleigh.

'So where are we going tonight, can you guess?'

Kayleigh shouts, 'McDonalds!' at the top of her voice, grinning from ear to ear.

'That's right and guess what, Mummy is getting none, it's all going in my tum.' He turned to face Kayleigh again. 'Do you think Mummy will be hungry?' Should we get her some when we are there?' Thinking he could still use any excuse for a return visit.

Kayleigh paused for a second 'No Daddy. Mummy won't be hungry; she's going out for dinner tonight.'

Stirling felt his daughter's words hit him like a sledgehammer. He struggled to hide his panic. 'Is that right baby? Did Mummy say where she was going for dinner?' They'd arrived at McDonalds drive thru, and he was happy for the distraction from his own inner demons.

'Hello Lochlan speaking, how can I help?'

'Alright chief. Can we have a Big Tasty meal, with bacon, fries and Irn Bru and a cabbage happy meal.'

Kayleigh was giggling along. 'No Daddy. Not cabbage. Nuggets.'

Lochlan was quick on the speaker. 'Extra turnip with that?'

'Yes please chief, lots of turnip please.'

Stirling giggled away to himself as Kayleigh leant over to correct her silly Daddy's gargantuan error, shouting for chicken nuggets and a Fruit Shoot.

'Just pop round to the first window.'

Stirling was still winding up Kayleigh, but she quickly spotted that the screen confirmed her chicken nuggets. 'You are a smart wee cookie aren't you?'

Stirling picked up their order and sped off up the road, trying to get home before their chips went cold.

Kayleigh ran off across the grass and into the close as Stirling locked the car and balanced her bags, their food and a drink holder all in one hand. She held the door for him, eager to get into the house.

Running into the living room, Kayleigh immediately demanded 'Bluey' as Stirling tossed her bags into her room and laid their food in front of them.

The two of them sat quietly eating their chips as Stirling found Bluey for Kayleigh. His mind was still on Sarah and her mystery meal.

'So did your Mummy say where she was going for her dinner? Was she having McDonalds too?'

Kayleigh was transfixed by the television, offering a quick no as she continued watching her programme. 'She was going to tell you,' she suddenly remembered between chips. 'She told Nanny that she was going to tell you tonight.'

Stirling's brain was working overtime. Who was she going for dinner with? And then it dawned on him. She was going out for dinner... A dinner date. Stirling's heart sank; the McDonalds suddenly feeling limp in his mouth. He tossed the remainder of the burger into the brown paper bag and picked up his phone, scrolling through his messages. He clicked the phone off and began clearing the table, stroking Kayleigh's head as he did so.

He sat there for about an hour as she watched her show, imagining various potential couplings of Sarah with other men, tormenting himself.

Eventually Stirling got himself together, took a deep sigh and closed the blinds, before running Kayleigh a bath. Sitting on the toilet as she played with her toys outside the door, Stirling felt a thought form in his throat. It was really final this time, Sarah hadn't ever shown interest in anyone else previously, even after they had broke up. This felt like a watershed moment. Stirling felt a tear form in his eye which he wiped away as Kayleigh came prancing into the bathroom naked.

'Bath time Daddy!' she shouted as Stirling swished the water to create more of her favourite bubbles.

Stirling sat and daydreamed, watching Kayleigh wash her doll's hair in the bath.

Stirling dried her hair before laying out her unicorn pyjamas. Smelling the Johnson's baby soap in her hair, he helped her into her night clothes and choked back a sob he could feel trying to catch him. Stirling kissed her on the head, and she gave her daddy a massive hug, before insisting he read her a bedtime story.

As she fell asleep, Stirling closed her door and began to tidy away the rubbish from earlier, as well as making himself a tea. Leaning back against the worktop in the kitchen, before he knew it his phone was out and he was scrolling through Sarah's social media. Facebook, nothing, Instagram, nothing, Tik Tok, nothing. Every time he hoped to see her smiling face and a group of her pals celebrating some aunt's birthday or some girls leaving work, but none materialised.

Stirling slumped onto the sofa, mindlessly flipping from CBeebies to Sky Sports News. The silence felt unbearable. After a while, he found himself standing outside Kayleigh's room, peeking in to make sure she was asleep. Her steady breaths calmed him for a moment. He brushed her hair back from her face and whispered, 'Love you, princess.'

Then his gaze fell on her pink fairy bag. Hesitating, he unzipped it and slid out her iPad. Sitting back in the living room, his hands hovered over the screen. Don't do this, he told himself, but the temptation gnawed at him. He tapped open the Find My Friends app. The map loaded slowly, and his chest tightened as a familiar dot pinged to life: Fabio's Italian restaurant on Corstorphine Road. His worst fears were confirmed in an instant, this was a date.

He sat back on the sofa, defeated. He silently replaced the iPad in Kayleigh's bag and gave her head another stroke as he left. Leaning against the other side of the door, his shoulders began to shake, and the tears started to flow. This was all is his fault; he'd lost the only thing he wanted before he knew he even wanted it again.

His phone buzzed, yanking him from the spiral of thoughts. Jack's name flashed on the screen, a momentary escape. He answered, trying to sound normal.

'What's up, man?'

'You got a number for that boy who delivers?' Jack's voice was breezy, oblivious to Stirling's mood.

Stirling smirked despite everything. 'Who, Richard?'

'Aye, that's it: Richard Gear! Man, I've been racking my brain trying to remember. Closest I got was Michael Caine.'

A chuckle escaped before Stirling could stop it.

'You're a daft cunt, Jack. I sent you his number last week.'

'I deleted it, didn't I? Thought I was stopping. Guess that's going well, eh?'

Jack's tone was self-deprecating, but Stirling heard the all too familiar undertone of defeat.

'Just send me the number, pal. You wanting some for Friday next week tae?

'Aye, why no. Fuck it.' Stirling's words and thoughts in unison this time.

Stirling sent Jack the number for Richard Gear and watched the screen blink with a standard thumbs-up reply. With a sigh, he dropped the phone onto the sofa and slumped down beside it, staring at the ceiling as the weight of the evening settled back over him.

28

Week Nine

Jack arrived at the Community Centre earlier than usual; he could see Ryan's car, but he wasn't waiting outside as per, and Dave hadn't arrived yet.

He made his way inside and grabbed a seat in the corridor, noticing that the karate class was still on. He pulled out his phone and started scrolling, eventually interrupted when the disabled toilet door flew open and out came Ryan, looked flushed.

'No trust a fart these days, chief?' rattled Jack as soon as Ryan approached his seat.

Ryan looked deep in thought as to how to reply, settling on a humourless 'very funny' instead.

Jack laughed to himself regardless. 'How have you been doing, pal – you shagging that Katrina yet?'

Ryan contorted with the awkwardness of Jack's direct questioning before Jack comforted him with, 'I'm only joking, big man. You still doing the metal detecting?'

Ryan ignored Jack's first question but replied more gratefully to his second, 'I am that, every Sunday. It's amazing what you find!'

Just then, Dave breezed into the waiting room. 'Hi guys. Nice to see you both.'

Lucy joined them, nodding around the room as she entered and leant against the wall while the three guys waited for Sensei Jamieson to call his class to an end.

Jack picked up his earlier conversation with Ryan. 'So you still looking for that ring of yours?' he asked.

'Yeah, still looking for the ring but we've found so many coins and even a rusty old set of handcuffs!'

Jack couldn't help himself. 'You dirty dog!'

Dave started laughing before Ryan continued, 'I'm sure if it's out there, we'll find it. The detector has even picked up tiny earing studs.'

Lucy was stuck to the wall, the image of the ring in Katrina's bag shining bright like a diamond in her mind.

Sensei Jamieson called his class to an end with an 'oosaaaa', and the class started to filter out. Jack prepared himself for Kevin's appearance outside, still cognisant of the beating he'd threatened to take out on Stirling. They all stood up and Dave greeted Sensei Jamieson cheerily as he passed. Before the early arrivals slipped into the hall, Tony arrived to greet Kevin at the door as the rest of the groups exchanged tenancy of the hall. Tony and Kevin stood talking just long enough to let the last few members enter the room. Tony awkwardly brushed off Kevin's attempt at a hug before loudly instructing him to pick up some KY jelly on his way home.

'And dinnae bother flossing, I'll give you a help with that when I get in'.

Tony strode into the hall as Dave had started laying out the circle of trust, plonking himself down on the first chair available whilst Jack and Ryan helped to assemble the remaining chairs under Dave's direction. Ryan was quieter than usual but still keen to develop under Dave's resistant tutelage. 'Dave, why do you lay the chairs out in a circle? Is there a thought to it?'

Dave continued filing out the plastic chairs before confirming, 'Mainly so that we can all see each other, Ryan, but I like to think of the circle as representing the bond of the group, the bond of trust and unity.'

Ryan accepted this answer but was clearly disappointed there wasn't more to it. Dave felt a bit guilty thinking that he could have entertained him a bit longer but that was it, no magic circle effects or feng shui, just the opportunity for him to look into everyone's eyes and see the real story. Even when it was in contrast with what was sometimes said.

Lucy and Jack had already taken their seats before Tony joined them. Katrina and Stirling arrived soon after. Dave looked around the room before confirming once again that 'Derek won't be joining us as he's still touring the US'. He looked around again to see who was missing, just as Millie walked through the door and rattled off her apologies.

'I'm sorry I'm late, Dave. I've been so busy trying to get everything ready for the launch this week I didn't think I'd make it.'

Dave seemed content that all were present or accounted for, and began. 'Hello everyone and thanks for coming along. It's good to see you all again, and well done for continuing with your challenge with romance. This week we will open in the usual manner by going round with a check-in for all members of the group, and we'll then move onto some aspects relating to our love language and how certain activities or actions can sometimes be interpreted as love, and how to spot them yourself. Katrina, are you able to start us off this week?'

Dave watched as Katrina fumbled with her bag and self nervously. She was agitated, Dave wondered if Ryan had missed metal-detecting again this week. She began to apologise while muttering to herself. Dave asked her to take a deep breath and calm down, and the room fell silent as she began her confession.

'Ok Dave. Well, my first admission is that I've not been single all this time; in person yes but not in spirit. I did come over from Ireland and my boyfriend Jimmy was separated from me as he committed a crime and has been in prison ever since the first week I come over.'

Dave, taken aback by her frank admission, tried to interrupt but Katrina was still in full flow as further admissions kept on coming.

'At first I sat at home alone and time slipped away. I've visited the various prisons over the years and spoke with Jimmy every week. It wasn't until I saw the post for this group that anything summarised how I'd felt all that time. I came along for comfort initially, maybe even curiosity but then I liked it, liked everyone, and it made sense. I drew some comfort but each week my lie just got further and further from the truth '

Dave was delighted – he'd been right all along. He was hiding his best

'I told you so' face. Katrina continued to explain that she'd only meant to come along a few times, but then made connections in the group and felt that she'd become invested in people's lives, and didn't want it to end.

Katrina started to cry as Dave shuffled nervously in his seat. Eventually, he collected a hanky from his suit jacket and went over to console Katrina, reassuring her that she'd clearly had issues with romance and was just as welcome here as anyone else. He told her that it had never been a pre-requisite that anyone be single; just that members were aware of the risks associated with romance.

Katrina was still upset and asked if she should leave. Dave reminded her that everyone has secrets, and this was only ever meant to be a safe space to share them and even then only if she, or anyone, wanted to.

Stirling couldn't help himself any longer. 'What did he do?'

Dave told Stirling it wasn't his place to dig further. Katrina reassured both Dave and Stirling that it was fine, that she knew she had some explaining to do.

'It's okay. It's okay. It was a horrible case of misguided jealousy and Jimmy killed a young man, right in front of me. He headbutted him and he hit the pavement; he was gone in an instant. I remember checking his pulse and looking up at Jimmy. I've retraced and revisited that moment a million times and wished it turned out differently...'

Stirling couldn't contain himself.

'Fuck sake! Ah mean wow... ah mean, I dunno what I mean. Are you okay?'

Dave looked over at Stirling, who quickly followed up with 'I'll shut up – sorry Dave.'

Katrina went on to explain how Jimmy had almost served his time and how his most recent parole hearing had been successful. Even though she thought she should stop coming after that, Dave encouraged her to keep attending and thanked her for sharing. Only then did he think about Ryan who hadn't really engaged with the conversation at all.

Millie was still checking that Katrina was okay before she started her own check-in, with a thanks from Dave. Millie was busy with her plans for her forthcoming launch event, taking the opportunity to remind everyone that it was this Friday, which didn't receive much of a response. Interactions with her ex had settled down and with her focusing on her event, she didn't even appear fazed that a colleague had pointed out that Stevie had liked a post about it. Dave wasn't convinced this single action shouldn't be given more merit or even concern.

'Do you think he might turn up?' he asked Millie, not wanting to spook her.

Dave wasn't surprised when Stirling leapt in to provide her with some support, bravely suggesting that if he did turn up, she wouldn't have anything to worry about – but that Stevie would.

Dave thanked Stirling and asked Millie, again, if she thought he might turn up unannounced. Millie appeared to shrug off the suggestion, merely surmising that there would be plenty of people around even if he did appear and that he'd only end up embarrassing himself if he did.

Dave could tell the rest of the room were less convinced. Tony was next to settle any nerves that were bubbling underneath.

'Don't you worry Millie, me and Kevin will be coming along. He knows how to handle any idiots causing a scene – together we're like Right Said Fred meets the Legion of Doom. We'll probably burst him and then ride him... Plus, you have your 6ft 5 streak of pish there to help with spotting him!'

Dave was still perturbed while Millie only focused on the fact they were both coming along and how lovely of them it was to do so. Eventually he lost the trail of his questioning as Tony confirmed that it was the first official event that they'd attended which wasn't a 100% LGBTQ gathering, saying it'd be a new experience for them not being surrounding by dykes and poofs.

Millie took the opportunity to thank Tony again and made sure to remind everyone that they were welcome to bring along their own plus-ones. Dave immediately wondered if Katrina's jailbird boyfriend might get day release.

He looked next to Stirling who was still sporting the remnants of a black eye. Stirling ran through his weekly check-in, suggesting that he and Sarah had finally reached a point of closure which he was now accepting and looking forward from. Still, he was upset by the realisation that Kayleigh would now definitely be growing up in two separate houses.

Dave wasn't sure if Stirling was more buoyant at the prospect of quickly replacing Sarah with Millie, and whether this might have aided the apparently convivial nature of their final parting of ways.

He moved round to Jack, who was grinning maniacally. Before Dave even had a chance to ask, Jack countered with 'Are you sure, Dave?'

Dave confirmed he was always sure, before the group strapped in for another Jack roller coaster.

Jack's report wasn't quite of his usual calibre, suggesting that his dug Cal winning best of breed at a dog show in Gretna had been the highlight of a week largely filled by Jack Daniels, cola and FIFA, occasionally punctuated with a few online chats which Dave could tell had been with Lucy, judging by the way she seemed to perk up at there mention.

Dave wasn't sure if he was pleased or disappointed with Jack's more banal summary; a feeling which appeared to be shared by the rest of the room.

Jack picked up on the air of disappointment, defending himself with a defiant,

'Even the devil takes a rest sometime, folks.'

Dave knew Jack well enough to know that his devilish side was alive and well, and that his black magic was clearly working on Lucy. He finished off by checking if that was Jack's first place at a dog show, which it had been – Jack was delighted that the long drive south had been rewarded by a rosette.

Lucy was still laughing even after Jack had finished. Clearly smitten, Dave asked if she could check-in as she too adopted their party line, running through an uneventful week with the Samaritans and the kids spending time with her Mum and Dad. Dave had asked how her volunteer work was going and was delighted to hear that she appeared to be growing in confidence, and even felt a bit of pride when she said her kids had been asking about her work, and how no longer felt like just another single mum on benefits. Dave couldn't resist the temptation to remind her of her personal rights and to keep her attachment style at the forefront of her mind – he didn't know if this was for her benefit or Jack's.

Dave glanced over at him and then back to Lucy as Lucy assured them both that she wasn't looking for romance. Dave knew what Jack heard, and it was that she was looking for something else. Tony was next to check-in.

'Hello everyone. My week has been going good thanks. After we spoke last week, I had a chat with my ex-wife and I've opened up to her about my pooftership.'

Dave simply nodded, considering himself and the group now immune to Tony's unique turns of phrase when it came to his sexuality.

'She was supportive, suggested that the clues were there and that my wearing her pants was always a cause for concern for her. I'm just glad she never found any shite on her dildo.'

Some of the room grimaced, while Jack laughed out loud. Dave tried to reign Tony back in a bit, asking how things might be conveyed to his daughters.

'We've come up with a plan to tell the girls together in a few months, before the summer holidays, letting them get their university work out the way first. Strange thing thou, when I was leaving her boyfriend turned up and I was all right to him – he'd obviously been well briefed on how I could have been – but I couldn't help thinking I recognised him from somewhere. I might need to check if he's swinging both ways. Could be sharing more than a dildo with my ex-wife in the future!'

Dave praised the positive steps which Tony had taken, and the giant leaps he'd made in a matter of weeks, which Tony thanked him for pointing out. Dave couldn't help but think there was still a sense of conflict within Tony hiding behind these outbursts, as if his indoctrinated homophobia prevented him from accepting even himself. He weighed up the chances of reasoning with Tony further and then quickly decided to move on.

Ryan was next to run through his week for the group. Still sombre from Katrina's earlier revelations, Dave listened as he described lessons he'd learned within the group and how much he was looking forward to tonight's session on love languages. He described how they had been beach-combing this week and found a rusty old set of handcuffs complete with the key – Jack quickly suggesting that he knew he'd left them somewhere. Ryan forced a laugh as Dave fought off the urge to ask for his take on Katrina's secret relationship. Dave sat for a second waiting for Ryan to go further, but he seemed to be done. Dave was sure Ryan had probably mentally added Katrina to his list of previous heartbreaks already, but didn't want to push him.

With that, Dave spoke to the full group from his seat. 'Now we've completed our check-ins for this week, we'll move onto our next session if you're all happy to proceed?'

The room nodded along as Dave pulled back his seat and primed his blue pen for the whiteboard, writing 'Love Languages' on the board.

'This week's session will look at the how we look for love and the five primary acts of romance which we can interpret as romantic notions.' He uncapped his pen and wrote the following five groups on the board:

Receiving gifts

Acts of service

Words of affirmation

Quality time

Physical touch

Dave recapped his pen before addressing the group again. 'These are the five groups which people who have an issue with romance can be easily duped into believing are expressions of love – love languages, as we will call them tonight. Let's look at each individually and explore areas where we may have had experience or seen examples of where others have been duped by them. Firstly, let's consider receiving gifts. Now, what the item itself can be is irrelevant, as it's often the act itself that is considered the 'tell' by someone who is inadvertently looking for the signs of romance. Has anyone received a gift before or given one innocently, where the recipient then incorrectly assumed a love interest?'

Jack raised his hand. Dave sighed, before asking, 'Yes. Jack?'

'Well Dave, one time I bought a girl a double ended dildo and she wrongfully assumed it was for us and totally went off on one. That was a mistake on her part – I'd expected her to use it with another female. Even after I explained, she wasn't happy,' Jack said, in all seriousness.

Dave thanked him for the example, replying, 'Thanks Jack. Maybe in that case, the gift itself represented sexual intention. Anyone else have anything less obvious which has then led to an issue?'

Dave's attention shifted around the room while the group thought about potential responses.

Slowly, Katrina came to life. 'I once got bought a record player for Christmas with a selection of my favourite records from another teacher at the school. I'd only really spoke to him occasionally over lunch in the staff room, and it felt a bit of a big gift between colleagues.'

Dave was delighted someone had come up with a relevant example that didn't involve dildos. 'Thanks Katrina. And how did you react?'

'Well, initially it was wrapped up, so I didn't really know what to react to, and then when I took it home and opened it, I didn't really know what to say – it seemed like too much, but I'd opened it then. When we were back in school the following week, I'd tried to not make a thing of it. He then approached me and asked if I'd opened it. Jesus, thinking back now... it was so awkward! I just said I did thanks, and then he pushed for a response on how much I liked it, and then I said I loved it, and then he asked me out for a drink one night and I rejected him flat. The conversation stopped and that was, pretty much, that – our lunchtime chats stopped and he was never really the same with me again.'

Dave was still thinking before summarising, 'In that instance he was demonstrating the language of love pro-actively via the purchase of gifts, even though the feeling wasn't returned. Is there anything in advance of this that might have led him to believe that you too had been demonstrating the 'language of love'?

Katrina looked puzzled but then the reality dawned on her. 'He'd misinterpreted the chats we'd been having as something else.'

Dave was chuffed. 'Exactly that,' he said triumphantly. 'The quality time he thought you both were sharing was enough for him to up the ante. Great example, thanks Katrina. Anyone else?'

The room paused again as the group studiously racked their brains. Dave proceed to describe the next item listed. 'Maybe think on this one here,' he said tapping the board at acts of service. 'This is when someone is doing something for you that they think you would like.'

Just as soon as Jack moved to speak, Dave cut him off. 'Not necessarily physically but even something a bit more innocent such as watering the plant on your desk in the office, or offering to watch your pet when you're on holiday – anything you'd probably interpret as 'being nice', some people can misconstrue as budding romance.'

Stirling was feeling mischievous so he ventured, 'Like helping someone find an engagement ring'.

Katrina looked furious, but Ryan reacted very calmly, even before Dave could interject, 'Absolutely, and it's a good thing we both know exactly where we stand as the search for the ring could tick two boxes, maybe even three...'

Ryan continued to chalk them up in his mind before carrying on. 'So the act of service would be Katrina helping me with the ring-finding, quality time – that's the time we spend together each Sunday – receiving gifts would be the various items we find on our way. I'm pleased to report in this instance it's three strikes not out. We are very much just friends.'

Katrina looked relieved and Stirling looked disappointed, hoping to have stirred up a bit more of a reaction – Dave was too. He continued looking for other examples before noticing that time was up.

'Ah, sorry guys I've gone and lost track of time, that's us finished for this week unfortunately. We can continue with our piece on the language of love next week and in the meantime, I hope to see most of you at Millie's launch on Friday. Thanks everyone for sharing and taking part this week, it's been a pleasure. Good to see the group supporting one another. For those that can't make it on Friday, we'll hope to see you here next week.'

Dave clipped up his pen and popped it in the pack as the group packed up slowly and grouped into small chats between themselves before making their way home.

Jack caught up with Stirling as they both walked out.

'Alright sir. What's happening with you? We going out after Millie's thing on Friday. I got that stuff off your pal, Richard, by the way' Jack nodded with the suggestion of a wink.

Stirling was in a confident mood. 'Only place I'll be going afterwards is back to mine with Millie! But a wee livener would be good; what did you get, one between us or wan each?'

Jack was almost offended. 'One each, surely' It's only Friday!'

'Right, one each it is then. Text me your details and I'll transfer over the money.'

'Good man,' confirmed Jack as Stirling opened his car door. Both of them waving farewell to Katrina and Millie as they walked past.

'See you Friday, ladies!' Jack announced, this time fully winking in Stirling's direction.

29

Launch Night

At the very top of Buchanan Street was the Royal Concert Hall, a glorious venue with ornate styling and the whiff of being very upmarket indeed. A stone's throw from Adler and Stevenson's Head Office, it was the location for Millie Singh's first launch event and fashion show. There was a real buzz in the air, more so than usual, as the fashion industry press had suggested that Adler and Stevenson's next big thing was here.

George Adler patrolled the event's champagne reception like a well-coiffed peacock, his boyfriend Nic in tow, as was the lesser spotted Billy Stevenson who was preening the star of the night – Miss Millie Singh.

Millie always looked immaculate but tonight she'd gone for 30s class and had executed it with aplomb. She was nervous, nervous but excited; everyone she knew, everyone she loved was here. The venue was already filling when Millie's parents arrived; George was quick to greet them and whisk them straight to the table of waiting fluted glasses.

She looked up and Katrina had arrived alongside Ryan, Tony and Kevin. She waved them over as she was under George's specific instructions 'to wait here and look your usual radiant self'. They shimmied over. Tony was first to greet her, offering her a warm hug and telling her she looked prime for a riding, which Kevin confirmed with an awkward smile. Katrina and Ryan each gave her a hug whilst they all eagerly scooped up the free champagne.

'This is awfully posh,' announced Katrina in her warm Irish accent. Just as they were getting freshly acquainted in a very different setting to normal, Jack, Stirling and Dave arrived, and quickly made a beeline for a familiar face, bounding over with more than a hint of bustling energy.

Stirling was quick to compliment Millie. 'You look amazing, hen. How are you feeling?'

Millie smiled coyly before replying 'Thanks. I'm nervous, but excited too. I just wish we could fast forward through to when it's done and I can trust myself to have a glass of champagne or two!'

'Have you no had one yet?' offered Stirling.

'No thanks. Not just now. I only need two and I'm feeling tipsy.'

Stirling headed over and collected a couple of glasses before Jack addressed the group. 'Check you guys all dressed up. It's like one of us has got court or something. I feel like I'm at a wedding!'

Millie was beckoned over by George who had been speaking with her parents but was now chatting to some of the fashion house reps who'd travelled up from London for the show.

'I need to get to work. Thanks so much everyone for coming. It really means a lot.'

Stirling caught her just as he was returning with glasses for him and Jack. 'Sure I can't tempt you?' he said with a wink.

'Maybe later,' Millie flirted, as she left the group.

At that, Stirling noticed Lucy who was making her way in. The group gravitated away from the main reception, as Dave collected a champagne for Lucy as well as spotting an orange juice for himself. They made their way over to the group, greeting each other warmly while Jack slunk over to collect a few more champagnes, coming back with another extra one for Lucy.

They chatted away while waiters floated between the guests with trays of miniature street food, which was all Indian/Scottish fusion at Mr. Adler's suggestion: Haggis pakora, square sausage samosas and pots of curry all labelled as tandoori radge, all washed down with small glasses of Buckfast lassi.

Almost an hour of free champagne guzzling had passed before Mr. Adler loudly drew everyone's attention towards himself. 'Hello!' he said while clinking his glass. 'May I say you all look fabulous. Can I firstly give thanks from all of us at Adler and Stevenson for coming along, and secondly please let's have a warm round of applause for Millie Singh ahead of her first launch night.' The crowd cheered wildly, Jack and Stirling opting for some wolf whistles, while the remainder clapped enthusiastically. Millie swayed with slight embarrassment at the attention and half waved to the crowd before Mr. Adler invited everyone into the main hall and the start of the show.

The crowd made their way into the main hall, and Millie felt like she was having an outer body experience as the words flowed from her mouth, the crowd responded, and the models began to flow out from backstage, accompanied by classic disco remixes from the DJ. The atmosphere crackled and the crowd buzzed as every new outfit and model appeared. By the time they had finished, no one was in any doubt that it had been a tremendous success.

George, Billy, and Millie came out to riotous applause alongside all of the models. Millie was mobbed and engulfed by her friends and family who raced to congratulate her. Dave, Lucy, Stirling, Tony, Katrina, Ryan, Kevin, and Jack were all still milling around as one – Millie came over to thank them again for coming, intermittently disturbed by more well-wishers as she attempted to talk to them. Eventually there was a seconds gap in her attention as they subconsciously stood in a circle around each other. Millie smiled and relaxed in that one moment.

'I'm so so glad you're all here for me. I just want to stay with you all now and watch everybody else'.

At that, another well-wisher disturbed her seconds relief and pulled her away from their makeshift circle of trust.

She shook her head before being whisked away turning to confirm 'There's an after-show party over at St Jude's, everyone is heading there next. There's a tab for all of you; we might get a proper chance to catch up then. This is mad!'

At that George and Billy came over with some official looking guests, and Dave turned to the rest of his group. 'Well guys, my night's drawing to a close.

I can give any of you that aren't going to the after party a lift home... but you'll need to leave now.'

Jack and Lucy were deep in conversation before Jack announced, apparently for both of them, 'We're staying', Stirling was a definite stayer whilst Ryan and Katrina were in a three-way debate – Katrina had already had way too much champagne and was trying to matchmake Ryan with every single-looking woman in the room. Tony and Kevin were in high spirits too, but decided that they'd probably enjoy the Polo Lounge better than St Jude's, so were going to leave. Katrina, in a momentary flash of sobriety, concluded that she was going home. Ryan joined them and they each hugged one another and said their farewells, before heading off to their selected venues.

Jack, Stirling, and Lucy were at St Jude's in five minutes. There was already a queue but as soon as they announced they were here for the Adler and Stevenson after party, they were whisked to the front and pointed into the direction of a series of booths. They were the first to arrive and were greeted with bottles of Grey Goose on each table alongside buckets of mixers on ice.

Jack poured them three generous glasses before topping them up with cola. Lucy nipped off to the toilet before Jack and Stirling carried out a brief coke update.

'Much you got left?' asked Jack.

'Bout 2 lines pal. I had a flipping nightmare. I went into the toilet at the concert hall and the toilets were so busy I didn't want to chop one out.'

'What happened?' asked Jack curiously.

Stirling laughed. 'I just dropped the straw in the bag and thought a took a tiny wee sniff...half the fucking bag flew up ma nose.'

Jack shook his head. 'Rookie mistake. You should have dipped a key in. What's the plan tonight?'

Stirling's eyes bulged before he reaffirmed his original stance. 'Sticking with plan A.'

'Good man,' replied Jack before Stirling enquired about his own plans.

Jack tapped his nose and winked, 'Lucy's no kids tonight.'

At that, Lucy returned to the table and announced that the rest of the party were arriving before she squeezed into the booth between Jack and Stirling. Jack downed his vodka coke before quickly pouring another large glug of vodka in his glass and adding a splash from the open can of cola. 'The night is young!'

George arrived at the booth with Nic initially, alongside Millie and some of her colleagues, who remarked that they'd found the vodka okay with a friendly enough laugh that still somehow managed to look down it's nose at them. The VIP area soon filled up and eventually Stirling managed to catch Millie's eye as she wandered over. She was a lot more relaxed than she'd appeared earlier but still looked stunning.

'Well done you,' he announced.

'Thanks so much' responded Millie, before she continued, 'I can't believe how well it's gone. I've got trips to London already planned and Mr. Adler is already talking about the next launch. So exciting! Thanks so much for coming.'

'No problem at all,' replied Stirling, noticing how dry his mouth was. 'I'm needing a water or something, can I get you anything?'

'Yeah that would be good. Thanks, Stirling.'

He headed off to the bar, and Millie grabbed a seat along from Lucy and Jack who both turned to greet her. Lucy started by admiring her lovely dress, and Jack continued by confirming that the scran was first class.

'Where's Stirling off to?' he asked.

Millie turned to check he was on his way to the bar and looked stunned. She turned back to Jack, her voice trembling. 'Oh my god. He's here.'

Jack said, 'I thought you said he was at the bar?'

Millie continued without looking back, 'Not Stirling. It's Stevie!'

Jack looked around, not knowing who he was looking for, before another guy approached their booth. He was sharply dressed and looked like a pretty sound guy, not anything like Jack had pictured originally.

'Alright pal. How are you doing?' asked Jack, still not sure who he was speaking to.

'I hope I'm not intruding,' Stevie said, a little nervously.

At that, Stirling returned from the bar with a couple of glasses. He didn't recognise the guy at the table so brushed him aside as he gave Millie her water.

Stirling immediately noticed the atmosphere around the table. 'Has something happened?'

Millie confirmed something, or rather someone, had happened with an introduction. 'This is Stevie.'

Stirling drew him a look. 'Who Stevie, Stevie?'

Stevie responded, 'Just the one Stevie. Cheers pal. But it's all right; I've been called worse.'

Stirling never even responded, but instead immediately looked to Millie. 'Are you okay?'

'I'm fine. I better go and speak with George though.'

She left the table and the four were left sitting in silence, which was only broken when Jack asked if anyone wanted a top up, lifting a glass out for Stevie. Lucy and Stirling nodded while Stevie declined the offer.

'Sorry pal. I'm driving.'

Jack poured drinks for Stirling and Lucy, which they refilled again while making awkward small talk. Stirling said very little. Eventually Millie made it back over to let everyone know that Billy, George and Nic were all leaving. They each thanked them for a lovely night and for coming along, before George noticed their new guest – he pulled Millie aside and gave her a hug before departing.

Millie came back to the table. 'Hi guys. I think I'm going to call it a night; it's been a busy one for me.'

Stirling's faltered with his disappointment before Stevie was first to respond. 'I'll give you a lift.'

Millie replied, 'I'll get a taxi.'

But Stevie wouldn't let it go. 'But I've got the car there, don't be daft.'

Stirling spoke up, 'She told you she'll get a taxi,' he said sternly before adding. 'Do you want me to walk you to the taxi rank, Millie?'

Millie sat quietly. Stevie didn't..

'Who they fuck are you like, the taxi marshall? I've said I've got the car there. I'll make sure she gets home safe.'

At that, Millie picked up her bag and slammed it on the table.

'I said I'll get a taxi,' she yelled before storming out of the club. Stevie followed with Stirling hot on his tail.

Stevie caught up with Millie, who was crying. Stirling pushed Stevie out the way, saying, 'See if you've hurt her...' He didn't even finish his sentence when he felt Stevie's fist connect with his nose; he hit the deck and could feel the texture of the wet gravel on the pavement against the side of his face. He felt like his nose had been punched clean off his face, seeing blood pouring out onto the pavement before everything went black.

He slowly opened his eyes. There was an old couple checking he was okay, and he heard Jack shouting in the distance as he stared ahead, almost in soft focus, watching Millie as she dropped Stevie's hand and opened the door of a bright blue Subaru – the same bright blue Subaru he'd seen a few weeks earlier. The pain then hit him and he realised Jack was helping him to his feet while the couple and Lucy were fussing around him too.

'Are you okay?' asked Lucy. 'You poor thing,' she said, mopping up some of his blood with a handkerchief and looking in her bag for something more substantial to stem the flow of blood from his nose.

Jack shouted loudly, clearly a bit panic-stricken. 'Stirling, speak to me!'

Stirling was now sitting upright, still watching Millie, and not responding to those fussing around him. He caught Millie's eye as the car pulled away – she mouthed sorry as the car sped away.

Stirling brought his attention back to those around him. 'Fuck's sake. Fucking, fuck fuck sake,' he yelled.

Lucy was kneeling in front of him, dabbing him with a packet of hankies. 'You've had a sore one there. Don't worry, there's an ambulance on its way.'

Jack was at her side. 'You okay sir? What happened?'

Stirling was defeated. The bleeding from his nose had stemmed but a blood red bogey bubbled as he laughed at the absurd position he found himself in. 'That didn't go to plan, did it? She fucked off with that cunt Stevie.'

'Aww fuck sake man,' Jack tried to console his big pal.

An ambulance pulled up, giving a quick blast of its siren before two paramedics promptly jumped out and took over from his volunteer helpers.

Lucy and Jack watched him get into the ambulance before waving him off, with Jack saying he'd call him tomorrow.

Stirling arrived at the hospital within about fifteen minutes; he'd been cleaned up and was feeling a bit more like himself.

The paramedic checked him over one last time. 'You doing okay pal? That's our bit done. You'll survive but we've asked reception to get a doctor to have a look at your nose and check if its' broken. Plus you might need a dressing on those grazes,' he advised.

Stirling thanked them for their help. 'No problem guys. Thanks very much for everything.'

The paramedics left and Stirling looked around the reception, it was full of post-drunk drunks sat sombre alone, crying kids with frazzled mothers and old couples not sure if it was the weekend or pension day – it looked like a bomb had gone off in LIDL.

He hoped it wouldn't be long, but after waiting unattended for two hours, Stirling decided to phone himself a taxi and went home alone.

He'd suffered a suspected nose break, a badly grazed face, and a severe whack to his pride. Plans A, B and C hadn't worked out for Stirling.

30

The Morning After

Stirling was already on his fourth wank of the morning. He'd now officially given up on trying to visualise Millie into bed via Indian porn on Pornhub, returning to the safe obtainable prospect of the good, old fashioned, British MILF. He'd been unable to sleep all night and, as a result, only able to perform two tasks: internet searches and masturbation, and very occasionally both combined. The heady mix of a cocaine come down and rejection had left him rooted, rejected, and ripping the head clean off it. A text hit the mobile in his hand, interrupting a BBW from Buckinghamshire getting into a black cab. He grimaced as he checked the sender: Jack. He opened it tentatively, it read succinctly, 'R U OK?'

Stirling looked at it for what seemed an eternity, laid back and thought of a response but then decided better, eventually settling for silence. He returned to the Buckinghamshire BBW, maybe even a BBBW he thought, getting in her taxi, pulled the duvet over and started another wank. The fleeting rush of his climax failed to resolve any of the comedown or rejection pain. He placed the phone on his pine bed side table and grabbed the almost empty glass of water, savouring the last few drops, pretending to himself that it had actually quenched his thirst to save him obtaining a refill; that task was for later, he thought to himself. Saving the sustenance of one haggis pakora in 24 hours for more wanking.

He lifted his phone again. It was three fifty-seven of the pm. He still couldn't muster the motivation to move yet, and so decided on another search of Pornhub. Suddenly, his phone started ringing, and it was Jack again. He watched the call drift through each ring as it settled back to silence. Stirling still wasn't ready to text anyone, let alone actually speak to someone. This was the fear in effect, classic symptoms. But by the time his ringtone had stopped, he'd lost his wank appetite and returned the phone to his bed side table, pulled the duvet over his head, and sighed heavily. He knew he would feel better by around Wednesday.

He began mentally preparing for work tomorrow. His mental preparation was abruptly shattered by a wrap at the door. Stirling, still naked, stood up and peered around the corner at the vestibule door which was hiding the front door proper, hoping that this was a figment of his overactive imagination. It went again and then the doorbell, a few times. He resigned himself to answering it. He picked up a pair of swimming shorts and pulled them on quickly, shouting at his very unwelcome visitor 'This better be the fucking police' as he opened the vestibule door only to be greeted by Jack's beady eyes staring at him through his letter box.

'Just the fashion police big chap.'

Stirling opened the door, and immediately turned around, headed back into the living room before plonking himself defeatedly on the sofa. Jack was in high spirits 'You doing a few lengths this morning?' he asked.

Stirling was rubbing his head, puzzled by the question before he looked down at his shorts and made the connection. 'Nah man. Very funny, am rough as fuck. I'd flung them on to answer the door.'

Jack laughed. 'I didn't actually think you had a flume out to the private pool'. Still giggling away, Jack threw himself down on the adjacent armchair and swung his legs over one arm. 'I thought you'd be a bit tender today. When did you get out of the hospital?'

Stirling sighed again, as if the recollection were too much for him, he rubbed his chest and then started to put together a timeline for Jack. 'I reckon the ambulance got there about one-ish and then they filled in a few forms. By three o'clock, I was still there. I couldn't get a signal on my phone, and it was full of bams. I eventually jumped behind reception and used their phone to call myself a taxi and came hame.'

Jack looked at Stirling's face studiously. 'You should maybe still get that checked out. That snib on you wasn't exactly your best feature in the first place but whatever that Stevie boy did hasn't fixed it.'

Stirling got up and looked at the mirror. It was as bad as he remembered. He poked and prodded himself whilst trying to sniff via both nostrils. 'I think it'll be fine man. It's mainly swelling. I tried to take a line when I got back last night. I tried to sniff, and it went half up my nostril and then fell back out on the plate. Canny even get a sniff man'

Jack laughed. 'A trooper man; still trying to take lines through a broken beak, class. You must be a bit better. You looked gubbed on that pavement man. I was shouting at you, trying to get you to respond but you were just dazed staring into space.'

Stirling winced again as he sat back on the sofa. He was still feeling his nose when he clarified for Jack what had happened 'I know man. I could hear you, but I was too busy watching Millie, walking away, hand in hand with that Stevie cunt. Climbing into his big daft car and driving away. She never even turned back never mind check I was all right. What kind of fucking cow does that? I'm trying to defend her. I'm trying to defend her FROM HIM. But naw, he decks me and she fucks off with him. It's no right man. Fucking bint. I mean all that pish about him stalking her and that. Pure cow material.'

Jack nodded through Stirling's recollection; but when he spoke, he adopted a more serious tone as if to help steer Stirling away from any further drama. 'That was a bad craic man. Better off without lassies like that. Some of them just love all that drama. He's a fucking nutter and she's a glutton for punishment. Best steering well clear chief.'

Stirling wasn't feeling any better but clearly appreciated the camaraderie declaring proudly, 'That's me back on the white, British birds from now on.'

Jack laughed. 'Were you ever off them like?'

Stirling thought for a second before replying, 'No. No really. But I've re-prioritised my preferences.'

'Wise move, big man. You get yourself up The Blue Oyster with Tony and Bruce Lee.' They both laughed, but Stirling stopped when he could spot a certain impatience in Jack by the way he kept nodding along, as if to get him to wrap up his story. Then Jack edged forward on his seat. 'You no wanting to ask what I got up to?'

Stirling got up and headed into the kitchen before gesturing to Jack if he wanted a tea.

Jack shook his head and Stirling carried on before shouting back from the kitchen 'You weren't scouting around the various hospitals to see if I was dying then?'

Jack stretched out on the chair. 'Well, I thought about that first, but well, I'd seen you into the hands of some healthcare professionals. And no-one likes someone interfering when professionals are involved, eh?'

'Aye right. So where did you go then?'

'Where did I no go, big chap,' announced Jack proudly. 'Well first me and Lucy carefully assisted you into the ambulance. As soon as the ambulance left, she's said to me what's your plan now? I says to her, "Well, what do you want to do." She's right back at me with, "What do YOU want to do?" I took my chance and said well I was thinking a few drinks and then back to mine. She then played her trump card and told me she'd got a hotel through there for the night, on account of her Mum staying over with her kids and her deserving a night out and time to recover. She then said how about we skip the drinks and head back there.'

Stirling shook his head. 'Ya jammy bastard. I'm getting carted off with a broken nose and you're riding that wee dirty from the group'

'Indeed, my friend,' confirmed Jack smugly, 'and dirty she definitely fuckin is! What a ride. Honestly man, I never slept; every time we stopped, she was back on me. At one point she said you can fuck me up the arse if you want.'

'And did you?' interrupted Stirling, greedily hoovering up every word.

'Nah man. We'd no johnnies and I wasn't wanting shite all over my knob. I hate that.'

Stirling nodded along in agreement, despite knowing he'd never had anal sex before and couldn't corroborate his distaste.

'It got till about lunchtime today and we'd been riding for hours when her

Mam phoned and she'd said she'd best get back for her kids. We headed for a coffee downstairs in her hotel after she'd checked out and then we walked to the train station. We sat there for 20 minutes before getting on the train. I'm sat on the train and I can feel her hand in my pocket rubbing the head of my cock. Next thing, we were in the toilets and I'm getting a blow job off her. Honestly man, my filth radar was bang on; she was asking me to pull her hair, tell her she was my slut and all that. Right up my street that was. I'd still ride her again, even right know.'

Stirling was sat deep in thought. He'd seen a new side to Lucy. Previously, she'd thought she'd just have a slack fanny on account of her turning out a couple of kids. 'Good ride then?' he ventured.

Jack looked deep in deliberation before announcing his decision, as if he was opening an envelope at the Oscars, 'One of the best. In fact, thee best. I kid you not. There it is ... the best.'

'Ya spawny, lucky bastard. I'm rolling about Buchanan Street with my nose hinging off ma face and you end up riding all night in a hotel, and then a blowjob on the train. Are you meant to be cheering me up here?

Jack continued smugly, 'Wait till I tell you this tae, see that last wee bit of gear I had: snorted off her naval.'

Stirling was stunned. 'You didnae?' he checked, before they volleyed back and forth their confirmation.

'I did.'

'You didnae.'

'I did. I snorted a line of her naval and then started licking her pussy.'
'Fair play to you Jack man. You're a fucking legend ma man. A dirty bastard but a fucking legend right enough'

Jack was delighted with himself, his work here was done. 'Anyway, big chap, I'm off to get some sleep and get ready for the morra. I'll let you get back to the residents pool. You gonna come along to the RA group tomorrow?'

Stirling stood up to let Jack out whilst confirming,

'I'll be there. If anything, just to check if Millie's there and to set her straight on how pish I thought that was.'

Jack was stood on the doorstep now. 'Do you think she'll make an appearance?'

'I wouldn't think so. Not this week anyway,' replied Stirling whilst he was stood, ducked, in the vestibule. In fact, he couldn't bring himself to say it out loud, but he quietly believed that might be the last he'd see of Millie Singh.

'Good riddance. Onwards and upwards, get yourself on that mad shaggers website man. That's the place for you chief!' encouraged Jack.

Stirling was tempted but wasn't showing Jack 'And pick up your cast offs' he offered before bidding his farewell. 'See you later.... shagger'

Jack strutted off up by the steps and round by the garages whilst Stirling opened the browser in his phone and returned to bed.

* * *

Lucy was walking back from the station. Before she'd even got two steps off the train, she was on her phone to her best friend Claire who, incidentally, worked with Tony at Atholl Safety.

'What a night we had Claire, honestly, such a gentleman. He took my hand as we walked along to my hotel after we'd helped his friend into the ambulance; yeah he was after a girl from that group I go to an on Monday and her ex-boyfriend turned up. It didn't end well for him! But, anyway, it did leave me and Jack together. Well, we just talked and talked all the way back to the hotel. I was laughing so much and then, in bed, he just held me all night. He even took us for a coffee in the morning and carried my case down the stairs, always checking after me – so attentive and so easy to talk with. Do you know that way when you just seem to click with someone and conversation just flows. It was just like that. I know, yeah I hope so. My legs are like wee baby giraffes. I think I've got the butterflies'

'What was that? Obviously, I did, it was amazing. He knew what he was doing, I tell you, and we done it for hours, and then again in the morning. After we had a coffee, we walked up to the train and he told me he'd had an amazing time and hoped we could see each other again soon and that's me now on my way back to the kids. Yeah, my Mum's there, well I'll see you on

Thursday. Catch you soon, take care babe.'

Lucy removed the phone from her ear, slipped it into her denim jacket pocket and swung open the gate. She bounced up the path and opened the door, and within seconds each of the kids took it in turns to embrace her as she tried to get inside. 'Give me a minute, Give me a minute' she told them, only half meaning it, as she dumped her case at the bottom of the stairs.

Her Mum was sat in the kitchen.

'Have they been good?' Lucy shouted through as she hung her jacket up on the banister.

'They've been good as gold. You're in a good mood. Good night, was it?'

'It was that,' replied Lucy. 'A little bit of drama with one of the guys in the group but apart from that the show was excellent, all very fancy, and then some dancing and plenty drinks.'

'Some drama? How? What happened' asked her Mum.

Already it seemed like old news, but Lucy recounted the whole sorry story of the lanky guy from the group, and the abusive ex, the ambulance lights and the heap poor Stirling was left in.

'Guys fighting over girls, it was exactly the same in my day. I remember Shug Neary taking a black eye off yer Dad for trying it on with me one night up Rosie O'Grady's. None of them fighting over you?'

Lucy blushed a bit before conceding, 'Well, someone did walk me back to my hotel and we swapped numbers.'

'That's lovely... I hope you used protection!'

Lucy reacted with mock embarrassment. 'Mum! He was the perfect gent and I never put out on the first night.' But Lucy's Mum was having none of it.

'Yeah and I'm sure that's how you ended up with these two. Two gentleman and you the budding nun!' Lucy blushed a bright shade of red, real this time, as her Mum backed off towards the kettle. 'Cup of tea? I could warm the kettle off your face! What was this gentleman's name then?'

'His name was Jack, if you must know. And he was a gentleman, compared to some nowadays, anyway.'

Janet laid down a hot cup of steaming tea in front of her. 'Good for you,

you deserve to have some fun. I'll be heading off soon, I'm meeting Karen tonight for a few drinks up in Falkirk. Might get a Jack of my own to have some fun with!'

'Mum. TMI! I don't even want to think about that. As far as I want to believe you've never been with anyone since Dad died.'

Lucy's Mum had a glint in her eye. 'That's right enough, dearest daughter. Haven't even looked at another man.... I prefer it from behind anyway.'

Lucy about spat out her tea and covered her ears. 'Right, that's enough. I don't want to hear anymore. You best get heading up to see Karen and I better get the kids dressed. Late to bed last night, was it?'

Lucy's Mum sighed, but Lucy refused to allow her to explain further for fear of what profanity might emerge.

'It's fine. Thanks Mum,' she said moving her empty teacup to the sink, collecting her Mum's jacket from the staircase in the hall, and trying her best to force her out the door.

'See you then,' her mum wrestled back.

'Bye kids!'

With that, Little Archie ran down the stairs as fast as he could to give her a hug at the door before she set off on her way. But as the two of them embraced, Lucy had already checked her phone. She had a text from Jack already, she didn't want to appear too keen so was already training herself to delay her reply, whilst working on said reply and not waiting too long. She read the text.

Just checked on Stirling, he's doing good. Hope you got back to your Mum okay. Look forward to catching up again soon. Xx.

Two kisses she thought to herself, he was definitely on her page as she locked her phone and decided it was time to give her Mum that final push out the door so she could get the kids settled into a full-on pyjama day.

31

Week Ten

Dave was finishing off his evening meal with Morag and the kids. They were all very excited having booked a holiday to Tenerife following the realisation of Dave's share options with Scottish Spinsters. He was already trying to curtail the rogue spender in Morag, well aware that she operated in stealth, she was trying to encourage him to have their back garden landscaped, but Dave saw this as a slippery slope into twenty grand territory. He was looking to spend half that.

Dave looked at his watch and found an emergency exit in the shape of tonight's meeting. He polished off the last few pieces of frying steak and, in one singular movement, collected his plate, cutlery and glass and placed them into the dishwasher. He then bent over and conceded that he'd get a few quotes for landscaping before kissing Morag and bidding them all his goodbyes. He grabbed his keys from the kitchen worktop and headed off to the car, only stopping to say goodbye to Misty. 'See you later baby' he gushed as he stroked the dog's ears and squished up her face.

Misty paused expectantly at the door as Dave left apologising and assuring her that he'd be back soon, as he pulled the door quietly behind him. He opened the car door, fired everything up before the car dash flashed up with two warnings: service overdue and oil change due. Got to get them booked, he thought to himself, then instantly remembered he'd already forgotten his notes.

* * *

Ryan greeted Dave in his usual manner and was still as pleased with himself as ever. Dave succinctly responded with a quick 'Ryan' before making his way into the hall, where he found Tony already waiting.

'I never knew you were here Tony' said Ryan as the main door closed behind him, clearly worried, Dave thought, that Tony had seen him and thought he was waiting outside for any particular reason.

Dave took a seat whilst Tony explained his early attendance. 'Kevin's car is in the garage getting some work done. I'd come down early to drop him off but then realised it didn't make sense to head home and come back again, so I thought I'd just hang back to watch his class from the window.' Tony turned back to look through the window again. 'He can fight like fuck but has some arse on him.'

Dave was busy setting a reminder in his phone to book his service and oil change.

Ryan still replied apologetically. 'I'd been outside for 15 minutes, too. Sorry I never even noticed your car, or I'd have popped my head in.'

Tony never even looked away from the window. 'It's fine. Ryan, I've enjoyed the view!'

Dave patted his thighs accompanied by a 'right then' absolutely delighted with himself that he'd set a reminder to phone the garage. 'Good to see you all on Friday. What a wonderful show it was too. Were you out late, Tony? See any more of the rest of them?'

Tony was still stood staring in the door window of the hall and only half turned to respond. 'I'm not too sure, Dave. After you guys left we left pretty much straight away, deciding that The Polo Lounge probably wasn't the scene for Jack and Stirling, so we left them to it. I think they were headed to the after party, it was at a place called Fire Burner or something like that.'

Ryan thanked Dave for the lift home, as if he'd suddenly just remembered it'd happened. Dave gave him a quick side eye before confirming it was no problem. At that, Stirling arrived in the waiting room with all the gusto that a six-foot five overgrown casual with matching black eyes can, just as Sensei

Jamieson called his class to a halt.

Tony backed away from the doors as Kevin's class left in single file, followed soon after by the man himself. Ryan greeted Stirling before even noticing the black eyes and swollen nose that accompanied him. His, 'Hi Stirling,' followed up immediately with 'good heavens. What on earth has happened to you? Are you okay?'

Before Stirling had a chance to reply, Sensei Jamieson paused to examine the damage, surmising that whoever did it, 'meant to hurt him' with his expert eye.

Stirling was quick to respond. 'I have to admit, it hurt a lot more than the last direct I'd had to the face.'

'That's because I never wanted to hurt you,' Kevin retorted. 'Just remind you.'

'I suppose I should say thanks in that case, cos this is not good,' Stirling left it at that, which was admirable as he was still clearly holding back some comment that Dave could see bubbling up in his brain-damaged head.

Dave continued unstacking the chairs and laying them out in the circle of trust, waiting for the last few stragglers to make it into the hall. But, despite the group not being underway yet, he was still keen to get the story from Stirling as soon as possible. 'As long as you are okay, though?' he asked.

Stirling took his seat and confirmed he'd be fine. 'I'll survive Dave.'

Suddenly, bursting through the door in a wave of apologies, came Katrina. 'I'm so sorry to anyone I offended on Friday night. I was sooo drunk. I'm so embarrassed by myself.'

Dave lied and said he thought she was fine whilst the rest of the group settled for the same tone, apart from Stirling who asked if 'she'd shat herself in a car wash on Saturday?'

The group all laughed apart from Ryan who gave a patronising, 'Thanks,' in return whilst Katrina settled for a far more polite, 'not quite,' as she took to her seat in the group. But before she could sit her arse down, she noticed Stirling's face.

'Have you been fighting with Mike Tyson. Look at your face?' she shrieked, her inner Irish mother coming to the fore.

'I'm fine,' said Stirling, 'it looks a lot worse than it really is.'

Dave looked around the room, he knew Derek wouldn't be here but had expected both Millie and Jack. He ushered the group towards silence, as he enquired about giving them five more minutes before starting.

'I messaged Jack last night. It was a screen shot of a guy with a beard in stockings, from that website he'd set me up on. He'd messaged asking if I wanted a blow job. Asked Jack if he'd already been there, but I didn't hear anything back.. WhatsApp says he's no even read it. It's no like him. I asked if he'd be here on Saturday and he was still coming along, so I've no idea what's happened.'

'And he messaged me after he left Stirling's, and he's no been online since then,' interjected Lucy, seeming more panicked than was even necessary.

Dave thought to himself that he must have been back on it Saturday night and then shattered and had probably crashed out before running in late to work today. He'd be fine. 'Anyone heard from Millie?' Dave looked around the circle, again at blank faces and shaking heads.

'I don't think she'll be back,' Stirling volunteered. 'On account of her walking off hand in hand with her ex after he'd knocked me out.'

'Oh right' said Dave, 'that doesn't look good then. Hopefully she's okay. I'll email them both later and offer them the opportunity to return, reminding them that our door is always open.'

Dave assumed that Jack had finally shagged Lucy and was now thinking better of it, but and as for Millie; his spider sense had probably been right all along.

He kicked off proceedings.

'Hello everyone and welcome to Romantics Anonymous. Thanks all for coming and well done. I hope you are all well, we've already heard a bit from some of the group but if we could all check in in the customary manner that would be much appreciated. Katrina, could you please start us off this week?'

Katrina took the opportunity; mainly to continue to proclaim her innocence and repeated apologies for her antics on Friday night. Dave couldn't remember anything that she'd done or said which was particularly bad and assumed Katrina's fear was for what she could have or even thought about saying with a drink in her. So instead, Dave enquired about her plans for her and Jimmy's reunion.

'Just to be together will be lovely without the guards watching our every move, like we are smuggling drugs to each other. And to start the life we'd always planned. It'll take him some time to get re-acquainted to life nowadays and I guess a lot of his friends will resurface now that he's back.' She finished off by sheepishly offering her apologies for not coming along for the next few weeks whilst enquiring if she'd be welcome back. Dave noticed there was no mention of metal detectors.

Deciding to himself that the main motivation behind his disdain for Katrina had been the lack of honesty, which had now surfaced in abundance, Dave confirmed she'd be welcome to come back along and that he hoped everything went to plan.

Next Dave looked over at Lucy who still looked a bit desolate. Dave cursed Jack for his roguish ways. He must have known she'd be all in. Lucy wasn't exactly the type where you could wipe your cock on the sheets and skip back to life without a second's thought. He's probably best avoiding the fallout, he thought.

'And what about you Lucy, are you able to share with the group this week?'

Lucy took as deep a breath her defeated posture could allow. 'Well Dave, even just this weekend I've found myself mistaking the 'language of love' and probably getting carried away with myself. It's amazing how quickly it can grab you and the minute you think you're wise to it, bang it catches you right when you were least expecting it'

Dave caught Stirling's eye who nodded back as if he'd read Dave's mind.

'Thanks for sharing Lucy and you're totally right. That's how addiction can work and with something as omnipresent as romance it can be difficult both seeing it coming ... as well as utterly convincing in terms of its suggestions and your interpretations. Was there anything particular about this episode which caught you unaware?'

Lucy lamented over the time her, and Jack had spent both leading up to and immediately after what Dave thought had probably been a night of unbridled Jack after Millie's fashion show. The only missing element being Jack's name, which she never confirmed – despite everyone in the room already having made the obvious connection.

She then confirmed a full return to non-practicing Lesbianism and that her and men were done.

Dave had heard this before but hoped she maybe would take heed a bit further this time. He liked Jack a lot, but could have easily predicted the circumstances which had unfolded here. Dave looked back at Stirling again who took a sharp intake of breath as Dave asked him to proceed with his check-in too.

'Cheers, Dave. Well, where to start this week? Much like Lucy was saying just a second ago, convincing yourself and reading someone else's intentions incorrectly can be a right bastard.'

Dave felt sorry for Stirling. He was a good lad and a far better option for Millie than her on off partner Stevie. He'd seen it happen way too many times before. Nice guy likes girl, girl likes nasty prick. Good guy gets left standing. Dave probably knew this better than most having played both roles in previous romances.

'Thanks for sharing, Stirling. That's very brave of you and I'm sure the hurt goes beyond the face, remember it takes two people to consider the language of love and sometimes when someone thinks the easiest thing to do; to remain ambiguous that really isn't helping.'

Stirling clearly read between the lines but didn't react to it kindly. 'Thanks Dave kick a man when he's down. So I've been a daft cunt cos she was never interested? I must look like a right fanny.'

Dave was quick to try and dilute his interpretation to a more palatable taste 'Sorry Stirling. I never meant it like that. I meant in more general terms when we want to see something we look for evidence or proof that it hasn't happened rather than it has and it can be amazing how quick the brain can build a dossier of supporting evidence. You've nothing to feel ashamed or down about, its about moving forwards and you are in the right place to do that. As I said earlier it takes a brave person to come here and share with the group and your honesty wont just help you but helps each and everyone of us.'

Lucy rubbed Stirling's knee as he accepted a small round of applause from the room. Dave was thankful for the support of the group, and he watched as Stirling's face resolved and accepted Dave's diluted revision.

Tony was next. He had come out to his daughters, almost prompted by their suggestion and it had gone far better than he had anticipated. He hadn't been sure his ex hadn't had a hand in it but was pleased that the threat of them finding out through other means had been lifted. He had reassured both of them that he was still their mad Dad, and that if anyone crossed them he'd still batter them but probably shag them as well, now. If he liked the look of them, of course.

This was typical Tony, Dave thought. His mask would get popped on when things got challenging. 'How are you feeling now?'

'Yeah it was a bit emotional Dave, but it's another milestone passed. God bless her, India was checking that I was using protection and said she was worried about monkey pox and STD's.'

'Well, that's great, Tony. And have you been following their sound advice?'

No need to worry, Davey boy, Tony laughed. He reached into his pocket and pulled out a durex, which he held up and presented to the room. 'Ribbed for pleasure, he read before he added 'and better traction in the mud,' looking very much delighted with himself.

Tony continued, this time with a slightly more sombre tone.

'A difficult one though was bumping into Kevin's exes at the club we were in on Friday night. That was difficult for me. Felt like I was stood beside members of a club that I hadn't really been signed into yet. I ended up turning into a bit of a cunt about it all, but we got home to my flat and made up. Took all my frustrations out on his arsehole, pair cunt won't be delivering too many roundhouse kicks tonight.'

'It'll be new experiences for a while,' Dave said, 'and it's about taking in these experiences for what they are and always remembering to think about your personal rights. You can do what you want to do at whatever pace you feel inclined to. Also, it is important to be aware that the decline into romance can be fraught with danger. In many respects, Kevin is your first and you're not his, so be careful to remember he does have a past and that too could include you at some point.'

This seemed to strike a chord with Tony. 'I seem to be sailing along in this new life, new me, new immediate couple but I know that there is so much still to go through and seeing his exes really fucked me up a bit – especially because they were right freaky looking cunts. I was outside smoking a fag later on and one of them was drinking water out of a dug bowl dressed as a dug, so I sniffed his erse and asked if that's what he was after. He wasn't happy. Cunt needs to douche his arse better tae.'

Dave didn't know what to say to that and was in fact pleased when Tony didn't pause for a response.

'I've decided I won't be introducing Kevin to the girls just now. I don't want any more upheaval or changes when they've already had enough. Being introduced to your newly gay Dad's new boyfriend is a head fuck I don't think they'd be able to handle just yet. '

Dave was on more comfortable ground with the sentiment of the last statement. He reassured Tony that this was a sensible outlook and that whilst he had been comfortable with the pace of change it was good that he was being mindful of his daughter's reaction in that respect.

Then it was onto Ryan. Dave had thought Ryan was quiet on Friday night. Half expecting him to fly off the rails at Katrina's revelation regarding her secret Jimmy. If anything, he was disappointed in the frustratingly nice Ryan continuing to be just that, frustratingly nice. He looked over at him and Ryan started to check-in without any prompt necessary.

'As you are all aware I've been a regular here for sometime now my skirmishes with romance have left me bruised a bit emotionally and now I've been acutely aware of the potential damage caused by romance and my own particular notions so I've been careful to protect myself. This week I had a lovely night out, with most of you, at Millie's launch on Friday and I really wish she was here so that I could tell her how impressed I really was and following that I was back out on Sunday with Katrina as we went looking for my ring. We've tried around the rock pools and most of the beach along past Hawes Pier but still nothing. We went for a dinner along at the lobster pot in Blackness afterwards, it was lovely. I had the scampi and Katrina had the lobster macaroni.'

Dave continued to be frustrated with frustratingly nice Ryan. And his temporary relief in disdain for Katrina had recovered.

'It was only a shame,' Ryan added, 'that we hadn't all had another opportunity to congratulate Millie on her efforts last week.'

Dave heard Stirling tutting. Dave was unsure if this was directed at Ryan's niceness or the query whether Millie now deserved it. He thought that he probably agreed with both, regardless, and let it slide unchecked.

'Thanks Ryan. It was good night on Friday and it's a shame we've not managed to congratulate her but hopefully we can catch up next week. That's unfortunate that you've still not located the ring but after a few years it was always a long shot, good that you had a nice meal though.'

With check ins complete, Dave took the opportunity to deliver his next line, well aware of the connection to his previous statement. 'As a recap; last week we looked at the language of love and the ways that differing acts can be picked up or misconstrued as acts or words which are representing someone as looking for romance.'

Dave pushed back his chair and turned to the board:

'Receiving gifts

Acts of service

Words of affirmation

Quality time

Physical touch'

Dave asked if someone could remind me where they'd got to the week prior.

Ryan pushed his hand up in the air willingly, Katrina a little less cautiously. Dave opted for Katrina, hoping that having to say them out loud would force her to recognise what she'd done. It was one thing stringing poor Ryan along when Jimmy was a secret but giving him a send-off lunch was just cruel.

But Katrina never shirked the invite. 'Last week we covered the top two before briefly branching out into others but we definitely covered the top two.'

Dave thanked Katrina and began by revisiting words of affirmation. Dave asked the room if anyone could give him some examples of where words of affirmation could be misinterpreted as looking for romance.

'I think I've recently become a sucker for the language of love,' Stirling bemoaned. 'The words of affirmation could be when you're looking for a sign that someone's interested, and their reactions or words lead you to think there may be more there or that they are on the same page as yourself.

Tony was quick to shorten this answer to just three words. 'A fucking Tease.'

Dave tapped his pen on the board waiting for other responses.

Katrina was next to suggest something. 'It's when someone speaks using positive terms and the other party interprets the positive terms to be alluded to them.'

Dave pointed the pen in Katrina's direction confirming this was correct and thanked Tony and Stirling for their responses. 'Phrases such as, it's so lovely to see you or responding to someone with you're the best are both innocent statements, but to the right ears these can be seen as affirming someone's romantic interest.'

Dave then tapped the board at the fourth item on his list.

'And these can often work in tandem with the following item on our list: the sharing of quality time. Has anyone any idea how the sharing of quality time can end up being mistaken for romantic interest?'

Dave looked over at Katrina who seemed to bow her head.

'At the end of any unsuccessful date,' Lucy piped in. 'The awkward end to someone giving you a lift or a walk home which is just an actual lift or walk home is a nightmare.'

Katrina was cooing in agreement 'Oooooh, that's so it, not that I've had that many dates, but the unexpected date is another one. Where you're on the page that something platonic is happening and then they try to get a bit more than friendly. Awkward is definitely the word!'

Dave took umbrage at Katrina's description, wondering if this was aimed at Ryan purposefully. He still thanked them both, suggesting they were two good examples all be it through slightly gritted teeth. He then asked if any of the guys had any examples from their perspective?

Tony suggested that he used to be a firm believer that sustained eye contact was sufficient quality time and conclusive evidence of someone wanting more.

'The weird stare work for you often Tony?' Lucy laughed.

'Put it this way, if it resulted in someone accepting a lift home, they were as good as getting it.'

Lucy delved a bit closer to home with her next example. She herself had recently had an experience where she'd thought that some quality time was a forerunner to maybe something else, but her bubble had been burst. 'And I can say that confidently, because he's not here.'

There was a bit of a delay whilst her admission silenced the room awkwardly.

Dave allowed the silence to roll on until he couldn't bear the groups discomfort any longer. 'Thanks Lucy. Our last heading here is physical touch and that can be fairly innocent connections or even accidental touching, where a very willing recipient interprets that action as intentional and a sure-fire sign of romance'

Lucy snapped back at his last offering 'Yip, that one too. There was definitely physical touching!'

Dave thanked Lucy for her contribution before confirming that any single item listed can be seen as an indicator of romantic want, and that any combination of them only serves to further build the case in confirmation.

'Like that teacher I mentioned last week' Katrina chimed in. Stirling, too, could also see his own previous misinterpretation.

'I totally see where these has landed me in trouble before. It's fascinating how your mind plays tricks on you. I remember one time being in the cinema and the girl I was with kept running her leg up against mine, I was sat thinking she does that one more time and she's up for it. Bingo, one more time, I put my hand on said leg and she freaked out, slapped me, and stormed out!'

Tony laughed. 'I bet she was wanting more, but she got fed up waiting.'

Katrina scowled and asked why guys were like that. 'Why does everything have to lead to sex for you lot?'

Tony smirked, already antagonising both Lucy and Kat.

'Because that's how we're wired,' Tony answered, not afraid to give a response.

'Some want shagged and others want to be shagging. It's much easier with guys cos we all know we're all after one of those two things. You women are too much drama.'

'We're the dramatic ones are we?' Lucy jumped in with both feet. 'Why are guys all liars? Just lie and lie, connive and convince until they get into your pants and then nothing just silence and then onto the next. It's disgusting.'

Katrina clapped her hands. 'Well said, Lucy.'

'So tell me this, right,' Stirling said, raising a hand to try and quieten the girls. 'Why if it's not happening, would you then string us along? If you know we're only after one thing, and you know it's not happening, why continue?'

Katrina eyed up Stirling suspiciously. 'Continue with what?'

Dave wanted to step in and throw in a comment regards Katrina and Ryan's Sunday metal detecting session but opted for the fifth amendment and watched the conversation unravel as Stirling, Tony, Katrina and Lucy suggested example after example where one was leading each other on until each one was standing in front of their chair.

'It's interesting to see how many interpretations of who should or shouldn't act in a certain way in any given combination of circumstances that can or could all lead to romance. Unfortunately, we'll not resolve that today,' he said, packing away his pens, 'but it's vitally important that, particularly when we have had issues with romance in the past ourselves that we remain acutely aware of how these signs can be miscommunicated on both sides.'

That had been his main point and Dave, for one, was happy with how it had been delivered. The rest of them looked less than thrilled.

32

Ghosted

Dave's phone rang sharply, cutting through the post-session quiet. Stirling, who had been chatting with him, paused mid-sentence as Dave answered.

'Hello? Yes, speaking,' Dave said, his tone immediately taut. His expression darkened as he listened. 'His mum called you? Okay. Absolutely, do what you need to. I'll head there now.'

He hung up, his movements suddenly rushed.

'That was the police. Jack's mum hasn't heard from him since Friday. They're heading to his flat now to break down the door.'

Stirling blinked, the words hitting him like a blow.

'What? Why?'

'They think something's wrong,' Dave said, pulling on his jacket.

'I've got to go. Can you handle tidying up the chairs?'

'Of course,' Stirling stammered.

'But let me know as soon as you hear something, aye?'

Dave nodded, already moving toward the door. Stirling stood for a moment, processing the conversation, before turning back to the half-circle of chairs. His hands worked automatically, stacking them, but his thoughts were elsewhere, spiralling toward Jack. Something felt wrong, badly wrong.

He dropped the chairs into their stack and made a beeline for Lucy, who was lingering by the exit with Katrina. They were deep in conversation, their voices rising and falling in animated lively tones.

'Lucy,' Stirling interrupted, his voice urgent.

'Sorry, Katrina, can I grab her for a minute?'

Katrina gave a curious look but waved them off.

'She's all yours. See you next week.'

As they stepped outside into the brisk air, Lucy hugged her arms against the chill.

'What's this about? Did Jack send you to do his dirty work?'

'No,' Stirling said, his voice low. 'You really haven't heard from Jack, have you?'

Lucy rolled her eyes, her irritation obvious.

'Not since Saturday. He texted me, I replied, and then... nothing. Clearly gone off the idea after he got what he wanted.' Her voice faltered. 'Why?'

'Dave just got a call from the police. They're at Jack's flat, his mum hasn't heard from him either. He's on his way over there now.'

Lucy's full demeanor immediately shifted from spurned faux indifference to a mix of confusion and dread.

'What? Do they think something's happened? Has he gone missing?'

'I don't know,' Stirling admitted. 'But I'm going up to his flat. Do you want to come tae?'

Lucy hesitated for a moment before nodding. She climbed into the passenger seat of Stirling's car, her hands trembling as she fumbled with the seat belt. Stirling started the engine, reversing sharply out of the car park, jolting Lucy back and forth as he did.

As they drove, Lucy stared at her phone, scrolling through her unanswered texts to Jack.

'I didn't want to push him,' she murmured. 'I thought he needed space, and now...' her voice tapered off.

'I'm sure it's nothing,' Stirling said, trying to convince himself. He barely registered her words as he focused on navigating the dark streets.

They pulled into the car park by Jack's flat, where the sight of Dave's car, a police van, a fire engine, and a black transit van made Lucy's breath hitch. Stirling parked and the two of them climbed out, their movements staccato as if their limbs didn't agree with where they were headed.

Dave was standing with two police officers near the garages adjacent to Jack's flat. He glanced at them briefly, his face pale and drawn, before turning back to the police.

'Dave?' Stirling asked, not wanting to interrupt but too worried not to.

Dave shook his head and raised a hand as if to say, not now. Lucy and Stirling exchanged a worried glance but still approached cautiously.

They hovered nearby as Dave talked with the police, occasionally breaking off to allow one of the officers to talk into his radio. They weren't close enough to hear what was being said but the occasional word drifted over and churned up Stirling's panic further.

'What's fucking happening?' he eventually demanded, his voice trembling as the dread began to engulf him. Lucy was frozen quiet, shivering in silence. Her shaking had become uncontrollable.

'Someone tell us fucking something, anything?'

Dave turned to him, his shoulders sagging.

'Stirling, it's Jack'.

Stirling dropped to his hunkers and cradled his head in his hands. Catching the full weight of all his worst fears with it.

'It cannae be Jack, Dave'.

Lucy was still shaking, now violent in her disbelief.

'What do you mean Dave? Has he done something wrong?'

'Lucy...' He opened his arms, and she stepped into them, tears already streaming down his face.

'Jack's gone,' he said softly, his voice cracking with emotion. 'They found him in his bed earlier tonight. He'd... he'd collapsed. The police are with his mum, they had to wait until the other officers were with her.'

Lucy let out a wail, collapsing against Dave as her sobs echoed in the cold air. Stirling stood up, his mind still racing. Images of Jack flashing in his mind and all competing with the horrible reality in front of him here and now: laughing, joking, always full of life.

'What happened?' He finally asked, not even sure if he wanted to know.

One of the officers stepped towards him.

'We can't confirm anything until we've conducted a full post-mortem, but it appears he passed away in his sleep. There were no immediate signs of foul play.'

Stirling nodded numbly, unable to process the actual words. Lucy clung to Dave, shaking as she cried.

The taller of the two police officers stood back to take a call on his radio. Before indicating to his colleague that they were needed elsewhere. Dave broke off from Lucy and thanked them both for their help. They exchanged some details before Dave confirmed he'd wait until the flat was secured. After watching them leave, Dave looked at Stirling.

'There was ching on Friday night, wasn't there?'

Stirling felt the colour drain from his face. It felt like it drained further still, out his body and legs and down out of his feet. He hesitated, then nodded. Dave asked how much he'd had. Stirling looked up as he tried to think back, cycling through sketchy memories like a poorly recorded video before remembering that Jack had told him he'd had a few more lines off of Lucy's naval.

'Probably about half a gram whilst we were out, maybe took the rest later. aye we had about a gram each.'

Dave rolled his bottom lip as if to say he didn't know.

'The police didn't mention anything, but they'll probably need to carry out a toxicology report.'

Dave's conclusion done nothing to alley Stirling's fears.

Lucy looked up at him, her face streaked with tears.

'Why didn't I call him? Why didn't I push harder?' Her voice cracked. 'Maybe I could've done something.'

Stirling didn't have an answer. He crouched beside her, his own tears falling freely.

A white van pulled into the car park, its headlights cutting through the gloom. The joiner stepped out, holding a toolbox.

'Looking for flat number four?'

Dave waved him over, then turned to Stirling and Lucy.

'I need to get him fixing the door. Are you two going to be okay?'

Lucy nodded weakly, though she was far from okay. Stirling helped her to her feet, and they walked back to his car in silence.

Inside, Stirling stared blankly at the windscreen, his hands back on his head rather than the steering wheel. 'I just can't believe it,' he said finally. 'Jack gone. It doesn't feel real.'

Lucy scrolled through her messages again, tears dripping onto her phone screen.

'I just wish... I just wish I'd sent more. Maybe he'd still be here.'

Stirling reached over, resting a hand on her arm. 'It's not your fault,' he said quietly, though he wasn't sure he believed it for himself.

The joiner was returning to his van for tools and bowed his head as Stirling drove away from the garages. Stirling bowed in return and turned on the radio before deciding he wasn't ready for any songs. He switched it back off, Lucy agreed silently.

Back in the empty car park at Trinity House, they sat for another moment, the realities of tonight spinning somewhere between them.

'What do we do now?' Stirling asked, his voice trembling.

Lucy shook her head, still staring at the messages on her phone.

'I don't want to admit it's real,' she whispered. 'I can't.'

Lucy started to cry, and Stirling leaned over to give her a hug. Stirling moved himself over to make it easier for him to comfort her, feeling the gear stick sticking into his midriff as he did. He moved back into his seat as the gear stick sprung back into place and Lucy pulled away.

'Oh shit! I need to get home. The kids...' She grabbed her things and hesitated by the door.

'Sorry Stirling. I don't even have your number.'

They exchanged numbers and Stirling, caught up in the emotion of it all, struggled to save her in his contacts. Lucy eventually took the phone off him and hit save. They smiled at one another, just briefly, the first time they'd smiled since leaving the meeting that night and then Lucy began to cry again.

Stirling sat alone in the dark, staring at the empty car park. Memories of Jack flooded his mind: his laugh, his wit, his boundless energy. And then the tears came again, unstoppable this time. He cried until he couldn't anymore, then wiped his face, took a deep breath, and started the car.

It was time to go home.

33

Tastes Like Freedom

Kat pulled up to the car park about 8:30am. Jimmy had said that he should be out by about quarter to nine. As his release day fell on a Sunday, he was getting out a few days early, a bonus which Kat hadn't wanted to count on, having counted down the days, hours, minutes and seconds until right now. She didn't know whether to sit in the car or wait at the doors, and for a minute or two found herself hovering over the door handle, frozen in place. In the end opting to hang about outside her car, hoping to get closer. She continually checked herself. She wanted everything to be perfect for Jimmy, she wanted to be perfect for him. She almost couldn't believe it was so near.

She watched the doors swing open and her heart skipped a beat, only to be disappointed when someone else left before him. Strangely though, the guy headed straight towards her.

'Are you Kat?'

'Yes', she replied tentatively.

'Ah, that's great hen. Jimmy said you'd be able to drop me off in Condorrat, on account of that being on your way.'

Kat looked up nervously as the doors opened again, and there he was, her Jimmy. He ducked out between the swishing doors, accompanied by a warden who handed him a clear bag of his meagre possessions. She watched as him and the warden exchanged a few words before the warden returned inside, leaving her Jimmy a free man. She caught his eye and he flashed her a smile, before taking in a lung full of freedom. He'd had a fresh shave and haircut, and was wearing almost the same outfit he'd worn to court all those years ago: Tan Timberland boots, boot cut stonewash jeans, and a navy blue Harrington jacket. Jimmy looked like he'd tried to squeeze into his former younger self, only reasonably successfully. For a second Kat stood watching and waited for the emotion to hit her, but nothing arrived. She had built up to this day for so long that her passive emotions at the sight of her Jimmy, now finally free from prison, had caught her by surprise. She had expected more from herself.

She started off walking towards him at pace and was soon running, leaving her proposed passenger stood by the car as she neared her Jimmy. 'Jimmy' she called, waving as she got closer. Jimmy was striding towards her, purposefully as if he was taking in the moment. Kat collapsed on him and he picked her up as they embraced.

'It's so good to see you, Jimmy McGovern,' Kat gushed, as she caught her breath and kissed him again trying to jump start her feelings. Jimmy caught up her hand in his and they both started towards the car park, clearly not wanting to spend a second longer by those gates.

'Is it this way?' he checked, before continuing with her. 'Let's get away from here sharpish.' Kat followed his lead, hand in hand. She watched his every move. She finally had her Jimmy back, it didn't feel real but it also didn't feel right, not yet anyway.

As they approached her car, Kat pointed towards their proposed passenger. 'What's he doing here?' Jimmy asked Kat.

Kat felt a hint of panic. 'He said we were to give him a lift to Condorrat.'

Jimmy laughed. 'Chancing bastard. He's no getting a lift anywhere. Hoy you, you've got your BFH, get yourself tae fuck, you're getting a lift nowhere.'

'Aww come on big man. What's 10 minutes out your road? I'll get you some blues when you drop me.'

The guy chattered on as Jimmy brushed him aside and climbed into the passenger seat. He readjusted the chair as Kat slipped into the driver's seat. Jimmy lowered the window and leaned out. 'Bus stations that way pal. Catch you on the dark side,' before he raised two fingers out the open window.

As Kat exited the car park, she reached over and stroked Jimmy's leg. She continued to act through motions she'd expected to happen naturally. Her inner voice stayed eerily quiet.

All the way home Jimmy talked excitedly about anything, from how busy the roads were to how many new brands of cars there were. Deliberating over the pronunciation of Hyundai. Meanwhile Kat ran through their itinerary for the next few days. She had planned a day's shopping, a day out visiting South Queensferry, meals, romantic walks. Jimmy lapped up the prospect of everything she mentioned.

They arrived in Camelon and pulled up to Jimmy's flat. Jimmy looked up at it but seemed reluctant to get out of the car. 'Honestly. It feels weird thinking you've been longer in ma flat than ah was ever in it. I canny believe it, how could your heart take so much?' Kat started to cry and her hand stayed gripped around the handbrake. Jimmy reached over and gave her a hug. 'Come on, let's get inside. I can't believe we're here.' Jimmy skipped out the passenger seat, slung his bag over his shoulder and opened Kat's door, before lifting her from her feet and carrying her down the path. Kat's tears immediately turned to shrieks of laughter. 'Ah've no thought this through,' Jimmy said. 'You've goat the keys!.'

Jimmy put Kat back on her feet. She opened the door and stepped inside, Jimmy followed, as she walked up the stairs she could feel his hands on her bum. She didn't run from it though, in fact, she paused on the landing and let him catch her, let his hands rove around her, until finally she turned to face him. They were almost level, Jimmy losing a few inches by standing on a lower step. His hands were all over her as they kissed, and she only broke away to lead him to the bedroom. She wanted her physical feelings to address her lingering emotional distance.

Before they did anything, she pulled the blind down and turned around to face Jimmy, slipping out of her dress as she walked towards him. 'I want you inside me Jimmy McGovern.'

Jimmy had his shirt off before she'd finished her sentence, and his jeans down at his ankles, but was struggling to get one trouser leg over his boot and off his foot. 'Fuck it!,' he announced as he fell on top of Kat and onto the bed with one boot still attached to the trailing edge of his bootcut denim jeans. Kat could feel his hard cock pressed against her wet knickers. She kissed him slowly, feeling his eager tongue in her mouth as she arched her back and wrapped her legs round him. Jimmy fumbled with her bra strap before he gave up and flipped out her breasts from each cup and sucked on them greedily. 'Hey,' Kat warned him as he gripped them too tightly. Jimmy whispered an apology before kissing her midriff and then removing her knickers. He gasped as he caught a glimpse of her glistening want.

'You are fucking gorgeous. Kat. I fucking love you.' Jimmy slowly licked her pussy, immersing himself in her want. By the time he climbed up her body his face was soaked with her. His cock twitched in anticipation as Kat manipulated her body to guide him inside her. Jimmy gasped as he filled her wet wanton sex.

'Oya fucker,' he exclaimed as Kat writhed on the bed, enjoying his hard cock inside her. Jimmy began fucking her, holding her tight as he reacquainted himself with his lover, faster and faster until he let out a grunt which almost became a sigh and collapsed on top of her.

Kat could feel him burst inside her and she didn't want to let it go. She held him tight as she grinded out every single gasp of her pent-up lust for Jimmy. Whimpering in tongues as she let herself go and pulsed out her satisfaction, all over the sheets. Jimmy kissed her again, before he laid down next to her, both blushed with satisfaction.

Kat rolled herself up in her duvet and curled up next to Jimmy. 'I've missed and wanted you for so long. I never thought you'd come back.'

Jimmy's eyes narrowed. 'Was there ever anybody else?'

'No, don't be daft. Never, I've only ever wanted you, Jimmy McGovern. Nobody could ever make love to me like you.' Jimmy's ego was back restored, and Kat curled her head up into his chest. 'What about you? You never take up a sissy in the prison?'

Jimmy laughed. 'You'd be surprised at how many propositions I did have. LGBTQ Scotland is alive and well in the Scottish Prison Service, well not so much of the L, unfortunately.'

Kat slapped Jimmy gently before returning to her position curled up against his chest. 'What time is it?' she asked.

Jimmy looked around to the alarm clock on the bedside table, '11:37. How?'

'We've got some shopping to do. You're going to need to get a new wardrobe Mr McGovern. Fashions moved on a bit in 11 years!!'

'Steady on. I've got feelings you know,' remarked Jimmy as he kissed her on the head. 'First things first thou, I'm going to have a shower.' Kat prevented him rising, moaning as he tried to slip out the other side of the bed.

'Just a minute more' she asked. Jimmy slipped her grasp before raising his leg, still bearing an inside turned-out leg of his jeans wedged around his hidden boot. Kat looked up as he fought to get them off. 'You've made a mess of that have you not?'

'I got too excited,' explained Jimmy as he finally managed to expose the laces of his timberland boot. He took out the laces, before releasing the denims to the bed which then slipped off on the floor. As he made his way to the shower, Jimmy smiled and stopped to pat Sounness in the hallway. 'Hiya pal, you must be the bluenose.'

Jimmy pulled the cord for the shower and closed the door as the window steamed up. he began belting out Daddy's uniform much to the dismay of Kat who'd moved to the kitchen wearing her robe. 'You'll not need to watch for picking up the soap in that shower,' she called.

'You can come in and get it for me!'

Kat opened the door and dropped the robe. 'We've got a lot of catching up to do,' she said as she closed the door behind her.

34

Two Bridges

Kat and Jimmy were walking along between the bridges, but Jimmy walked with something approaching a limp.

'These are too fucking tight. You can see my baws.'

'That's the style these days,' Kat laughed. 'You look lovely.'

'I feel like that Russell Brand.'

Kat's phone started ringing, it was Dave from Romantics Anonymous. She looked at it and Jimmy looked at her. 'It's Dave, from that group I told you about,' explained Kat not rushing to pick up the call.

'Well, answer the boy then,' encouraged Jimmy. It rang off and Kat put the phone in her bag.

'That's strange. He never phones. I'll try him again in a bit, the group's maybe not on tomorrow because the holiday.' She picked up Jimmy's hand and walked along towards the Orocco Pier restaurant.

They looked at the menu outside for a bit. Jimmy wasn't entirely sure about the value on offer 'Robbing bastards' he muttered to Kat as she elbowed him and continued to read the menu trying not to let on that she'd been here just a few weeks earlier with Ryan.

'Hello Kat' said a familiar voice. She didn't want to look up and talk to him, but Kat had to look away from the menu. 'Oh … Ryan,' Kat confirmed nervously. He had a bag and a metal detector and the most shocked look of upset on his face.

'Hi Kat. Have you heard from Dave.'

But she didn't answer. She was already halfway through introducing Jimmy. who nodded and waved politely, but neither of his introductions were acknowledged.

'Kat, has Dave called you.'

Kat was a bit taken aback by his rudeness, and stumbled into a response, 'I had a missed call just a minute ago. Is everything okay?'

Ryan seemed to steady himself for a second. Kat was aware that Jimmy was now growling at the poor man, and she knew he would be aware too, but then he began to explain, almost silently. 'Sorry Kat and I'm sorry Jimmy. It's nice to meet you at last, I've just received some bad news regards one of our friends. Sorry Kat but Jack Stewart passed away.'

Kat looked confused by Ryan's announcement. 'Who? Jack from the group? Jack's not dead.'

'Sorry Kat. I still can't believe it myself, but it's true. He was found dead in his flat on Monday, just after last week's meeting.

Kat was stunned by this news her thoughts of Jack's constant smile and it's sudden passing rocked her. In an instant she realised how much the group meant to her, she felt instantly ashamed for trading off their friendships as a pastime. Jimmy gave her a hug. 'Are you okay, Kat?'

'Yeah. I'll be fine, just a bit of a shock. In fact, a total shock. I don't know what to say. Poor Jack. That must have been why Dave was calling. To let me know.' Kat removed the phone from her bag as if she had to confirm.

'Yeah,' Ryan said, he'd called me just as I'd started out on the rock pools. I just stood for five minutes in silence and decided I would pack up early today. I don't know what to do, I just couldn't really face it afterwards.'

Kat felt lost in the news. 'We were just heading in for some lunch, you're free to join us if you like?'

Ryan looked poised to accept before Jimmy's face turned the invite down for him. 'I don't think I can today. I'm going to get myself home.' He offered out his hand to Jimmy.

'Nice to meet you. Hopefully, we'll meet again in better circumstances.'

'Cheers,' Jimmy nodded. 'You too.'

Ryan gave Kat a slight hug and bid them both farewell. Kat and Jimmy turned back to the menu, and now silently deciding life was too short to worry about the prices, they headed into the restaurant.

* * *

'This is nice' said Jimmy looking out to the Forth. The waiter had kindly sat them on a table on the terrace, with the rail bridge towering at their side. 'Ninth wonder of the world that is. Feat of engineering genius.'

Kat, however, was not able to appreciate the sights or the summer sun.

'Do you think I should call Dave back?'

Jimmy just shrugged.

'So the poor boy who's died. Do they know what happened? I hate to sound ominous but when you spend your life living like I have for the past few years, you tend to jump to suspicious suggestions when faced with a premature death.'

'He was a right bubbly guy,' Kat said, barely acknowledging Jimmy's question. 'Dead chatty. Always talking about mad sex parties and getting himself into weird positions.' Jimmy made a face at the double entendre.

'No like those positions,' corrected Kat,

'like having affairs and threesomes and stuff.'

Jimmy raised both eyebrows and Kat knew exactly what he was suggesting.

'Hmmm, does sound dodgy when I say it out loud. I'll phone Dave later and see if he knows anymore.'

Jimmy smiled back and tried to pull her focus back to their nice wee lunch. He looked through the menu and clearly tried to hold his tongue about the prices.

'What was the story with that guy?'

Kat was still thinking about Jack and what might have happened to him. 'Who?'

'Ryan,' Jimmy replied sternly.

'The metal detectors, Sunday afternoon. What's the story with him then?'

Kat realised that needed a bit of explanation too, but before she could launch into it the waiter in a shirt and tie came over. 'Are you guys ready?'

Kat looked at Jimmy and Jimmy looked at Kat and then Kat asked for five more minutes.

As the waiter walked off, Kat tried to explain.

'Well, Ryan lost a ring. Which he was going to propose to Susan with. In fact, Ryan threw away the ring and, well, he told the group. And we'd offered to help him find it.'

Kat could see Jimmy's brain working quicker than his reply.

'So the group is helping him find the ring that he threw away?'

Kat listened back to Jimmy's interpretation and realised the missing elements, she tried again.

'Sorry. Ryan bought the ring to propose to Susan but Susan ended things with him before he got a chance to. He threw the ring into the sea when he was upset, here in South Queensferry, and now he is trying to get it back.'

Jimmy looked up from his menu.

'He threw it into the sea and he's back looking along the beach, is he dense or whit?'

'Yeah, the daft eejit was feeling upset. He regrets it now.'

Jimmy looked at Kat blankly. 'And were you helping him look for it?'

Kat felt herself blush as she looked around the empty restaurant.

'Yeah, I came down and gave him a hand, but to no avail.'

Jimmy looked decidedly unimpressed.

'So he's now coming down himself? Was no one else daft enough to give the sad cunt a hand? Just you?'

'Noooo,' said Kat, 'my friend Agnes came down to give him a help as well. Why are you getting so annoyed?'

Jimmy folded up his menu and threw it down on the table, clearly becoming agitated with a story he couldn't quite grasp.

'So, let me get this right, you're coming down here to search for the boys engagement ring whilst everybody else doesn't actually bother.' Kat nodded.

'That's a bit weird is it no? Do you no think?'

The waiter came back to take their order. Jimmy ordered the steak whilst Kat opted for the crayfish macaroni, and as they told the waiter what they wanted they didn't give off a hint of the agitation they were both feeling. As soon as the waiter delivered their drinks, the two of them got back to their conversation.

'So what about the deid pervert, what's his story?'

Kat looked over the bridges and towards the Forth. She pictured her and Ryan laughing as they walked along the beach each Sunday.

'He wasn't a pervert.' She snapped.

Jimmy stopped chewing his steak and looks at Kat.

'You'd said he was up tae all sorts, does that no make um a pervert then?'

Kat was still looking out the window when Jimmy gripped his cutlery and booted her shin under the table. 'What is out that fucking window? I'm just out the fucking jail and you've been fucking about with perverts and jumping about with some geek metal detecting!?! I'll tell you whit, you can apologise now or I'll head out there and volley the geek cunt alright. All right? Did ye fucking hear me? There will be no more fucking metal detecting or blubbering on about your pervert pals.'

Jimmy grabbed her arm and held it against the table, staring at her as she winced and mouthed an apology. They both continued with their lunch in silence.

35

Route Sixty-Seven

Derek was stood at the baggage carousel, still not entirely sure if this was the right one but reassured by the presence of the family that he'd seen boarding the flight several hours, earlier in Los Angeles. He looked down and patted his stomach, which was slightly protruding over his trousers.

'Those burgers catch up with you eventually Mr Horn' Patricia mentioned, catching his brief moment of self-analysis.

Derek sighed.

'Looks like it, but they were just too tasty.'

Patricia laughed as Derek sighed again and leaned against a pillar before staring forlornly at the rubber flaps where the cases, he was willing to appear, eventually would.

Derek knew Patricia was far more patient. That was just one of the many reasons he needed her in his life. Every instance he'd be ready to flare up, she'd be there to talk him back down and round.

Ever since young Tiger had a fibral convulsion, when he was just a toddler. Patricia saved Tiger that night, in Derek's eyes. Despite what the consultant had to say at the hospital later. Patricia was the one who'd wait, analyse and then act, Derek had always been far more impetuous.

'What do they do with the bags?' Gasped Derek exasperatedly.

'It took them long enough to get us off the plane and then for us to walk through the maze, that is this airport. The bags should be here already!

This is supposed to be business class.' Scoffed Derek, loud enough so that someone could here, not anyone in particular, just someone.

Patricia leaned in, towards him, smiled knowingly and gave him a hug as she reassured him that they wouldn't be long.

'Where's that carefree Derek that threw caution to the wind and took me on the trip of a lifetime?' Is he gone already?'

Derek hugged Patricia back and kissed her on the lips. Resting his hands on her hips and resisting the temptation to grab her bum. Patricia had put on a bit of weight too, but unlike Derek's protruding gut, it was working for her. Big time, he thought.

A siren buzzed and the conveyer belt jolted into action. Derek broke off from their hug before, yet another inexplicable delay ensued. Finally, their cases began to appear in fits and starts.

Derek watched as they individually made their entrance and then he followed them like a hawk. Eager to catch each on the first circulation, as if they might return to the abyss and be lost into the annals of Edinburgh Airport forever.

Edinburgh Airport was far smaller than Los Angeles and the fervent service culture they'd become accustomed to in America, now too severely lacking. They had been greeted by a grunt at security without so much as a 'have a nice day'. Derek had commented that they could take a leaf out of the Americans book for service twice already and they'd only been landed forty-five minutes.

Once Derek had collected the cases, counter checked them and then balanced them all on a trolley which Patricia had steadied for them. They made their way through nothing to declare.

Patricia was still chatting over the burger joints they'd habited over the past week.

Initially their trip had been Derek's usual overpowering show of wealth and continued attempts to dissuade any suggestion that this trip had been done on any sort of budget or shoestring. That was until one night, whilst they travelled along Route 66 and misjudged their timings. Both starving hungry, they'd been forced to pull into a traditional American diner somewhere in Arizona. Initially they felt like they'd walked into a fifties b movie set and when the waitress, fully decked in garish pink, stood hand on hip and chewed gum whilst collecting their order; They hadn't hoped for much. But the burger and fries they'd had that night were amazing. 'A culinary delight.' Derek had tried to remark to the same waitress who'd came to check on their meal mid-bite.

'What yall saying?'

'A culinary delight' Derek tried again.

'Yall gonna have to try English Mr, I aint sure what language you think you be talking'.

Eventually Derek adopted a fake American accent and provided her with a solid:

'These burger patties are damn awesome little lady'.

The waitress sparked into recognition.

'Well that's great to hear. Thanks for eating at Red Flames yall'.

After she waltzed off. Patricia was still laughing, like proper laughing. Derek hadn't made her laugh like that for years. As a result, he wasn't ready to give up on his accent, in fact he was already growing attached to making Patricia laugh all over again.

'I aint sure my pants won't burst with these mighty fine burgers you got here mam'.

Patricia was playfully asking him to stop but he was hooked.

'I aint stopping till the you be back in that trailer park pretty lady. When I'm through with this fine patty I'm gonna get started on that fine ass mam'.

Patricia tried to quieten him down as the waitress approached again. Derek in full yanky doodle and dandy flow.

'This is the finest damn burger joint this side of Mississippi mam. Could I trouble you for another glass of this mighty sweet beverage?'

Coming right up' confirmed the waitress, who's name appeared to be Shirelle according to the small talk she subsequently shared with Patricia.

After that night the trip took a change of pace. Derek relaxed and the more Derek relaxed, the more Patricia had laughed. It had been one of many funny happy moments they shared. And the sex they had in the RV was, Derek thought to himself, the most impressive performance he'd put in since he was in his twenties. Aided and abetted somewhat by his alter ego Bob whose persona he drifted into more often than he was Derek since that night in the burger joint.

As they stood and waited for James to collect them at the airport car park. Patricia had pulled out a wide brim cowboy hat which they'd picked up on one of their many stops along the route, which did the trick and Bob resurfaced yet again.

James pulled up in the same large black people carrier which had dropped them off a few weeks earlier. James had been a bit taken aback by Derek's cowboy hat and even more surprised when Derek confirmed this 'aint no city cab' before Patricia smiled at James knowingly. They all helped load the cases back into the boot, or the trunk as Derek described it.

Derek happily chatted away whilst James moaned about the parking charges at the airport and described how he'd sat waiting to hear from them to then minimise the absurd fees which had been recently introduced. The car weaved through Edinburgh on its way along to Morningside.

Derek turned back towards Patricia when the noise of the cobbled roads and the more comfortable surroundings of Morningside greeted them. Morningside was a village before the city swallowed it up, fiercely retaining its distinction through its inhabitant's insistence that they lived in Morningside rather than Edinburgh.

The car turned into the street and carefully edged along their driveway until they arrived at the front door. Derek and Patricia's home was an immaculately presented Victorian Villa with stunning period features and a huge arched front door, which had only really used for greeting guests.

Patricia asked James to take them further along the drive and nearer to the side entrance, suggesting that it might be more practical for them to avoid the steps and drop the heavy cases directly into the utility room. James duly obliged.

Derek left the car as James unloaded the cases and Patricia remarked that arranging the cleaner to come in yesterday had been a wise move and that, judging by the bags adjacent to the bins, Tiger had enjoyed the liberty of his first lengthy stint home alone.

Derek lugged each of the cases into the side doorway and placed them neatly alongside one another in their spacious utility room. Patricia made off into the house to check on Tiger and returned to find Derek in the kitchen slumped against the kitchen island.

'What's up Derek?' she asked.

Derek had been picking up messages and emails, which he'd purposefully avoided during their time away. He'd had bad news and wasn't ready for it. He welled up as Patricia approached him again.

'What is it honey? Has something happened?

Derek was nodding but unable to get his words out. Eventually he started to cry and Patricia held him tight until he eventually managed to find his voice and explain what had happened.

'It's Jack, the chap from the groups I'd been attending. He's passed away unexpectedly'.

Patricia was consoling him tenderly. Chatting through with him what might have happened tentatively.

Derek brushed away his tears and took in a big gulp of air before he then exhaled up and into his fringe.

'His poor family and friends. He was only young; he could have only been mid 40s at most'.

Patricia suggested that he get in touch with Dave and then reminded Derek that it was Monday and that he could probably make the group if he felt able. Derek paused for a second, looked at Patricia and thought to himself that he loved her more than he ever had in his full life. She was the nicest person he'd ever known as well as his best friend.

He gave her a hug and agreed that he should go along, before suggesting that he venture out and collect burgers for them to have for tea tonight.

36

Unraveling

Kat and Jimmy hadn't spoken for two days. Katrina had gone back to work and now she felt herself race to get back home each night, just to endure more silent treatment. She parked her car and hurried up the stairs to the flat. She'd lived as a prison widower too long she thought to herself. Jimmy was right; She'd stop attending the group, then she'd sell the ring, she thought to herself, they could make a new start together.. She opened the latch and called out to Jimmy.

'Hello!' Jimmy was quiet. 'Are you there Jimmy?'

'Yeah, I'm here. What the fuck's with all the excitement? Happy with yourself are you?'

Kat took off her scarf as she wandered through to the living room, talking as she walked 'Well, I've been thinking about it, and you're right I'll stop with the group and we can make a new start together from here.' Jimmy rolled his eyes but still offered her the chance to share her plan. Kat was slightly taken aback. 'Well, if you're going to be like that, then I'll not tell you,' she said teasingly.

Jimmy was having none of it. 'Oh well, nothing new there. You never told me about your secret group for 11years and now you can't keep it to yourself for five minutes.'

Kat felt his words with the manner he intended. 'And what do you mean by that Jimmy McGovern?' she asked. Jimmy had re-opened the fight he was spoiling for. He narrowed his eyes and screwed up his face as he looked up at her.

'I mean if you can keep all that to yourself for so long. What else have you been doing behind my back whilst I've been in the fucking jail?'

Kat was hurt, but defiantly she continued. 'Jimmy. That was the only company I had some weeks. I kept my distance and waited for you all that time. Never once did I miss a visiting time. How dare you, you can sleep on the couch tonight.'

Jimmy rose to his feet. 'Nah, I think you'll find if anybody is sleeping on my couch, it'll be you, if I let you.'

Kat recoiled before biting back, 'Your couch went to the tip 10 years ago, along with all the other rubbish you left me with. I've paid for, decorated, and looked after this place myself. Building a home for us.'

Jimmy walked close to her. 'Living rent free for 11 years at my expense more like. Entertaining anyone that'd give you half a look from your daft wee group.' Jimmy marched past her into the bedroom and slammed the door.

Sounness looked startled and climbed up on the arm of the sofa as if to encourage Kat to sit down. She was stunned, she spun around and flung the door back open, Sounness bounced quickly off the arm of the sofa and back to safety. She stood in the doorway and looked towards Jimmy who was laid on the bed. 'Does that make you a big man because you can slam a door? Does that make you feel good about yourself?'

Jimmy sat up in the bed and scowled at her. 'Do you no take a fucking hint? Do you know what makes me feel good about myself? Knowing that I'll no be taken for a fucking mug by a daft cow who runs off to her singles group. Sizing up your next ride after mourning your last are you?' Kat looked at Jimmy indignantly before Jimmy carried on. 'Aye. Just as I thought. Gutted you'll no have that dirty wee cunt running about after you anymore aren't you? Do you know what? I'm glad one of they fuckers is deed or I'd have done it myself. I can do another 11 years nae bother. I'd be as well in there, the way you carry on.'

Kat started to cry. She couldn't hide the emotion anymore and began pleading with Jimmy to see sense. She felt as if her Jimmy had slipped away and been replaced by this monster in front of her, as if he was possessed. 'Why are you being like this? Has something happened?'

'Has something happened? You're asking me? I had a wee search through your room and found your pals ring and your record player with the wee card. You've had a fair bit interest whilst I've been incarcerated, haven't you? And I bet that's only the half off it.' Jimmy flung over her empty bag onto the floor and held the ring up in front of her. 'Get yourself tae fuck out of my house.'

Kat knelt to pick up her bag, she was staring at the discarded contents before looking up at Jimmy. 'I can't believe you'd do that.'

Jimmy stood up from the bed and began shouting loudly, more animated. 'You can't believe what I'd do? When you've been fucking dating half that fucking school where you work. Lapping up perverts stories and loving your wee beach trips with the geeky cunt!?!??'

Kat shook her head, and her body trembled with upset as she looked up through her tears at ... Jimmy. Was this even Jimmy? 'I don't need to explain myself. If you were interested in the truth, you'll see how much my heart ached for you, for 11 years. And all I'd waited for this?'

'Nah you got what you were waiting for the minute I walked through the door and then you couldn't wait to get back to your dating group again' replied Jimmy. 'Do you know what. You can get tae fuck. Fuck off round to Ryan's house or anyone of they cunts that want on next, that's if they haven't already.'

Kat made her way to the cupboard and pulled out her large suitcase. she laid it on the bed and started piling her clothes into it. Jimmy continued baiting her as she laid her clothes in the case.

'That's it get your stuff and get to fuck. Ya Fenian whore, fuck off back to Ireland. My pals were right about you.'

Kat tried to ignore his jibes, continuing to fill the case with her belongings, almost randomly. Once filled, she zipped up the case and pulled it off the bed. She grabbed her coat and rewrapped her scarf around her. Jimmy was in the kitchen, but he came back through before she could get to the door.

'Where are you going to go with that?' he asked.

Katrina ignored him. He seemed to now realise she was serious. His tone shifted. 'Kat. I'm sorry. I got carried away, ah mean I've been in jail and you're wanting to head along to your group. It wound me up, I love you.'

Kat looked up at him, a tear still in her eye. 'And I love you Jimmy McGovern. More than you could ever know, now can you get out of my way?'

Jimmy stood firm. Kat tried to squeeze past him. He kicked the case back into the hallway.

'Jimmy,' she cried. 'Will you just let me go?'

Jimmy pushed her back towards the wall, leaned into her face and sneered menacingly. 'You're no leaving here tonight.'

Katrina pushed back and wrestled past him, making her way for the door. But Jimmy ran after her, then pushed her against the door as she tried to open it. The force made her face collide with the door and her nose burst on impact. Katrina screamed in horror. 'Jimmy!! What have you done? I'm phoning the police.' Blood dripped along the carpet as Kat held her nose trying to stem the blood. The front of her pink jacket was immediately drenched as her upper lip began to swell.

'Katrina. I'm sorry doll, I'm so sorry. I was trying to close the door. I just didn't want you to leave. Dinnae phone the polis, they'll put me back inside. We can sort this out, I love you.'

Katrina went to the bathroom, and before cleaning anything or trying to stem the blood she looked in the mirror at her face. Jimmy was stood at the door watching her, full of remorse. He began to cry. 'I didn't want any of this to happen. I just didn't want you to go to that fucking group.'

'Jimmy. You've smashed up my face, ruined my jacket and all you can think about is your fragile ego and your daft jealousy for nothing. This isn't what I want, none of it.' She bristled, blood still dripping from her nose in the bathroom. Jimmy approached her and rolled some toilet roll up with his hand and began to catch the spots of blood, slowly gaslighting her as he dabbed her face.

'You've caught yourself a beauty there. Here let me get you some ice.'

Katrina sat on the toilet whilst Jimmy went to get her some ice. He wrapped it in a tea towel and brought it with a basin.

'I'm sorry, Katrina. I love you, I really do.'

Kat looked up at him as he patted her swollen nose.

'I loved you too.'

She took Jimmy's hand away from her face and left the bathroom. She picked up the ring from the kitchen worktop and turned to him.

'But I'm better than this. No one has the right to treat anyone like this. We're finished Jimmy. I will not ever love you like I did, you've changed and to be honest. I wish you were still in jail.'

Jimmy followed her, wrestling her case off her at the top of the stairs. But she continued without it. He howled at the top of his voice and threw her case after her.

'Fucking Fenian whore, I've knew it all along.'

She drove for around an hour and ended up at South Queensferry again. She didn't know where else to go. Parked up looking over the bridges she suddenly worried about Sounness and Dana, but she knew she couldn't go back tonight. She started to think about Ryan, his disappointment when their walks finished, her own disappointment. She thought about Jack and how upset she was at his passing. The upset consumed her from inside, everything was too much. Her tears tasted salty on her swollen lip. From nowhere she realised it was Monday. She was going to call Dave back. The RA meeting would be on tonight and she wasn't waiting for Jimmy McGovern ever again.

37

Week Eleven - Ryan's week

Rather than waiting outside, Ryan bound through the front doors of the Trinity Centre and headed straight into the waiting area. He opened the door and sat down in the reception area by himself. He hadn't been sure if anyone was going to arrive when Stirling swung through the door

'Alright Ryan?' he asked as he sat down.

'I wasn't sure if we'd all be here tonight. I just thought I'd take the chance that someone might be here.'

'I was just sat wondering if anyone else would come along too. I wasn't even sure if I wanted anyone else to, because I don't know what to say. It just doesn't seem real that Jack's not here, I mean it's Jack.'

Stirling sighed. 'I know man. That's about all I've had to say for about a week now.'

Both sat in silence, listening as Sensei Jamieson brought his class to a halt, the floors squeaking as the class hurriedly gathered their belongings and joined the exit line.

Ryan and Stirling lifted their heads as the door opened and the class made their way out. Sensei Jamieson's voice bellowing out the instructions for next week until he reached the doorway. 'Oh hello guys. Sorry I didn't know you were here. Sorry to hear about your friend. I heard the other day from Tony. What a shame for Jack, he was a real character and a big miss for everyone.'

Ryan and Stirling stood up. Kevin patted Stirling's arm as he made his way into the hall.

Ryan sighed before announcing wearily that he supposed they better get started and began pulling out the chairs from their stacks. Stirling followed Ryan's lead nervously before asking,

'No Dave tonight?'

'Yeah. He couldn't face it, yet. He'd asked me to step in. I thought getting together might help some of us. Obviously not Dave, but everyone has their ways of coping.'

Ryan kept up with Stirling, laying out the chairs for the group. He felt a lump fill in his throat as he debated whether to lay out a seat for Jack, croaking as he tried to explain to Stirling what he was thinking. Stirling burst into tears. Katrina had arrived just as Ryan was consoling him. Ryan gave Katrina a look which she immediately understood was enquiring about her face, she shook her head and left him to settle Stirling. Stirling composed himself and then upset himself all over again as he tried to explain why he'd got upset in the first place. Ryan just patted his back.

'It's fine, here take a seat and I'll finish laying these out.'

Ryan stood back from the circle and watched as Stirling sat down before he looked over at Katrina. What had happened to her face, he thought. He waved almost in apology. Katrina moved over to Stirling's side, rubbing his arm, and whispered along in agreement. 'It's so sad. It's okay to cry, don't worry. There's nothing to apologise for.' Stirling looked up at her 'Thanks Kat. But what's happened to your face? Are you okay?' Kat hushed him quiet.

'Don't you worry about me. I'll be fine'.

Tony arrived soon after, walking in with Lucy who'd clearly been upset too.

She took one look at the circle and burst into tears. 'I knew this was a mistake. He should be here! I just hoped it was all a nightmare and he'd be here. A horrific bad dream. I can't take that it's not!' Tony grabbed her and gave her a hug. Derek arrived and quietly sidestepped them as he came through the doors, looking around the room and politely smiling and tried his best to say sorry without speaking. Lucy breathed in and brushed her hair back before sniffing up some of her upset, enough to grab herself a seat.

Ryan stood up in front of the room. Looking round everyone as he began to address them. 'Hello everyone. I better begin by letting you know that Dave won't make it along tonight. He didn't think he was able to, not tonight, and I must admit I'm beginning to understand why.' Ryan took a deep breath and had another look around the room. 'I'm sorry. This is tough. I've sat with a distant stare for days now, a distant stare into nothing. I've just tried to understand why. Why is it that the one person who gave me hope or the sense that confidence would help me, is gone? How can this happen to the luckiest person in the room? He was a winner, and I wanted to be winning. Is this it? Can no one get lucky? I was thinking it was just me. Does life just snatch it all back when you think you're eventually winning? Jack gave me inspiration. Inspiration to try, to try again at love, at life even. To put it out there and not be transfixed about the fear of rejection or failing or even falling, in love with someone again. I couldn't do what Jack did in his life, I'm not charming enough or funny enough or even brave enough but the way he put himself out there, sort of, let me believe I could do it, a tiny bit. That was never discussed in the group here, but it was how I seen him and how he helped me. And now he's not here.' Ryan looked as if he was resurfacing for air as he took another deep breath and his eyes filled with tears. He sat down as Katrina leaned over and held his hand.

'Well done,' she mouthed. Ryan looked closely at her battered face. He went to ask again, before she pointed to Lucy who was sobbing quietly.

Ryan, a bit more composed, addressed the room again.

'Let's try and give some support to everyone in the room, for our benefit and for Jack. Grief is truly painful. Katrina, are you okay to share with the group? Anything from your week or memories or thoughts about Jack, whatever helps you.'

Ryan only realised that he'd still been holding Katrina's hand when she slipped hers away to begin her check in.

'You'll all be wondering why I'm sporting a red nose and a fat lip. And I have to tell you all firstly that I'm fine. I could sit and tell you all that I'd fell and bumped into a door, because that's almost what happened. But I'm hurt because Jimmy pushed me. He pushed me and threatened me, he's kicked me and abused me. I've realised that prison had kept me safe from a man who's mask I'd never been with long enough to see slip '

Ryan was furious. He could feel his blood boiling inside as he continued to watch her speaking.

She explained why she'd come back tonight and how Jimmy's jealousy about the group had been a real eye opener for her, whilst Jack's untimely passing proved the catalyst for her to realise that life is really too short. A lesson she wished she'd learned a long time before.

Ryan felt himself watching her, impressed by her grace - even amidst such a personal and physical challenge with Jimmy. Katrina continued with her check-in.

'The hurt I'd felt as soon as I'd heard that Jack had passed was totally crushing. It wasn't until that very moment that I realised how much of a special bond we all have here, trying to watch out for each other as we deal with the most important of all our emotions.'

Ryan picked up her hand again as she continued to talk with the group.

'I never realised how important these groups were for me and even when I felt like I would sacrifice them. Which, I'm sorry to say, I'd decided to do. I knew it felt wrong. It felt wrong to turn away from my emotions which were hurting for Jack as much as it felt wrong to have the emotions I had for someone else so carelessly discarded, mocked and questioned. I'm sorry that I nearly gave up on you all for someone who didn't even appreciate my love.'

'The sudden vacuum I felt, as soon as I heard about Jack, hit me hard. It's been a tough week but I'm happy to be here with you all tonight.'

Ryan thanked Katrina for her lovely sentiment as he looked towards Stirling who looked broken. Ryan softly asked him if he thought he was able to say a few words too.

'I will try Ryan. As Katrina and yourself have both said. It hurts so bad, and seeing his friends outside his flat last week. I mean, I don't think they can even understand that he'd affected us all as much as them. I've sat with

Jack right into the very small hours and shared a lot of personal insight and despite everyone having this view of Jack always being involved with these mad antics. The one thing that he always was, was a good guy. And that doesn't even sound enough, but when it came down to the crunch, regardless of the situation and in any situation. Jack was a good man.'

'He was indeed that,' Ryan agreed. But then it was time for Lucy. She had looked unwell since she came in, her eyes flickering and looking faint. He asked her if she was okay, again.

At first she said she wasn't sure. Not sure is she was okay. Not sure if she should because she felt so guilty. Then she snapped back at herself loudly. 'Selfish even!.'

Ryan reminded Lucy that she didn't have to share if she felt uncomfortable.

Lucy let out a painful wail. Then started muttering randomly. Katrina rushed over to console her as she began crying violently. Kat produced a hanky which Lucy blew into. Catching a brief moment of lucidity, she began to try again.

'I feel really guilty; me and Jack spent a night together and I found myself hoping it as something more. I'd text him and not heard back and I'd assumed that he'd patched me. I thought the worst of him and I can't stop crying about that. I mean what does that make me, thinking ill of the dead when they aren't even dead yet.'

'Take your time,' Ryan said.

Stirling put a hand on her thigh.

'How many times have I got to tell you. You can't beat yourself up for liking the guy and that was it. I done the very same. I was texting him but assumed he was having more fun somewhere else. You were upset because you liked him and that's nothing to be ashamed or feel guilty about.'

'Because ultimately that's what your actions meant,' Ryan added. 'You liked him and you were hurt because he ... he never got the chance to let you know he liked you back.'

'And I'll tell you whit. He did tell me too. He came and saw me afterwards and said he had an amazing night. He was buzzing.' Confirmed Stirling.

Lucy began crying again, eventually settling back into her check-in.

253

'Thanks guys. I think I've been focusing on that part to stop myself looking stupid for being this upset because I liked him. I'd spent one night with him and I read a lot more into it, hoping that maybe he did too. The fact that I'll never know what could have been, I just don't know.' She shrugged as she appeared to give up on the turmoil for a second.

Katrina was next to try and appease Lucy. Ryan listened as her beautiful Irish voice curled around every syllable. 'That's it Lucy, you just don't know. No one else knows apart from Jack and you and the four walls. Whatever happened there happened to you both and whatever it was, well it went on for as long as it possibly could. You cared about him and he cared about you. You make decisions about someone in an instant, and it's only you that know that yourself. I know that, I've made one tonight.'

Lucy confirmed that she really did as she leaned quietly back into her seat. Ryan was happy that she seemed placated from her guilt. He'd asked Katrina if she'd like to say a few words, secretly revelling in her tone. He could listen to her all day he thought.

'I was just thinking much along the same lines with what you were saying earlier. In this setting you really draw inspiration and support from the group. I loved Jack's stories, I have to say I looked forward to them a lot more than anyone else's.'

Ryan caught himself watching her as she finished up. Coughing himself back into the room, he followed up with a few words of his own in an attempt at disguising his doe eyes, quickly suggesting that they all loved Jack's stories. He described how they were other worldly, like a film happening but in real life. They gave them all that hope or that notion that there could be more to life, not necessarily a lesbian tryst on the hotel floor or a swingers party but just that unknown element of life, which Jack embraced.

Katrina summarised this as the joie de vivre. But Ryan never knew what that meant.

Ryan wasn't sure if he'd ever seen Derek not wearing a suit before, he looked incredibly relaxed he thought to himself, before realising that this was just in contrast to usual Derek.

When Ryan asked if he would like to speak, he immediately apologised with his hands raised. His maroon v neck and chino's belied his suntan.

'Sorry it doesn't feel right sharing any good news amidst the past week's events so I'd just wanted to sit in the background, When I first heard I knew I wanted to come along, for all the reasons Katrina mentioned earlier. I'll probably save the vacation stories for another day. We've more important things to catch up on this week.'

Ryan was pleased, but then felt guilty for feeling pleased about Derek not wanting to share his holiday memories tonight.

'I totally understand Derek but you did say some good news there and well if there is anything we could all be doing with is good news. Again, no pressure, but if you can give us a snippet? Would the rest of the group be okay with that.'

Derek almost appeared bashful as the rest of the group encouraged him further.

'Well, the trip went really well and myself and Patricia eventually renewed our vows at the end of our trip. Right there in the little chapel in Las Vegas, ceremony conducted by the Elvis reincarnate himself. We had a lovely trip, the motorhome was amazing and all the stops, sights and ...it was just amazing. Really was the trip of a lifetime, with the love of my lifetime. I'll bore you all with the photos and more details at another time but that's how it went!'

Ryan thanked Derek for sharing his good news and was surprised when the room managed a spontaneous round of applause which he half-halfheartedly joined in with.

Derek was raising his hand stopping Ryan before he moved on, suggesting he did have another story which he thought might be worth sharing.

'Jack called me out for parking in the disabled bay,' he said and leaned forward.

'It was my first week at Romantics Anonymous, and he was arriving just as I was running late. I pulled up and parked in the bay before I hopped out the car and offered Jack a "Hello." Jack's said to me. "Alright chief, your blue badge seems to have falling off the window there.'

Derek's Jack impression was funny enough on its own thought Ryan as he wondered what Derek actually thought he sounded like.

'So I then replied, the only badge I need is the one on the front. That lets me park wherever I need. Jack then approached the front of the vehicle, before he studiously looked at the badge and then looked back up at me before asking how small it was then? I countered enquiring what did he mean and pointed, "there's the badge on the front."'

'He then said, "Aye, you've got your small cock badge on the front I was just wondering how small it was to be classified as a disability?"'

The room broke into reluctant laughter. As Derek mustered a chortle which brimmed with his own self-satisfaction.

'Called me well there I thought, after a while. But I never gave up parking there. You see, I didn't want to acknowledge my defeat, particularly to Jack and his lurid tales of swingers clubs and such like. It was still awkward for the first few weeks before I realised I'd met more than my match. Jack didn't care who you thought you were and as Stirling said, Jack was a good man. Who transcended all levels. A top chap indeed.'

Ryan was pleased that Derek had lightened the tone and hoped that the group could have taken the opportunity to share some of the lighter moments of Jack's life, but he was still filled with some trepidation for what Tony could be about to say.

Tony launched right into his weekly check-in, not ever being one to stand on ceremony.

'I'd really just like to echo most of what's been said already. Just like Del Boy said there, Jack never had any change in the way he dealt with anyone or anything, after everything that has happened this year. I remember him asking me about Kevin just the exact same way we'd have spoken about his or my attempted exploits at a sex life previously. Deadly serious, one day he caught up with me in the car park, he said "Tony I've been meaning to ask are guys better at blow jobs?" I said who's going first like, me or you.'

Tony went on to describe how Jack seemed to qualify his thesis on the basis that men knew better what men were looking for. In much the same fashion that we give ourselves the best wank. Jack had then stopped for a second to think before warning Tony that 'Big Kev could rip the heid clean off it, with they big karate hands' before giving a quick demo of Jack's best karate chop.

"Must be like getting a wank of off Wreck it Ralph."'

Tony looked emotional despite the light tone to his story, clearly catching a lump in his throat as he described how he was 'still laughing when I got home, but to me that meant a lot. You know that he was just the same, it really didn't matter to him who I was riding. '

Ryan stood up cagily, as if he was too small for the space in front of him. He nervously bounced as he apologised for not following the usual format. 'I thought this might have been the best for everyone.'

Katrina was first to thank him as she looked up at him affectionately. 'I would just like to say well done you, tonight couldn't have been easy and you've handled it brilliantly.'

The rest of the group offered their own thanks and then started to pack up. But then Lucy, who'd been quietly staring into space since her break down, suddenly sparked into life.

'Wait, wait, wait. Can I have a just a minute to say something?' she asked.

Ryan retook his seat and assured her it was fine whilst he encouraged the rest of the room to return to their seats too with a wave of his hands.

'I just wanted to add that Jack lived his life to the fullest he could, every adventure, every misadventure, every half chance to get the best out of his life he tried and that's a real inspiring legacy to leave for us all. And well, hearing how he's called things out and been congratulated for this has me contemplating calling something that has bothered me, and I don't know why but ... Aww I just don't want to blurt it out.'

'Thanks Lucy,' Ryan said, 'we've all been sharing stories about how Jack was but that doesn't mean we need to change who we are. But if you have something on your mind and feel that Jack's inspired you to share then go for it.'

And she did.

'Well a few weeks ago. I mean. Now, I know that you and Katrina have been searching for a pink diamond ring and, well, I met Katrina a few weeks back and we had a coffee and something fell out her bag. Have you got something

257

to tell Ryan, Katrina?'

'About my bag?' Katrina said, biting down on her thumb. Ryan couldn't work out what they were saying. His mouth hung open, ready to speak, but couldn't quite put the words together.

'No Kat not about your bag.... about your search. About the ring that you are still looking for... the platinum pink diamond ring?'

Ryan's confusion turned to panic as he realised the strong inference of Lucy's questioning. He turned to Kat himself. 'What is actually happening? Do you know something about the ring Kat?'

Katrina looked deep in thought. She looked at Lucy and suddenly she went from chewing on her fingers to smiling. A weight seemed to be lifted. 'Thanks Lucy and, in some way I think I have to say thanks to Jack too and to you Ryan, obviously' and Maybe an apology as well but first please won't you let me explain.'

She stood up from her chair and turned towards Ryan.

'I've loved every minute of your company Ryan Alexander, you are the kindest sweetest, most considerate man I didn't even know existed. You're not trying to get anything, you are the most selfless and sweetest hearted person I've ever met. Now Lucy's right. I do have something to tell you...'

She stopped for a minute, before taking a few steps towards him.

'The very first week we went searching, as you tidied up our names scrawled out in the sand, my friend Agnes, who had all the beach combing kit found your ring. She dropped it in my hand and I asked her to leave it with me. I got it cleaned initially, and then we went again, and then we went looking again and I loved your company so much that I thought if I give him this ring it'll all be over. So, I've kept it in my bag and pondered how I would tell you and now I've decided I'll tell you this way.

Katrina dropped to her knee and produced Ryan's platinum pink diamond ring from her closed hand. She looked up at Ryan, who had remained almost transfixed throughout the last five minutes unsure about where his misfortune would turn this time. Her eyes caught his and with them locked on each other she asked him 'Ryan Alexander will you marry me?'

Ryan looked down at her with tears in his eyes. 'You want to marry me?

Are you sure?

'Yes' shouted Katrina but it's me down on one knee here asking you, you bloody eejit. Will you marry me?'

'Yes. Of course, I will. Right away if you want. Right now in fact.'

The two of them embraced on the floor in a hug and a kiss, before they enormity of what had happened seemed to hit Ryan and he climbed back onto his seat. Katrina held his hand. Ryan looked at his engagement ring, before looking at her hand and pulled it up to his face to kiss it and then with his other hand slid on the engagement ring.

The group were cheering and wailing. There was tears and laughter, there were spontaneous bouts of laughing tears and even more hugs. They gathered around the two of them, congratulating them both. Lucy sat back down, not even sure if what happened just happened.

The rest of the group returned to their seats in what felt like an anti-climax. Ryan turned to Lucy and thanked her for sharing before talking to the group 'Well who knew that one of the saddest days times and days of my life would become one of my happiest. Thanks to all of you for sharing this week, I never thought it would ever work out like this but this week had been magical and I think Mr. Stewart will have had a hand in this one way or another.'

He looked up as if he was trying to tilt tears back into his head whilst talking to their dead friend.

'I genuinely hope you're up there I hope you're laughing at how I've royally fucked my first and only chance at chairing Romantics Anonymous by getting engaged in the circle of trust. I don't quite know how I'm going to tell Dave yet, but needless to say I don't think I'll be back in charge next week. I'm going to go and walk out with my fiancé and I hope to see you all next week when we can catch up again.'

Ryan took Katrina's hand and strode out the room. He got to reception before he turned to Katrina, 'Where do we go now? I mean whose car do we take?'

Katrina laughed at him, kissed him, and said, 'You take your car and I'll take mine. I'll follow you and we can go to yours. Please don't shit yourself this time!' She paused for a second. 'Listen I will need to get my things from Jimmy's flat, will you come with me? He's out of control and I'm a bit frightened.'

Ryan looked at her, put his arms around her shoulders and said to her that she will never feel like that again. She believed him.

Lucy and Stirling were still talking as they waved goodbye to Katrina and Ryan.

'Am I having some kind of hallucination?' Lucy asked.

'If you are,' Stirling said, it's good stuff.'

'I don't know what that was but I think I needed it,'

Stirling half shook his head and partially agreed, still bemused as to how they even got there. Derek left and patted Stirling on the back as he went, before giving Lucy a quick hug. Stirling laughed as Derek's Mercedes badge rolled into view.

'He did like you by the way,' Stirling said to Lucy. 'He might not have proposed to you in front of a room full of romantic addicts but you never know. He maybe would have.'

Lucy smiled. 'Thanks Stirling. If you need to talk, just give me a call anytime.'

She thought she caught the tail end of a shooting star and turned to see no one else was there to see it but felt as if someone else did.

38

So Close Yet So Faro

Stevie walked out onto the apartment terrace. Millie and him checked into Club Albufeira and hired a black BMW convertible for their stay. Their plan was to have a few days chill together. It had been a while since they'd had some time, just the pair of them. Stevie agreed to stop using and had a longer-term plan to stop dealing. He'd told Millie it wasn't just as simple as stopping, he'd need to find another source of income, for a start. Millie pretended to understand. She was just delighted to have her Stevie back, her proper Stevie. Not one continually wrapped up in everyone else's plans, who needed what and who needing paying, or who needed dealt with. Millie told Stevie this was the only way they'd get back together and Stevie had accepted, stopped taking gear and stopped drinking that same day.

Now, 24 days in, he was beginning to feel the benefit, his appetite had recovered fully and he was loving his food. 'Where are we eating tonight?' He called through to Millie. 'Are you okay with the old town tonight?'

Millie was busy getting herself ready, she was enjoying every minute wrapped up in Stevie's company with no distractions. She'd even gave him a blow job on their first night, and they'd ended up falling between two single beds while having sex afterwards. They paused only to take breath before Stevie finished her off on the floor.

Millie called back through. 'What about that place at the front of the strip, sea foody place?'

Stevie was delighted he'd dropped enough hints about the seafood and fish rice dish that she'd finally relented. 'Great. Should be fine to walk up. We can have a walk around the square first.' Stevie walked into the apartment and grabbed one of the non-alcoholic Sagres from the fridge. 'Are you wanting anything?'

Millie shook her head. 'How's that?' she asked, pouting and posing in Stevie's direction. 'Gorgeous,' replied Stevie.

* * *

Stevie was still getting to grips with the convertible roof. It was automatic, but the directions were in what he thought was Portuguese, he'd already worried it'd become stuck midway between open and closed a few times. He'd ran ahead to the car park to get it sorted, but when he arrived there was a deep gauge and a scrape along the sill of the bottom of the car. Stevie took a deep breath; he's looked at it several times, checking with his recall and then completed an elaborate spot the difference in his brain.

'What's up handsome?' Millie asked, sauntering up behind him.

Stevie's knelt down feeling the scrape on the bottom of the car.

'I've only gone and bumped the fucking car babe.'

Millie stood back and squinted, but it didn't take much to spot it.

'Oh, that looks bad, where did that happen?'

Stevie racked his brain. 'I dunno. Must have been on the way over from the airport.'

'It's not bad,' Millie consoled him. 'What do you think we should do?'

Stevie had already decided he'd be having his seafood dinner, and he wasn't delaying it for some car. 'I'll call them tomorrow. I'll tell them we've bumped it out here, we've got insurance but you need to tell them as soon as it happens, one of my pals Binny had a bump in Ibiza, he had left it till dropping the car back and that had voided his insurance. Ended up costing him three thousand pounds to get it all sorted.' Stevie climbed over the passenger seat, put down the roof, adjusted the radio until he heard Kiss FM and then, eventually, settled into the driver's seat. They then set off for dinner.

After dinner. Stevie and Millie walked hand in hand along the winding streets and down to the main square. They grabbed a seat in the old town and Millie had a few cocktails whilst Stevie enjoyed a few mocktails. A girl played acoustic covers in the street, whilst they had their drinks and they were eventually joined by an old couple from Bristol who insisted on buying them a round. Millie was so chuffed when Stevie continued his abstinence, even explaining to the barmaid how he was an idiot on the drink and better off without it. She then returned with a flavoured shot for them both, non-alcoholic for Stevie. They left after a good hour's people watching and grabbed an ice cream as they walked back up the hill towards the car. Several times along the way Stevie was asked, in an increasingly elaborate and less discrete manner, if he wanted drugs. Again, Millie flushed with pride as Stevie rejected their approaches.

'Can you imagine me doing that down Buchanan Street on a Friday afternoon Mills? I'd be huckled in 10 minutes. Brazen, I bet their stuff is shite tae.'

Stevie looked up at Millie who'd paused for a second.

'It's all shite like, but different standards of shite. My shite was the best shite. Their shite is just shite, shite.'

They'd reached the car and Stevie beeped the doors open and took another look at the damage on the sill before he jumped in the driver's seat waiting for Millie who watched the roof slowly retract. Millie climbed in and clicked in her seatbelt.

'Thank you,' Millie said. 'I've had a lovely night.'

Stevie winked before replying. 'I've had worse Saturdays.'

The next morning Stevie drove the car along to get fuel and as he travelled back, he searched the road trying to look for a potential crime scene, where he could confidently say that the car had been bumped. He found a sunken drain cover next to a roundabout off the Avenue de Ferreries. He drove close to have a look and then drove on, turning into the hotel and parking up before calling the hire company. He explained what had happened, being careful not to over-elaborate and checked his insurance was fully comp, which it was.

He parked up the car and returned to the apartment. Millie was waiting in the terrace. 'All sorted, babe,' he announced, arriving into their apartment and planting a kiss on the top of her head.

'Good. You feel better now?' she asked.

'Yeah' said Stevie. 'Feel like I'm 90% covered now.'

His phone buzzed and he'd received an email from them summarising his conversation with the added element of requiring a police record of the incident. Stevie didn't have a fond relationship with the police. He called the rental company. They confirmed he'd need to go to the police station with his documents to help create the record. Stevie sat for a moment and waited for Millie to react to his silence.

'What's up?' asked Millie eventually.

'The car hire company want us to go to the police station, I'm not sure I can go.'

Millie looked at him over her sunglasses. 'Why not?'

'After that trouble we had back at the flat, I'd been lifted and I didn't follow up. I think I might have a warrant out for me,' responded Stevie tentatively. He paused for a second and then followed up with, 'It's alright though. You're on the insurance too. Would you mind?'

'You're lucky I'm a good bird. Give me the forms.'

Stevie handed Millie the forms who then headed over to the police station.

She immediately realised she knew no Portuguese apart from 'Thanks' and that, that alone wouldn't be sufficient. She quickly googled a few phrases on her phone before addressing the guard at the desk, 'Pour la voca ingles.' The officer looked confused.

'Can you speak English please? He asked Millie.

Millie continued with her best, slowest English which was still a challenge for the Portuguese guards. She described the situation which Stevie had created and suggested that she needed a police report on account of the insurers advising her of no cover, hoping for a common enemy in the shape of an insurance company. By then there were several Portuguese officers in the main reception each looking Millie up and down and then checking the goings on with the duty sergeant who appeared frustrated with the story provided. Millie felt uncomfortable. They were insisting that officers would accompany her to the scene, and already Millie was thinking this would be a means of getting her to commit to his lie under oath and then incriminate herself when they later found the video footage, showing she hadn't even been driving the car never mind hitting the drain, the kerb or even got close to the side of the road. Millie's fears then began to drift as the three male officers accompanied her the short distance in their vehicle to the Avenue de Ferreries. They found the spot where Millie claimed the damage happened and then took some pictures. Millie sat in the back, not sure whether she was about to be raped or arrested. She was relieved when they all got back in the car and drove back to the station.

The duty sergeant looked over the photographs before completing the accident report for her.

Half an hour later, she bounced into the apartment. Stevie was in their room and hadn't noticed her come back. So, to try and scare him, she crept to their room where she could hear him breathing. When she came around the door, she saw he was going through her case.

'Ahem. Find anything interesting there?'

Stevie looked flustered, he blushed and closed the case before admitting that he'd been wanking in her dirty underwear. Millie shook her head.

'You're a total pervert. You should have been arrested for that never mind your crazy insurance effort.'

She handed Stevie the form, and he grabbed it off her, running his finger across each detail.

'Right that all looks in line. I've been thinking though, the excess is fifteen hundred euros. There's no way that damage will cost fifteen hundred euros. I've text Sami, he knows a few guys out here and one of them has said they'll fix it for a couple of hunner Euros.'

Millie looked up at Stevie. 'You mean I've stood at that police station for two hours for absolutely nothing?' she said, slapping Stevie on the chest.

Stevie laughed. 'There's only one problem babe. Sami's pal can't fix it till Tuesday and we're heading home tomorrow. I've checked and there is a flight back on Thursday night, plus I can extend the hire for a further two days for 60 euro. The flight back is only £35 and the apartment another 75 euro. Even with that we're still saving nearly a grand.'

Millie looked deep in thought. 'I can't stay till Tuesday I need to be back to work on Monday morning.'

Stevie looked over at her. 'It's fine, babe. You go back on Sunday as planned. I'll drop you at the airport on Sunday and then get the car fixed Monday/Tuesday and back home Tuesday night. You can get me at the airport on Tuesday night?'

Millie nodded tentatively.

'No bad, you getting a few days more in the sun,' she said slumping on to a chair on the balcony.

'I don't want to go home tomorrow.' She made a face like a spoiled child.

Stevie joined her at the table and sat opposite her.

'It's only two days and I'll be back to get you, babe.'

Millie was still forlorn, she let out a big sigh and took a drink from her glass of water. Stevie sat back on his chair and let his sunglasses fall onto his nose as he leaned back.

* * *

Their alarm was buzzing for about fifteen minutes when Millie's' apple watch finally woke her. She nudged Stevie awake as she got up for the shower. 'We need to get going. I'll be late and have to ruin your plans.'

Stevie was still laid on the bed looking tired. 'What plans are they?' he asked screwing up his face.

'I don't know, plans for your two days on the Algarve! Relax, I'm only joking.' Stevie got up and pulled on his shorts and t shirt. Millie grabbed her case, before Stevie offered to carry it for her..

At the airport. Stevie dropped her at the main entrance, leaving the car with the hazards flashing, as he helped her out with her case. They hugged and Stevie kissed her 'phone me when you get back and let me know you're okay,' he asked. Millie kissed him and made her way into departures, stopping to wave off Stevie as she did.

In the airport, Millie was joined by a stag do heading back to Glasgow. She did her best to keep out of their way. She made her way through security, but quickly became uncomfortable as two well-built guys on their own kept on watching her and trying to make eye contact. She grabbed herself a coffee and then moved seats, only for them to follow her and then sit at the adjacent table. She tried to look busy on her phone. When one of the guys approached her, he asked if the seat next to her was taken. Millie lied that it was and that she was waiting for her boyfriend. The unwelcome stranger asked if that was Steven Anderson, as the other guy stood up from his table and flashed her an ID card, as he approached.

'Policia Seguranca Publica, could you please come with us Miss Singh? We have some questions relating to your stay, in Portugal, as well as information relating to controlled substances which maybe in your luggage.'

Millie's last few days with Stevie raced through her brain as realisation hit her.

39

A Burnt Toast

The War Office was a typical old man's pub. Local legend suggested that the unofficial name by which it was now known was due to its re-purposing during the war as an enlisting office. Stories surrounding the sobering thought of revelers waking up, after a night on the beer, on their way to Dunkirk had been widely exaggerated but still accepted.

It was here that Stirling met up with Jack's friends Craig and Wilson as well as his old pal's Shaun and Al. The collective purpose was to catch up and raise a toast to Jack's memory.

Stirling had arrived to find them already one pint in and midway through their shared grief counselling session.

'Alright, Stretch?' offered Al, standing up to give him a hug as he arrived.

'Have you been on a fucking moon bed?' he asked, on account of Stirling looking so white.

Stirling raised his eyebrows even higher and suggested he hadn't slept much these past few days. The rest all shared the same style of welcome: genuine care hidden in a lock knife of banter.

Stirling had been off work for a few days and decided that he'd continue this unofficial period of leave until after the funeral. Bereavement leave was officially for close family, but his pals were Stirling's closest family.

Craig was in full flow as Stirling pulled over a stool to sit round their table.

'I was laughing to myself yesterday remembering the time he hired and drove a bus through to the cup final for us. We couldn't find a bus to take us all through and there he was complete with captains' hat.'

Wilson pitched in further. 'Mind he took us home via the longest detour ever. The drive back was actually better than the final!'

Craig agreed that there were so many funny memories. He recounted a tale where Jack had been seeing a new girlfriend and missed their pal's baby's head wetting because he'd taken his new girlfriend and her Mum to see 42nd Street at the playhouse.

'We called him Leroy for months after that, so we did'

Al raised his pint to Jack and the others duly followed. Wilson raised his to the bold Leroy.

Shaun was off next with more memories of Jack. Telling the boys about the time he'd played him at golf, but not before reminding everyone that, at one stage, he could've been a top, top golfer.

'We were getting into a deep conversation, and I'd asked him if he'd ever wanted kids. Jack joked that he probably had plenty he didn't know about before he took this right serious tone. 'Shaun,' he said, 'I just don't think I'm meant to have kids. I've thought about it, thought about it a lot and well, it's just never happened. I can't say it's a regret, but I do see everyone else moving on. I just fill my time by doing anything I want. It would probably be different if I did have a son or wee lassie but, in the meantime, I just fill my life doing everything you can't.' Jack took a draw of his joint and left the spliff in his mouth, swung his 7 iron and curled a neat shot onto the edge of the green which rolled up towards the hole. He pulled the joint from his mouth and looked at me and announced, 'Like that' before he strode off up the fairway laughing.'

'That was him, a total legend.'

Stirling shook his head.

'It still hasn't sunk in. I don't think it ever will' he drunk up his pint as Al patted his shoulder.

Wilson got another round of drinks in, and they continued to share stories for a few hours. Eventually, Craig gestured Stirling towards the pub toilets, and they'd shared a couple of lines. They came back to the table to find another round of pints waiting for them accompanied by a round of shots.

Al told them about a time where they'd gone to the Premier League of Darts with Jack and he'd suddenly took off one shoe and began singing shoes off for Gary Anderson. Soon enough, the whole hall all joined in with one shoe held aloft for their hero.

'He was some boy,' announced Craig. 'One of the best. In fact, thee best'. They all charged their glasses once more and downed their shots in unison. Some regulars in the pub looked around at the unusually spirited drinking for a Thursday evening.

Craig passed the bag of ching onto Al in an attempted clandestine manner that became anything other than that. Al came back from the toilet just as the barman called last orders, which prompted them to decide to share taxis up to Falkirk and into a nightclub called City.

Quickly inside, Craig was first to remark on the madness that they now found themselves in. 'Last time I was here was with Jack to see Ultrasonic and now I'm here on a Thursday night to toast his memory, it's just no right'.

Stirling reassured him that it was all in the name of toasting their pal, who'd more than approve. 'He'd be right in the thick of it if he could. Always was.'

The nightclub had just one dance floor open, on account of it being midweek, and everyone appeared to be drinking from the same promotion. Wilson left soon after finishing his first drink and bid fond drunken farewells to each of them, reminding them that he'd soon see them all at Jack's funeral. The heady mix of broken sleep propped up by amphetamine and multiple drinks had already caught up with Stirling. He was holding himself with all the substance of an empty tracksuit.

Craig and Al watched him briefly limber up as a hefty wallflower, who'd lingered in their shadow all night, made her way over to Stirling. Much to their obvious amusement, to everyone apart from Stirling, he had welcomed the approach.

Stirling chatted animatedly with his new friend until he was soon dragged onto the dance floor.

'What's shur name again?' Stirling attempted, not even hearing a response due to the loudness of the music.

After multiple attempts at crude sign language and repeated motioning by him for her to shout in his ear. He still couldn't hear what she was saying but eventually nodded and got back to dancing. He momentarily lingered about in a semi self-dance as she chatted with a friend, who then departed leaving them alone. He looked up and over to Al and Craig who gave him a thumbs-up, as he continued what he thought was dancing.

Stirling was lost in the music and revelling in her company. Grinding up against her, until they began simultaneously groping each other. Suddenly they were kissing on the dance floor and Stirling felt his cock surge with want.

'Do you wanna go back to ma place?' Stirling offered, before she motioned that she couldn't hear him. Eventually he leaned in and yelled the same into her ear, she turned and nodded.

As they left the dance floor, Stirling felt his phone vibrate in his pocket. He stared at it blankly before confirming it was Al and swiped the screen in order to accept his call. He put a finger in one ear and pressed the phone against the other.

'What is it pal? I love you man.' He said drunkenly.

'Where are you going with her?' asked Al, getting to the point.

'What? Where are you?' replied Stirling, spinning on his axis, looking around, and confused regards his pal's location.

'I'm right fucking above you, man. Look up the stairs. I can see you. I'm looking right at you. What are you thinking?' protested Al.

Stirling still couldn't hear him but Al continued.

'She'll eat you alive, in fact, it looks like she's still no digested her last victim.'

'What? replied Stirling, 'I've pulled man I'm leaving the now.'

Al continue to protest helplessly. 'Like I'm no saying she's big but when she was coming in the bouncers tried to break her up'

Stirling wasn't listening, he clasped his phone to his chest as he raised his free hand to his forehead and attempted to scan round the nightclub, before missing his head as he tried to re-engage with the conversation. His new friend moved into his flailing arm before he stumbled backwards, catching him slightly before they began kissing again. Stirling only then remembered he still had his phone in his hand.

He then took multiple attempts to slide the phone back into his jacket. Finally negotiating it safely into his pocket before waving ambiguously to the whole nightclub and then leaving arm in arm with his new friend.

In the taxi, Stirling's admirer was like an octopus all over him. Stirling was mute apart from the occasional hint of encouragement.

They arrived shortly after, outside Stirling's flat. Stirling threw the taxi driver the last twenty note in his pocket before she pulled him out of the car. She then frog-marched Stirling up the stairs and frisked him as he fumbled for his door keys, eventually operating his arm like a puppeteer to open his front door.

Inside the dark of the hallway, she asked her way to the bedroom, kissing him wildly as he motioned towards the direction of the bed. Soon after, they were both in it.

Stirling, somehow, removed her bra with one hand. She broke off from their kiss to tell him that was the first time somebody had taken off her bra in twenty years and that her pants were already soaked.

* * *

In the morning, Stirling woke in a haze. He was rough, and memories of the night before trickled back selectively into his consciousness before he could even open his eyes. When he did, he noticed himself somehow higher up on the mattress than he'd ever been in his own bed before. Confused, he then noticed the body laid next to him.

He slipped out of his bed and tiptoed silently to the bathroom, turning back to catch a glimpse. He closed the bathroom door quietly behind him and clasped his head in his hands as he stared at himself in the mirror. He needed to think quickly. He decided to take the opportunity to shower, taking time to wash his cock with shampoo, conditioner, and shower gel.

After he'd showered, he stood with the towel draped round him. He weighed up options on how to escape this predicament before an idea struck him. I'll say I'm working, he thought triumphantly.

He took a deep breath and returned to his bedroom, confident in his plan as his bed partner stirred. He quickly offered a brisk good morning before he activated his master plan, trying not to make eye contact throughout.

'Sorry doll. I'm working this morning. I need to get going, Can I give you a lift anywhere?'

She sat up on the bed and reached for a packet of cigarettes.

'Aye, you canny smoke in here. Plus, I really need to get going'.

'Can I not even get a cup of tea?' she asked.

'You've no got time for a glass of water, pal. I'll get sacked if I'm late again.' Stirling lied, eager to get on his way.

She climbed out of his bed, which screeched with relief as she made her way to her feet in stages. Stirling finally caught her eye and the way she looked back at him. Defeated, almost. This struck a chord in him somewhere, somewhere where he thought of Lucy in the group and the way she'd described Keith casting her aside thoughtlessly, alongside the times his mother sat alone, after his Dad had left, listening relentlessly to Annie Lennox's no more I love you's. A wave of shame and guilt collided and washed over him, what was he doing? He thought to himself. He wasn't that guy.

'Oh hang on. It's fucking Friday. What am I thinking, I'm off the day' He countered, whilst she was stood fixing her bra straps. She looked at him unconvinced.

Stirling sat down on the edge of the bed whilst he began climbing of his dickhead high horse.

'Here how about you have a shower and I'll get you that cup of tea..... '

'Veronica' she interjected.

'Stirling' he replied, laughing at himself before releasing she hadn't joined in.

'Nice to meet you, Veronica. Do you want me to turn it on for you?'

'I think you did enough turning on last night' she replied before a flicker of a smile cracked across her face.

'I'll get you a towel' Stirling announced, bouncing up off the bed and past Veronica who then followed him half naked up the hallway with the remainder of her clothes bundled up tightly against her chest.

'Right well. You get yourself in the shower and I'll get sorting the tea. How do you take it?' Stirling smiled as he slid the towel into her hands alongside her bundle of clothes.

Veronica suggested she'd maybe taken it a few ways the night previous before she then asked for two sugars and milk.

She followed up with a cheerfully remembered please as she closed the bathroom door behind her.

'Two and Coo. Coming up' shouted back Stirling as he made his way into the kitchen.

Veronica was a while in the shower. Enough time for Stirling to make up a couple of slices of toast and lay out two cups of tea on the wee dining table in the living room.

Veronica smiled as she sat with her towel tied around and tucked over her breasts.

'You don't happen to have a hair dryer?' she asked.

Stirling rubbed his hair. 'For this? Sorry Veronica. I can get you another towel?'

Stirling leapt up and retrieved a smaller towel from the hallway cupboard then watched as she wrapped up her hair in a makeshift turban.

'You feel better now?' Veronica asked as Stirling greedily polished off his second slice of toast, and then washed it down with a gulp of tea. Stirling quickly realised he hadn't stirred it properly and had caught a mouthful of lumpy molten sugar.

'Sorry. I dinnae think I've stirred them properly' he apologised, getting up to retrieve a teaspoon from the kitchen whilst voicing a noise of distaste.

Veronica thanked him as he sat back down and stirred her tea.

'You look rough' She offered.

'Thanks' replied Stirling sarcastically. 'I've felt better. I'm not going to lie. You doing okay?'

'I'm fine thanks. Look I've got something to tell you Stirling... I'm married'.

Stirling was delighted but tried to hide the honest reaction from his face. Inside he was dancing like he'd sunk a hole in one at the Masters. He responded tentatively.

'Oh I see. How's that working out?'

'Well. It's gone 9am, and he's not text. So clearly he's not missing me. I could be, well I suppose I am literally anywhere. He just doesn't care anymore. I'm just a cleaner and housewife these days.'

'That's not so good. Maybe he just trusts you?' suggested Stirling, trying to be positive.

'Yeah maybe, I don't normally do this type of thing. It was just nice to feel wanted and.....' Veronica started to cry.

'God look at the mess of me.'

Stirling got up and grabbed some kitchen roll before he asked if she'd like more tea, as he switched the kettle back on presumptuously.

Veronica thanked him as he returned and gave her a few sheets, which she duly used to dab her eyes and blow her nose. She held them midway in front of her as she looked around for a bin.

Stirling held out his hand and collected them for her, before dispensing in the kitchen bin. The boak slightly catching him as he felt the warm squidginess of her collected snot. He stepped on the pedal of the bin and discarded them, noticing the used condoms in the bin as he did. This was a win, which he hadn't recalled. He patted himself on the back as he slid back the cupboard door and prepped two further teas.

'Can you leave the bag in mine. I like it strong' Veronica called through to Stirling from the living room table.

'Nae bother' Replied Stirling. Now delighted with the way events were unfolding. He danced a wee shimmy as he lobbed his tea bag into the bin. Then took a double take at her retained tea bag before shrugging his shoulders and making his way back through.

Stirling laid the two cups down on the table, one with the tea bag still bobbling like a buoy at sea. He couldn't handle that, he thought to himself.

'So how long have you been married V? Any kids?'

Veronica took a sip of her tea. '8 years this Christmas and I have one kid, a wee boy. How about you?'

'Yeah. I've a wee girl' Stirling laughed, nodding around at the collection of pink fairy castles and dolls collected in a pile.

'Where will you say you've been?' Stirling enquired.

'At my sisters. I'd already text her to let her know. She was with me last night but left whilst we were dancing'.

'Dancing?' Stirling nearly spat out his tea, he hadn't recalled dancing yet.

'Oh yeah. Really dancing' replied Veronica whilst adopting a fake northern English accent for extra emphasis.

Stirling laughed awkwardly. Still not comfortable with his exploits, particularly the dancing. He wasn't a dancer.

Veronica paused for a minute. 'Thanks for this, and last night. It's been lovely, I've not felt like this in years.'

Stirling felt somewhat bashful. 'Eh. Thanks to you too'.

Veronica smiled, before she added.

'Would you mind if we kept this between us?'

Stirling looked up to Jack and winked back at Veronica as he promised not to breathe a word. Motioning a zip seal closing around his mouth, as he did.

'Thanks. Is that lift still on offer? Veronica asked Stirling.

Stirling thought for a second, but then confirmed it was. Collecting the four empty mugs and two saucers from the table, before he laid them in the sink and collected his keys.

He waited by the table as Veronica finished getting ready in the bedroom. Soon after presenting herself at his living room door.

Stirling looked up. 'Come on then V. Let's get you back to reality'.

Stirling squeezed past her before he opened the door and stood back to hold it open for her. Veronica thanked him and they made their way down the close stairs towards the street and Stirling's car.

'Where are we off to?' Stirling asked, as Veronica slung the passenger door wide open. She then got in the passenger seat and immediately reached for the under-seat slider. 'Langlees', she announced.

Stirling then listened in silence as she arranged the cover story, with

276

her sister, as to her supposed whereabouts. Stirling took an alternative, disjointed route, hoping that he'd throw off any ability Veronica had to remember where he'd lived, just in case some crackpot jealous husband suddenly emerged. He eventually dropped her off at the end of what was her sister's street, despite being assured that it had been fine to drop her at the door. Langlees looked like the Gaza Strip after a visit from the IDF.

Veronica left the car and leaned back in to say thanks. Stirling suggested he might see her around, whilst taking a mental note to never frequent City, Falkirk, any bars, or even public, ever again. She shouted back thanks, closed the car door and made her way up the street.

Stirling sat, alone in the car, for a minute and took stock.

His friend had died.

Sarah was seeing someone else.

Millie was back with Stevie.

And he was now having one-night stands with married mothers who he'd rather not have fucked. A MMWHRNHF was some distance from a MILF, never mind a Millie.

He drove back home in half the time that his elaborate route had taken him to get there. He sprinted upstairs and pulled the flat door shut behind him. He sat on the sofa: guilt followed relief, followed shame, as his delayed hangover fully caught up with him. He needed to tidy the house and remove any further memory of his exploits.

He got up and stripped the sheets from his bed, the stench of their sex reminded him of the pungent taste of her vagina as he rushed to the bathroom. He remembered removing a ball of toilet paper from her pubic hair with his tongue, prompting him to wretch deeper until the memory of that taste was replaced with bile.

Convinced circumstances had now been fully resolved and any evidence now removed, he slumped back on the sofa and waited for time to take over. He now felt safe enough to check his phone. The WhatsApp group, which he'd created to organise last night's drinks, was now awash with queries as to how his night had ensued. He decided that he fell asleep in the taxi and she'd gone straight home. He could only have ever told Jack the truth about this.

40

Week Twelve

Dave hadn't been the same since Jack's death. He'd barely worked and all mention of the wondrous plans which him and Morag were to embark upon following the realisation of his share options from Scottish Spinsters had ground to a halt, although he knew she'd be biding her time. He'd largely sat and stared either into space or into cyber space. He'd returned to work this week like a zombie going through the motions.

The waft of beige chicken nuggets was making its way into his makeshift office. Morag was making dinner early. Dave was hoping, rather than expecting, that he'd get back to the RA meetings this week. He'd found the lack of engagement cycle he was spiralling into wasn't good. He'd seen it happen with others and could, in the third person, see it in himself. Worse was the temptation to drink, he hadn't trusted himself to catch up with Stirling and Jack's friends this week and then felt guilty for not going.

Morag knocked at the door.

'Hello' stifled Dave, pretending to be disturbed from something.

Morag slid open the door. 'Hiya. Could I interest you in something to eat?'

Dave thought for a second before responding, as if galvanised by Morag's kind offer but his nose having already detected the culinary delights on offer. 'You know what, I will Morag. I'm going to get some dinner and I will make my way along to the Trinity Centre for the RA meeting tonight.'

Morag smiled back at Dave, he knew letting her help was the best for them both. He knew only too well she intrinsically linked his recovery from this spiral to a recovery for her spending plans.

Dave sat down to dinner, feeling almost like a stranger. The kind eyes from his boys made him feel guilty for his recent departure as a functioning family element. He asked the boys how school was and what they'd been up to with their friends as if he was an estranged uncle who had popped in with a yearly Christmas card to resolve his conscience. Christmas, he suddenly thought. It was almost December already. Dave was probing for Christmas gift ideas and was relieved when Morag helped out with conversation, encouraging the boys to answer their dad. Him and Morag locked eyes, that was love, real love and he knew it. He held her hand as the boys squabbled over who was getting what this year.

Dave had been sitting on the news for about a week but hadn't been able to share. He didn't know if he was angry, upset or not even capable of processing good news yet. Either way he was ready now. 'You'll no believe what's happened,' he said. Morag, cocked a squint. 'Ryan and Katrina have only gone and got engaged at the last meeting.'

'Ryan? and Katrina?' Morag accentuated her questions with an exaggerated expression, driving home her disbelief.

Dave laughed as he leaned back on his chair. 'Yip. That's them. Apparently, Katrina had been harbouring a thing for Ryan, which had built during their time metal detecting and she's only gone and popped the question ... in front of the group ... and with Ryan's lost ring!'

Morag looked actually surprised, and Dave was delighted with her reactions, reminding him that not only did they share a brain sometimes but they often had the same cynical view of events. 'I thought Katrina was waiting for the murderer?'

Dave agreed. 'I thought she only came along to address the boredom and hurt of her own forced breakup, but maybe there was more to it.'

'And Ryan. Was his issue not committing too early?'

Dave was already nodding '55 days! 55 days and he'd been ready to propose to Susan. By my calculations Katrina's proposal beats that!'

Morag laughed. 'Was this to be expected. You miss one week and the group take leave of their senses?'

Dave looked as if he'd been fishing for a shark and caught a whale. 'Ha-ha. That's what you'd think but the nature of it is actually fantastic because this is against both of their failings. Katrina trapped waiting for the wrong man and Ryan now battle weary from his eager commitment efforts have gone full circle. I think this is fantastic.'

Morag looked even more perplexed 'Fantastic?'

'Yes. Absolutely fantastic. As Gary Barlow would say.'

'You've all gone mad. The Romantics Anonymous have become the romantic addicts.' Morag quipped.

Dave was looking at Morag as if she'd struck gold. 'Romantic Addicts Morag? That's good' Dave was scribbling it down. I mean Romantics Anonymous served a purpose but Romantic Addicts has a better ring to it.' Dave was delighted to feel so animated again. Morag smiled and confirmed she was off to clean up the plates as Dave made his way back into his emails. He'd emailed Millie Singh regarding Jack's funeral, but had not heard back from her.

He printed off his notes for tonight and switched off his laptop. Dave collected his briefcase from the foot of his desk and shouted goodbye to Morag and the kids, taking the time to dutifully relay his goodbyes onto Misty.

He left and got behind the wheel of the car, he'd turned the stereo and started drumming along to the stray cat strut as he made his way to the Trinity Centre, delighted with himself that there hadn't been a single flashed reminder as he made his way to the group. Today was a better day.

Arriving at the Trinity Centre, Dave parked up and pulled his case over from the passenger seat. 'You alright Dave?' enquired Stirling as he locked the car and joined him walking towards the centre.

Without waiting for his response Stirling carried on 'Did you hear the funeral's next week? The coroner finally got back to the family and recorded their results; transpires it was heart related, just like his Dad.'

Dave nodded agreement but wasn't fully aware of what Stirling was actually saying, catching himself, he explained further 'I was speaking with his Mum, Cathy, yesterday. Do you know I'd never met her until then and she knew all about me, all about you, all about everyone in Jack's life. '

Stirling had a look of slight panic on his face. Prompting Dave to re-assure him that clearly, he never meant everything, everything. But everything he could and should have shared with his Mum. Stirling laughed with relief as they carried on their way up the steps. Stirling finally relaxed enough to respond.

'That's nice that. I tell ma Mam nothing, I don't even think she knows me, and my ex are.... Well just that! Exes'

Stirling pulled open the door whilst Dave paused to greet Ryan and Katrina, who'd arrived in unison, congratulating then both on their recent engagement.

'What happened Ryan? One week I left you in charge and Romantics Anonymous has become Romantic Addicts!' He knew fine well that wasn't going to be the last time he stole Morag's line.

'It wasn't my fault, it was all this one,' Ryan announced, prodding Katrina who bashfully swooned in Ryan's direction.

'All my fault? What can I say. I'd fallen for him. I must be an eejit'

After handshakes and hugs, they made their way into the centre as Sensei Jamieson was bringing his class to a halt. They picked seats dotted around the waiting area, Stirling was relaying the details regards Jack's funeral onto Ryan and Katrina as Derek arrived.

Dave looked up from his phone, in order to greet him. He was enquiring about his trip across America and checking how things were with Patricia when Kevin Jamieson opened the door and his class made their way out the hall.

As his class left, Tony arrived. Neither even exchanged a glance as the class followed their Sensei out into the car park.

* * *

'Hello everyone. Sorry I couldn't make last week, with such sad circumstances surrounding Jack's sudden death I just couldn't bring myself here.

Thanks very much for Ryan deputising and I understand it was an eventful week.'

Dave looked at them both and squirmed at the guilt which appeared to flush over Ryan's face. It looked like he somehow thought that he'd sullied the group's reputation and was about to face a tribunal. Dave was quick to reassure him. 'All I can say is that I'm delighted for you both and what a fitting memory for Jack, within the group, that from bad news springs new hope and happiness. I'm sure all the group wish you all the best of luck and I expect we'll all get a mention in the wedding speeches!'

Dave went on to confirm the funeral date as well as the coroner's findings to the rest of the group.

Dave moved onto this week's check-ins, starting with Ryan, who seemed to have a perma-grin attached to his face. Dave noticed that Katrina had left her usual spot to sit alongside her new fiancé.

'Hello everyone. Well, what can I say? After a few years coming along here and trying my best not to get swept up in romance. One week I get the chance to help others by chairing the group, and end up engaged. What can I add to that? The last week was great. I spoke with Katrina's family and we've been making arrangements to go over and see them, plus we've been getting to know each other's tastes and habits. I'm definitely the cook in the relationship. Aside from that, Katrina has been busy with work and it's been interesting to hear all about it. We did have a long chat this week and again this evening about how we will manage things with Jimmy and we went and picked her stuff up. He never said a word to either of us.'

Dave watched as throughout his check-in, Ryan, was looking over at Katrina as if to make sure he got it right. Brushing off his discomfort from Ryan's approval seeking, Dave thanked Ryan for sharing. 'I'm surprised you didn't need a few weeks with Sensei Jamieson before going to collect Katrina's possessions from Jimmy.'

Dave was soon listening to Katrina run over her own version of the same events whilst thinking over whether they'd be both able to continue coming along to the group. He'd never had a couple that were together in the group, certainly not that he was aware off. Ryan was watching her every word and nodding along.

Dave drifted off, thinking if Jack and Lucy had been a couple too. Laughing at himself as he pondered if it could have been a marriage counselling session he was chairing instead.

His attention came back to Katrina who was signing off on her update. 'I'd like to think we can be a real success story for Romantics Anonymous and that our outcome is, however unexpected, one that shows there is a route back to love and romance, even for the most disillusioned and risk averse.'

Dave felt inclined to comment, it was his usual means of making up for any lapse in interest. He went for 'What a lovely way to describe yourself.' Immediately realising that he didn't mean disillusioned and risk averse as the look on Katrina's face appeared to have taken it. Dave decided to move quickly on. 'I must ask, have you been back to the beach?'

Katrina was delighted to confirm that they had been but that they were also branching out to new beaches and new treasures, rather than the same beach and a treasure which was already found.

Ryan touched Katrina's hand and confirmed that she was 'his treasure.'

It was in that moment that Dave decided that a minimum of one of them had to go. He'd need to make a motion, made even more awkward by Katrina and Ryan's positions there as Secretary and Treasurer. But he was certain that was an issue to tackle post funeral. He'd see how the weeks developed and make a decision from there but he wasn't comfortable with this dynamic. This was an EGM issue.

Dave could feel Stirling looking over at him as he was still deep in thought. He apologised and asked Stirling for his check-in.

Stirling's head space was all wrapped up in what had happened to Jack. He'd gone out with some friends last week to try and share some memories of Jack but all that it done was highlight how much Jack's already been missed for him especially. Dave enquired further with Stirling regards the situation at home but it transpired that things hadn't gone well for Stirling there recently either.

'I'd been spending a lot more time with my daughter recently. Sarah has started a new relationship and that's not really went down well with

Kayleigh, as a result she's been spending more time at mine.'

'And how have you been feeling about that?' enquired Dave.

'I think she could have been a bit more honest with Kayleigh and let her know, it put me in a difficult position as she was asking me and I eventually phoned her to ask and then confirm for Kayleigh. She was upset and I could just reassure her that I would always be there for her and always be her Dad, but that with the age of her new Mum's boyfriend she might be looking at a new granddad'

Derek chortled loudly as Kat sniggered away to herself. Dave remained expressionless, suggesting that this was an innocuous comment, all things considered.

Stirling didn't agree.

'Yeah but she went and told her Mum. Thinking it was hilarious. My ex did not. Apparently, I'm getting involved to make things difficult for her but I'm no, I'm just making sure things are fine for Kayleigh first and foremost. You never know these days'

Dave reassured Stirling that Sarah had the same focus on Kayleigh, even as much as he did. But, he stressed, he mustn't let jealousy get in the way of what could be a very sensitive time, particularly for Kayleigh.

'Absolutely Dave, especially having a wee lassie and hearing about all the freaks and pedos out in the world today. I've already been conducting my own background checks'

Dave shook his head. 'I'm sure Sarah has her best interests at heart, even as much as you, and sharing your concerns and seeking re-assurance directly with her Mum shouldn't be an issue.'

Dave could see Tony limbering up to respond, he grimaced hoping Tony didn't make things any worse.

'It's tough though, Stirling. I mean after everything I've been through, in terms of being a poof and all that, leaving the house and watching my daughters growing up, I still have the pure rage tucked away inside that someone else could be there, in MY family home. I know how you feel, if you need to talk yourself down from doing something mental – give me a call. I've been there.'

Stirling thanked Tony, as did Dave before he encouraged Stirling to keep going, reminding him that he'd had a rough few weeks but that he was doing great. Stirling didn't look convinced.

Lucy hadn't really lifted her head the whole time they'd been here, opting just to stare at her feet. But it was now her time to check in.

Lucy sounded to have had a few weeks similar to Dave. The same few weeks but without the support of a Morag. She'd let the housework get on top of her and had hoped that now the kids were back at school she'd get back with it.

Dave asked if that was likely to happen and if she'd been back to her role at the Samaritans.

Lucy had said she didn't think she was ready for that yet and maybe needed more of their help than vice versa. She started to cry as she said that even the mention of his funeral made it seem all the more permanent.

Dave didn't know if he was ready to be cruel and kind here but knew that someone had to be.

'I understand that too Lucy, if I'm honest I'd felt the same way but the funeral is usually one of the main milestones of recovery for grief. Because it is just that, permanent, as much as none of us want it to be. It is.'

Dave could feel himself listening to himself, both as the group leader and sitting beside Lucy in the exact same moment – it was as if he was talking to Lucy and himself at once.

'Hopefully we can all pull together and go through the healing process together, it's often the talking and the memories discussed that help that part of the process and, if anything, Jack provided us with plenty of those. How is everything else are you coping okay?'

Lucy was shaking her head already.

'I've been a shell. The kids deserve better. But I just can't get out of it.'

'That's natural, Lucy, and it's difficult to keep going. If I could give you just one bit of advice, it's just do one thing. If it's to wash one cup, put away one set of towels or to clean one room. Sometimes one will just be enough to make a start and you'll do a lot more, and other times doing just one is enough anyway. Give it a try and see how you get on.'

Lucy thanked Dave before he thanked her back for sharing. He gave her a long look as she lifted her head slightly.

Seconds later, Tony was beginning his weekly check in suggesting that his week had been clouded by the same recent events affecting everyone else, but seemed reluctant to share anything else. Dave though recalled how him and Kevin hadn't even exchanged glances at reception earlier.

'How are things with Kevin?'

Tony appeared to be uncomfortably wrestling with something.

'I don't know. It's a hard one, and if I'm honest I don't even know if it is really a problem at all.'

Dave reassured Tony that he could share as much or as little as he felt he wanted.

Tony didn't need much more encouragement.

'It's Kevin. I'm constantly bursting his balls as he's always working. Every Saturday it's somebody's first dan, or grading or black belt exams and, to tell you the truth. I'm fucking annoyed with it. I feel like bursting into they classes and telling them tae fuck off so's that I can get my hole on a Saturday afternoon. I've now started to have some thoughts about how quickly I've entered a relationship with Kevin and how I have the right to no be happy but I'm not being rash and I'm no being a dick about it. We're talking about it and it'll either work out or it won't. That is it. That's where I am.'

Dave was impressed that Tony was considering a lot of influencing factors here, as well as the potential impacts of his own feelings. This was progress, even if Tony didn't really see it. Dave asked if there had been anything specific - aside from the Saturday working which could be giving him that feeling.

Tony admitted that there had been a few times where he wondered if he'd played the field enough before settling into things with Kevin. Even more so now when they are continually bumping into Ex's of his.

'Are straight relationships somehow different to gay ones?' Tony asked.

'I don't fucking know. But I can tell you ones got all the same fucking headaches and grief that I had with women. I'm just better at handling it.'

'How do you think Kevin feels when you talk about fact that you've slept with women previously?' Tony sat quietly as Dave followed up his question.

'I mean. You've effectively had double the potential humans to sleep with.'

Tony pondered that for a minute or two. 'Aye right ah suppose ah hadn't really thought much of that. If he had settled down sooner then he would have had less partners – true.'

Dave nodded along enthusiastically, grateful that the penny was starting to drop for Tony. Then Tony carried on a bit more...

'But seeing where he's been, and with who, gives me the boak a wee bit. Cunts dressed like dugs and that. I'm out walking with Kevin and we walk passed someone walking a dug and I'm watching to see if he's eyeing it up. I'm thinking a wee dug would be nice to have for walks and all that, but I'm wanting a cockapoo, no him thinking about his cock all poo. Sakes man.'

'I think you're safe on the dog front,'

Dave said before suggesting that Tony might want to consider that his new social grouping will be largely Kevin's and that can often be a problem when someone starts a new relationship. People tend to adopt their new partner's social group.

'Maybe,'

'This might be a chance for you to spend a bit more time with your old friends and family, either with Kevin or alone.'

Dave watched the cogs turning in Tony's brain, until it seemed like everything suddenly clicked into place.

'That is the case. I have delved more into Kevin's world recently and I should probably spend some time finding myself too. I don't think I feel as welcome down the pub as I did previously. When I am there I'm sure the boys think I'm rattling the gear cos I'm always in the cubicle, I just dinnae want them thinking I'm sizing up there cocks in the gents. I'm no. Well not all the time anyway.'

'Remember, we can't control how other people think. Don't worry what they are thinking. It really is none of your business and vice versa it's none of theirs either.'

Katrina was listening along before she pitched in too. 'You need to find some space for yourself Tony. It might not be your old social groupings, but you should at least try. There will also be an opportunity to spend time with your daughters and making new friends too. You've got to find time for yourself, it will be good for both of you.'

Dave thanked Tony for sharing with the group and Katrina for her advice too. 'There are a lot of things that will be new to you but the dynamic of relationships work the same regardless of who you are, you can identify genetically as a lampshade and be attracted to trains but you still need to spend time doing your own thing and being yourself.'

'You know what,' Tony said, 'maybe I'll get myself a wee dug.'

'Or just get a costume for Kevin and kill two birds with one stone,' Stirling quipped.

Tony just looked at him as Dave checked if Derek was doing okay and welcomed him back to the group.

Derek was happy to follow up on last week's update, delving more into him and Patricia's trip along route 66. Describing how things had really turned a corner for them both and how he felt that their relationship was stronger than it had ever been. He went on to describe how his offer to sell the business had been accepted alongside his suggested period of working just one day a week post sale, also that him and Patricia had been looking forward to what she was describing as a fresh start for them both.

Dave enquired what their longer term plans were, and Derek confirmed that this was likely to include a lot more travel, a lot of making up for lost time as well as making sure Tiger had everything, he needed for success himself.

Dave assumed Tiger was Derek's son's name and not a reference to himself. He thanked him for his contribution as well as the wider group, as he took his place by the whiteboard.

'Tonight we'll pick up on a new topic which will be looking at reward pathways and how they can they can lead us into romantic addiction.'

'Can anyone help us get started by describing what they think our brain reward pathways might be or do?'

Stirling was first to answer. 'Yes Dave, these are the areas which light up when we take drugs... apparently.'

'100%. The reward pathways are like receptors for different feelings and different substances. Ultimately these are what drive our behaviour. When an addiction is hitting our reward pathways not only can it be difficult to stop, it can quickly become destructive. Tonight we will be talking about the signs which can lead you to realise you are acting impulsively as well as how you can avoid the pleasure trap.'

Dave removed the cap from his pen and wrote up the heading: The pleasure trap.

'We are all naturally provided with a reward path. As I mentioned earlier, this path is designed to motivate us to do things that are good for us, to eat/drink, survive and procreate. So the body and brain combine to make these things feel good and as a result encourage these very behaviours.'

'Problem with us romantic addicts is that our biology works too good, so we're biologically very efficient and our system is prioritising the romantic reward above everything else. Does anyone know what could happen if you continue on this path?'

'You'll become a bunny boiler?' Lucy ventured.

That's right, but beyond that where would we eventually end up if we continued to prioritise that particularly need above the others, those for feeding, drinking and being safe?'

Derek offered up that we'd be dead.

'That's exactly right, Derek, but thankfully we don't let that happen. But what we do then is fall into the pleasure trap. Let me draw you a diagram of what can happen.'

Insert graph.

'At point 1, this is the normal, happy, in a relationship status. But for a romantic addicts, this is where they go, here at point 2. Then by point 3, they aren't feeling like it was the same as it was at the start, even though it is, so they get annoyed make it feel worse. Then they do the something to jump start the cycle again. This cycle can continue for ever and is really difficult to stop.'

Dave asked the room if they had any examples of the actions people with a romantic addiction can take to get them back to point 1.

'Having a baby?' Lucy ventured.

Dave wrote it on the board. 'That's right. Many people do try to recapture that initial relationship buzz by creating a new focus such as a baby.'

'Moving house or changing their life setting?' Derek suggested.

Again, Dave wrote it on the board.

'Getting engaged or married,' Ryan added which appeared to rile Katrina.

Dave noted this under those suggested previously.

'Maybe creating arguments?' Tony said. 'So that they can then make back up again?'

But Stirling was stumped. What about flirting with someone else?'

Dave asked how he meant.

'Well, sometimes people, I'm no saying me, might flirt with someone else almost to gain their interest, just so that they can get their partner a wee bit worried. You know, make them step it up a bit.'

Dave agreed again and wrote this in the board. But when he turned back around, the room looked dejected as if Dave had just written a bad report card for the group.

Derek was first to break the silence 'Do we all need an intervention?'

41

A Busted Flush

'Why won't you let me go? I'm not going to going anywhere. You can drive me there and pick me up. You need to let me leave the house sometime. I've told you I love you.'

Millie was pleading with Stevie to let her attend Jack's funeral. Stevie hadn't let her out of the flat alone since he returned from Portugal. He'd returned via a ferry having been tipped off that he was about to get lifted at the airport. Millie getting arrested hadn't been in his plan, but he also didn't want her spooked by their intervention. He'd already lost her once and wasn't prepared to lose her again. He could tell she didn't trust him and he hated that. He wouldn't do anything to put her in jeopardy, ever. He just needed her to see that.

Since Stevie's' return, Millie spent every waking hour making plans to escape; whilst he appeared to spend every hour awake making sure she didn't. It was an unspoken Mexican stand-off, which she felt he was winning. When she woke up, Stevie was sitting by their bed watching her sleep. She pretended she was still sleeping but she could feel his eyes on her, piercing the darkness with his stare. It was a silent threat for her to remain exactly where she was.

Stevie wasn't entertaining the notion. 'You only knew the boy for five minutes. I've already told you you're no going. That big daft cunt will be there and I dinnae want to have to break his huge beak all over again.'

Millie looked at him pleadingly. 'But Jack's dead and these people helped me when I was really down.' She took his hand gently and moved closer to him, wielding all her feminine persuasion. Stevie began kissing her as he stood up, taking her head in his hands as he devoured her greedily, shaping her body with his hands until they rested on her pert bottom. He pulled up her dress around her hips and slipped his hands inside her knickers whilst they kissed, tugging them aside as he bluntly rubbed at her dry pussy. He could tell Millie was faking interest. He laid her back on the bed, and continued the rouse by pulling her knickers off. He lay on top of her as they intermittently kissed one another, pulling at his jeans and boxers. Unfurling his hard cock, he asked her if she wanted to fuck. Millie nodded and Stevie roughly fucked her pussy, reveling in the faked approval as he knowingly took her against her bodies will, her fake want yielding as he bluntly entered her. He spat obscenities until he finally came inside her.

His salty venomous fuck had nipped at Millie, she turned into the foetal position before trying to look natural again. Stevie sat up on the bed beside her.

'You never even wanted that, did you? You think I'm fucking daft.'

He started laughing.

Millie lay defeated, she was trapped and mentally tired. She mildly attempted a retort but the defeat had left her spent

'Why do you enjoy hurting me?'

'You think I'm enjoying this? You pretending to want to have sex with your boyfriend just so you can go and mark the passing of one of they sad lonely cunts. Good riddance I say, another lonely cunt dead. Nae loss.'

Millie pulled the covers back over her. She fixated on her discarded knickers, lying in a ball on the floor, as if the vision encapsulated the desperate position she'd now found herself in.

She was working from home on account of her being unwell with an illness which Stevie had created for her, which needed multiple hospital visits and even more rest in order to cover for her elongated holiday and her time with the Portuguese police. She hadn't seen her Mum or Dad in three weeks, since she'd told them she was going back. The lack of social interaction was weakening her spirit and the constant focus of Stevie had worn her down.

Stevie was looking out of the window. He'd sparked a cigarette and kicked an ashtray along to his feet to catch his ash.

'I just want us to be happy and by that I mean you happy with me. That's not too much to ask for really?'

Millie sat there quietly.

'I mean is it?' he demanded more loudly.

Millie, broken, agreed meekly.

'Yes. That's all I want too, just to be happy with you.'

'Well you might want to tell your fanny that eh?'

Stevie stood up and took another draw of his cigarette, scowling at Millie as he passed. He left the bedroom and Millie retrained her focus on her knickers laid on the floor. She needed to escape.

Slowly contemplating her every move. Millie picked up her phone, dialled 999 and hit 55 as soon as she heard a voice, then laid the phone face down on her bedside table. She serenely made her way toward her cupboard and pulled out her black dress, laid it on the bed and picked a towel up from the back of the door. She walked through the hallway and passed the kitchen.

Stevie was there, moving bags of white powder across a digital scale. He looked at her with mocking disgust. Millie sighed and pulled the bathroom door behind her. Locking the door and pulling back the shower curtain as she put both taps on full. She then sat with her back against the door and listened as the water crashed off the plastic shower curtain, enjoying the white noise.

She couldn't be sure if she heard a knock at the door but she definitely heard Stevie's reaction.

'Cunts,' he whispered, leaving the door unanswered. She visualised his every step, hearing him bundle up the white powder from the kitchen and approaching the bathroom. She braced herself as she felt him try the handle.

'Millie, it's the polis. Open the door,' he whispered pleadingly.

Millie put her hands against her ears and pulled her knees up to her chest. She felt him push the door again, eventually barging against it as the lock burst from its hinges. Thankfully, the door swung back closed behind her back. Stevie must have tried one last time as the front door burst open.

'Strathclyde Police,' was yelled as Stevie slid against the bathroom door, a tub of white powder under each arm. Millie watched as the tension against the hinges gasped and relaxed before she climbed into the shower. She heard the mumbled noise of an altercation and focused on the warm water and soap against her skin, enjoying the fresh aroma of the lather as she washed Stevie out of her life one last time.

42

Funeral

Lucy sat waiting for the first site of a recognised car before she was even prepared to leave the vehicle. She watched, disappointed, as strangers greeted each other with warm vigorous handshakes and wild smiles as they took the opportunity to catch up. She was fixing the magic tree against her rear-view mirror. She regretted touching it as the pungent smell of pine stuck to her fingers.

As the car park filled up, she noticed Derek's Mercedes arrive, taking that cue to look as if she had just arrived herself after throwing him a quick wave. She slung her bag over her shoulder, closed the door, and waited at the end of her car for Derek to walk by. She had only been stood a second when Millie appeared at her side.

'Hello Lovely, how are you doing?'

Millie startled Lucy with her sudden appearance.

'Hello Millie, I didn't realise you were coming. Thank you.'

Millie shook her head before giving her a light hug.

'I wanted to come along, but I didn't think I'd get to. It's been a strange couple of weeks.'

Millie choked and the tremble of a cry overcame her.

Lucy looked at her intently.

'Are you okay, lovely? What's happened?'

Millie composed herself and she tried to reassure Lucy that she was fine.

Lucy hugged her again. Millie shook off her thoughts and smiled as Derek met them both with a hug.

'Have you been here long?' he asked.

Millie looked thankful for the distraction and confirmed she'd only just arrived.

'Has anyone else arrived yet?'

Lucy looked over and raised her hand to wave as she noticed Ryan and Katrina approaching them.

At that, Tony and Kevin arrived in Kevin's car. Sensei Jamieson rolled down the window and shouted to the group of them,

'Are you okay guys? I'm dropping Tony and then picking him up from the social club later. Do any of you want a lift?'

Tony sat in the passenger seat fixing his tie before greeting the group. He hugged all the girls and shook hands with Ryan and Derek.

'Is that us?' he asked.

Lucy confirmed it was.

Stirling was going along with some of his friends and Dave had been asked to do a reading, so they'd catch them after. At that, Derek asked if they should head in and find a seat. Lucy was shaking ferociously, more than the cold was affecting her. She tried to make herself shake, as she'd once been told this was the best way to stop yourself, somehow. It seemed to work fleetingly as she trailed inside, behind the others.

She awkwardly found a space in the middle of a room full of strangers, before she spotted Stirling across the room. Stirling gave her a nod and made his way over to her.

'Hiya. You doing okay? You look freezing.'

'I just can't stop shaking. I was sick all morning and couldn't eat a thing.'

Tony, who was standing next to her and clearly listening in, decided to offer some words of support.

'Don't drink any cola. If you've no eaten and drink cola you might shite yourself.'

Lucy stifled a laugh whilst Stirling brushed it off as just Tony. Then Lucy moved closer to Stirling.

'Look who's here.'

Stirling hadn't noticed her before. He instantly puffed his chest out and stood a few inches taller, looking her way long enough to catch a glance back and nodding whilst simultaneously asking Lucy:

'How is she?'

'Not good I don't think. I mean given the circumstances it's difficult to gauge but I think she's upset, like at something else, other than the obvious.'

Stirling waved over at Millie and fixed his tie. '

You going to be okay?' he asked Lucy, still watching Millie.

She wasn't sure but reassured Stirling she was fine.

A guy wearing a formal black suit, who Lucy assumed was the funeral staff, approached those at the front of the hall, opened a door and the crowd began to dissipate, trickling slowly through the door and accepting a booklet from an older lady wearing a black and grey two piece. Lucy watched Stirling hang back, remembering that he was to help carry the coffin in. She watched as Stirling and Millie finally exchanged glances.

She accepted her white booklet and stared at Jack's smiling face which was emblazoned on the cover. His smile was infectious, she thought, holding back a lump in her throat with all her might. She looked around the room, amazed to see just so many people without recognising anyone. Along the pews she spotted Dave and who she assumed to be his wife, Morag, who had led the group into the hall and gauged what was far enough back from the front to allow space for family and close friends. Lucy was not quite sure how close she should put herself.

She wanted to be in the front row, grieving him like his widow but she hung back doubting where she stood in Jack's wider life. Looking around her as the hall filled up, she felt herself drifting back to her own Father's funeral. She remembered how she couldn't find a tear that day, however much she tried. That weight of expectation wasn't with her today.

She felt Dave nudging her arm. 'Hi Lucy, are you okay?'

'I'm fine Dave. You?'

'Not too bad, thanks. Good turn out for him. It's nice to see so many people coming along to pay their respects.'

'It is,' agreed Lucy as Millie looked along at her.

Taking in the group all dressed in black, she suddenly thought that she'd never have pictured this group of people together at a funeral in her wildest imagination. Now it was happening, however much she wanted to stop it all.

The doors opened and Lucy turned to see Stirling carrying Jack's coffin alongside one of the guys she'd met that night outside his flat.

The hush was broken by the sound of music. It seemed to play for ever as Stirling and Jack's body made their way to the front of the hall. She felt the tears as the words resonated through her. Turning to look at Dave when the chorus kicked in with Straight to Hell boy.

Dave whispered, 'It was Jack's choice, he was very specific about the music that would be played at his funeral. I think he was trying to be funny.'

All Dave could do was shrug his shoulders. The song continued, almost hypnotizing Lucy as her mind wandered to fantasies of where Jack and her might have gone, wondering if she'd missed out on love. The chorus reverberated around her. She didn't want Jack to go to Hell, she wanted to find out what could have been. The wild nights that could have lasted for ever. She tried to hold back the tears but began crying as Millie put her arm round her. She took a hanky from her whilst apologising. The song ended and a lady stood up to address the service.

Lucy's mind wandered again, and she found herself staring out the window, feeling insignificant. She wondered if people thought of her as stupidly mourning a guy that she'd had one night with as if it was the love of her life. She wondered if she thought that of herself. The guy spoke about Jack as if it was someone different to her recollections: Talked about his school mates and family members she never knew. He then guided the service to song words in the white booklet with Jack's face on it. 'Jack had been a keen music fan all his life and it was part of his very own wishes that we sing two of his favourite songs as part of this afternoon's service,' she announced.

Lucy braced herself as the piano introduction to Don't Look Back in Anger started. Noel Gallagher's voice opened up the song and some in the crowd began to join in. Eventually, the whole hall was singing in unison. Tears streamed down Lucy's face as she sang and looked round to see the full hall in voice and sporadic drops of tears. Some of the guys in the crowd began shouting Jack's name as the song tailed off. 'Go on Jack,' shouted one. The song faded off gradually to silence as everyone hugged each other.

The celebrant returned to the front of the hall. Lucy didn't even notice as Dave took to the stage just alongside Jack's coffin. Lucy couldn't believe he was right there. Her Jack, just quietly sat in the wooden box as his friends and family all sang and cried their hearts out for him. She watched Dave take to the stage and tried to listen intently. Dave cleared his throat before making reference to his grey suit, letting everyone know about a time Jack had left shortly after arriving at a black-tie event on account of his wearing a grey suit. He stood at the lectern, cleared his throat again, looked around the room and then began to address the rest of the service.

'This might sound a bit odd but I'm absolutely honoured to be speaking here, devastated but honoured that amongst the hundreds of people who loved Jack that I'm the one who gets to stand here and tell you about how great he was. I was speaking to his mum, Cathy, a few days ago and she was asking about numbers; she did a sort of double take when I suggested there would be hundreds of people here. I'm not surprised to say I was right. That speaks volumes to how Jack made friends in every situation. Another thing I took from that same conversation was how aware she was of everyone in his life. He shared everything with her and that felt special to me. I suppose confirmation that our relationships with Jack was something I talk a lot about ... love. '

Lucy watched Dave continue with his speech, knowing that she definitely loved Jack.

'Jack had a lot of love and a lot given in return. A friend asked me what I thought his best quality was, and I have to say it was his ability to get out of any potentially bad situation with a positive outcome. And you know how he got away with it? Because whoever spoke with Jack wanted to believe in him. You wanted him to always be right. You always wanted him to be okay, even today, just now, despite knowing it's impossible, I'm still willing and wanting him to walk through those doors and laugh at us all. And again, he'd get away with it because we all want him to be okay. I'm not a religious person but if there is anything up there, I hope he's having fun already and, if not, well there's few that can say they crammed as much life into their time here as he did.'

Lucy watched as Dave looked up and around the room, as if he was taking the opportunity to check everyone was okay with what had he'd said. Before he nodded to himself, turned the page and carried on with his eulogy.

'It's too often said but Jack was the life and soul of the party. Jack had the ingrained want to make sure everyone had a good time. That was him, always keen to entertain, always ready with just enough infectious nonsense to make it happen. I remember one time being with him in a nightclub and managed to get full groups of people talking to us like they were pirates, because he'd told them it was National Pirate Day. Another time he'd squared off a football pitch amidst the hoards at T in the Park, and was charging 50p to beat the goalie, which was me, with a beach ball. Even at a festival, he was trying to make sure everyone had a good time. More about that in a bit.'

'But on a personal level, Jack always gave me advice that made me feel better, that reassurance that I was doing the right thing. He was the friend that boosted your confidence. The friend that always took your side. The friend that I will never give up...'

Dave stopped as he choked and held back what looked like a wash of tears brewing. His voice was breaking with emotion as he picked back up with his speech.

'. . . the friend I needed five minutes before speaking to you all today.'

The celebrant went over to check Dave, but he assured her he was okay, waving her off with his hand. As he apologised to the rest of the hall, Lucy said, 'It's okay, Dave,' out loud. She never even noticed it come out her mouth. Dave chuckled awkwardly which seemed to crack open his emotions all over again before he stifled them back in and thanked her. Lucy sat transfixed, now holding Morag's hand as they both watched Dave carry on.

'As much as I could stand here all day and lament stories of him pranking me with an electric shock pen as I signed share papers, or about him beating me at every single sport we ever played, I'll just leave you with this one. One time me and Morag were at T in the Park, and he'd offered to pick us up. As we left, he was continually texting and then calling, but the reception was terrible. We're walking about car parks aimlessly and eventually he gets me on the phone. He says, 'I'm in car park F.' I couldn't believe it. I said, 'I can see it,' So I'm dragging Morag over the hill, and when we finally get a proper view of car park F we notice there are hundreds and hundreds of cars amongst thousands of people. And, on top of it all, it was pitch black. He was still badgering me on the phone. 'Are you in car park F yet? Are you here?' Honestly, I couldn't match his excitement. I was a bit despondent at the prospect of finding him amongst the hundreds of cars in the pitch black, but finally I reluctantly confirmed I was there, thinking we would still be hours trying to find him. That's when he announced, 'Watch this.' At that, the car park lit up as someone let off a massive orange flare. I'm looking over at it, still with my phone in my hand. He announces, severely chuffed with himself, 'Can you see me now?' It wasn't too long before it dawned on me that the fizzing noise behind his laughter was that same flare in front of me. I could see my pal, proudly grinning with his flare alight. How I wish I could light a flare to bring you back home today, Jack.'

Dave finally let go of his tears as Morag rushed to the front to collect and console her husband. As she did, the service began spontaneously clapping. As Dave and Morag made their way back to the pew, he was congratulated and back patted numerous times. Lucy watched them contently, imagining her and Jack walking hand in hand. 'You doing okay, hen?' Dave whispered as he took his seat once more.

The celebrant addressed the crowd next. Asking if they would join in one more time as we sing Jack's next song. Caledonia by Dougie MacLean began playing and the service joined in again quietly, until the volume rose in the feverish chorus. The pall bearers lifted Jack's coffin and began walking back through the centre of the church as the song continued. Lucy broke down and couldn't sing; she wasn't ready for him to leave the room. She felt sick again and had to get air. She slipped out a side door and left the church, watching from a distance as they loaded Jack's coffin back into the hearse. She watched the service leave the hall.

Katrina ran over to collect her, gave her a long hug and took her hand as they walked back to the group. 'Are you going to be okay to drive, hunny?' Lucy nodded. And they made their way to their cars, with Derek shouting over that they could come with him if they wanted. Lucy, Katrina, and Ryan all took him up on the offer. They made small talk between each other but Lucy could only manage a stare out the window.

By the time they arrived at the cemetery. The service seemed to have grown. Cars were parked up everywhere. Luckily, Derek had no qualms about parking in the disabled section. 'This is my own personal dedication.'

Lucy stood with Katrina, Ryan, and Derek as they watched Stirling and his friends lower Jack's coffin into the ground. Flowers made out in his name were left aside the plot. She listened as the undertaker ran through the last few bits: Ashes to ashes, dust to dust, all that. She joined others and tossed a rose onto his coffin, holding back her emotions again as others threw in handfuls of mud. She didn't feel that today was somehow enough, that she was ready for it to be over. The finality of his burial sat as heavy on her as it would do on that wooden box. She imagined his body in the cold, and she wanted to climb in beside him and warm him up, to breathe life back into him, to give her and him the opportunity they had back again. She turned to walk back to Derek's car alone, but after only a step she couldn't hold it anymore. She wailed, and the others quietly put a hand on her back to steady her walk to the motor.

43

The Wake

Stirling walked awkwardly across the pub with the chair held at everyone else's head height. He put it down by Katrina, gave her a quick look, then peeled off to the bar where Dave was standing with Tony. The two of them were talking about the service, but Stirling watched as Katrina expertly caught Millie's eye, waved her over, and landed her right in the seat Stirling had just rescued. 'I'll be back in a second, boys.'

Pulling his long body into itself as best he could to avoid tipping trays of carefully carried mourning pints, he arrived as casually as he could back at Katrina and Millie's table. 'What you having?' he asked.

Millie pondered for a second, apparently unaware of Stirling's perilously loose place in queue. 'I'll have a gin, ginger beer, and rhubarb.' Stirling returned to the bar confidently, but wasn't entirely sure the social club would cater for such.

'This is Stirling,' remarked Dave to a group of newcomers who were all praising him for his speech. Dave's arm was wrapped around the back of an older woman. 'This is Jack's mum.' Stirling gave her a long hug and she remarked that he'd talked a lot about him and thanked him for coming.

Jack's mum gave Dave another hug, then made her way over to a table which sat with Jack's picture adorning it. She was joined by a small group of pensioners, very much the minority in the room. Stirling watched her quietly sit down, wanting to go over and say more but not wanting to intervene.

The barman took Stirling's order, and didn't even blink when he catered for Millie's requested drink.

By the time he got back with the drinks, Lucy had joined the table and the three girls were busy in full chat. Stirling nodded Ryan's way. 'What are you two wanting?' Stirling asked as he put Millie's on the table.

'She'll have a white wine, I'll have a non-alcoholic beer. I've got the car.'

Stirling returned to the bar. Time pressured by his pint on the table, he was cursing Ryan's feeble order which he tried to whisper to the barman so as not to draw attention. He didn't want to be the guy ordering the alcohol-free beer. Not today. He was seeing Jack off in style.

Groups joined other groups as the hall filled and a buffet opened. Stirling made his way back again with Katrina and Ryan's drinks. Millie smiled a silent thank you as she sipped on her gin and rhubarb. He sighed and took a large gulp of his pint. Dave looked over to him with a grin. 'You been waiting for that?'

'Aye, too right Dave. I'm no one for tea and scones'

The drinks continued to flow. Round after round as some of the groups made their departure. Lucy, who'd hardly touched her first drink was first to leave. She hugged everyone and blew kisses as she made her way to the exit, stopping by Jack's mum and family before heading for the door.

A lassie from one of the other tables had a bluetooth speaker and appeared to be the self-appointed selector. Stirling watched her fend off requests until the speaker crackled into life and Don't Look Back in Anger filled the hall once more. A group of guys sang along at first until everyone was joining in.

Stirling had been talking over old memories with Ryan and Dave when Katrina and Millie paired off to the toilet together. Tony was getting drunk. He leaned over to Stirling asked if he was going to be offering Millie a wee shoulder to cry on. Stirling laughed him off, thinking what a prick he actually was.

Derek took a round from the table, but Stirling waved him off.

'I've still got half a pint here, Derek.'

'Well, a half chaser, then?'

'Tell you what, Derek, what about a Cheeky Vimto.' Back from the toilet,

Katrina and Millie joined in and asking for one each too. Derek was puzzled.

'I didn't think they'd be such a big call for soft drinks today.'

'Naw,' Stirling laughed, 'it's a shot man. It's port and blue wicked.'

Derek was aghast. 'Port and what?!'

Stirling repeated the instruction. 'They're lovely Derek. Tastes like Vimto, hence the name. Get yourself one too' he suggested. Derek trudged off to the bar disappointed with the uncouth order he'd had to deliver to the barman.

Dave had been over speaking with the girl on the Bluetooth speaker when he re-joined the table. 'Dave. Tell Derek you're wanting a Cheeky Vimto' and pointed over to him stood politely waiting behind someone at the open bar.' Dave headed in the general bar direction as Stirling slid over to Tony. 'You wanting a wee cheeky line to go with your cheeky Vimto?' he suggested, cagily looking over his shoulder.

Tony was off his seat before he even answered. 'Cocks away, gay incoming' as he swung open the toilet door.

Stirling, instantly regretting the prospect of sharing a cubicle with him, pulled out the bag and started chopping out lines for the pair of them. He gave Tony a rolled up twenty and watched as he struggled to power a sniff strong enough to hold the powder up his actual nose. 'What are you daen man?' Stirling knew this was a worse idea than the bad idea he already thought it was. Eventually, he got the note back and hoovered up the full line for himself in one swoop. Tony tried again, tilting his head back as if he was having eye drops inserted, theatrically sniffing as he did. Finally, he dislodged the note and triumphantly reported that he'd got it. Stirling opened the door to the cubicle, and felt slightly embarrassed to find an older boy washing his hands.

'Nothing to worry about,' Tony reassured the guy. 'Just been sucking each other's cocks.'

'Fuck sake man,' Stirling shook his head.

'Alright fine. Just me sucking yours, again.'

They made it back to the table as Derek was laying out a tray of cheeky Vimtos. 'Good lad, Derek. Good lad. Did you get one for yourself?' asked Stirling.

Derek rolled his eyes. 'No, MacAllan 12 year old malt for me. I'm not seeing the attraction of a cheeky Vimto, Stirling. It's a desecrated port, mixed with diabetes and alcopops. You enjoy yours though.'

Later. Ryan had managed to peel Katrina away despite her remonstrations that Irish wakes last for days. He offered to take Millie home, but she declined the invitation on the basis that her Dad was already on his way and that she lived in the opposite direction. Stirling's ears had pricked up on the basis that there was no Stevie and his cheeky Vimto coloured Subaru coming to pick her up.

'Nae Stevie tonight?' Stirling said.

Millie looked a bit drunk. 'No Stevie ever,' she announced with a swipe of her hand. 'He'll be away for a very long time.'

Stirling slid along the seats up alongside her. 'What's happened, are you okay?' Millie passed it off as a long story whilst simultaneously beginning to tell Stirling what had happened. While she spoke, Stirling waved Dave away as he took another order for drinks at the bar. As she gave him the details, he felt guilty for feeling delighted. But this was the best news he'd heard all day; Millie and Stevie split up, Stevie arrested; he wondered if Jack was already working his magic upstairs for him.

Millie's phone buzzed in her bag. Stirling watched as she fumbled inside and picked it up. Her Dad was outside.

'Are you going to be okay?' Stirling asked again, and stood up with her as she reassembled her bag and wrestled her jacket off the back of a chair.

'Right I'd best get going,' Millie announced, trying to sober herself sensibly. 'Thanks Stirling.' Stirling reached in and gave her a hug, and as the two of them tried to kiss each other's cheek, Millie turned and Stirling inadvertently kissed her lips. Just for a fleeting glorious second. He was quick to apologise and then hugged her close. He could smell her perfume and feel her slender body. He wanted to hold her all night. She broke off and blew kisses goodbye across the table as the rest of the group replied with their own. Stirling watched her every move, he wanted to say so much to her. Stop her in her tracks and tell her he'd be there for her. He watched her leave, fixated on her.

Tony broke his focus. 'You just making a deposit in the wank bank big baws?'

Stirling bashfully sipped his pint but didn't answer.

'That's Derek heading off soon too,' Dave said. 'Where are we headed?' Stirling had never seen Dave so animated. Tony was non-committal, and loosely suggested that he was probably heading home but that Kevin was picking him up. Derek was stood, jacket on, smiling across to the last remaining group who were huddled around the Bluetooth speaker. La Prima Estate blared as some of the guys threw imaginary beach balls around the hall. Stirling looked around before deciding his time was up too. Derek led them to the waiting taxi. Stirling asked what he was doing with his car. Derek told him Patricia would run him back down in the morning to collect it. He'd already checked at the bar and there were cameras. Stirling laughed to himself, thinking he hadn't asked.

44

The After Wake

Stirling struggled for his keys as Dave looked up and down the street.

'I'm sure I've been up here once before,' Dave said, 'but I had no idea where I was. Had to walk to the phone box that used to be over the road and phone a taxi. All I could do was describe the surroundings until the boy could work out where I was.'

Stirling was only half listening. Finally, the door clicked open and he made his way up the stairs as Dave tracked behind. Dave seemed to comment on every landing. 'They keep it quite neat outside their doors, I like that, shows a bit of pride.' Stirling was only mildly patronised. He was more embarrassed to find a box full of empty coronas and a pair of old timberlands only recognisable by their general shape behind the mud at his own door. Stirling apologised for the mess before he let them both in.

Stirling was delighted to find his flat much tidier than he remembered. Since the departure of his last visitor he'd embarked on what must have been a deep clean, trying to rid both site and memory of his recent conquest. Stirling headed straight for the fridge, produced two bottles of corona and popped them both open with his lighter, chuffed with the pop as each lid whistled against the kitchen wall. He sat both of them on the table before asking Dave what he wanted on music wise.

'Young Hearts – Candy Staton,' was the shout from Dave. Stirling, mildly impressed by his drinking partners selection, duly obliged. He hooked

Spotify up to his TV sound bar before turning it down slightly, remembering it was gone 12 already.

Stirling scrolled through his phone for the tune, then remembered to text Millie: Hope you got home safe x. He had a message from Lucy which he read but didn't reply. She was apologising for leaving early. Dave drank his beer whilst looking over Stirling's collection of Kayleigh's toys sat in a box adjacent to the fire. Stirling had meant to put them back in her room but she eventually brought them back through. It was a never ending battle he had no intention of winning.

Stirling was deep in thought. 'Do you think Lucy's alright, Dave?'

Dave drank his beer before responding. 'I think so. She's got the kids to keep her going. I think today was a bit much for her, mainly because she holds it together with the kids. This was her time to think about Jack in isolation. It was tough for everyone. I struggled.'

'Really? Your speech was brilliant Dave. I couldn't have done it.'

'To be honest Stirling, I didn't say as much as I could. Jack was an old friend. Well before Romantics Anonymous.'

'I never realised that you and Jack went way back Dave?'

Dave chuckled. 'We worked together for a bit and me and Jack used to run about in similar crowds. We had similar interests. Jack used to get us some hash back in the 90s. I was a bit of a lad back then.'

Stirling was delighted at Dave's revelation. 'Wait a second,' he demanded and headed off in search of his rolling tray he kept tucked away in a cupboard in the kitchen. Eventually he produced a plastic tray adorned by a ripped rizla packet, some broken cigarette filters, and a bag of green grass. He sat it on the table to Dave's nostalgic delight.

'Grass. Can I smell it?' Dave lifted the bag and took a sniff. Stirling watching his face light up. 'Ahhh. That reminds me of Amsterdam. Can I roll one? It's been a while.'

Stirling passed the tray over to Dave who proceeded to roll a joint, setting the skins in a manner Stirling hadn't seen before, one horizontal with no glue. He wasn't expecting much better than a sleeping bag when Dave produced a mini cone that Snoop Doggy Dog would have been happy with.

'Still got it, Dave' remarked Stirling as he handed him a lighter.

Dave sparked it up and took a big draw and exhaled dramatically. Stirling was watching Dave smoking a joint not sure if this was really happening. Thankfully, he accepted the nervous pass as he laid the ashtray in front of him. He was already worried that Dave might end up whitying.

'Mind if I put on another one?' Dave said. Stirling took a draw and passed him his phone.

'Help yourself Dave, you're the guest'

Dave put on some Desmond Dekker and rested half the joint in the ash tray. He talked some shite about the 90s clubs him and Jack had went to. Stirling nodded along, bouncing off him with his own stories. Before long, he went to the bathroom to have himself another line. He snorted it quickly before returning to the table, not sure whether he should say to Dave. Eventually he decided not to. When her returned, Dave asked him about Millie.

'Poor lassie has had a nightmare, Dave. She'd had to get that Stevie lifted, had her trapped in the house for days.'

'Wow, that Stevie is a whole lot of trouble. She'd be better off without him.'

Stirling couldn't wait to tell Dave. 'I kissed her tonight. By accident, like, but I did kiss her.'

Dave tapped his hand on the table. 'I knew it. From the minute she walked in I seen your eyes light up.'

Stirling wasn't as bashful this time. 'Aye, it's been strange, Dave. With things ending with Sarah the way they did and then me thinking I could have got back with her. It's all been a bit all over the place. But you're right, I did like her straight away.'

'Love at first sight?' asked Dave, sparking up the joint again.

'Ah dunno Dave. It's difficult, I was thinking she was keen but then she went back to Stevie before. You know what it's like, sometimes you just canny win.'

Dave looked as if he still thinking. 'So what was it that happened between you and your ex?'

'Aww Dave, I had a nightmare. She'd gave me an ultimatum after a weekend where I'd went mental, it was her or the ching. She'd had enough'

Dave passed him back the joint. 'And you didn't stop?'

'Nah I didn't but worse than that, I left two lines of gear lying on the coffee table one morning for her and Kayleigh to find, laid out in front of me whilst I was sparked out. Talk about best intentions, my plan was to rattle them both and then make breakfast. To say she wasn't happy was an understatement, I knew I'd fucked it there and then.'

Dave just shook his head and continued to flick through songs on Spotify.

'Here I used to listen to this with Jack after a night out. It was the theme tune to a series called Boon.'

Stirling sat waiting as Dave sang along animatedly. Eventually, joining in as the pair of them danced around the living room.

'Hi Ho Silver. Talking Lone ranger. He's riding on down. To rescue me,' they both screeched.

'Jack's had this on a few times when we were back at his. Classic. Here give me a shot.'

Stirling watched Dave dancing around as the song continued. He'd found his next song already, he couldn't wait. Abruptly he cut Dave's moment in half.

'What about this one,' shouted Stirling, standing up in anticipation.

Dave looked disappointed until the first few bars of *Maybe Tomorrow* burst through Stirling's speaker. Dave cheered, before him and Stirling grabbed a hat, travelled light and sang along hobo style.

A dull thud from the flat above prompted Stirling to turn it down and simultaneously hush Dave who was still singing along. They both returned to the table slightly out of breath.

Stirling pulled out his bag of ching, confident him and Dave were bonding this time. Dave's eyes lit up.

'Stirling what are you doing to me? Is that what I think it is?'

Stirling nodded before Dave offered him money. Stirling refused, only relenting to allow Dave to get them more beers from his fridge. Stirling chopped out two lines on the table.

The pair of them sat as the hours rolled into one another, skipping each other's songs, and chatting over stories of Jack and their collective exploits.

Stirling professed his love for Millie. Dave encouraged him to go for it, but Stirling looked forlorn.

'Honestly Stirling. I can't tell you how much I owe to Jack. There was so much more I could have said today but, well, you can't fit everything in.'

Stirling stood up and hugged him enthusiastically.

'He was one in a million was Jack, a legend.' Dave charged his glass as they both saluted Jack's memory.

Stirling sat back down as Dave continued. 'Me and Morag split up, years ago. I was with someone else. Whirlwind romance, head over heels. The whole hog. It was difficult; kids were young but I was smitten. Jack phoned me one night out of nowhere he told me that Morag had offered to sleep with him. To hurt me. Thinking he would do it.'

Stirling was amazed at this revelation. Even more so when Dave told him he didn't do it.

'He told me she'd arrived in floods of tears, apparently looking for me. To be fair, I had said I was staying at his. She'd turned up to seduce me. Lingerie on under a dress. Jack's recollection was that she took the dress off and lay on the living room floor. Upset that I was at another woman's house. Morag asked Jack to fuck her.'

Stirling put on Sympathy for the Devil by the Rolling Stones. Dave looked up disappointedly from his story. Stirling apologised and assured him he was still listening. Dave carried on.

'Well, Jack then threw her a blanket and asked her to cover up and stop being daft. He sat with her as she poured her heart out. Told her he'd have a word with me and the rest, as they say is history.'

'So that prompted you to go back?' Stirling was far from convinced.

Dave snorted a line off the table which Stirling had laid out for him, before answering, 'In a roundabout way. Yes, it was the catalyst. I'd broken her, pushed her to the very edge and she'd do anything to win me back. Anything at her disposal and she was desperate, the mother of my kids. I'd done that. It was then I realised that everything I'd wanted was back home. The path I was on was a fantasy, it was then I realised I had a problem - I went cold turkey and went back.'

Stirling was still thinking that over, before helping himself to another line.

Changing the subject Dave looked up at Stirling. 'How much of that stuff are you going through?'

Stirling thought to himself for a bit before Dave encouraged him to tell the truth. Stirling paused for a bit pretending to count up in his head 'About 4 bags a month, sometimes 5.'

'So that's what four maybe five hundred pound a month. And that's part of the reason you and Sarah split up?'

Stirling was already nodding. 'I know what you're going to say, Dave.'

Dave carried on, despite Stirling trying to throw him off the case. 'So, let's think about this for a bit. Sarah kicked you out. Why do you think that was?'

Stirling was growing frustrated. 'Because I'd lied to her, because I'd fucked up our holiday plans'.

Dave snapped back at him 'No Stirling. Think about it deeper than that man. What was her motivation?' Did she do it to kick you out or did she want you to stop?'

Stirling sighed. 'Aye man she wanted me to stop hammering the gear.' Stirling tapped the rolled up note on the table, disappointed with himself, as the penny dropped.

'But you didn't. So, she wasn't enough to make you stop then. All of it: splitting up with her, breaking up the family home, selling the house, letting her move back in with Kayleigh to her Mum and Dads. All of that so you could keep on having a smoke and a few lines. Is that right?'

'Alright Dave. Steady on with the lecture'

'Look Stirling. I'm no saying anything. I'm just laying out the facts. Because if you think you're going to get with Millie, after she's been watching that daft boy Stevie run about shifting kilos of the stuff, she's no going to be impressed by your couple of bags and your quarter of grass. Is she?'

Stirling leaned back on his chair.

'So, what are you saying exactly Dave? I should get mare!'

'Not at all. What I'm saying Stirling is everything you need to impress Millie, you already have. A decent job, a nice wee flat in a quiet area, you're a good dad to your daughter. Nice guy, funny. The only thing that's going to fuck it up for you, again, will be your having a wee line and a wee smoke, being one of the boys. Threatening to punch Stevie out every time he comes near isn't going to work.'

Stirling shook his head.

'It will. I'll protect her from that wee dick. I'll volley him up and down the place'

Dave sighed again.

'Stirling. I'll tell you what, because your big, right, you'd probably give him a sore one once, but that boy is a psycho. There are three types of bams in the world; sad, mad and bad. With the first two you've got half a chance because there's an external influence there, something's made them that way.... But with bad, and that's what Stevie is, you'll have a war and he'll win. More ching, more badness, less to risk, he's no got the start that you've got. The good in you he'll never have'

'You need to win Millie over on a different level, don't compete with Stevie on his level, don't even sink to it. She wants a sensible boy now: a good laugh, safe. Stirling, if you're serious about this lassie, you're going to have to give it up, that's the only way it'll work. Believe me, I've been there... That's the first smoke and first lines I've had in nearly 3 years and it's a wee laugh, a reminiscent trip down memory lane for my dead pal. See if I was you, I'd take that bag and empty it down the sink. Make a fresh start, if you're serious about her. You could do it. You're in a different league and that's what she's after now.'

'I canny though Dave,' muttered Stirling

'You can.'

'Naw, I canny, Dave.'

'If you wanted to you could.'

'I really couldn't, Dave.'

Stirling held up the bag.

'It's already empty.'

Dave conceded he was indeed correct as Stirling stuck his tongue out with a smile and then into the empty bag. Stirling put out his hand across the table and Dave grabbed it firmly.

'Thanks Dave. I've got it, I hear what you're saying.'

'That's' good. I hope you have and if you haven't well there will be someone else, some other equally daft lassie somewhere prepared to take you on. Eventually, she'll want you to stop as well, they all will, and they aren't all working against you. They want you to stop because you're a good lad. Stop pretending your anything else. Why would you?'

Stirling's eyes filled up.

'Fuck sake Dave. I've been a daft big cunt.'

Dave comforted him, tightening his grip on his hand.

'You have, but we all have. The trick is spotting it yourself before you balls up everything. You're still a young man. Some boys go through their life and never do it. Jack didn't, great guy and never grew up. '

Dave appeared to summon himself a taxi out of nowhere and suddenly it was light outside. Dave pulled on his coat and helped Stirling put the bottles away in the kitchen.

'I'm going to get some grief from Morag when I get back. I'm going to have to tell her you were in a bad way and I was looking out for you. Cheers to you and Jack. I've had a one last blow out.'

'He was some boy. I still canny really believe he's gone. I still expect him to announce it was some big hoax, an elaborate wind up.'

Dave patted his back as he opened the door.

'Thing is, he would have got away with it too. '

Before he made it to the stairs, Dave turned on the landing. 'Oh Stirling. See when you went for a line when we first came in, and you weren't telling me you were on the lines.'

Stirling smiled at Dave from the door.

'Ha-ha, you knew?'

Dave looked back at him.

'Come on Stirling. Obviously I knew. Anyway, I was picking a song when wee Millie text you back to say she was fine. Put a kiss on it too.'

Stirling's head was in his phone and as he shouted cheers to Dave. He kicked the door closed and turned back into the kitchen. He ran himself a large glass of water and toasted it to Jack as checked the blinds to watch Dave's taxi pull away. That had indeed been a send-off. He stared at the kiss on his text and closed the screen. He knew he was going to be better than Stevie.

45

The Morning After, The After Wake

Dave stumbled out of the taxi, the driver's pitying look burning into his back as he tried to navigate the driveway. He'd spilled his life story (unedited) to the poor man, as if the fare came with free therapy. Now, standing in front of his house, it seemed bigger, brighter, and altogether too judgmental. He was drunk, and the edge of a comedown was already itching at him. This was an old friend he wasn't keen to reacquaint with.

Morag's face replayed in his mind like a looping news headline: the way her eyes softened when she asked if he was sure he didn't want her to drive. The kiss she'd left on his cheek, gentle and resigned, as though she already knew he'd crumble. The sickening relief he'd felt as the Corona slid down his throat, numbing the constant churn of emotions he couldn't name. Every memory was a jab of guilt, a stark reminder of his failure.

He hadn't just fallen off the wagon; he'd dived nose first into the shite. What was worse than a failed non-drinker? Like doing something for an achievement is understandable but he couldn't even NOT do something. And not doing something was all he'd felt good at for the past, he totted up the number in his head. 850 days. 850 fucking days sober, worn proudly like a badge of honour, washed away in one night.

He'd carried that number like proof to his old drinking pals that he was still one of the boys, just teetering on the brink of a bender. But now? He was back to being the dafty who couldn't be trusted to stop at one. He knew it was a slippery slope, Dave couldn't even watch a box set without binging.

He slid the key into the door and twisted it slowly, listening to each barrel falling into place before he slipped inside and pulled the door shut. The snib lock loudly clattering back into place like a grass.

Inside, the hallway felt huge. Dave rarely lingered there, and tonight it seemed almost mocking. The house was far grander than anything he'd dreamed of as a kid. Getting there had been a blur, and it had all felt a bit more precarious since he'd given up his crutches.

The kitchen was no better. Morag's occasional vodka bottle in the cupboard beckoned, its presence taunting him. He opened the door and stared at the bastard, just long enough to challenge himself, then slammed it shut. He grabbed a glass from the counter, ran the tap as if he was flushing out legionella, and then carried his full glass of water into the hallway.

He stopped outside the bedroom door, hand hovering over the handle. But he couldn't bring himself to face Morag, not like this. Instead, he crept into the spare room and collapsed onto the bed, hoping that sleep would be his friend.

It wasn't.

He lay there for the rest of the morning, tossing and turning. The way his pals all seemed to smile bigger when he had a beer in his hand - now leered into his face menacingly. He listened, like a guest, as the boys and Morag had breakfast. Rattling through an existential crisis from under a single duvet. Practicing what he'd say to Morag, rehearsing every excuse he'd prepared.

It's what Jack would've wanted.

Stirling needed a shoulder to cry on.

When the door finally cracked open, all he could manage was a weak,

'I couldn't say no.'

Morag stepped inside and sat beside him. Her touch was soft, a balm against the chaos in his head. She hugged him as he sat upright, and Dave, mortified, grew a full hard on the very instant she began comforting him.

'Its fine'

She reassured him, over and over, as he wept through the remnants of his failed abstinence. He spilled out the full story like she'd already agreed a plea bargain; the joints, the ching... before long he was telling her how Stirling had probably given up the gear.

Morag listened and stroked his ego back to full health, despite rejecting his advances (twice). When he finally ran out of words, she asked quietly,

'What would you tell Stirling if he'd been sober for 850 days and slipped after his best friend died?'

Dave blinked, the question catching him off guard. 'I see what you did there.'

'But seriously,' she pressed. 'What would you say?'

Dave thought for a moment. 'I'd probably say... well done. You set a new personal best. Now see if you can beat it next time.'

'That'll do for me,' Morag said, her lips curling into nearly a smile as she stood.

Dave watched her leave, her grace amplifying the mess of his own emotions. He lay back down, exhaustion pulling at him and determined that he would indeed set a new personal best. Then had a wank and fell asleep.

46

Week Twelve and a Half

'You in the dog house, Dave?' shouted Stirling as Dave walked from his car to the Trinity Centre.

'Just a wee bit Stirling. To be honest, I think Morag was secretly pleased I still had it in me. But still, she had go through the motions of being upset, just to make sure I don't slip back into my old ways. You see I've got a medical condition which means that when I get started, I just can't stop... It's called being a fucking legend! Anyway a few days and progress on my share options put paid to any lingering sulk that might have been happening. How's you? Did you phone wee Millie?'

Stirling was still holding the door open for Tony who was jogging to prevent Stirling waiting any longer.

Watching on, Dave wondered if Tony's jog was actually slower than his walk.

'Yeah, doing good Dave. I gave her a call and she was doing fine, and I've not had a smoke or a line since.'

'Good lad, keep it up. I know it's no easy you having the same condition as myself'

Dave winked as Tony finally made it to the door.

'What's this?' he asked, half catching the end of their conversation.

Dave watched Stirling shine as he described to Tony how he'd given it all up. Dave nodded to Sensei Jamieson as his class left, then watched Kevin,

Tony and Stirling all get caught up together. He made his way inside and laid out the circle of trust, proud of his work.

Next to arrive was Lucy, alongside Derek and Katrina minus Ryan. Katrina's appearance didn't surprise Dave, of course it would have been Ryan to drop out, on account of him being the better person.

Millie then arrived, immaculate as ever, and made her way to a seat. Not next to Stirling, Dave noted, but he did notice a few exchanged smiles.

Tony was first to check-in. Tony had had a strange week where his suspicions regarding his wife's new partner had ended, though in his opinion still true, as the guy had finished with her all of a sudden, just before Christmas too. She'd been upset when Tony had been to see the girls and blurted out that it was over. Tony had then provided more than a shoulder to cry on.

'You see she was greeting away, and I was consoling her, next thing she was kissing me and well one thing led to another, and I ended up pumping her. I feel rotten about it. I mean, I don't even fancy her. I mean, I don't even fancy women and I just did it.'

Dave asked him how he was feeling afterwards. Tony had been filled with remorse and guilt, saying that he'd been cold and distant with Kevin.

'Ah mean, I just want to tell him. Get it out the way.'

Lucy never even gave Dave time to think of a response.

'No, no, no Tony. That's crazy. Exes don't count in that respect. You made a mistake and well – it's not as if you've slept with anyone new. Put that down to a mistake and move on!'

Katrina agreed.

'Absolutely Lucy, love. She's right, Tony. Buy him a case of his favourite beer. give him a bloody good blow job and move on. She probably needed it on account of the breakup, you've done your bit now just let it lie.'

Dave sat watching as if he was umpiring a tennis match.

'How do you feel about that advice? He asked Tony.

'Would that be a possibility for you?'

Tony seemed a bit stunned, he stuttered a bit before responding..

'I mean. Well. Aye. I can't believe I did it though, I keep getting mental images of us together and I don't know whether to wank it out or cut it off.'

Dave gave him a third option by suggesting he follow Katrina and Lucy's advice and maybe focus on Kevin for a bit. Tony agreed. Dave was pleased to have resolved this so happily. He was still unsure why Katrina had come along minus Ryan, he set aside the notion to ask for now and moved onto Stirling for his check-in.

Dave surveyed the groups reactions as Stirling described how he'd decided to move on from drugs and move forward with a healthier outlook regarding life and relationships. There were no rounds of applause or slapping of backs, but Dave could sense that Stirling was committed to a new plan. Dave was delighted to see progress in him and hoped that something could happen for him and Millie, even just enough of an incentive to keep him on the straight and narrow.

Dave looked over to Katrina who had been sat to Stirling's left. He started off by asking the question on everyone's lips.

'Where is Ryan?.'

Katrina was quick to let everyone know. Her and Ryan had gone back to collect more of her things from Jim's flat, the last few bits. In between times, Jimmy had been texting her all levels of abuse and ringing her phone incessantly. Ryan had been dead calm about it all, letting her know it would all blow over. 'He'll run out of steam once he accepts it's over' he'd been saying.

Katrina folded her legs and tucked her hair behind her ear as she began to explain what happened when they went around.

'We were stood at the door, waiting for an answer when Jimmy just started launching the last of my things down the stairs and out the window. And understandably, I start getting really angry about it. I start shouting back up at Jimmy, calling him all the names under the sun whilst trying to grab anything that landed nearby. All the time, Ryan just stood there by the door, calm as you like.'

'Eventually Jimmy came down the stairs to trade more insults with me, before he started on Ryan. Jimmy stood at the doorway and called me a Fenian whore. He looked at Ryan and said "I bet you're one of those as well, a Fenian cuckold." He asked Ryan if he wanted him to take us both upstairs so that he could shag me properly in front of him. That's when Ryan snapped. Ryan started punching him repeatedly in the face. Jimmy backed away, shocked initially, and then came back at him. But Ryan swept him onto his back and headbutted him on the floor. He started punching him again. As I was watching, it looked like sparks were flying off Jim's head. It was his blood. Ryan was screaming at him to apologise. He dragged him over to my feet, told him to beg for forgiveness, and booted him in the side of the head until he did. Jimmy was begging away and crying as Ryan told him to get back in the house and then, casual as you like, he helped me pack the rest of my stuff into my car.'

Dave had been listening intently, as had the rest of the group, impressed and surprised that Ryan even had it in him. But he was still unsure where Ryan was.

'Is Ryan okay now?'

Katrina explained that he was fine. That they'd got home and unpacked their things and she'd helped clean the blood off Ryan's hands when the police arrived. Jimmy had made a complaint and accused Ryan of assault. He had been arrested this afternoon pending a court appearance tomorrow.

Tony summarised the groups feelings best.

'What a prick that Jimmy is by the way.'

Dave asked Katrina how she was feeling. She was obviously worried that he was in the cells but long enough in the tooth to realise it was a first offence against a convicted murderer. To even the most suspicious cop it was clear what had happened. The police that had arrested Ryan were both very apologetic and assured her that he'd be fine.

Dave thanked Katrina for checking in and asked her if she or Ryan could let him know when he was released from custody, and what was happening next.

Dave next moved onto Millie. Millie described her ordeal at the hands of Stevie and how that had also ended with the police's involvement. She took the time to thank the group and Dave specifically for some of the advice she'd picked up which ultimately kept her safe and manged to help her remove herself from a horrible situation.

Then it was Derek. Derek had received a message through his colleagues that the receptionist from their clients had been asking him to get in touch. She'd emailed a few times whilst he was away with Patricia, but he'd ignored and deleted them.

'She was becoming a nuisance. She was literally coming at me from every conceivable angle. I was collecting messages from our marketing team through our website, emails direct, emails from my colleagues. Messages via LinkedIn. After we got back, I thought, I must put a stop to this now.'

Dave watched as Derek pulled and adjusted his shirt from under his pullover sleeves. Dave had never seen Derek lose his composure, but he looked close to doing so today. He was stretching his neck in a circular motion which was already red from him stroking it.

'I'd decided I'd call her and put a stop to it once and for all. I mean I know she'd been smitten but it was becoming ridiculous. I was going to warn here that I'd need to involve the police if she didn't give up.'

Derek steadied himself. Dave asked if he was okay. Derek didn't look sure. He paused for a second and then carried on with his check-in.

'I'd called her and she answered immediately. Initially she was her usual self, very over friendly asking how I had been and making innocuous small talk. Suggested that she'd been trying to get in touch with me. It was then I adopted a firmer tone with her. Look Dannii these calls and messages have to stop. We're finished. It's been over for a long time. It was never anything serious. She began crying and suggested it was, I took the opportunity to close this down. Using my words purposefully. I said Dannii there was never anything serious from my side. Never. It was then she said I've got something to tell you...... I can't even bring myself to say it out loud.'

Dave asked Derek to take his time. Reminding him that he didn't have to say anymore if it was difficult.

'Thanks David. But I do need help here. Just give me a second.'

It was then Derek dropped the unexploded bomb which had recently unearthed itself.

'She then told me she was pregnant with my baby.'

There were gasps around the circle. As Derek slouched forward and cradled his full face in his hands. He continued from behind his hands, as if he was too scared to watch his own horror movie.

'She's adamant that it's mine. Patricia accepting me back after what I'd done was one thing but my sullying Tiger's inheritance with a bastard child wouldn't be a recoverable situation. Not ever.'

Tony was trying to offer some advice suggesting that he offer to pay her off. That he pays maintenance for life in advance and tell her that he didn't want anything to do with the baby.

Derek had been mainly focused on preventing the baby making the journey through to term. Even admitting that he'd thought about arranging an accident which he knew was ludicrous. Stirling was next to offer some encouragement.

'Have you asked for a DNA test yet?'

Derek slowly pulled his head up from his hands, stretching each of his facial features as he revealed his ashen face fully again to the group.

'I will Stirling. I mean thanks, I'll get on that.'

Dave was being careful with his words. Re-assuring Derek that he still had options, and that was the important thing in these situations and within this group. To remind each other that we have options.

'This might seem insurmountable but you'll get there Derek. Progress with establishing the facts first, both the pregnancy and the legitimacy of her claims.

Derek was becoming angry at himself.

'I've always been so careful with contracts. In this situation she has more rights than even Patricia has if she was in the same position. I just want it to go away. The timing, well there was never a good time. But we've just renewed our marriage vows, I'm settling down for early retirement.... Not another stab at parenthood with an unwanted child.'

Dave could sympathise with Derek's plight as could the rest of the group, but not Lucy she looked agitated. All of a sudden she sprung to life with her views.

'And have none of you thought about the poor girl,' Lucy interjected.

'How she's feeling through all this? Alone with a baby on the way and no dad interested.'

'It was a stupid affair,' Derek protested. 'It wasn't anything serious. It wasn't meant to lead to this.'

Lucy was becoming more and more upset.

'Do you know how it feels to be having a baby with no dad around, no one to share it with. No one else in the world happy about the pride she's carrying in her baby. Because I do. I'm living that nightmare right now.'

Katrina tried calming her down. She went over to give her a hug and sat next to her, reminding her that her two kids are all very much loved and that everyone wanted nothing but the best for them.

'And if the Dad's in their life don't want to be involved, that's their loss.'

Lucy broke free from Katrina's hug and wiped away her tears.

'Yeah, but this one's Dad never had the choice, did he?'

She pointed to her belly and then re-engaged with Katrina's hug.

Dave wasn't sure if he'd heard correctly, and the rest of the room looked around blankly apart from Derek. Derek went on to speak.

'That was my check-in finished really. I'm just lost to know what's the best thing to do for me. I feel like if Patricia finds out that we'll be done for ever and I don't think that my heart can take that. The truth is I want her more than any baby, more than anything.'

Dave was keeping tabs on Lucy who was still sobbing into Katrina's arms. Dave told Derek that he might want to try discussing some legal and payment terms with his former acquaintance and see if there were arrangements that could be made that way. But then it was Lucy's turn to check in.

'Are you okay, Lucy?'

Lucy burst into tears.

'I'm pregnant with Jack's baby and I don't know what to do.'

Dave felt pride and agony pass as he swallowed them both, thinking of Jack; The Peter Pan that never grew old, and here was his baby at long last. He didn't know what to tell her. Single mother of two, another one on the way. Dave decided to congratulate her, not knowing if that's what she wanted to hear.

Lucy thanked Dave before she carried on with her check-in.

'I think I needed to hear that, Dave. I just don't know what to say to his friends or family. I mean, I hope they'd be happy that they have a piece of Jack remaining but with me, a single mum of two. It's hardly the legacy they'd wanted for him. I wanted to say to his Mum at the funeral so bad, but I didn't want to disappoint them anymore.'

Millie tried to console her, and Dave was delighted to have another viewpoint wondering if his was skewed by his friendship with Jack. Lucy looked up as Millie was describing the situation for her.

'Think about it yourself. And I know it's difficult but far off in the future imagine that your Archie passes away and you have no grandchildren. No partner, your broken-hearted and lost, nothing to live for. Then this beautiful, kind-hearted, woman that loved your son with her big, big heart, comes along with news that she's carrying his unborn child. Just think about that for a second, if you can. Can you?'

Lucy lifted her head and sniffed with the glimmer of a smile brewing on her face. Millie carried on..

'If you can put yourself in her shoes, for just a second, and imagine how she will feel to have a small piece of her Jack left for the world. And with that an amazing Mum, a beautiful big sister and their big brother to help him do all the things his Dad would have loved to have done. Lucy, from my angle here you couldn't answer all of her prayers but you've got pretty damn close.'

Dave was delighted that Millie shared the same view as him. Stirling was agreeing too , as were Katrina and Tony. Dave eventually did speak.

'I'll tell you what. What about if I take you round to Jack's mum's place. We'll let her know the happy news. If that's okay?'

Lucy's full smile sparkled through her blotchy face. She remembered to apologise to Derek who shook it off.

Dave was already putting on his jacket.

'We were going to look over the symptoms of Romantic Addiction but I've decided that can wait till next week. Thanks everyone for coming along. See you all next week.'

Dave was already walking to the door with his keys in his hand. leaving the group to assemble the chairs.

He stopped to encourage Lucy to hurry up. Who was busy fending off hugs from the rest of the group.

'You ready? Let's go and share the good news. I can't wait to see her face'.
THE END.

Printed in Dunstable, United Kingdom